PRAISE FOR FERGUS McNEILL

‘a startling thriller ... a treat for fans of gritty crime’

— THE SUNDAY MIRROR

‘pacey, page-turning ... one of the freshest voices in recent crime fiction’

— TOM BROMLEY

‘seamlessly elegant high-concept crime’

— SOPHIE HANNAH

UP CLOSE AND FATAL

Fergus McNeill

1

Tom's Journal

It's a foggy April morning in upstate New York, and I'm staring out the window of a Greyhound bus, on my way to meet a murderer. He's not in jail, and nobody knows who he is, not even me.

The weather's strange and uncertain. The sun's a faint circle of cold white, lost in the pale grey sky. Walls of mist roll across the tree-lined slopes. This is a ghost of a landscape, fading in and out of view. We pass farms... a white wooden house, with its broad porch and steep-pitched roof... rows of rusting mailboxes at the end of lonely dirt tracks. Now and then, there's a huddled small town, or a forgotten gas station. And then the trees close in again, and I see my own face – messy hair, tired eyes, stubble shadowing my jawline – a nervous reflection flickering in the glass.

I've been told to get off at a little place in the middle of nowhere and await further instructions. Part of me is eager, impatient to get there... but part of me wants to hunch down in my seat and stay on the damn bus.

Leaning back against the creaking leather headrest, I let my eyes close for a minute, listening to the steady rumble of the road, the thin beat of music bleeding from the earphones of the kid sitting in front of me. It's already been a long day, and I'm tired and tense and cold. The message came through just a few minutes after midnight, and there was no chance of getting any sleep after that.

His voice has that Southern-accented warmth to it, a calm dignity that I find deeply unnerving. We've spoken twice on the phone – once when he first laid out his proposal, and again when he called to get my answer – and he's always been so polite. Even when he warned me about the 'severe' consequences if I disobeyed his instructions, he sounded like the maître d' at a good restaurant, smiling as he confirmed who would be getting what. It was only afterwards that I found myself thinking about just how 'severe' those consequences could be.

I could pretend that this whole thing was just an elaborate hoax, somebody's idea of a practical joke, or a big old fuck-you from someone who doesn't like what I write. They say a journalist isn't doing his job unless he ruffles a few feathers, and I've certainly done that... but, sitting here now, I don't have any doubts. All my instincts tell me this is real.

My fingers begin tapping out a nervous rhythm on the worn leather of the empty seat beside me, and I have to force myself to be still, taking a slow breath, trying to relax. It's natural to be scared. This is a million miles outside my comfort zone and, if it's genuine, then I'm taking an insane risk by coming out here... but I know the importance of what I'm doing.

The bus slows as it rounds a bend, then drops a gear, climbing between the tall pines that crowd in along the edge of the road. I glance down at my watch. Not long until I find out who's waiting for me, here in the grey morning wilderness.

I think he'll be older than me, probably the wrong side of forty, but it's hard to be sure from just a voice on the phone. He speaks with a quiet confidence, and he calls himself "J"; at first, I thought he meant his name was Jay, but now I think it's just an initial. Other than that, I don't know much about the man I'm going to meet. Only what he's done.

Then again, he doesn't know about the two unmarked police vehicles, shadowing the bus, just a few cars back. He may think I'm just another journalist, willing to do anything for a story, but I'm better than that.

I'm going to catch a killer.

THREE WEEKS EARLIER

2

It was past midnight, but this bit of the Lower East Side was never quiet. Rivington Street was like a long, deep trench, as though the crowded city blocks had reluctantly moved aside just enough to let it through. Tom made his way around the people that still cluttered the uneven sidewalk, drifting through the laughter and snatches of conversation. Smells of cooking and beer mingled with cigarette smoke and perfume. Above him, old tenement buildings framed the night sky, their faces muzzled with an ironwork mesh of fire-escapes.

He slowed by the mini-mart on the corner, then turned and went inside. From the cramped neon aisles, he picked up a six-pack of beer and a bag of pretzels, then walked back round to the counter, where the balding Puerto Rican owner greeted him with a broad grin.

'Hey. Lookin' good tonight.'

Tom gave him a blank stare, then remembered that he was still wearing the tuxedo.

'Oh, right.' Nodding, he handed over his money, then pulled awkwardly at the bow tie to loosen it. 'I was at a work thing, uptown. There was a dress code.'

The balding man laughed and handed over his change.

'With that British accent? You're like James Bond or something.'

Tom pocketed the money and picked up his things.

'Yeah, James Bond.' He managed a wry smile. 'That's me.'

Emerging from the shop doorway, he stopped to pull off the ridiculous tie and thrust it deep into his pocket. Then, undoing the top button of his shirt, he moved on.

He was glad they still invited him to the press awards, even minor events like the one tonight, but it was a long time since he'd been shortlisted for anything. So many new faces, idealistic and relevant and young. He reminded himself that being thirty-seven wasn't old, but the evening had still left him feeling tired. Yesterday's news.

At the end of the block, he turned the corner and walked the last few yards, past the familiar swirls of graffiti on the steel shutters, fumbling in his pocket for his keys. Once inside the relative quiet of the building lobby, he yawned and went over to check his mailbox, taking out the clutch of envelopes without looking at them.

At least he was still working. There were plenty of commissions at the moment, and the money was okay. What did it matter if the stories weren't his, or if some of the features were a bit dull? It wasn't as if he had to prove himself anymore. Keeping busy, that was the main thing now.

He turned towards the elevator, then changed his mind and walked round to the stairs. It was an imposing old building – five stories tall, with a basement parking garage underneath – and his tired footsteps echoed round the stairwell as he climbed slowly to the third floor. One of the hallway lights was still flickering as he passed it – the lease had promised a live-in supervisor, but he'd never seen any evidence of maintenance, or of anything being fixed. Stopping outside his own apartment, he drew out his keys again, listening to the raised voices coming from somewhere above – a man and a woman, arguing. Shaking his head, he let himself in, then bolted the door.

It was a relief to kick off his shoes and get out of the tuxedo. Pulling on a t-shirt, he padded through to the small living room area. A large TV dominated one wall, with a leather sofa opposite it, and a small kitchen counter filled the corner by the door. At the far end of the room, a single window looked out onto the building across the street, with a sleek glass-topped desk in front of it. The apartment was certainly cramped, even compared to the places he'd had back in London before he ever came to the States. But at least the rent was manageable, by New York standards, and he didn't really need much space, not since the break-up.

The couple upstairs were still arguing, so he put on some music, just loud enough to drown out their noise and his thoughts. Taking one of the beers, he shoved the rest into the fridge, then grabbed the bag of pretzels from the counter and went over to his desk. He had work to do.

When he glanced up at the clock in the corner of his laptop screen, two hours had passed, and it was almost 3am. He screwed his eyes shut and rubbed them, blocking out the words he'd written, letting his body tilt back into the chair. Yawning, he got to his feet and stretched. Another clickbait article about gang crime for *The Herald* – and probably another lecture from its editor for trying to explore a complex subject instead of just spoon-feeding the readers what they wanted to hear – but it was almost done, and he'd earned himself a break. Peering down into the street below, he saw a young couple making out in a doorway, kissing then pausing to stare into each other's eyes. They looked happy, oblivious to the world around them; just two people, sharing a moment together. Sighing, he turned away.

Walking over to the fridge, he got himself another beer, taking a sip as he idly sorted through the pile of mail he'd left on the counter. One of the envelopes caught his eye – cream-colored, with the name and address handwritten in neat capitals. Turning it over in his hands, he worked a finger under the flap and opened it to reveal a carefully folded piece of paper, and what appeared to be a driver's license. Curious, he took it out and studied it. A New York state driver's license, issued to Elizabeth Jane Reeves – the small photograph showed a young woman with straight brown hair, but her face wasn't any more familiar than her name. He drew out the piece of paper and unfolded it, frowning as he read the words written in the same neat hand as the address.

1.
2.
3.
4. LIZZIE REEVES
5.
6. DUNCAN BAUMANN
7.
8.
9. DARYL HIRSCH
10.

WAIT.

Tom checked the envelope once again, but there was no mistake – it was definitely addressed to him. The license appeared to be genuine, and it was still valid, with a few months left before it expired.

Shaking his head, he thought for a moment, then turned and walked over to his desk.

Elizabeth Reeves...

. . .

He brought up a new window on his laptop, typed in the name and hit the *Search* button. A moment later, his eyes widened, and he leaned forward, staring at the screen.

3

Tom sat, hunched forward over a small table in the corner of the deli, his eyes on the door. He'd ordered a cappuccino and an oatmeal bar when he got here, and both still sat in front of him, untouched. He watched as three more people came in – the place was starting to get busy with the lunchtime crowd – and he was about to check his watch again when the familiar broad figure finally appeared in the doorway.

Leo was a big man in his forties, short black hair neatly swept back, looking comfortable in his dark grey suit. Seeing Tom, his strong features split into a smile, and he walked over to the table.

'Hey, buddy. Sorry I'm late.' Leo gave him a firm pat on the shoulder, while glancing round at the other tables. 'You been waiting long?'

'No,' Tom lied. 'I just got here myself.'

'That's great.'

The big man turned to squint up at the menu boards, then glanced back down at Tom. 'Can I get you anything, or are you all set?'

'No, I'm good. Thanks.'

'Okay... be right back.'

Tom watched him as he walked over to the counter. They'd first met six years ago, when Leo had been one of the detectives on a murder case that he was writing about. The pair of them had got on well, and they'd kept in touch ever since, quietly helping each other out with bits of information, watching each other's backs.

A few moments later, Leo returned with a sandwich and a soda. Pulling up a chair, he sat down opposite Tom and shot him an enquiring look.

'So... how's it going?' he asked. 'It's been a while.'

'Yeah.' Tom hesitated, wondering how long it had been. 'I think I was writing up the Lipman case?'

'That's the one,' Leo nodded, tearing back the paper from his sandwich. 'You still doing the true-crime investigative stuff? I haven't heard from you in a while, so...'

'I'm doing a little of everything.' Tom gave him an awkward smile. 'Mostly it's just feature articles for the nationals just now. That's where the money is.'

Leo took a bite of his sandwich.

'Gotta pay the bills, huh?' he said.

Tom shrugged. 'Child support isn't getting any cheaper.'

Leo nodded sympathetically as he ate. 'How old is your boy now?'

Tom did a brief mental calculation, swallowing a momentary flutter of panic as he wondered if he'd missed a birthday.

'Five,' he said, quickly. 'Zak's five.'

'Five? Jeez, they get old so fast.'

'Yeah,' Tom sighed. 'Tell me about it.'

He wondered what Zak was doing right now, how tall he was... Kids changed so quickly at this age, and it had been some time since he'd visited. After the break-up, he'd told Samaria that he wanted to be involved, but Boston was a four-hundred-mile round trip and with things the way they were, the way he'd been feeling...

He found that Leo was looking at him and forced a grin.

'How about your two?' he asked.

'Donnie's six and Bella's eight,' Leo said. 'Eight years old, can you believe that?'

'Time flies,' Tom smiled.

'Yeah, well, I love 'em to death... even though Bella can be a giant pain in the ass.' The big man paused, then grinned. 'Takes after her mother.'

A man in an apron appeared at his shoulder, noisily gathering up empty cups from the next table onto a tray. He gave them a brief nod, then went back towards the counter.

'Anyway...' Leo took a gulp of his soda. 'I can't stay for too long, and you said you had something you wanted to run by me?'

'Oh. Yeah, that's right...' Caught off guard, Tom hurriedly lifted his bag from under the table and set it on his knees to open it. 'It's kind of weird but... well, this came to me in the mail.'

He took out a clear plastic folder. Inside, the unfolded piece of paper and the driver's license were visible, along with the handwritten envelope.

Leo leaned forward slightly to look, but made no attempt to reach for it.

'Who's this...' He squinted at the name on the license. '...Elizabeth Reeves?'

Tom placed the folder on the table between them.

'That's what I wondered,' he said. 'Took me a while to find her, but I did some online searching. Her body was found a couple of years back, beside some lake up near Syracuse.'

Leo continued to peer at the license. 'She was murdered?'

Tom waited for him to look up. 'Yeah.'

'Did they catch the guy who did it?'

Tom shook his head. 'I dug up what I could from the local press reports, and her ex-boyfriend was a suspect for a while, but the police were never able to make a case against him.'

Leo appeared to consider this.

'So... what are you thinking?' he mused. 'You think maybe *he* sent her license to you?'

Tom shrugged.

'Maybe, but then there's also this...' He turned the plastic folder over to reveal the words written on the paper.

Leo scanned the page and frowned.

'Who are these people?' he asked.

'Well, searching for them was more difficult, because I only had names, no other information or I.D. to work on...'

'But...?'

Tom leaned forward, lowering his voice.

'But I *did* find that each of those names corresponds to a murder victim.' He paused, then added, 'And though they were killed in different states, over a couple of years, all three deaths happened in the same order as they're listed here.'

Leo stared at him, then slowly leaned back in his chair.

'Shit.'

'Yeah.'

'A list of victims...'

'That's what I was thinking, yeah.'

Leo picked up the plastic folder, leaning closer to stare at the letter within.

'And these other numbers... they could be additional victims,' he said to himself.

'They could.'

Leo set the folder carefully on the table and tapped it with his finger.

'Okay if I take this?' he asked. 'I doubt there's any prints on it, but Forensics may want to take a look.'

'Of course,' Tom replied. 'That's why I brought it.'

Leo sat in silence for a moment.

'I'll check these names and see what's on file, but...' He sighed and shook his head. 'If local law-enforcement *had* established any connection between the victims, they'd have bumped it to the Feds by now.'

'I know,' Tom said. 'I'd just be really interested to hear about anything you can turn up.'

'You got it.' Leo picked up the folder again. 'So, you're thinking whoever sent this, maybe they had something to do with the deaths?'

Tom took a deep breath and let it out slowly.

'I think it's a possibility,' he said. 'Don't you?'

Leo frowned, then gazed intently at him.

'But why you?' he asked slowly. 'Why's he sending all this to *you?*'

Tom sat back in his chair, his foot tapping nervously under the table.

'Yeah,' he mused. 'That's what *I* want to know.'

4

Tom lay sprawled lengthwise along his sofa, idly scrolling through different shows on Netflix, the TV remote resting on his chest.

The regular FaceTime call with Zak earlier in the evening had left him emotionally drained, as it always did. Seeing that mischievous face with the mess of dark curls, listening as his little boy babbled excitedly about TV shows he didn't recognise and toys that meant nothing to him, Tom was painfully aware of the distance between them.

In the days following the split, he'd told himself that the miles didn't mean anything, that he'd get his head together and make things right – but as time went on, he worried more and more that he was losing touch with his son. He felt a sudden pang of regret, wishing he could feel that closeness that other parents seemed to take for granted, see that excited light of recognition in his son's eyes... and then, tonight, just as Zak had asked him to tell him a story, and there had been a moment of real connection between them, Samaira had interrupted and said that it was bedtime.

Now it was after midnight. Tom shook his head, forcing

himself to think of something – *anything* – else. His thoughts drifted back to earlier, to the driver's license he'd given to Leo... and the person who had sent it.

He lay there for a while, staring blankly at the screen, then realized that he'd scrolled all the way to the end of his list and back round to the beginning again. Sighing, he aimed the remote to switch off the TV, then let his head relax back onto the arm of the sofa, so he could gaze up at the ceiling.

He'd never heard of Elizabeth Reeves, or any of the other names on the list, but someone had sent this to him, and there had to be a reason.

He rubbed his eyes then slowly pushed himself up into a sitting position. It was frustrating to know so little. After a moment, he got wearily to his feet and went over to the desk. Dropping into his chair, he woke his laptop and clicked on the next article in the search listings – another archived news report from one of the local networks. Leaning forward, he began to read.

OTISCO LAKESHORE BODY IDENTIFIED

SYRACUSE, NY – The Onondaga County Medical Examiner's Office has formally identified the body of a woman found near Otisco Lake as that of local university researcher Elizabeth Reeves. The 27-year-old, from Eastside, had been missing since last month. Her remains were discovered on Saturday morning by a conservation worker near the shore of Otisco Lake, approximately 20 miles southwest of the city. Detectives are treating her death as suspicious, and have asked anyone with information about Miss Reeves to contact them via the Syracuse Police Department website. Anonymous phone tips can be left on the Department's Crime Tip line.

Staff at Syracuse University paid tribute to their colleague, *describing her as "a dedicated person who inspired everyone around her" and "a passionate campaigner for civil liberties". Miss Reeves, who was a keen runner, raised over $3000 for charity last year when she took part in the Empire State Marathon...*

Tom slumped back in his chair and rubbed his eyes again. It was just like all the other pieces he'd read – a lazy rewording of the official police report, with some trite comments from friends and co-workers. That wasn't journalism. To grasp the meaning of Lizzie Reeves' death required some understanding of her life – what she was like, who she really *was* – before she was reduced to a murder statistic. Whoever wrote this crap brought nothing new to the story, no insight, no truth.

Shaking his head, he clicked to dismiss the news article, and sat there thinking. He knew from experience that murder victims weren't always saints, or honor students, or passionate campaigners who "inspired everyone". Just for once, he wanted to read that the victim had been "a selfish man who wasn't particularly liked". Yawning, he gently closed the lid of his laptop. It hadn't been a very productive evening – there was still a piece outstanding for *The Tribune* – but he'd catch up on work tomorrow. For now, he was done.

Taking his empty glass over to the kitchen counter, he went through to the bathroom, then switched off the lights. In the bedroom, he stooped to put his phone on charge, before sitting down on the edge of the bed. Just as he was bending forward to pull his shoes off, the phone began to ring.

Tom groaned, then froze as he remembered the time. It was almost 1am now... who would be calling this late? For a sickening moment he felt panic, certain that it was Samaira, that something was wrong with Zak – but when he snatched up his phone he saw a number he didn't recognise. Bowing his head in relief, he tapped the *Answer* button and lifted the handset to his ear.

'Hello?'

At first, there was silence. Then an unfamiliar voice spoke – rich and pleasant, with a warm Southern accent.

'Did you receive my letter?'

'Letter?'

For a moment, Tom was completely wrong-footed, wondering if this was another stupid marketing call, or just a misdialed number. Then he felt the hairs stand up on the back of his neck as it dawned on him. 'Oh, you mean... the letter with the hand-written envelope?'

There was a pause.

'That's right... Tom.'

Tom sat up straight, chilled by the mention of his own name.

'Do you know who I am?' the voice asked.

Swallowing hard, Tom took a breath, doing his best to sound calm.

'Are you the person who killed Elizabeth Reeves?'

The voice ignored his question.

'I'm a great admirer of your writing, Tom. You seem to have a knack for getting at the truth of a story without becoming distracted by all the titillating details of violence, or wallowing in pointless emotions.'

Tom pressed the phone hard against his ear, feeling the clammy sweat from his palm on the back of the handset.

'Why did you send me that driver's license?' he asked.

There was another brief pause, as though the answer to his question was being carefully considered.

'I believe it's important that a man understands who he's dealing with. Don't you?'

Tom frowned.

'And just who *am* I dealing with?' he demanded. 'Who are you?'

'Now *that*...' The voice changed in tone, as though whoever was speaking had allowed themselves to smile. 'Well, that is *the* question, isn't it? But the answer isn't a simple one, and it would require time and effort to discover the truth.'

'Everything requires time and effort,' Tom retorted, rubbing his eyes. 'That doesn't worry me.'

'Perhaps it should,' the voice said, softly. 'But if you're *sure* you want to know, I mean *really* know...'

Tom hesitated, sensing the warning in this, then hated himself for wavering. When had he become so cautious, so timid?

'I want to know,' he insisted.

'Very well. I'll be in touch.'

The line went dead.

5

They were in a small meeting room with glass walls on the fifth floor of the main Police Department building. The door was closed, but it didn't quite keep out the sounds of the open-plan office outside, just blurred them into an indistinct babble of voices.

Sitting across the table from Tom, Leo leaned back and rubbed his jaw.

'And that's all he said?'

Tom shifted uncomfortably on his chair, one foot tapping nervously against the other as he stared at his friend.

'Isn't that enough?'

He'd been trying to reach Leo all morning, without success. In the end, he'd taken a cab over here and sat downstairs until his friend had a few minutes free.

Leo bit his lip thoughtfully, then gave a slight shrug.

'He never actually admitted to killing Lizzie Reeves...'

Tom sighed.

'Next time I'll be sure to ask for a signed confession.'

Leo held up his hands. 'Sorry,' he said. 'I just like to be clear about things.'

'Well, it seems clear enough to me,' Tom muttered. A night of disturbed sleep had left him feeling impatient.

'Okay. So you tried to call him back?'

'I tried, but the number wasn't working. Probably a burner phone, and he could have tossed it right after the call.'

Leo nodded.

'Well, whoever he is, he certainly seems to be a fan of your writing...'

'Yeah.' Tom gave him a wry smile. 'Yeah, that's very comforting.'

Leo regarded him thoughtfully.

'You've done a lot of true crime features...' He leaned forward. 'You think maybe it's someone you've written about?'

Tom shook his head.

'I wondered about that, but most of the people I've reported on were either dead or in jail, and this... this doesn't *feel* like someone who's got a problem about something I've written.'

Leo considered this. 'Well, then maybe it's someone who wants their story told.'

Tom looked at him and nodded. 'That's what I've been saying...'

'...but that doesn't automatically make him a murderer,' Leo said, interrupting. 'I mean... what if it's some armchair detective, who's cooked up a theory about the Reeves case? Or someone who just wants to see their name in print?'

'No.' Tom took a deep breath. He'd been over it repeatedly in his mind, and there was something significant here, he was certain of it. 'Come on, Leo, you know me. I'm not some hack who sees spooks in every shadow. You know the kind of people I've dealt with, the situations I've been in. I *spoke* to this guy on the phone. You really think I'd be chasing this if I wasn't convinced?'

Leo stared at him, then acquiesced. 'No, I don't.'

'So what is it?' Tom pressed. 'Why are you giving me a hard

time? Why does it feel like you're pushing back against everything I say?'

Leo sighed.

'Because *I'm* not the person you need to persuade here,' he said, getting to his feet.

On the wall behind her desk, Lieutenant Gina Lopez had three framed commendations, and a faded child's painting of a police car. Wearing a smart grey suit and a carefully neutral expression, she paused to rub her eyes, then replaced her glasses and focused on Tom once more.

'And he *definitely* confirmed that he was the person who sent you the list?'

Tom held her gaze and nodded.

'The list and the driver's license, yeah.'

'But there was no direct reference to Reeves, or any of the other names on that list, during the call?'

'Only when I asked him if he was the one who killed her,' Tom replied, then added, 'which he didn't make any attempt to deny.'

Lopez studied him for a moment, then leaned back in her chair and glanced at Leo.

'You're strangely quiet, Moretti,' she said, thoughtfully. 'Where are you on all this?'

Leo hesitated.

'I agree, it's not enough to be sure of anything,' he conceded. 'But I trust Tom. And he's not the kind of guy who cries wolf.'

Gina's face remained impassive, but she sighed and turned towards the window.

'Bottom line? That driver's license is the only tangible thing you have right now. The rest is just...' She shook her head slowly, then appeared to reach a decision. 'Find someone we can speak to in Syracuse, someone who actually worked the

Reeves case. I need to know more about the investigation, and how that license could have wound up here, before I can make any real sense of this.'

Leo sat up.

'Sure thing,' he nodded. 'I'll get on it.'

'Thanks,' Tom said, relieved that Leo's boss had listened to them and hadn't discounted anything. 'I appreciate it.'

Gina regarded him calmly, her face giving nothing away.

'Don't thank me just yet,' she said.

Tom followed Leo down the corridor.

'So, what's the deal with the Lieutenant?' he asked, once they were far enough away from her office. 'I was trying to figure out how that went but I couldn't get any sort of read on her.'

'She's a good cop,' Leo replied. 'She's smart, gets things done.'

'Good to know. Hey, before I go, any word from Forensics? Did they get anything off the driver's license?'

Leo slowed and shook his head.

'Way too soon for that,' he said. 'But I *did* do some digging on those names from the list. You were right about them all being murder victims and I pulled the files to see if there was anything that stood out...'

'And?' Tom gazed at him expectantly.

Leo leaned in close, lowering his voice.

'Okay, so Elizabeth Reeves was found on a lake shore, about twenty minutes outside Syracuse,' he explained. 'The body wasn't in great shape – it's an isolated spot, and she'd been out in the open for a while – but she didn't drown. There was clear trauma to the head, like somebody had laid into her with a piece of pipe. It wasn't pretty, and it definitely wasn't an accident.'

'Right. Her boyfriend?'

Leo gave a slight shrug. 'It was an on-off relationship. He had a couple of priors for possession, but nothing violent. Local PD picked him up, because there was nobody else in the frame, but they never really figured him for the killer.'

Tom looked at him.

'That's it?' he asked.

Leo shrugged.

'Hey, you work the evidence however you can, but things don't always pan out. You know how it is.'

'Yeah, I guess so.' Tom sighed. 'What about the other two names? Anything on them?'

'Duncan Baumann was an interesting one,' Leo said, brightening. 'He's just some nobody, a minor city official up in Mitchel, South Dakota. Then one day, he goes out into the woods and gets shot in the head with a hunting rifle. Bang! Now it *could* have been a tragic accident – I mean, it does happen sometimes – except for one thing.'

Tom stared at him.

'What?'

'There was a note on the body,' Leo explained. 'A piece of paper, folded into the guy's pocket, written in neat little capital letters. It said, "OLD DEBTS MUST BE PAID". Pretty wild, huh?'

'Debts.' Tom frowned. 'Was he into anyone for money or...?'

'Who knows? There was a big investigation into the guy, and into his past, but...' Leo shrugged. 'No debts, no nothing. I requested a handwriting comparison with the letter that you received so we'll see if anything comes back.'

Tom considered this, trying to find a connection between the victims.

'What about the last one... Daryl Hirsch?'

Leo's expression darkened.

'Well, it was written up as a robbery,' he said slowly. 'Hirsch was found beside his car in a furniture store parking lot in Michigan. Multiple stab wounds. Whoever did it took his wallet, jewelry, phone...'

'But?' Tom prompted.

'But this furniture store was closed up, gone out of business. If it was a robbery, fair enough, but what was Hirsch even doing there? I'm thinking maybe it was something else, like maybe he was meeting someone... but nobody seems to know.'

Tom stood in silence for a moment, trying to make sense of it. They couldn't just be random deaths. They *had* to be linked, somehow.

Leo straightened up and clapped him on the shoulder. 'They did have one thing in common, though...'

Their gaze met. 'What's that?'

'They're all still unsolved,' Leo said. 'Whoever killed these people is still out there.'

Tom gave his friend a chilly smile. 'You're very reassuring, you know that?'

6

Kendra lived above a nail spa in an old, grey-brick building near Canal Street. Sitting across from her at the small table in her apartment, Tom set his fork down on the plate and turned towards the window. Outside, the rain pattered steadily on the glass and a distant police siren blared. Absently, he wondered if Leo and Lopez knew more than they were letting on, whether the crime lab would turn up anything useful from the driver's license or the letter...

'Hey.' Kendra leaned forward. 'Everything okay?'

Tom found her deep brown eyes studying him. She'd been his neighbor when he first moved to New York, one of his first American friends, one of the few people who'd been genuinely sympathetic about his depression. Perhaps that was why she was one of the few people he still felt comfortable talking to.

'Yeah.'

'You sure?' She arched an eyebrow at him. ''Cos you've been really quiet this evening.'

'Sorry,' Tom said, forcing a smile. 'I didn't sleep well last night, and today I... well, my head's been all over the place.'

Kendra narrowed her eyes. She pushed back her chair and got to her feet.

'Well, so long as it's not a comment about my cooking, then I guess that's all right.'

'No.' Tom looked up at her. 'No, really, this was great. Thank you.'

'Good.' Kendra reached for the bottle he'd brought and slid it across the table to him. 'Pour us both another drink then.'

Tom watched as she gathered up the plates and disappeared through to the tiny kitchen, then leaned over to refill both their glasses. Her apartment felt cluttered but comfortable – a tall wooden carving of an African woman, with Kendra's hospital ID lanyard hanging from its outstretched hand; the ornate Persian rug that had belonged to her mother; Polaroid photos of friends, arranged in a jumbled mosaic on the wall – everything obviously precious, everything obviously her.

'So, what kept you up last night?' Kendra called through from the kitchen. 'Did you finally hook up with that woman from *The Gazette*?'

Tom's face split into a wry smile. 'Remember I told you how we ended up sharing a cab after the Carbon Zero event? Well, a few days ago I ran into her again, at the press awards, and she completely blanked me.' He sighed. 'Clearly didn't remember me, didn't have a clue who I was.'

Kendra walked back over to the table.

'Her not knowing you *might* improve your chances,' she smiled, sweetly.

'Stop trying to cheer me up,' Tom grinned, as he slid one of the glasses towards her.

He'd often wondered about himself and Kendra. They got on so well, and they were both single just now, but she'd always been very clear that they were just friends. Thinking about some of the guys she'd dated, he couldn't really figure what her type was. All he knew for sure was that it wasn't him.

'So?' She reached for her drink. 'What kept you awake?'

He briefly considered telling her, wondering how he could do so without freaking her out. Being contacted by a potential killer wasn't the sort of thing that people took lightly. How could he explain to her why it mattered so much, and what it could mean for his career?

'It's just... it's this thing I'm working on. A possible story.' Pausing, he shook his head. 'I think it could be important but... well, I've got some reservations about it.'

Kendra frowned, as though she were trying to read his face. 'What does your gut tell you?'

Lowering his eyes, Tom picked up his glass.

'My gut tells me that this kind of opportunity won't come around again,' he replied. 'That if I let it go by, I'll always wonder if I made a huge mistake.'

Kendra looked thoughtful. 'What's that saying? That we only regret the things we *didn't* do?'

Tom knocked back his drink and raised his glass to her.

'No regrets,' he smiled, hoping it was true.

They sat on the couch together and Kendra put on a movie while they finished the bottle.

'How's Zak doing?' she asked.

Tom managed a slight shrug. 'He's doing okay, I guess.'

'You *guess?*'

'I speak to him on FaceTime, and I buy him things but it's... it's difficult, y'know?' Tom avoided her eyes. How could he figure out fatherhood when he still hadn't figured out what was wrong with himself? 'I want to be part of his life, I want him to like me... but how do you even do that? Sometimes I just feel like he's growing up without me.'

Kendra gave a soft sigh. 'Maybe that's because he is.'

Tom glanced over at her. 'I'm just not sure that I'm ready...'

'He's a little kid, Tom. It's not like he can wait for you, is it? And if you're not there, then he *is* gonna grow up without you.' She shifted on the couch so she could face him. 'If you want to be part of his life, then you've gotta be there for him, ready or not. Otherwise, you're gonna miss it.'

Tom held her gaze for a moment, then looked away.

'You talk a lot, you know that?'

Kendra smiled and reached for the wine bottle.

'My bad,' she grinned. 'I'm sure it's all *Samaira's* fault. Is that what you wanted me to say?'

She offered him the bottle.

Tom made a face, then held out his glass as she refilled it.

'You enjoy mocking me, don't you?'

She put her arm around him and gave him a sympathetic squeeze. 'I really do,' she whispered.

Kendra had to work in the morning, so it wasn't late when he left her apartment and stepped out onto the shining wet sidewalk. There were no cabs in sight, but the rain had stopped and he was feeling pleasantly buzzed from the drinks. He managed to catch a bus, and eased into his seat, gazing out through the glass as the rain-washed streets slid by. Somehow, he always felt better after talking to Kendra. Did she get something similar from spending time with him? He hoped so. Dimly, he wondered what he brought to her life, and why she'd stayed friends with him, when so many of their mutual acquaintances had sided with Samaira after the break-up. Whatever the reason, he was grateful. A smile touched his face as he thought about her, idly wondering what little gift he could get her to say thank you...

There was a buzzing in his pocket. Yawning, he reached inside his jacket and drew the phone out, lifting it to his ear as he stared out at the lights of the city.

'Hello?'

'Good evening, Tom.'

He stiffened as he recognized the voice, gripping the back of the seat in front of him. 'Oh, er.... hi.'

There was a slight pause, as if the person on the other end of the line was amused to have caught him off guard. 'Have you been thinking about our last conversation?'

Tom screwed his eyes shut. 'Of course I have.'

'And do you still want to know?' the voice pressed. '*Really* know?'

Tom twisted his body towards the window, cupping a hand over the mouthpiece.

'I said so, didn't I?' he hissed.

There was another pause.

'It *will* mean travelling,' the voice warned. 'You may be away for several weeks.'

'Away?' Tom frowned. He'd been uneasy about speaking on the phone, getting too close to the killer... but travelling? Was this man suggesting that they should actually *meet?*

'Is that a problem?'

'No, it's just...' Tom pressed his forehead against the cold glass, desperately trying to shake off the alcoholic fog. 'Where would I be going?'

'Are you starting to have second thoughts?'

'No... No, I'm just trying to understand the risk, that's all.'

'Oh, we'll *both* be taking risks, Tom.'

There was a sound that might have been a soft chuckle. 'But I don't intend to kill you, if that's what you're thinking. At the end of our journey, you'll be free to walk away... and with one *hell* of a story.'

There it was! He'd wondered if the caller might be someone who craved attention – someone who wanted a journalist to take an interest in them – and this seemed to confirm it. Tom gulped down a breath, his thoughts stumbling ahead of him.

What a story it could be... and who better than him to tell it?

'Well?' the voice pushed him.

The temptation and fear were both overwhelming – because if this offer was real, then the danger was real too.

'Can you...' He rubbed his eyes, trying to think. 'Can you tell me more about how this would work, about what we'd –?'

'You just need to *decide*, Tom.' There was a note of challenge in the voice now. 'Do you want this or not?'

Tom stared out at the blur of anonymous figures on the sidewalks, dim shadows slipping away into the night. If he said no, the opportunity would be gone forever, and he'd spend the rest of his life wondering what might have been. He clenched his fist, knowing that he had to say something...

'Yes. I want it.'

It was the only answer he could give. And anyway, he had friends in the police department. They would help him, protect him. He would figure something out.

'Well, I just need to know that you understand: if you *do* agree to do this, there's no backing out – no way out, under any circumstances whatsoever. The consequences would be... *severe.*'

'What do you mean, "severe"? What sort of consequences?'

The voice ignored his questions.

'Do you *understand*, Tom?'

Tom hesitated, trying to think of something he could say, something that would tip the balance in his favor ... but it was no use. Swallowing hard, he replied, 'I understand.'

'And you still wish to proceed?'

He took another breath, screwing up his courage.

'I do.'

For a moment, neither of them spoke, then the voice was in his ear again, sounding pleased.

'That's good, Tom. I knew you'd make the right choice.'

Tom found that he was nodding in agreement, and forced himself to sit still.

'So now, will you... will you tell me who you are?'

There was a momentary pause.

'You can call me J,' the voice replied. 'But that's not really what you want to know, is it now? You want to know how that young woman ended up on her back beside the lake. You want to know *why...*'

'So tell me,' Tom urged. 'I'm listening.'

'Good.' There was a soft chuckle. 'Enjoy the rest of your evening, Tom.'

'No, wait, I...'

The line went dead.

Tom slumped back in his seat, staring down at the phone in his hand, wondering what he'd just agreed to.

Travelling... a journey...

He frowned, trying to clear his head, trying to recall everything that the killer had said. Opening the Notes app on his phone, he began tapping in what he could remember, knowing how much might depend on it.

One hell of a story... no backing out...

The bus slowed suddenly for a sharp corner, the unfamiliar motion jolting Tom back to the present. He sat up and looked around, blinking stupidly as he tried to work out if he'd missed his stop. Where the hell *was* he?

Flustered, he got unsteadily to his feet and took a few swaying steps towards the door, peering out the windows, and wondering if he'd gone too far.

7

It was mid-afternoon and Tom was working when he heard a knock. Putting his eye to the peephole he saw Leo standing there, his imposing figure filling the hallway.

'Hey,' Tom said, unbolting the door and pulling it wide open. 'Come in.'

'Sorry I couldn't make it this morning.' Leo stepped over the threshold and gave an apologetic shrug. 'A couple of things came up, you know how it is.'

'It's okay. Don't worry about it.'

He shut the door, then turned to find Leo watching – those keen eyes taking in the multiple locks before sweeping round the apartment, the way so many detectives seemed to – observing, cataloguing, contemplating.

'You want a drink?'

'No, I'm good, thanks.'

Leo paced slowly across the room to peer out of the window. His looming silhouette made the whole apartment feel small.

'I prefer this to the place you had in Brooklyn,' he said,

turning and looking round the room once more. 'You been here long?'

'I think it's been...' Tom paused, trying to work out the dates. 'Yeah, it must be a little over three years now. When Samaira left, I just... needed to move, so I took the first thing I could get. But after a while – well, I suppose I wanted to be closer to things again.'

'Yeah, I get that,' Leo agreed. 'Anyway, it's a change of scene from the diners and bars where I usually see you.'

'True enough.' Tom gestured towards the sofa. 'Have a seat.'

'Thanks.' Leo sat down, spreading his arms out on either side of him, effectively filling all the space. 'So, I assume you haven't heard anything new from the guy today?'

'Nothing since last night's call,' Tom said, drawing over his desk chair.

'All right.' Leo hunched forward, clasping his hands in front of him. 'Then let's start with his voice. Anything you can remember, anything at all?'

'Well...' Tom did his best to summon the memory of the phone call, and hear the voice again.

We'll both be taking risks, Tom.

'You said he had a Southern accent?' Leo prompted, taking a small notepad from his pocket and flipping it open.

'Yeah, it was like...' Tom paused, then frowned. 'I'm not so good on which accent comes from which state, but it was definitely from the South.'

'Did he sound *like* anyone?' Leo asked, jotting down a couple of words that Tom assumed were probably *Southern accent*. 'Maybe somebody famous?'

Tom thought for a moment.

'You remember Kevin Spacey in *House of Cards*?' he said. 'It was a bit like that, only softer. Less pronounced.'

'Got it,' Leo said, writing *Kevin Spacey*. 'Any feelings on his age?'

'Hard to say, but I think he was older than me,' Tom said, slowly. 'It wasn't that his voice was weak or anything... more the *way* he spoke.'

Leo considered this. 'Did he sound educated?'

'Yes, that's a good way of describing it,' Tom replied. 'Not upper-class, just well-spoken.'

'OK. When he spoke to you, did you pick up any emotion from his voice? Was he angry? Excited?'

Tom shook his head.

'Just the opposite,' he said, recalling the unsettling manner and tone. 'He was calm. I mean *really* calm, like everything was under control.'

Leo's face remained impassive, but his eyes were fixed on Tom.

'What about background noise?' he asked. 'Were there any distinctive sounds? Anything you could pick out?'

Tom made a face. 'I've been over it and over it in my head but –'

'Just try,' Leo urged. 'Even one little thing could turn out to be important.'

'I was on a bus when I took the call. It was noisy, difficult to hear...'

'Then how about the previous call?' Leo pressed. 'Anything that comes to mind? Did he sound like he was outdoors maybe?'

Tom concentrated, trying to think back. 'Well... the call was quite clear, and I don't recall any background noise, so I guess he was probably indoors.'

'Nothing else? Nothing at all?'

'Sorry.'

Leo jotted another note down in his pad, then looked at Tom.

'How did he get your number?' he asked. 'Are you easy to find online? Or would our guy have contacted one of the newspapers you work for?'

'My number's listed all over the place,' Tom said. 'It's in several business and media directories, so it wouldn't have been difficult for him to...'

He paused, then stiffened.

'Shit! Forget about the *number*, how the hell did he get my *address?*'

He glanced at Leo, who was watching him steadily, and remembered the professional way that the detective had been assessing the security of his door locks and windows. 'This guy knows where I *live*, Leo.'

Leo held his gaze. 'Yeah,' he said. 'You only just picking up on that *now?*'

Tom's shoulders sagged, and he slumped back into his desk chair.

'I figured you'd realized that already,' Leo said, shooting him a look of concern. 'Something got you off your game? You getting rusty?'

Tom hung his head. How the hell *had* he missed it? Maybe he'd spent too long taking easy-money jobs where he didn't have to think. Or maybe it was the anti-depressants that he'd reluctantly started taking just to get him through the break-up... and that he was somehow still taking now.

'Shit,' he muttered. 'The bastard knows where I live.'

'He said he didn't plan on killing you,' Leo reminded him. 'So – y'know – that's something.'

Tom glared at him. 'Well, let's hope he's a man of his word.'

They sat there in silence for a time. Eventually, Leo cleared his throat.

'Is there anything else?' he asked. 'Anything at all?'

Tom swallowed his nerves and forced himself to think, running through the conversation once more in his mind.

Travelling... no backing out... consequences...

He lifted his head, staring at Leo.

'Did you see the scene photos of Lizzie Reeves?' he asked. 'Where she was found?'

'Yeah, I saw them. Her body was by the side of a lake, with the head injuries, like I told you...'

'Was she lying on her front or on her back when they found her?'

'On her back. Why?'

Tom clenched his fists as the meaning of this sank in.

'He *said* that. He said it when he called last night... that she was on her back!'

Leo narrowed his eyes.

'But in the notes you sent over, he only talked about her ending up *beside* the lake...'

'No, I remember,' Tom said, excitedly. 'He said, "You want to know how that young woman ended up *on her back* beside the lake."'

'You're sure about this?'

'I can hear him saying it!' Tom tapped a finger against the side of his head. 'I'm absolutely sure.'

Leo sat back, making the sofa creak, his expression more serious.

'I mean, it doesn't *prove* he killed her...' he said, eventually.

Tom finished his sentence for him. '...But it seems a lot more likely now.'

Leo regarded him thoughtfully. 'Maybe it does.'

'And,' Tom added, 'if he killed *one* of the people on that list...'

'Yeah, but you don't have enough to make *that* leap,' Leo cautioned. 'For now, those are just names on a list.'

Tom paused, feeling frustrated. 'You know that something like forty percent of homicides never get solved, right?' he argued. 'That's a *scary* number. You don't think there's room for a few serial killers to hide, in among all those unsolved cases?'

Leo shook his head.

'What I think, or what you think? It doesn't change anything. This guy knows things he shouldn't, about the Reeves murder? Sure, *that* might be something. But then we got a set of names that may or may not be connected... one don't make the other true.'

Tom scowled, then his shoulders dropped. 'And the other two deaths were out of state,' he said. 'We don't have enough to get the Feds involved.'

'Exactly,' Leo replied. 'For now, all I can do is poke around the Reeves case, and check out anything you bring me.'

'I'm sorry. It's just...'

There *was* something here, he felt sure of it, but Leo was still a cop, and cops could only do so much without evidence. He gave his friend a wry smile. 'Anything on the driver's license?'

'Nothing except your prints,' Leo replied. 'I'm still waiting on the handwriting, but as soon as I hear back I'll let you know.'

Nothing.

In spite of all the hints, in spite of everything they'd put together, they had nothing. Whoever he was, J hadn't given them anything they could use to find him. He could be anyone, anywhere.

'You okay, Tom?'

He blinked and found that Leo was watching him with obvious concern.

'Try to keep it together... it's gonna be alright.'

'Yeah.' Tom swallowed, but his mouth was dry. 'Yeah, I know.'

'If you're worried...' Leo glanced around the apartment. 'I dunno, maybe stay someplace else for a couple of days? Just until we can figure out what we're dealing with.'

Tom got to his feet and turned towards the window, staring out at the building opposite, wondering what he could do, where he could go. He had a couple of friends he might stay with, here in the city – but that would potentially mean putting them at risk. Boston was out for the same reason. He briefly considered checking into a hotel, but really, what would be the point? He couldn't afford it for long, and he'd have to come home sooner or later... and then he'd be right back where he started.

'No,' he said, quietly. 'Running and hiding won't solve anything.'

Behind him, he heard the detective sigh.

'You got a better idea?'

Tom stared down into the street, watching a cyclist weaving in and out of a line of cars. A woman was standing in the doorway of the creperie opposite, eating, while her dog looked up at her hungrily.

This was his neighborhood, his *home*. He didn't want to live here in a state of constant worry, waiting for another phone call... or, worse, a knock on the door.

He frowned. Up until now, he'd been focused on getting the story – but what if he *was* the story?

What if *he* could help to stop this murderer?

He blurted it out before he could stop himself: 'Do you think we could catch him? Y'know, if I agreed to meet him?'

Leo gave him a wary look.

'If you agreed to *meet* him?'

'It's the only avenue we have open to us right now,' Tom reasoned. 'And you said it yourself – unless we get another lead...'

Leo looked grave.

'Think about what you're saying here, Tom. If this guy is what you think he is, you'd be sticking your head in the lion's mouth. I mean, I get that you wanna help, but come on... this isn't like writing about something after the fact; this is lining yourself up to be the next victim! You don't wanna take risks like that.'

'If this guy is what I think he is, I'm *already* at risk,' Tom argued. 'I'm on his radar, Leo, and he knows where I live. I'd rather do something about that, than just sit around, waiting for him to pay me a visit.'

And being part of the operation that caught the killer would make the story so much stronger.

Leo's expression was still troubled.

'This is a bad idea, Tom,' he growled. 'I mean, even if we could get you some protection – try and keep tabs on you – there's still no way to guarantee your safety. The fact that you're even talking about it shows you've been out of the game too long. You don't have to do this. You don't have to prove anything.'

It was a low blow, but Tom knew his friend was just trying to protect him. He held up his hands.

'Okay, okay,' he said. 'Just in theory – hypothetically-speaking – how do you reckon this might play out? Come on, Leo, humor me.'

Leo didn't respond at first, then he slowly lifted his head.

'Hypothetically,' he replied, thoughtful now. 'Well, he's *got* to assume that you're talking to the cops, so if he wants to meet you then he'd have to figure some way of getting you on your own.'

'Maybe that's what he meant when he talked about travelling?'

'Maybe. It could mean you leaving the country, in which case we're screwed – no way to plan for that, or protect you, and no jurisdiction for us.'

'True,' Tom admitted. 'But what if it was here in the States?'

Leo made a face that wasn't encouraging.

'Still a bunch of problems,' he mused. 'This isn't like some old *Dirty Harry* movie, where the bad guy runs the cop back and forth all over town, just to make sure he isn't being followed. Our killer needs a way to meet you where we can't follow. Somewhere we can't see, or can't go...'

He trailed off, deep in concentration.

'Well, he must have *some* kind of plan,' Tom said. 'Otherwise he wouldn't have contacted me.'

Leo shot him a bleak look.

'Oh yeah. And that's doesn't make me feel any better, thinking how he's probably got it all worked out... and we don't.'

'So, we come up with our *own* plan,' Tom said firmly. 'Come *on*, Leo. Don't you want to be the detective who stops this guy?'

Leo gave him a withering look.

'Of *course* I want him stopped...'

'And your boss will help us, right?'

'She's gonna think you're batshit crazy.'

'But then you'll tell her about the caller knowing details of Lizzie Reeves' murder,' Tom reminded him. 'Then she'll *have* to take it seriously.'

The determination in his voice was obvious. Leo sat in silence for a while, then sighed in resignation.

'Well, if we're even gonna *consider* this, the first thing we'll need to figure out is how we can follow you,' he said. 'We have to keep track of your location, at all times, no matter where this guy tells you to go...'

8

Tom's Journal

I don't know why, but things have changed for me since Leo's visit. I didn't notice it at first, with all the planning and preparation, but it's been a week now, and I'm definitely feeling more positive. I've been eating a bit better and drinking a bit less, and I've even hit a couple of the daily exercise goals on my smartwatch – something I've not done in months.

Even Zak seemed to pick up on my mood when we spoke on FaceTime yesterday. At first, he wanted to tell me about his latest Little League game – being English, I didn't grow up with baseball, so all I can really do is offer him general encouragement – but then we got onto cartoons and Lego and things were a lot less awkward. We must have talked for almost an hour. Samaira checked in on us a couple of times, appearing surprised and pleased that neither of us wanted to end the call. And, when we finally did finish, Zak told me that he loved me before I said it to him, which hasn't happened for a long time. Maybe I'm just imagining it, but they say kids can tune into their parents' emotions, and it really felt like that as we were talking.

He's certainly more perceptive than I thought, and it made me realize how important it is that I protect him from my own negativity.

I'm still not sure why I'm feeling better, especially with all these new concerns about a potential J meeting. Maybe part of it is just keeping myself busy, distracting myself from unwanted thoughts, but I suspect there's more to it than that. Kendra once told me that preparing for something – even if it's stressful – is often easier than just waiting for it to happen. Perhaps that's the case here. There's certainly been plenty of details to work out, and Leo is still a bit reluctant about the whole plan, though I think we've both kind of talked ourselves into it now.

His boss, Gina Lopez, wasn't easy to persuade. She grilled us both and asked a ton of questions: Why had he chosen me? Had I ever spoken with anyone who worked on the Reeves case? Did I believe that J was the real thing? Was there anyone out there who might want me dead? Why the hell had I agreed to do it?

Leo told me she was a good cop, but she's also got an incredible poker face, and I honestly couldn't figure out whether she was convinced or not, right up until the end of our talk. Since then, she's been working with us on a plan to keep me as safe as possible for a potential meeting, and figuring out how to take down our anonymous caller, assuming he actually shows up.

Anyway, we're probably as prepared as it's possible to be. The trap is ready, and I'm the bait. Now it's just a question of waiting.

9

There was a single soft chime – *1 new message*. Yawning, Tom paused the old episode of *Smiley's People* that he was watching and leaned over to retrieve his phone from the arm of the sofa. It had been two weeks since he'd heard from J and he was beginning to doubt whether anything more would come of it. Then he saw the new message was from an unrecognized number, and sat up straight, hurriedly tapping on the screen.

Tom,
Get off at Prattsville and walk north. At the bridge, turn right onto Maple Lane. About a mile out of town, there's a parking spot on the left side of the road. Be there at 1:30pm.
Travel light but bring your phone and a coat. Come alone.
See you tomorrow,
J.

At the bottom of the message there was a link to a bus company website. Tapping it, Tom found himself on a *Print Your Ticket* page. He hesitated, then got up and walked over to his desk. Checking that there was still paper in the tray, he followed the instructions on the phone screen, and waited as the printer clicked and whirred into life. After a moment, a single page slid out and he snatched it up, staring at it.

Your Ticket / Trip Itinerary

– – –

08:30AM (origin) NEW YORK, NY

Port Authority, 625 8th Ave, New York, NY 10018

– – –

12:36PM (destination) PRATTSVILLE, NY

Crnr Rte 23 & Washington St, Prattsville, NY 12468

– – –

Passengers: 1

Tom sank down into his desk chair, his heart racing. The trip was scheduled for tomorrow. And it was one way. Twisting around, he opened his laptop and typed *prattsville, ny* then hit the *Search* button. From the results, he selected a map option and stared at the screen. It looked like a tiny place, little more than a village, straddling a river in the forested wilderness of upstate New York, miles from any major town. Why was J sending him all the way out there?

Picking up his phone, he read the message again, then dialed Leo's number. It rang several times before he heard his friend pick up.

'Hello?'

'It's Tom,' he said, quickly. 'Listen, I just got a text message from J. He wants me to go and meet him... he's sent me a bus ticket for tomorrow morning.'

'*Tomorrow*?'

'He says I'm to go to some place called Prattsville, and there's walking instructions to a spot just outside the town. I'm supposed to bring my phone and a coat, and go there alone.'

'Where the hell is Prattsville?'

'Upstate New York. It's a little place in the middle of nowhere.'

'How did he send you a ticket?'

'It was a link to a prepaid bus ticket. The bus leaves Port Authority at eight-thirty tomorrow morning.'

'Eight-thirty!' Leo exclaimed. 'Jeez, that doesn't give us a lot of time.'

'I know,' Tom agreed, anxiously. 'Do you think you can still get the protection detail together? We've only got a few hours...'

'It's gonna be tight, but I'll try. Let me make some calls and I'll get back to you. For now, assume it's going ahead and start getting ready. You remember what we discussed?'

Tom closed his eyes and nodded. *This was really happening.* 'I remember.'

'Good.' Leo sounded more collected now, his training kicking into gear, a calm head in a crisis. 'Follow the plan, exactly as we discussed. No shortcuts and no screw-ups, okay? We need you prepared.'

'I will be,' Tom assured him.

'Good. I'll call you back in a while.'

Leo hung up.

Tom remained motionless for a moment, then put his phone on the desk and got slowly to his feet. Walking over to the kitchen counter, he poured himself a glass of Scotch and knocked it back.

He wondered where J was right now, what *he* must be thinking... how did he hope to arrange a meeting while avoiding capture? Was he really walking into their trap, or were they walking into his? Had the killer thought of something that they hadn't?

Focus!

Leo had told him to get ready, and that's what he had to do. Setting his glass down, Tom turned and walked through to the bedroom. The most crucial element of their plan was to ensure that Leo and the team could follow him at a distance, remaining out of sight until they were needed. To do that, they needed a way of tracking his location – something that would still work, even if J somehow managed to surprise them before Tom reached the rendezvous.

The GPS tracking device was sitting on his bedside table, a thin black cable connecting it to the power outlet. He checked that it was fully charged, then disconnected it and turned it over in his fingers; a small disc-shaped device, barely larger than a poker chip, finished in smooth grey plastic. Despite the size and weight, it could broadcast Tom's location every 30 seconds, for almost a week. And because of the size and weight, he'd be able to hide it in his clothing without anyone knowing it was there.

Moving over to the wardrobe, he pulled the door open. A coat would certainly have been easiest – there was plenty of room to hide things in the lining, and J had actually told him to bring one – but coats were the first things to be discarded, when going indoors or getting into a vehicle. No, he needed somewhere better, a hiding place that wouldn't be discarded, and wouldn't be discovered in a pat-down search. He stooped to retrieve a pair of sneakers, lifting them up to look at them. The upper parts were made of a breathable, padded material. With a pocket knife, he carefully made a clean, two-inch incision on the inner quarter panel, and gently eased the tracking device in between the layers of padding. When he was satisfied with the positioning, he used Krazy Glue to seal the slit, then inspected his work. Nobody would notice unless they knew it was there. Whatever happened, the police should always be able to find him. It was a reassuring thought.

Going back to the wardrobe, he grabbed a few clean t-shirts, along with some underwear and socks. He wasn't sure how long he'd be away – the killer might be waiting for him in Prattsville, or he might have to travel for days before they met – so he made sure to pack his anti-depressants as well as some basic toiletries.

He was just sliding his laptop into the bag, and checking he had his chargers, when the phone rang. Snatching it up, he saw Leo's name on the screen.

'Hello?'

'How are you getting on?' Leo asked. 'Is the tracker fully charged?'

'Everything's ready.' Tom forced himself to speak calmly. 'How about you? Did you manage to get hold of the protection team?'

'I spoke to Lopez and the team's in place. Lock'n'load, pal! We got the green light.'

It was grey and overcast as Tom stepped out onto the sidewalk. Pulling the lobby door closed behind him, he held his bag close to his body and hurried towards the street corner. He hadn't slept, and the early morning air felt cold, but he was glad to be on his way at last. Anything was better than pacing around his apartment, waiting.

He hailed a cab and slid into the back seat, tasting the sickly scent of air-freshener as he leaned forward and spoke to the driver through the glass partition.

'Port Authority please.'

The cab pulled away and Tom made himself sit back, keeping his bag on his lap as he stared out of the window at the neighborhood slipping by. Commuters were going to work, their faces masks of boredom as they hurried along, rushing to do the same things they did every day. So safe, so *monotonous*... He wondered how they could stand it.

Traffic was moving freely along West Houston and they were making good time. A thought came to him, and he took out his phone. Opening the messages screen, he brought up

Samaira's name, then hesitated. He couldn't tell her what he was *really* doing... and what else could he say that wouldn't be misinterpreted, stir up more tension between them? Frowning, he cancelled the message and brought up Kendra's name instead. They were supposed to be meeting up later in the week, and he felt as though he had to say *something...*

His thumb hovered over the keyboard, before he slowly tapped out a few words.

Hi. Unexpected work trip came up. Might be away for a few days. Tell you all about it when I get back. Tom.

He hit *Send* and slipped the phone back into his pocket, wondering what kind of story he'd have to tell when he did get back.

There was a lot more traffic when they turned onto 6th Avenue, and the cab slowed to a halt. Restless, Tom checked his watch again. He knew he had plenty of time – and there was still the long bus journey ahead of him, so he wasn't going to get to Prattsville any quicker – but he could feel his impatience growing. The cab crept forward, stopping and starting at intersections, as the buildings on either side of the street became steadily taller. They were opposite Macy's when he felt a vibration in his pocket and drew out his phone. It was Leo.

'Hey, buddy. How're you doing? You get any sleep?'

'An hour or so,' Tom lied. 'Where are you?'

'We're just heading over to Port Authority now,' Leo said. 'You on your way?'

'I'm in a cab.' Stifling a yawn, Tom gazed out at the endless succession of people, vehicles and storefronts. 'I'll be there soon.'

'Okay. We've spoken to local PD up in Greene County and explained the situation. They'll be keeping a low profile, but they'll be watching the roads around Prattsville.'

'Good to know.'

'There's a team of people who've got your back,' Leo assured him. 'Just remember what we talked about, and you'll be fine.'

The Port Authority Bus Terminal was an ugly, sprawling structure, like a huge multi-story car park, caged in behind a crisscross lattice of steel girders. It squatted on a series of giant columns, with shops and restaurants huddled beneath. The cab dropped him off on the opposite side of the street before pulling away and disappearing into the flow of passing traffic.

Tom glanced around uneasily, then made his way to the crosswalk, weaving through the steady stream of morning commuters. He strode through the delicious aroma from the bakeshop on the corner – normally, that would have made him hungry – but today he pressed on, pushing through the glass doors of the terminal building entrance. Inside, the place was a vast mall, with lines of illuminated storefronts, and the constant murmur of people.

Tom went to one of the information kiosks and checked his gate number, then glanced at his watch. There was still nearly an hour to kill. Taking out his phone, he noticed that he had missed a message from Kendra.

Lucky you! Have fun and call me when you're back. X

Perhaps he should have told her. Would she have pressured him not to go? Part of him hoped she would have, and part of him worried how she'd react when she inevitably found out. Once again, he was torn between his career and the people he cared about. Staring at the screen, he sighed then rubbed his eyes. He was just tired, that was all. A cup of coffee and he'd be okay.

Jamming the phone back into his pocket, he turned and went to find a Starbucks.

10

Gripping his bag tightly, Tom stepped off the escalator and walked towards the gate. His eyes darted left and right, searching the faces of everyone he passed, looking for a flicker of recognition. Was J here somewhere, watching him? Could he be one of the passengers on the bus? Standing in line, he glanced around, surreptitiously studying his fellow travelers. There were only two older men among them – one was overweight and balding, with a blue quilted coat; the other looked like a veteran, his military haircut shot through with grey, wearing a faded brown leather jacket. As they got on board, Tom did his best to see their faces, but neither looked round, and he couldn't get a clear view of them. He took his seat, a few rows from the front, and tried to settle himself in for the long journey.

Prattsville was four hours from New York. As the bus emerged from the noisy darkness of the Lincoln Tunnel, sweeping up and around to join the freeway, Tom gazed back across the Hudson to the jagged Manhattan skyline. It had been months since he'd left the city, and there was something odd about seeing it from the outside again, recognizing just how constrained his life had become. He hated the idea of being in a rut, of *settling*. Still, he was certainly out of his comfort zone now.

The bus rumbled north, gradually breaking free of the New Jersey sprawl to a tree-lined highway that swept along past a succession of anonymous towns. At each stop, Tom peered down at anyone waiting on the sidewalk, and watched carefully to see who was getting on and off. He wasn't certain what he was looking for – someone staring at him, or turning away suddenly – but he felt sure that he would know it when he saw it. Leo had thought it unlikely that the killer would risk boarding the bus but, even if he'd decided not to, he could be watching from somewhere along the route. There was still a long way to go.

And the man with the leather jacket was still on the bus, sitting somewhere behind him.

The skies gradually cleared and the sun made a brief appearance, warming his face. The hypnotic green blur of the passing landscape and the soothing motion of the bus made his eyelids feel heavy, as lack of sleep began to catch up with him. Frowning, he took a few deep breaths and forced himself to sit up, willing himself to stay alert.

An hour became two hours... two hours became three. The sun had disappeared again, and the weather was steadily closing in. Tom stared out at a misty grey landscape, pale and cold. *Bring a coat,* that's what he'd said...

They'd left the freeway far behind them. Now the bus was on a remote country road, winding its way deeper into the forested hills. The passing towns became smaller and less frequent, and there was almost no other traffic around. Glancing down at his phone, Tom noticed that the cellular service was dwindling.

Was that part of the reason the killer had brought him all the way out here, to prevent him communicating with anyone?

And if there was no signal, would his location tracker still work?

He stiffened, sitting up suddenly in his seat. Out here, in the middle of nowhere, he really didn't want to be alone. Gripping the phone, he considered texting Leo, then decided to call instead, needing the reassurance of his friend's voice. But there were other passengers around him, and he didn't want to be overheard...

He paused for a moment, trying to think clearly. There was a restroom at the back of the bus. He could lock himself in there and make a quick call – plus, walking to the back of the bus would give him a chance to get a proper look at his fellow travelers, including the man in the leather jacket.

Twisting around in his seat to check the restroom was free, he gathered up his bag, took a deep breath and got stiffly to his feet.

There were only two passengers in front of him – a teenage boy listening to music in the seat directly ahead of him, and a middle-aged woman with wavy blonde hair sitting up near the driver.

Okay...

Easing himself out from between the seats, he began to make his way towards the rear of the bus, eyes glancing left and right.

A young couple in their twenties – him with a downy beard, her with purple-framed glasses – huddled close as they watched something on an iPad, connected by a shared pair of earphones. On the opposite side, a woman in her thirties was lost in thought as she gazed out of her window.

One row further back was the balding man in the quilted jacket – asleep now, with a slack jaw and a peaceful expression – an open packet of cookies lying on the empty seat beside him.

In the next row, a goth girl sat with her head bowed, reading a book. Opposite her was a heavy-set woman with snowy-white hair and a pale blue cardigan; she looked up briefly as he passed, then went back to her magazine.

Two rows further back was the man in the leather jacket. He was leaning back in his seat, face turned towards the window, a backpack on the seat beside him. Tom slowed, peering down at him, but the man gave no reaction, seemingly focused on the passing scenery.

There was only one more passenger – a little old man with thick glasses and a wisp of fine white hair, who'd joined the bus at Bloomington. Tom stepped past him and entered the tiny restroom, quickly shutting the door and locking it.

He leaned against the wall and took a breath. Ten passengers, not including himself, and still only two who looked as though they might possibly fit the killer's voice.

He took a moment to compose himself, then drew out his phone, noting with some relief that he still had a signal. Tapping Leo's number, he turned his body away from the door and cupped his hand over the mouthpiece. It only rang once before being answered.

'Is everything okay?' Leo sounded concerned but, Tom realized, what they were doing was dangerous, and an unscheduled call *would* be worrying.

'Yeah, I'm all right.' Tom spoke in hushed tones. 'I just... wanted to check in, that's all.'

'Okay, sure, no problem,' Leo replied. 'We're about half a mile behind you right now.'

Tom breathed a silent sigh of relief.

'That's good to know,' he said. 'The tracker's working okay then?'

'Yeah, we know exactly where you are. Why?'

'Nothing,' Tom answered quickly, then added, 'I just saw that the cell service was getting a little patchy and I wondered if that would affect it.'

'No, you're good,' Leo assured him. 'I'm watching you all the time, and we ain't gonna lose you.'

Tom bowed his head. 'Thanks,' he murmured.

'Are you sure you're okay?'

'Yeah, it's just being stuck on this stupid bus...' Tom rubbed his eyes. 'Too much time to think, to imagine stuff, you know?'

'Just take it easy.' Leo's tone was calming now. 'You're doing fine.'

'I've been watching the other passengers, seeing who got on, who got off,' he said, glad to change the subject. 'There's ten people on here with me just now.'

'Anyone who looks like they might be a fit for the voice?'

'It's hard to tell,' Tom replied. 'There's two older men – an overweight bald guy with a blue quilted jacket, and a grey-haired guy in a brown leather jacket. Both of them got on in New York...'

'I *seriously* doubt that this guy would risk being on the bus with you,' Leo said. 'You just sit tight and keep your eyes open, okay? Everything's gonna work out.'

'Yeah, I know.' Tom felt annoyed at himself for sounding so anxious. 'Look, I'd better go...'

'Hang in there, buddy,' Leo said, gently. 'And remember, we're right behind you.'

'Thanks, Leo.'

Tom ended the call and slipped the phone back into his pocket. Conscious that other passengers might be expecting it, he flushed the toilet, then waved his hand under the dryer to start it. While he waited for it to finish, he leaned forward and peered at the tired-looking face in the small mirror above the sink.

Back in his seat, he put his bag down beside him and gazed out the window again, staring at the forested slopes that rose until they were lost in the mist.

Whoever this killer was, he was going to catch him.

11

Tom stepped down onto the side of the road. Behind him, he heard the soft hiss of the doors closing – nobody else was getting off here. Shouldering his bag, he moved across onto the paved sidewalk, then turned to look up at the windows as the bus pulled away. The man in the brown leather jacket glanced down at him briefly, but there was no recognition, nothing in his expression to indicate that he was anything other than a disinterested traveler. Tom watched the bus as it rumbled away down the long straight road, then exhaled.

So far, so good.

He gazed up at the low grey clouds, glad that he'd brought his coat, then took a moment to look around. Prattsville was a tiny little town, stretched out along a straight piece of road in a forested valley. The houses and stores were spaced apart with trees and mown lawns, and there were flower baskets hanging from the lampposts. On his right, was a neat little red-brick post office with the stars-and-stripes hanging from its flagpole, bright and bold against the overcast sky. On the other side of the street, beyond a gravel lot stacked with fertilizer sacks and wooden garden furniture, there was a big old-fashioned hardware store. A typical, out-of-the-way small town... definitely *not* the sort of place you'd expect to meet a killer.

Glancing down at his watch, he checked the time, then gripped the strap of his bag and started walking north. Many of the houses had raised wooden porches and flags in their front yards. There were a couple of small stores, and a tavern restaurant whose painted sign reminded passers-by that Tuesday was "Wings Night" and Thursday was "Taco Night".

Tom walked on, his eyes flicking left and right. He felt conspicuous out here, a lone person on a long, empty sidewalk, so noticeable after the crowded anonymity of the city. He'd known the risk he was taking, coming to meet a murderer, and had mentally prepared himself as well as he could... but he hadn't expected it to be so dreadfully quiet. He slowed, glancing back over his shoulder at the deserted road behind him. There was virtually no traffic through here. If the local police really *were* watching him, they were being very subtle about it.

There was a small church near the edge of town, with a white wooden belltower, and beyond it the asphalt bent round to the right in a long, sweeping curve. A quarter of a mile further on, past a final few houses, the road angled up and to the left, rising to a boxed girder bridge that carried it over the river. On the right, a smaller road continued along this side of the water.

Maple Lane.

Tom turned, taking one last look back towards the town. Then, adjusting the strap of his bag, he walked on.

For a while, the river was close by, a dull rushing sound that was somehow comforting as he trudged along, but he soon lost sight of it as the road began to climb into the woods. There were no sidewalks anymore, and steel guard rails lined the edge of the asphalt as it curved away to the left; he listened for the sound of oncoming cars amid the soft rustling of the trees, uneasy about being out here alone, and on foot. He walked on slowly, following the road as it continued to rise. The woods pressed in tightly on either side, though he still managed to catch an occasional glimpse of the river, now far below.

He was beginning to wonder how far he still had to go when he suddenly saw it: a parking spot on the left, just a few yards ahead. It was little more than a patch of dirt, a gap in the guard rails, but there could be no doubt about it. This was the place.

Tom stepped onto the dirt and peered down between the trees, but it was just a tangle of bushes and dense foliage. There was nobody here.

He checked the time again. It was twelve minutes past one – eighteen minutes to go. Pushing his hands into his pockets, he began to pace, back and forth along the dirt.

When he first heard the car, he froze. Pulse quickening, he remained absolutely still for a moment, trying to be sure... yes, it was definitely coming from the north, beyond the town. And it was getting nearer.

Tom drew himself up, standing straight as he turned towards the sound. Whatever he felt inside, he wasn't going to let the killer think that he was scared. First impressions mattered, and he was determined to meet this man on an equal footing.

And then he could see it, coming into view around a bend, further up the road. It was a blue pick-up truck, and it came down the hill towards him at speed. Tom squinted, trying to see the driver, but took a nervous step back when the truck showed no sign of stopping. He glimpsed a bearded man with a baseball cap as it roared past and continued down the hill towards the town.

Was that him?

He checked his watch. There were still a couple of minutes to go. Perhaps that was just a local person who happened to be passing. Until J chose to reveal himself, there was no way of knowing.

The noise of the pick-up truck faded, and all that remained was the restless sigh of the wind in the trees. Tom stared at his watch, counting down the final few seconds...

One-thirty.

He looked up, alert and eager, not sure whether he expected to see another car, or a hidden figure stepping out from among the trees...

Somewhere behind him, a phone rang.

Tom spun around, his eyes searching the wooded slope – but there was nobody there. The ringing continued, a thin, insistent tone against the soft rustling above him. Confused, he tried to pinpoint the sound. He couldn't see anyone, but it was close, very close. Tentatively, he moved forward, then turned a little to the left... it was directly in front of him now... right here, and yet...

He glanced down. At his feet, nestled in the rough grass at the edge of the dirt strip, there was something half-covered in leaves. Stooping, he reached down and picked up the small, clear plastic bag. Inside it, he could see a cheap prepaid phone, its screen illuminated, and some sort of black fabric pouch.

The phone continued to ring.

Opening the bag, Tom took out the phone and pressed the *Answer* button.

'Hello?'

'Hello Tom.' Something in J's voice sounded different, almost deflated.

'I'm here,' Tom prompted him. 'I'm at the parking –'

'When you look back on this moment,' J said, interrupting him suddenly. 'I want you to ask yourself: *why* did I involve the police?'

Tom blinked, and half-shook his head.

'What are you talking about?'

On the phone, J sighed with disappointment.

'I told you to *wait*, Tom. I told you in my letter. But I guess you just *couldn't* wait to talk about this, could you?'

'But... I did everything you said,' Tom protested. 'I'm here, just like you asked.'

'There are other journalists, Tom. No hard feelings.'

'But...'

'And I do hope you keep up the writing. Goodbye Tom.'

'No! *Wait...*'

The line went dead.

Tom stood by the roadside for a time, trying to process what had just happened. Was this some sort of trick? A test to see how he'd react? Or had he really come all the way out here, just to be told that he'd blown it?

After a moment, he reached for his phone, wanting to call Leo, but then stopped himself. What if J was watching him right now, waiting to see what he would do?

Frustrated, he turned this way and that, peering into the trees, but there was no sound or movement. Perhaps he really was alone. Lifting the clear plastic bag, he took out the black pouch and studied it for a moment, but it was empty. Sighing, he returned the phone and the pouch to the plastic bag and jammed everything into his coat pocket. Then, with a last glance around, he turned and started walking back down the hill towards town.

As he came to the first bend, he thought he could make out the sound of a car somewhere ahead, faint, but growing louder. He paused, briefly wondering if he should turn around and run back to the parking spot, but it was too far for him to make it in time. He stood and waited until the car came into view, tensing as it approached – but the driver was an elderly woman. She drove past without stopping.

Tom sighed.

What the hell was he even doing out here? He'd been excited at the prospect of a truly unique story, at the thought of a leading role in the capture of a killer. In a single stroke, it would have kickstarted his career, and put him on top again... all too good to be true.

Standing there by the roadside, he shook his head, then took out his phone and made the call. Leo answered on the first ring.

'Hi.'

'Where are you?' Tom asked.

'About half a mile away.' The anticipation was obvious in Leo's voice. 'Are you alone?'

'Yeah, he isn't coming.' Tom bowed his head. 'I think we've blown it.'

'Shit,' Leo sounded unhappy. 'Okay, just stay where you are. We'll come and pick you up.'

Moments later, the car came round the bend – a dark blue Dodge Charger – with Leo at the wheel and a serious-looking woman in the front seat beside him. They pulled over and Tom got in.

'Hey, pal.' Leo's eyes were watching him in the rear-view mirror. 'You okay?'

'Yeah,' Tom said, sighing as he put his bag on the seat beside him. 'I'm fine.'

'This is Alyssa Cunningham,' Leo said, as he eased the car into a tight U-turn. 'She works with me sometimes.'

Alyssa twisted round in her seat and nodded to him. She was in her thirties, dressed in a dark jacket, with an unreadable expression.

'Good to meet you,' she said calmly.

'You too,' Tom replied.

'So?' Leo demanded, as he accelerated down the road. 'You gonna keep us in suspense? What happened?'

Tom leaned back in his seat.

'I walked up there to the place, just like he said, and I got there with plenty of time to spare,' he explained. 'I only saw one vehicle, a blue pick-up truck...'

'Did you get the license plate?' Alyssa asked him.

Tom shook his head, feeling even worse.

'Don't worry about it.' Leo was still watching him in the mirror. 'We can speak with the local PD... I'm sure they can track it down.'

'Well, it didn't stop, and that was a bit earlier anyway,' Tom said. 'Then, at one-thirty, I was waiting at the parking spot, and I heard a phone ringing. I looked around but there was nobody there... then I saw this plastic bag, kind of hidden under some leaves.'

He rummaged in his coat pocket and drew out the bag, with the phone and the black pouch. Alyssa reached over to take it from him, holding it carefully by one corner as she peered at the contents.

'I saw there was a phone inside, so I answered it,' Tom continued. 'And it was J.'

'What did he say?' Leo asked.

'He said something about how I'd look back on this day and ask myself why I'd involved the police, and why hadn't I waited, like he told me to in his letter. He said that there were other journalists and... no hard feelings.'

Tom wondered who J would approach now. Who would get the story that he had lost?

'That's it?' Leo pressed.

'Pretty much.' Tom shrugged. 'He said that he hoped I kept writing, then he said goodbye and hung up on me.'

Leo drove in silence for a time, then smacked the steering wheel.

'Fuck!'

'So that's it,' Tom murmured. 'Somehow, we've blown it.'

Leo's eyes flashed at him in the mirror, then glanced across at the bag Alyssa was studying. 'What's that black pouch thing?'

'It's one of those secure wallets for phones,' she replied. 'It blocks any signals, in or out – cellular, Wi-Fi, everything.'

Tom frowned. 'The prepaid phone wasn't inside it,' he said. 'They were just... in the same plastic bag.'

'Oh, I don't think it was meant for the prepaid phone.' Alyssa looked over her shoulder at him. 'I think it was probably for yours. You know, blocking your phone so it couldn't be tracked, and providing this other one for you to receive your instructions?'

'Of course.'

J had obviously given this a lot of thought, Tom thought, preparing an elaborate plan that would have eventually allowed them to meet... but he had stumbled at the first obstacle. He'd failed.

12

Tom took another sip of coffee and set his cup down on the polished wooden table. He could see Leo outside, pacing back and forth in the diner's small parking lot, speaking into his phone.

'So how do you guys know each other?' Alyssa asked, slicing off a piece of pie with her fork. She was sitting directly opposite, and her calm eyes seemed to bore into him as she ate.

'We met a few years ago, when I was researching an unsolved murder for a book,' Tom explained. 'Did you ever hear of the Sonnenfeld case?'

'No.'

'Well, Leo was one of the detectives who'd been working on it, and we got talking.'

Alyssa raised an eyebrow. 'How did you ever persuade him to talk to you?'

'We just... helped each other out,' Tom said, shrugging. 'I'd pulled together a lot of background on my own, and I was able to give him some useful information.'

Alyssa appeared impressed.

'Did he catch the guy?'

'No,' Tom admitted. 'But we did manage to link two separate murders... and doing so helped to rule out the previous main suspect. That was pretty satisfying.'

'I guess.' Alyssa nodded thoughtfully, then turned her attention back to her food.

Tom traced a finger around the rim of his coffee cup. The Sonnenfeld case *had* been a good story, and it had done a lot for his career... but this one with J could have been so much more.

Behind him, he heard the door. Leo came over to the table and slumped down into a chair, his expression grim.

'The others aren't far,' he muttered, slipping his phone into his jacket pocket. 'They should be here in a few minutes.'

'Did you speak to the sheriff's department too?' Alyssa asked.

'Yeah, I've updated them on the situation, so they can stand their people down. I don't reckon they're gonna catch anyone today.'

He sat brooding over his coffee. Tom watched him for a moment, then leaned forward.

'At least we know that J's been here,' he said.

Leo glanced up.

'In the last day or so, yeah. That phone still had plenty of charge.'

'Exactly. But you don't think he's here now, do you?'

Leo gave him a bleak smile.

'I think he's *smart*. And if you're smart, and you know someone's about to close a trap on you, you get the hell out. Remember, he could have called from anywhere.'

'Okay, but what about the local police?' Tom pressed. 'This is a pretty quiet place. They might have noticed a strange car...'

'It depends when he dropped the phone off. He could have done it during the day yesterday, *before* he called you, and before I spoke to the sheriff's department.'

Tom considered this.

'You don't think he came back?' he asked. 'Today, I mean... to meet me?'

The idea that he'd been anxious for nothing, that J had already written him off, was somehow disappointing.

'*That* depends on what tipped him off,' Leo said, softly.

Alyssa gave him a sidelong glance.

'There's no way he knew we were following the bus,' she said. 'We stayed a long way back, you know that.'

'I do know that,' Leo said. 'No, I think maybe someone told him.'

Alyssa's glance turned into a hard stare. 'You don't think he found out from *our* end, do you?'

'No way.' Leo sounded adamant.

'Who, then?' Tom asked.

Leo looked uncomfortable, then turned back to Alyssa. 'It's only a theory but... I've been trying to figure out why our guy chose this place for a meeting, and now I'm asking myself if he might have a friend up here, maybe someone in the local PD. I mean, think about it... short notice? Out-of-the-way place like this? Of *course* I'm gonna call in some local backup. And as soon as I do, everyone involved knows we're coming.'

'Great,' she replied, without enthusiasm. 'So where does that leave us?'

'Nowhere.' Leo lapsed into a troubled silence.

'So, what's our next move?' Tom demanded. 'Do we speak to the local police or not?'

Leo pursed his lips. 'Not yet. I'm gonna speak to the Lieutenant first,' he said. 'See what she can dig up on the Green County officers and staff.'

'Oh, she's gonna *love* you for that,' Alyssa muttered. 'She burned a lot of favors pulling this together.'

'I know.' Leo bowed his head. 'It's a fucking mess.'

Tom shifted awkwardly in his seat. As much as he'd wanted this for himself, it was dawning on him that he'd put his friend in a difficult position too. He was glad when the waitress came over to their table.

'More coffee?' she asked, brightly.

'Thanks,' Leo murmured.

They sat there as she refilled the cups. Alyssa gestured out the window. 'The others are here.'

Outside in the parking lot, a dark blue SUV had pulled up, and a man and woman were getting out. He was in his thirties, stocky, with a trimmed beard; she was athletic, with her brown hair swept back in a ponytail. Both were dressed in casual nondescript clothes. As Tom watched, the back door opened, and another man got out – a familiar figure, with short, greying hair, and a brown leather jacket.

'That guy out there...' Tom said, turning back to the table. 'You had an undercover cop on the bus and you didn't *tell* me?'

Leo shrugged his broad shoulders. 'I told you I'd try and keep you safe,' he replied, simply.

It was getting dark by the time they got back to New York. Leo had seemed preoccupied, and Alyssa had chosen to ride in the SUV with the others, so it had been a quiet journey. As they passed through the toll plaza and approached the George Washington Bridge, Tom stifled a yawn.

'You really don't mind?' he asked again. 'You could always drop me in midtown if that's easier...'

'It's no problem.' Leo was still staring straight ahead, his face lit red from the taillights of the car in front. 'Anyway, it gives me time to think.'

'Well, if you're sure...'

The bridge rose up before them, a looming black structure against the glow of the evening sky, with soaring strings of lights draped between the dark towers. As the car climbed to pass over the river, they felt the regular *bump bump bump* of the concrete deck sections, and Tom gazed out at the twinkling Manhattan skyline.

'Sorry about the way things turned out,' he said.

Leo shot him a puzzled look.

'What have *you* got to be sorry about?' he asked.

'Well, I know it can't have been easy squaring things with Gina, and you both went to a lot of trouble on this...' Tom trailed off, then sighed. 'Oh... you know what I mean. I just really thought that something was going to happen today... that we might *catch* him.'

'It wasn't your fault,' Leo said flatly. 'And don't be so sure we won't catch this guy. Even if he's done talking to you, we know more about him now. We've got a possible connection between three murders that we didn't have before, we know he's been to Prattsville in the last few days, and we may get more about his location if we can track down where he called you from this afternoon. We ain't done with this guy.'

Tom nodded thoughtfully. The story hadn't gone the way he expected, or wanted – but maybe it wasn't quite over yet.

Leo dropped him off at the corner of Ludlow and Rivington.

'Really appreciate the door-to-door service,' Tom smiled as he got out and shouldered his bag.

'You can make it up to me tomorrow,' Leo told him. 'Buy me lunch and we'll figure out how we find this sonofabitch.'

'Sure thing,' Tom agreed. The idea that they might still be able to hunt J down was suddenly invigorating. 'What time?'

'I'll call and let you know.'

Tom watched the Dodge pull away and disappear around the corner. He stood for a moment, wondering if he should grab something to eat from the mini-mart, then decided against it. He was still feeling full from his meal at the Prattsville diner, and he really wanted to sit down and type up a few notes on the day, before last night's disrupted sleep finally caught up with him. Turning around, he walked eagerly along the block, let himself into the building lobby, and jogged up the stairs.

Things had seemed pretty bad when J had hung up on him, but Leo wasn't throwing in the towel, and neither was he. They *did* know more now – they knew where the killer had been, and when.

Walking down the hallway to his apartment, he reached into his pocket for his keys.

The more he thought about it, the more he felt that this aborted meeting could be crucial to finding their man. It was almost impossible to move around the country without leaving some sort of trail, digital or otherwise. They'd find out where the prepaid phone was purchased, which cell towers it had registered with... somebody would remember something, or there might be CCTV footage...

He slotted his key into the lock and pushed, but it didn't go far enough in to turn. Frowning, he tried again, then pulled it out to check it was the right key.

Had the lock jammed? Squatting down, he leaned forward to peer at the keyhole, when he sensed something moving behind him – but as he tried to turn around, a jolt of blazing agony hit him in the side of the neck, surging down through his limbs and up into his head. Mind and body went into spasm as the world contracted and he lurched forwards, banging into the door and collapsing in a twitching heap on the hallway floor.

13

For a time, he was unable to think, and there were only disjointed impressions... intense, clenching pain... a hand pressing something firmly over his mouth... being dragged across a rough carpet, wondering why his arms and legs wouldn't work...

He wanted to cry out, but his lips were sealed shut, and a shrieking sense of panic welled up inside him as he struggled to breathe through his nose. The floor seemed to move beneath him, and his stomach lurched as his wide eyes tried to focus... was he in the elevator?

Every part of him hurt... an exhausting, aching hurt that left him dazed and helpless. He was dimly aware of cooler air on his face, then something was pulled down over his head, and he was being dragged into an awful, terrifying darkness.

When he came to himself again, he was lying on a cold, hard surface that bumped and rattled against his skin. He felt the world shifting, swaying him from side to side, and the muffled sounds of an engine and wheels on the road slowly took shape in his mind. He was in a vehicle.

Instinctively, he tried to sit up. But though his painful muscles responded at last, he found that his arms were securely bound behind him and his legs were tied too.

I can't move.

A horror gripped him. Straining against his bonds, he writhed desperately, then finally slumped down again, sobbing with frustration, trying to inhale.

I can't move!

The air inside the bag that covered his face was warm and sickly, and he forced himself to lay still, suddenly afraid that he might suffocate if he struggled too much.

Mustn't panic, mustn't lose it...

But as he lay there, weeping in the darkness, he felt himself becoming more and more frightened.

Am I going to die? Oh God, am I going to die?

A sudden wave of grief surged through him, and his thoughts spiraled away. Zak... Samaira... all the stupid choices he'd made, all the things he hadn't done...

But there was nothing he could do now. He couldn't get free, he couldn't cry for help, he couldn't even breathe. It was unbearable. And, worst of all, no matter how frantic he became, he couldn't make this nightmare stop, he knew it would only continue...

His cheeks bulged as he choked against the gag taped over his mouth, twisting and jerking his body against the cold metal floor, banging his head until the exertion left him dazed and sweating, frantically sucking air through his nose – but the note of the engine didn't change, and the rumble of the road remained constant.

They weren't stopping.

. . .

Tom lost track of how many times the fear overwhelmed him, of how many times he thrashed around in frenzied desperation, but the strength was draining from him now. He lay there, battered and breathless, screwing his eyes shut to try and block out the endless darkness.

And then, there was a particularly jarring bump, and the motion of the vehicle changed. The road noise was different for a while, then he felt himself lurch forward as they came to a standstill, and the engine fell silent.

In his confusion, this sudden quiet was more terrifying than everything that had come before, and he fought for breath, straining to hear anything that would tell him what was happening.

For a moment, there was nothing. Then, he made out the metallic creak of a door opening and felt the weight of footsteps on the floor. He flinched as something touched him, then felt the warm fabric move across his face, as it was pulled up and off. He jerked his head backwards in the cold air, breathing fast through his nose as he blinked at the dim light.

There was a figure stooping over him, an indistinct silhouette that squatted down beside him and gently cradled his head. He blinked again, struggling to focus, trying to see who it was, even though he already knew.

'Good evening, Tom.' The voice was as calm as ever, with that same distinctive Southern accent. 'It's a pleasure to finally meet you.'

Tom tried to draw away, but firm hands gripped his shoulders and helped him up into a sitting position, where he froze, staring at his captor. They were in the back of a large van, with both the rear doors wide open. Outside, he could dimly make out the darkened expanse of a vacant lot, with a high razor-wire fence. The light of a nearby streetlamp was the only illumination.

J turned away and moved over towards the doors, the van

shifting and creaking with his weight. Dressed in work overalls, he was shorter than Tom had expected – around 5'10" or 5'11" – with a paunchy build and receding hairline that suggested a man in his early fifties. As he sat down somewhat stiffly on the floor, the light fell on an intelligent face with dark, glittering eyes, and he shifted uncomfortably before drawing a gun from one of his pockets. It made an ominous metallic clunk as he set it down beside him.

'I apologize for the subterfuge,' he said, glancing over at Tom. 'But a man in my position has to take certain precautions. I'm sure you can appreciate that.' He paused, then a faint smile touched his lips. 'Just as *I* can appreciate why you tried to involve the police.'

Trembling, Tom glanced around, his breathing fast and ragged. J appeared to study him for a moment, then leaned forward, stretching out a hand.

'Forgive me,' he said, then ripped the tape off Tom's mouth. 'There. That should be better.'

Gasping, Tom inhaled deeply, gulping down the cool night air.

'You must have been uncomfortable.' J's tone was one of regret and concern. 'Can I get you some water?'

Tom stared at him, then shook his head, groggily.

'What... what's happening?' he croaked.

A smile of profound satisfaction spread across J's face.

'What's *happening* is that we're starting our journey, Tom.'

He leaned back contentedly, resting his head against the interior of the van. 'You said you wanted to know who I am... that you were prepared to give your time, and dedicate yourself to learning the truth? Well, I'm gonna repay that commitment. I'm going to take you with me and give you an access-all-areas backstage pass. You're gonna see exactly what I do... and maybe understand the world a little better.' He paused, then chuckled to himself. 'Whatever happens, you'll have a *very* exclusive story at the end of it.'

Tom gaped at him in horror as the full magnitude of his situation began to dawn on him.

'Oh shit,' he whispered.

J looked up.

'What's the matter, Tom?' he asked. 'Not what you imagined? Did you think that you'd accept my proposition, then outsmart me and hand me over to your friends at the police department?' He gave Tom a mocking grin. 'Were you planning on being a hero?'

Raising his index finger, he wagged it back and forth in gentle admonition.

'No, no, no... we had an agreement. And I believe that a man should *honor* his agreements.'

Tom tensed and tried to shuffle backwards. The restraints were cutting into his wrists, but the real pain was the aching in his muscles and the pounding in his head.

'What... what the hell did you do to me?' he rasped.

'Oh, that was just a stun gun.' J reached inside his overalls and produced a rectangular black device, with two metal terminals protruding from one end. Holding it up for Tom to see, he pressed a button and a glaring arc of electricity crackled angrily across it. 'Fifty million volts... but don't worry, it's non-lethal. I expect you'll feel fine in an hour or two. Are you sure you wouldn't like some water?'

Tom shifted his weight slightly, trying to find a position that didn't hurt as much. His tongue felt thick and his mouth was dry.

'Water,' he whispered.

'Be right back.' J shuffled over to the door and clambered out of the van, disappearing from view. A moment later, he returned, stooping as he approached Tom and held a plastic bottle of water to his mouth. 'Here you go.'

Tom drank with some difficulty, swallowing hard as water trickled down his chin.

'Thanks,' he gasped, as J withdrew the bottle. It felt bizarre to acknowledge his captor, but somehow the courtesy of the older man seemed to demand it.

'Better?' J enquired, moving over to sit down beside the gun again.

Tom nodded, then hesitated, his eyes on the weapon.

'So you're... you're *not* going to kill me?' he asked, cautiously.

J followed Tom's gaze down to the gun, then looked up at him and smiled.

'As I told you before, I have no intention of killing you.'

Tom frowned. 'Then... I don't get it... how do you think this is going to...' He broke off, as a frightening possibility occurred to him. 'You're not going to keep me bound and gagged in the back of this van – are you?'

J shook his head. 'I don't think that'll be necessary.'

'Then...' He looked at J warily. 'I don't understand...'

J sat back against the interior of the van and sighed with weary patience.

'Allow me to explain,' he said. 'You're going to accompany me for a few weeks. During that time, you'll be free to observe, to interview me, and to write. Naturally, you'll have to follow my itinerary and instructions at all times. And you *won't* be able to contact anyone, or interfere with my work in any way. At the end of our journey, I'll release you from your obligations, and you'll be free to go and do as you please.'

Tom stared at him. 'But – why would I...?' He trailed off.

J lowered his eyes. 'If you recall, I *did* warn you that the penalties for non-compliance would be most severe.'

'Penalties...' Tom lifted his head slightly. 'So if I go to the cops, I'm a dead man, is that it?'

J dark eyes were shining as he answered, simply: 'Not *you*, Tom.'

Tom froze as his stomach began to twist into a cold knot.

'If I should be killed,' J continued, 'if I'm captured, if I'm hindered in any way whatsoever –' He fixed Tom in his gaze, '– then the people you care for most will die. Including your son.'

Tom choked. For a moment, the whole world seemed to stop, and he could only gape in frozen horror. Then a scream of animal rage exploded from him and he began to struggle wildly against his restraints.

'No! NO! Not Zak!'

Pain surged through him as he twisted and pulled, but he couldn't break free.

'The arrangements have already been made,' J continued, raising his voice to make himself heard. 'There's nothing either of us can do to change them... you just have to hope that I'm still around to give the cancellation order when we're done.'

'You sick FUCK!' Tom continued struggling and swearing, banging his feet on the floor and making the van shake, and all the time his captor sat patiently, watching him, waiting for him to wear himself out.

Eventually, when Tom was hoarse from shouting, and his head was bowed with exhaustion, J spoke again.

'Do you understand the rules, Tom?'

Tom glared at him.

'Fuck you!' he hissed.

J regarded him calmly.

'Do you understand the rules?'

'Rot in hell!'

'Do you understand the rules?'

J's tone made it clear that he would keep asking until he received a satisfactory answer. Tom slumped forward, too tired to fight any longer. For now, there was nothing he could do.

'I understand,' he snarled.

'And you agree to abide by them?' There was a note of warning in the way J said this.

'Yeah,' he growled.

J studied his face, then nodded. Rummaging in his overalls, he took out a small pocketknife and knelt by Tom's feet, where he carefully sawed at the plastic restraints until they snapped. Then, shuffling behind him, he freed his hands.

Tom gasped with relief, feeling his shoulder click as he brought his stiff arms forward and rubbed at his wounded wrists.

'I'm sorry, Tom, I truly am.' J moved around in front of him again, closing the knife and returning it to his pocket. 'But it's the only way this was ever going to work, you must see that.'

Tom glared up at him balefully, wanting to smash that calm face, to silence that awful voice.

'You sick fucking bastard...'

He trailed off as J stooped to pick up the gun. The older man straightened up, then turned around to face him and held out the weapon, grip first.

'What... what are you doing?' Tom stammered.

J met his gaze.

'I'm checking how well we understand each other.' He stretched out his arm, putting the gun within Tom's reach. 'Go ahead, take it.'

Tom hesitated, then instinctively snatched at the gun. It felt heavy in his hand, big and unwieldy, but he managed to get a hold of it, aiming at J as he found the trigger with his finger.

J made no attempt to move or reclaim the weapon.

'I wanted to get things straight between us, to clear the air before we go any further...'

He broke off as Tom aimed the gun directly at his face.

'What have you done with my son?'

Slowly, J raised his hands, palms outward. 'Nothing.'

'Don't *fucking* lie to me! What have you done with my son?'

'Nothing. I promise.' He was eerily calm. 'And nothing will happen, so long as you honor our agreement...'

Tom stiffened, trembling with frustration.

'...but that really is up to you,' J continued. 'You've got the gun, you can decide whether...'

'Is it loaded?' Tom snapped.

J gave him a long, serious look.

'It's loaded.'

Tom stared down the barrel, his finger pressing up against the trigger.

'How do I know you're not bluffing?' he demanded. After the initial shock of J's threat, his mind was racing. This could all be a trick...

'There's something you need to see,' J said, softly. 'I have a phone in my pocket, and I'm gonna take it out... nice and slow...'

Tom tensed at the movement.

'What the hell is this?' he snapped.

Tilting the phone so that Tom could see, J launched an app and tapped the screen. A low tone sounded once... twice... then the view changed.

'This is how you know I'm not bluffing.'

J held out the device to him, a bright rectangle in the gloom of the van. 'Look.'

Tightening his grip on the gun, Tom's eyes flickered briefly down to the screen.

'Do you recognize it?'

It was a narrow house with a steep pointed roof, pale blue slatted walls, and porch rails. The camera moved slightly, focusing on a small tree on one side of the wooden steps, then a blue mailbox on the other.

Samaira's house in Boston.

'I don't understand...' Tom swallowed, trying to keep his voice calm. 'You went to the house and filmed it?'

'No, Tom.'

There was a note of pity in the older man's voice now.

'This is *live*,' J explained. 'Your son is in there, right now... but he's perfectly safe, I promise you...'

Tom choked back a cry of anguish. Staring down at the screen, he shook his head, trying to make sense of what he was seeing, trying to think...

The house looked different to the last time he'd seen it, with newly painted shutters edging the upstairs windows, and hanging baskets on the porch.

'You want the camera a little closer?' J asked.

Tom frowned at him.

'Closer?'

To his horror, the view on the screen lifted slightly, then began to move, as though it was being walked towards the house.

'No!' Tom cried. 'No, stop!'

The view halted, steadied once more.

Someone was there at the house right now, and they could hear him.

Stricken, Tom could only stare at the screen as the enormity of what was happening crashed in on him.

'Oh God... no...' he whispered.

J nodded, then sighed.

'If you *do* decide to shoot me... well, again, I'm truly sorry.'

He bowed his head and waited.

Tom's finger was rigid against the trigger, his aching shoulders tightening until they burned. He had the killer – *literally*, had him in his sights.

But the killer had his son.

Slowly, he lowered the gun, and his eyes blurred with tears as the weight of the situation crashed in on him.

'Why the hell are you doing this to me?' he demanded, stifling a sob. 'What the fuck do you want?'

J glanced up, then very slowly held out his hand. He waited until Tom reluctantly gave him the gun, then put the safety on and released the clip, holding it up to show that it was indeed loaded. Replacing the clip, he slipped the weapon inside his overalls before speaking.

'You agreed to this, Tom,' he said. 'Remember? All I expect is for you to keep your word.'

'But why me?' Tom choked, rubbing his eyes.

J regarded him with some sympathy.

'It's a long story, Tom. We'll have time to talk, *plenty* of time... but not now.' He straightened up, his tone becoming brisk. 'Can I take it that you *do* intend to honor our agreement? You won't try and stop me, and you'll do *exactly* as I say?'

Tom gazed up at him bitterly. 'What choice do I have?'

'I just *gave* you a choice, Tom!' J snapped. 'Now I want your answer.'

'Okay,' Tom murmured, startled by the change in J's tone. 'I'll... I'll do what you want.'

'Well then, let's start by putting some distance between us and this van, before the police come looking for it.'

J reached out a hand and lifted Tom to his feet. 'We've got a long way to go tonight.'

Tom swayed, trying to steady himself. 'Where are we headed?' he asked.

'Places you might not wanna go,' J replied, softly. 'Places only I can take you.'

14

J eased himself down from the back of the van, then extended a hand back up to Tom.

'Here. Just... take it slow,' he advised.

Feeling numb and unsteady, Tom accepted the hand and clambered down. A wave of dizziness hit him, and he almost stumbled, but J had a firm hold on him.

'Where are we?' he asked, squinting at his surroundings. The van was parked in a remote corner of a large vacant lot. Dark trees obscured the view beyond the razor-wire fence and, as he turned, he could dimly make out the back of several low, windowless buildings.

'Trenton, New Jersey,' J said. He had carefully emptied out the contents of his pockets and was now undoing the overalls. Underneath, he was wearing a dark grey sweater and blue jeans. 'You'll need to change.'

'Change?' Tom asked. His thoughts were still fuzzy, and his limbs ached.

'Your clothes.' The older man looked at him expectantly, then inclined his head towards the back of the van. 'Take them off and leave them in there.'

'But...' Tom blinked. 'Why?'

'We're gonna have to alter your appearance, so it's best if you just leave the whole lot behind.' J sighed. 'Am I really going to have to explain *everything* I tell you to do?'

'No, but...' Tom glanced around, self-consciously. 'What will I wear?'

J stepped out of his overalls and indicated a large plastic bag, sitting on the ground at the side of the van.

'There are new things for you in there.'

'Oh.' Tom stared at the bag, then felt a glimmer of hope as he remembered the GPS tracker.

The police would find him! Maybe not right away, but tomorrow, when Leo couldn't get hold of him, he'd figure out what had happened and use the tracker to get the location and come for him...

He saw J watching him, and began to unbutton his shirt, wondering what to do about his shoes. He'd need to remove them to take his jeans off, but maybe if he changed quickly, he could get his shoes back on before J said anything.

Nervously, he undressed, stripping down to his socks and boxer shorts, before moving over to the bag and lifting out a new pair of black jeans.

'Underwear too,' J said, folding his overalls and tossing them into the van.

Tom looked over at him.

'You want me... naked?'

'Not especially,' J replied. 'But I do think it's best. Consider it a symbol of the transition to a... a new chapter of your life.' He flashed Tom a brief grin. 'And a way of ensuring you don't have any personal items hidden away.'

Tom hesitated, then leaned against the side of the van, balancing on one leg then the other, as he removed his socks. Slipping his shorts down, he kicked them off, then reached for the bag of clothes to find new underwear.

Beside him, J began to gather up his discarded clothing – shirt, jeans, socks, shoes...

'Hey!' Tom looked over hopefully, pointing. 'Let me keep my shoes.'

'Don't worry,' J replied. 'There's a brand-new pair at the bottom of that bag. Size nine, right?'

Tom stared at him helplessly.

'Um... yeah, but...' He trailed off, wondering how his captor had known the correct shoe size.

J threw the clothes and shoes into the van, then walked round to the cab. A moment later, he returned with Tom's bag.

'No, wait!' Tom cried out. 'My laptop's in that bag, I *need* that if I'm going to write...'

J silenced him with a look, tossing the bag into the back of the van, followed by Tom's wallet, and smashed-up phone.

'Hurry up and get dressed,' he said.

The new shoes felt tight as he laced them up. Getting unsteadily to his feet, Tom paused to breathe through a wave of nauseous panic. J had promised not to harm him, but what if he had made that promise to the others? What if this was all just part of the killer toying with his next victim?

Anxiously, he made his way towards the back of the van. The older man was crouched down with a small flashlight gripped between his teeth, working to fix new license plates.

Hope returned to Tom. J was changing *plates*, not changing vehicles! It didn't matter whether the tracker was on his person or in the heap of clothes in the back of the van. It would still lead Leo right to him.

And then he saw the gas can.

'Come and hold this light for me,' J scowled, glancing up at him. 'I can't see a damn thing.'

Tom moved around beside him and took the flashlight, his eyes still on the can.

'Fitting false plates?' he croaked, then cleared his throat. 'That's smart.'

'I'm glad you approve,' J said, grimacing as he tightened the second screw. 'Though, if we're gonna be accurate, I'm actually putting the real plates back on.'

He stooped to retrieve two other license plates that were lying by his feet, then slowly stood up.

'*These* are the false ones,' he explained, holding them out so Tom could see. 'A different plate number, though it *is* from another white Ford Transit Cargo, just like this one. I wouldn't want to make things *too* easy for your police friends.'

Tom shook his head, confused.

'But – why would you...?'

'When they find this van, with its *genuine* plates, there won't be anything to link it with you, or your disappearance, or the CCTV footage from the parking garage under your apartment building.'

Tom blinked, recalling vague images from earlier.

'You took me down in the elevator...' he said, slowly.

'Then loaded you into the back of the van and drove you right out.' He gave Tom a friendly pat on the shoulder. 'I truly am sorry about that.'

Tom nodded slightly, trying to assemble the disjointed memories.

Being dragged along the hallway... lying on the floor of the elevator... being dumped on the floor of the van...

'So now you've changed the plates back... so you can drive it without attracting any police attention...'

'Oh no,' J replied. 'No, I've changed the plates back because I'm gonna burn it.'

'What?' Tom's head snapped up. 'But...'

'We left New York in a white Ford Transit Cargo,' J

explained. 'Do you really think I'm going to continue our journey in that *same* vehicle, even if it has different plates?'

He stooped to pick up the gas can.

Tom stared in panic at the pile of clothing in the back of the van.

'But... my things...' he stammered. If the tracker burned now, Leo would have no way of finding him.

'Don't worry,' J reassured him. 'You'll get another laptop.'

'But there's files on there, things I haven't backed up...'

'That's unfortunate.'

Tom could only watch as he began systematically dousing the interior with gasoline, the pungent smell of it wafting out over him like fear.

'You need to take a few steps back,' J warned. He slammed the rear doors shut and moved around to the side of the van, bending over to stuff an old rag into the fuel filler. 'And be ready to move.'

Producing a lighter from his pocket, he ignited the rag, then immediately turned and strode towards Tom, grabbing him by the arm and dragging him away. They made their way quickly across the rough ground, J moving purposefully, Tom stumbling along beside him, until a sudden flash of yellow light lit up the empty lot, throwing long shadows out in front of them. There was a curious sound, like a pair of giant wings opening, and Tom twisted around just as the heat from the flames reached them, feeling the warmth on his face as he stared at the silhouette of the van, wreathed in fire.

His bag... his clothes... the tracker... all burning, all lost.

He stood for a moment, overwhelmed by what was happening, and the crushing realization that his safety net was gone. Nobody was coming to rescue him.

J placed a firm hand on his shoulder.

'We should go,' he said, quietly. 'This is a rough neighborhood, and there's dangerous people around.'

. . .

They squeezed through a gap in the fence at the far side of the lot, and picked their way between tangles of dark undergrowth beneath the trees. It wasn't easy, but J led the way with confidence, and before long they emerged onto a strip of cracked asphalt at the back of an old warehouse. Tucked away out of sight, in the shadows between stacks of corroded shipping containers, Tom made out the shape of a dark red Honda Accord.

J hurried towards it, rummaging in his pocket and drawing out his keys; the lights flashed orange as the doors unlocked.

'Get in,' he said, stowing some things in the trunk, then walking round to the driver's side.

Tom turned and briefly looked behind him. Beyond the trees, he could see the flickering glow from the fire, and a billowing plume of dark smoke rising into the night sky.

How would Leo find him now?

Shakily, he reached for the door handle and climbed into the passenger seat. J started the car and pulled it forward. They crept around the back of the warehouse and over an empty parking lot, before bumping down onto a quiet street. J glanced around cautiously, then seemed to relax a little, accelerating away through a neighborhood of boarded-up houses and derelict stores.

'You must be hungry,' he said, as they turned onto a main road and merged with the traffic. 'Are there any dietary considerations that I should be aware of?'

'I'm not hungry,' Tom replied, staring out at the street with glazed eyes. How had this happened? How had this man been able to turn the tables on him so quickly, so *completely?*

'Well, I wasn't gonna stop for a while anyway,' J said cheerfully, as he pulled out to overtake a bus. 'That'll give you some time to work on your appetite.'

Tom rubbed his eyes, trying to order his thoughts.

'Were you even there?' he asked. 'Up in Prattsville?'

J glanced over at him, then turned his eyes back to the road.

'Not today,' he replied.

'I don't understand,' Tom frowned. 'You had me go all that way... for nothing?'

'Not for nothing,' J said, calmly. 'I needed some time in your apartment, and I wanted to make sure you wouldn't be there.'

'My apartment?'

Tom stared at him in shock. J had broken into his place, gone through his things... *that* was how he'd known about the shoe size...

'I'm sorry about the damage to your door,' the older man continued. 'I'd be happy to reimburse you for the broken lock... and for your laptop, of course.'

'You sent me away so you'd have time to go through all my stuff?' Tom asked.

'That's right,' J replied, nodding. 'It also gave me time to set up the cameras.'

'Cameras?'

'Two miniature wireless spy-cams...' J chuckled to himself as he slowed for a red light. 'Didn't you wonder how I knew *exactly* when to step out behind you in the hallway?'

Tom shrank back in his seat. 'You... you thought of all that? Went to all that trouble?'

J slowly turned his head.

'How do you think I've remained at liberty for all this time, Tom?' His voice was suddenly very cold and very serious. 'Did you think I was just "lucky" or something?'

Tom swallowed hard, looking away as the light changed to green and the car eased forward into the darkness.

15

Tom kept his gaze averted from J as they crossed the dark water of the Delaware and drove west into Pennsylvania. He felt cold and numb, struggling to think clearly, fighting the weariness that threatened to drag him from waking nightmare into sleep.

The freeway cut through a landscape lined with silhouetted trees and illuminated billboards. Tom stared helplessly at the drivers of other cars – all blissfully unaware of what was happening in the next lane, just a few feet over from them – then he screwed his eyes shut and tried to wish himself away, anywhere but here.

Beside him, J yawned and shifted in his seat.

'So tell me, Tom... how long have you lived in the States?'

It was such a matter-of-fact question, the sort of thing people asked to make conversation or pass the time. Dazed, Tom shook his head.

'I moved over here...' He tried to think, '...eight years ago, I suppose.'

J nodded politely.

'And do you get back to England often?'

'I haven't been back for a few years, now.'

He hadn't gone back to see his family since the split from Samaira. It wasn't anybody's fault, but he just couldn't face the clinging sympathy, the painful questions about Zak, and the exhaustion of being relentlessly encouraged that "things will get better". He'd decided to wait until things *were* better... and he was still waiting.

'Do you miss it?' J asked.

Tom slumped back in his seat without replying. Right now, the thought of being five thousand miles away was more appealing than it had ever been.

After a while, J changed lanes, moving over to the right and taking the off-ramp to join the interstate. As they merged with the traffic, Tom frowned.

'We're going north?'

'That's right,' J replied, his eyes on the road.

Tom waited for him to say more, but he remained silent.

'Can you tell me where we're headed?' he pressed.

'There's a motel just outside Scranton, where I thought we'd stay tonight, but we'll stop and get something to eat before that...' J stifled a yawn, '...and some coffee.'

He spoke lightly, as though they were colleagues on some dreary business trip, rather than killer-and-hostage driving through the night to who-knew-where.

Tom glared at him, then rubbed his eyes. He'd been awake for 42 hours and nothing was making sense anymore.

'Look,' he said, doing his best to keep his voice steady. 'You're going to have to explain this to me, because I just... I still really don't understand what the bloody hell this is.'

Still watching the road, J gave a sympathetic nod, then appeared to consider for a moment.

'You know how sometimes, when a reporter is sent to cover the fighting in a war zone... sometimes they tag along with a military unit, travel with them, live with them?' He broke off. 'I think there's a word for it...'

'Embedded,' Tom prompted.

'That's it!' J patted the steering wheel, seeming pleased. 'They're *embedded* with that military unit, and they report the inside story, right from the heart of the action...'

Tom stared at him in disbelief.

'You're saying that I'm – embedded with a killer? With *you?*'

J shrugged his shoulders slightly. 'Well... yes. Isn't that the best way to understand? To get to the truth?'

'But...' Tom tried to grasp the idea. 'Why all *this?* If there's something you want me to know, why don't you just *tell* me?'

'Oh now, do you *hear* yourself, Tom?' he replied. 'Are you suggesting that I should type up a press release? Tell you what to write? When did you *ever* approach a story like that!'

The older man chuckled to himself, as though amused by the thought, then spoke again, his expression becoming earnest. 'Listen. You said you wanted to know – *really* know – who I am...'

'So who *are* you?' Tom demanded. 'And why are you doing this?'

J turned his eyes back to the road.

'I'm not looking for some self-serving biography,' he explained. 'If I just wanted someone to copy down what I say, I wouldn't have gone to all the trouble of getting you.'

'I don't get it, then,' Tom said, frustrated. 'What's the point of this if you won't answer my questions?'

'You're asking the *wrong* questions, focusing on things that are subjective, emotional...' J broke off. 'I appreciate this has been a difficult day for you, but you're better than that. One of the things I admire about your work is its truthfulness, the way you build a story on facts rather than opinions...'

'You want me to ask you about facts?' Tom snapped.

'Isn't that what *you* want too?'

'All right then.' Tom glared at him. 'Did you kill Lizzie Reeves? Is that *factual* enough for you?'

J fell silent for a time. 'Yes,' he said eventually. 'I killed her.'

It was Tom's turn to fall silent. Up until now, it had been an assumption, a belief. He hadn't really doubted that this man was a killer, but hearing the words sent a sudden thrill of nervous excitement through him.

'Can you tell me why?'

For a long time, J didn't respond. Only his hand moved, inching the steering wheel left and then right as they passed a slow truck.

'It isn't easy to explain,' he said, finally. 'But I can assure you she deserved it.' Taking a breath, he set his jaw and stared out at the road. 'They've all deserved it.'

All...

Tom glanced over at him.

'What about the other names on the list?' he asked. 'Duncan Baumann... Daryl Hirsch... did you kill them too?'

J's expression was unreadable. 'I did.'

Tom swallowed hard. His mind was racing now, veering from one thought to another, but he knew what he had to ask next.

'There were three names on that list, but *ten* numbers,' he said, carefully. 'You've killed ten people?'

J shook his head. 'No.'

'Oh.' Tom was caught between hope that J wasn't as prolific as he feared, and disappointment that he'd made a mistake. 'I thought –'

'It's more than ten.'

They'd been on the road for over an hour when J pulled off the interstate and followed the long looping ramp that led into the service plaza. He nosed the Honda into a parking bay, then switched off the engine and yawned.

'Let's go get something to eat,' he said.

Tom climbed out and stretched his weary limbs. Then, moving stiffly, he followed J across the gloomy parking lot towards the brightly lit entrance, shivering in the cold night air. It was a bizarre, prefabricated building, with a steeply raked metal roof and unconvincing fake stone cladding. As they pushed through the main doors, Tom instinctively patted his pockets and grimaced.

'My wallet,' he groaned. 'I've got no cash, no cards, nothing!'

'Oh, don't worry about that.' J gave him a friendly pat on the shoulder, and Tom was too exhausted to flinch. 'This is an all-expenses paid trip. Whatever you need, it's on me.'

Inside, the building was one giant food court, with harsh lights suspended from the high metal ceiling. Rows of identical chairs and tables filled the center of the space, with different fast-food concessions lining the walls. Most of them were closed for the night, but there was a 24-hour Roy Rogers, and J bought them both a grilled chicken sandwich and coffee. They made their way to a table and sat down.

'There you go,' J said, taking his food and sliding the tray across.

'Er... thanks,' Tom murmured.

'My pleasure...' He paused, studying Tom, then smiled. 'Given our... unique situation, I imagine it must feel strange to be courteous to me. But it speaks well of you, it truly does.'

Tom slowly unwrapped his sandwich.

'It's just...' He shrugged. 'Oh, I don't know – just a habit, I suppose.'

'Well, it's an admirable habit.'

They sat and ate. Tom found that he was hungry, and wolfed down his food while watching other people coming and going. Everyone looked tired – the bearded trucker in a baseball cap, the pale guy in a suit with his tie undone, the older couple who seemed unable to decide between Roy Rogers and Starbucks – and he suddenly felt terribly alone, sitting at the table with his captor. Leaning forward, he spoke with a low voice.

'How long are you going to... keep me with you?'

J glanced up from his food.

'Why Tom,' he said. 'We've only just met, and you're already asking about parting ways? A more sensitive person might find that hurtful.'

He raised an eyebrow, then shook his head and smiled.

'Don't worry,' he continued. 'It'll all be over in a few weeks.'

'A *few* weeks?' Tom frowned. They could drive from coast to coast in less than seven days. 'Where the hell are we going? Are we leaving the country?'

'Oh, I wouldn't attach too much significance to that,' J said, calmly. 'It's not about the destination, it's about the journey.'

They were getting ready to leave when the police officer came in. Gazing around the room, Tom froze when he saw her – a dark-haired woman in her thirties, with a sheriff's department uniform – and his eyes followed her as she walked over to the Starbucks and spoke to the man behind the counter. He felt a terrible urge to call out to her, to let her know that he'd been assaulted, that he'd been kidnapped, and that the man sitting opposite him was a murderer...

But he couldn't do it. Even if he was smart, even if he found some subtle way to attract her attention, the fear of losing Zak was too great a risk.

He felt J's eyes on him, and stiffened. The older man twisted in his chair to peer over at the Starbucks counter, then turned back with a faint smile.

'Having second thoughts, Tom?' he asked.

Tom gave him a blank look.

'What do you mean?'

J picked up his coffee and sipped it thoughtfully.

'It's your choice if you want to go and talk to her.' His voice was quiet but untroubled. 'Just like it was your choice before, when I gave you the gun.'

Tom glared at him helplessly for a moment, then clenched his fist in frustration and ground it down hard against the tabletop.

They sat in silence as the officer collected her coffee, then turned and made for the door.

'Last chance, Tom.' J's eyes seemed to bore into him. 'You can still catch her if you hurry.'

Tom stared after her.

He could run over there right now... he could have J arrested and make himself a hero... but he couldn't protect the people he cared about if a contract had already been taken out on them.

He sighed and bowed his head.

'Don't feel bad, Tom. You're just doing what any decent parent would do.'

J pushed his chair back and got to his feet. 'Come on. We've still got a way to go before we're done for the night. No rest for the wicked.'

16

It was well after midnight when they finally pulled off the interstate. J swept the car up onto a curving overpass, then looped around and down onto a side road, lit by a forest of tall signs with fast-food and gas station logos. Slowing, he turned off into a small motel – two long, low buildings that faced each other across a half-empty parking lot. Driving slowly to the end furthest from the road, he eased the car into a dark space and killed the engine. Then, reaching up to switch on the interior light, he took a bundle of credit cards from his pocket and sorted through them until he found the one that he wanted.

'You wait in the car,' he said, reaching up and flicking the light off. 'I'll be right back.'

He got out and slammed the door, a menacing figure in the gloom, stretching then walking back across the parking lot to the illuminated reception entrance.

Tom sat alone in the stillness of the darkened car, listening to the distant rushing noise of traffic from the interstate. The weariness was overwhelming now, and he rubbed his eyes as he stared out of the window at the shadowed motel buildings, trying to stay awake.

He could jump out right now, make a run for it, disappear into the darkness and get away... if it wasn't for the thought of what would happen to Zak.

Sighing, he undid his seatbelt and glanced at the inside of the car, twisting around to peer into the back. Despite being an older model, the Honda was spotless, and it had the smell of a recent professional cleaning. He checked the door pockets and flipped open the glove box, but everything was empty.

It had probably been bought recently.

A moment later, movement caught his eye, and he saw J coming back from reception, beckoning to him. Slowly, Tom got out, stiff and shivery as he straightened up and hugged himself in the cold night air.

'We're all set,' J told him, walking to the back of the car and opening the trunk. He took out two large sports bags and hefted one of them towards Tom. 'Here – this one's yours.'

The bag felt heavy. J slammed the trunk and locked the car.

'Come on, we're just over here.'

Tom followed as he led the way down the line of rooms. A few of them still had lights on behind their curtains... people inside, sleeping, fucking, watching TV, oblivious to who was checking in right beside them.

They halted outside a room with a darkened window. Fumbling with the key, J unlocked the door and pushed it open.

'After you,' he said, softly.

Too tired to argue, Tom stepped over the threshold, reaching out with his free hand to find the light switch and click it on. The room was long and low, with a small wooden table and chair by the window, two large double beds with floral comforters on the left-hand wall, and a desk with a TV on the right.

J pushed the door shut behind him and snapped the lock into place.

'What a day,' he smiled, tossing his bag onto the nearest bed. 'I'll take this one, you take that one, okay?'

Numb, Tom nodded and went to sit down on the other bed.

'Okay,' he said.

J gave a cavernous yawn, then wandered over to the desk and picked up the TV remote. He peered at it, then pointed it at the screen and began flipping through the channels. Finding a news network, he turned and went back to his bed, where he sat down and began easing his shoes off.

'Oh yeah,' he sighed, contentedly. 'That's better.'

Looking over at Tom, he pointed to the bag.

'I put a few things in there for you,' he said. 'Just some basics for now, but I figure you can tell me whatever else you need, and we can get you fixed up.'

Stirred from his half-daze, Tom picked up the bag and lifted it onto the bed. Unzipping it, he leaned over and looked inside.

It was mostly filled with clothes – jeans, shirts and sweat-shirts – all in his size, and all in plain, nondescript colors. There was also underwear, socks, and a small washbag containing deodorant, toothpaste and toothbrush. Underneath, he found a packet of pens and a set of lined notebooks. Frowning, he drew these out, and looked over at J.

'Not as fancy as your laptop,' J told him. 'But it should keep you going for a while.'

Shaking his head, Tom shoved the notebooks back into the bag.

'You really expect me to write?' he muttered. 'Should I be making notes on what it's like to be electrocuted, how it feels to be kidnapped?'

'Well, that's not for me to say,' J remarked, thoughtfully. 'But seeing how we're starting out on this journey, I wanted you to have what you needed, just in case you felt inspired. I won't look at what you write, unless you ask me to.'

He yawned again and got slowly to his feet. Walking past

Tom, he made his way through to the bathroom and shut the door.

Tom slumped back onto the bed and closed his eyes as the news anchor droned on about an argument between two politicians, regarding inappropriate comments made at a fundraising event. Next came a report about a car that had fallen from a bridge, disrupting rail services in northern Pennsylvania, and prompting outrage among delayed commuters. Finally, there was a piece about a white Hollywood actress who was now at the center of a cultural appropriation scandal after being cast in a role that might otherwise have gone to someone of Asian heritage. There was no mention of his abduction. It was too soon, of course, but that wasn't the problem.

"Journalist kidnapped."

Who would care about that? Unless something made people angry, it wasn't a big story – that was just the way things worked now. Feeling terribly alone, he rubbed his eyes and gazed up at the ceiling.

The door opened, and J emerged from the bathroom. Wearing just his shorts and a vest, he padded across the room and hung his clothes neatly over the back of the chair, then turned to look at Tom.

'Are you okay?' he asked.

Tom shrugged. In the circumstances, there didn't seem to be any other answer.

J studied him for a moment, then nodded sympathetically.

'It's been a long day for both of us,' he said, gently. 'Get some sleep, and we'll talk more in the morning.'

He moved over to his bed, pulled back the covers and sat down. Finding the switch panel above the nightstand, he flicked different switches until all the lights were off except for a reading lamp at Tom's side.

'Here,' he said, tossing the remote control over. 'Go ahead

and watch whatever you want. I can sleep through anything, so long as it's not too loud.'

Yawning again, he lay down, and rolled over.

'Goodnight, Tom.'

Tom sat on the bed watching him for some time, replaying the nightmare sequence of events, wondering how this man could attack him and abduct him... then just lay down and go to sleep as though nothing had happened.

He shut his eyes, hearing the slow, restful sound of the older man's breathing.

How could J be so... so *calm?* But of course, *he* wasn't the one being forced to share a room with a killer.

After a while, Tom got up and went through to the bathroom. Standing at the wash basin, he leaned forwards and peered at himself in the mirror. His face was grimy and sweaty from the ordeal in the van, and he wearily cleaned up, before switching off the bathroom light and going back through.

Sitting down heavily on the bed, he turned the TV off and stretched out, longing for rest. He was desperate to shut out the storm of thoughts that raged behind his eyelids, but it was no use. Propping himself up wearily, he leaned over to reach inside the bag, took out a notepad and pen, and slowly started to write.

17

Tom's Journal

I don't know why, but I just need to get some of this down on paper... it's too much for me to keep in my head, and this is the only way I can try to work through it all, try to process everything.

The clock on the TV reads 2:17am, and I'm sitting in a motel room, somewhere outside Scranton, Pennsylvania. There's a murderer sleeping in the next bed, just a few feet away from me, so close I can hear him breathing.

How can this be happening to me?

Everything's gone so wrong, and I don't know what to do. Yesterday, I was working with the police to draw out a killer and bring him to justice. Now, the life of my son, and the lives of the people I care about most, hang in the balance. If I don't go along with J, and do exactly what he says, they'll die. I keep thinking there must be some way out of this, something I can try, but I'm trapped.

There's a noise outside... muted conversation, uneven footsteps, a woman laughing at something. I want to tear open the door and shout for help, I want to warn them who's in here with me, but I can't. The sounds pass by the front of our room, then I hear another door closing and everything falls silent again, except for J's quiet breathing.

I lean back against the headboard. My neck and shoulders still ache from where he hit me with that stun gun, but the agony of the electricity was nothing compared to the horror of the van ride that followed, lying there helpless, bound and blindfolded... an endless waking nightmare.

And in a strange way, that's the same situation I find myself in now. My hands and feet may be untied, but I'm still bound in place. My gag may be gone, but I can't cry out. It's unbearable, and it's going to continue, and there's nothing I can do to stop it.

Somewhere in the far distance, a train horn echoes out across the night, lonely and mournful.

God help me... I don't know what I'm going to do.

18

Tom woke suddenly from a troubled sleep. For a moment, he wasn't sure where he was, confused by the unfamiliar feel of the bed, and the shaft of dazzling sunlight. Then he sat up with a jolt, as memories of the previous day came crashing in on him.

He stared around the motel room, blinking, holding up a hand to shield his eyes from the bright glare. The curtains had been drawn wide and the adjacent bed was empty, sheets turned back and crumpled.

'Good morning, Tom.'

J was standing in the bathroom doorway, with a toothbrush in his hand.

'Get dressed,' he said, turning back towards the sink. 'Then I'll buy you breakfast.'

They checked out of the hotel, and J went to hand in the key at reception. Tom carried their two large bags over to the car, where he put them down and waited. Absently he wondered what was in the older man's bag – weapons, perhaps, or information about previous victims – but before he could risk a look, J returned with two small paper cups of coffee.

'Here you go.' He handed over a cup, along with two creamers and some sugar sachets. 'I wasn't sure how you take it.'

Tom accepted the coffee and nodded his thanks.

'We'll find somewhere down the road to eat,' J told him, moving round to the driver's side and opening the door. 'There's not much here, and I prefer to avoid friendly questions from inquisitive hotel staff. The less conversation, the less people remember you.'

They got into the car. J drove back through the parking lot and turned onto the road, heading away from the interstate.

'Where are you taking me?' Tom asked.

'Today, we're heading south,' J explained. 'I have an appointment in Delaware, so we've got a couple of hundred miles to drive. Plenty of time to talk, and start getting to know each other.'

Tom frowned, thinking about the break-in at his apartment.

'I got the impression that you already knew me quite well,' he muttered.

J grinned. 'Well, I certainly know your writing, Tom,' he admitted. 'I know where you live, what books you have on your shelves, and what your shoe size is. And yes, I know a little about your family and friends...'

Tom stiffened, wondering who else apart from Zak he was referring to.

'...but I wouldn't say I *know* you,' J continued. 'Not the *real* you.'

He slowed down and pulled up at a stop light, then twisted round in his seat to gaze thoughtfully at Tom.

'There's an old saying: *you only really know a person when you've seen them at their worst.* Anyone can be good, or funny, or generous, when things are going their way. But you turn up the heat on someone, and you'll see what they're really made of.'

The light went green, and he nosed the car forward. 'So, I guess I'll get to know you soon enough.'

Tom sank back into his seat. 'And will I get to know you?' he asked.

J smiled to himself.

'That's why you're here,' he replied.

They stopped for breakfast a few miles down the road, at a small Denny's, tucked in between a furniture warehouse and an auto repair center. The place was busy – the air filled with murmured conversations, the rattle of cutlery, and the smell of cooking – but they managed to get a table by the window, and a cheerful waitress brought them coffee and took their order.

'So,' J said, watching her leave, then looking across the table at Tom. 'I'm curious: what makes an established British reporter abandon his job, his family and his friends, to start a life over here?'

Tom looked at him and hesitated, wondering why his captor had chosen to begin with this particular subject, and how much he already knew.

'Oh, come on, Tom,' J urged. 'I appreciate the circumstances of our meeting haven't been ideal, but there's no harm in us talking now, is there? And I really *am* interested in learning who my travelling companion is.'

Tom chose his words carefully. 'At the time, I think I just wanted to try something new, to be a part of something... bigger,' he lied.

The memories still stung him. It had been such a wrench to leave everything behind, but Samaira had been so supportive – so *encouraging* – that he'd ignored the nagging doubts he had and accepted the move. Looking back, that was probably when the depression started, but he'd ignored that too, throwing himself into his new career, so he didn't have time to think about anything else. Or to notice how the dynamic was changing between them.

'It was one of those opportunities that don't come along very often,' he continued. 'And it was New York, so when the chance came I just had to grab it.'

J nodded. 'Well, it certainly paid off with the Crawford story.'

'You read that?'

'Of course.' J picked up his coffee and took a sip. 'I remember following those articles you wrote for *The Post*, and I read the book you did too. Very impressive, very – truthful.'

'Er... thank you,' Tom said.

'You won several awards for that, didn't you?' J prompted.

'That's right. It did pretty well for me.'

'Crawford must have been a fascinating individual,' J mused. 'Did you ever meet him?'

Tom shook his head.

'I tried, but he refused all contact from the media.' He turned his face towards the window, thinking back, wishing he'd been able to get closer to the man. 'I saw him at his trial, of course, but...'

'But you never spoke to him?'

'No.'

'Well, I think it's impressive what you achieved, considering,' J said. 'I guess you had to rely on the police for most of your information?'

'Yes, I had a lot of help.'

Leo had kept him up to date on the case, and given him what he needed to piece the story together. Tom wondered how different things might have been otherwise.

'Well, your writing certainly gave a valuable insight into the investigation,' J told him. 'I found it extremely useful.'

Tom looked round sharply. *'Useful?'*

J watched him over the rim of the coffee cup, his dark eyes calm and unblinking.

'Maybe that was a poor choice of word.' He shrugged. 'Let's just say I followed the story with a certain... professional interest.'

Tom stared at him. There was something about J's manner – his quiet calm and easy-going politeness – that made it possible to forget who he was... *what* he was...

But not for long.

'I helped the police to get Crawford,' Tom said, scowling. 'I gave them access to all my research, things they might have missed... I *helped* them.'

J took another sip of coffee, then carefully set his cup down.

'Good for you,' he said.

After breakfast, they drove back to the interstate and headed south, retracing their route from the night before. Seen in daylight, the rolling landscape seemed bigger. Long tree-lined sections of road gave way to grassy terrain, with glimpses of scattered towns in the distance. Here and there, an elevated section of road would smooth out the contours between the hills, and occasional bridges leapt across the meandering river valleys.

Tom was slouched back in his seat, head resting against the passenger window, staring out at the forested horizon. After a while, he turned towards J.

'So tell me about her,' he said.

'Tell you about who?'

'Lizzie Reeves,' Tom said. 'Why'd you send me *her* driving license? Why not one of the others?'

J paused, then a faint smile spread across his face.

'That's a good first question, Tom,' he replied. 'I suppose I sent you her license because I thought it would get your attention. Partly, because she's a woman and – let's be honest – people just don't feel as much *sympathy* when something terrible happens to a man.' He allowed himself a bitter little chuckle before continuing. 'But mostly it was because hers was the only driver's license I had, and I thought that would be the best way to get you started. A license is a very personal thing, but it's also extremely *specific*, much more so than just a name. You understand?'

Tom nodded.

'I wouldn't have known *which* Elizabeth Reeves if I'd just had a name,' he agreed. 'But once I knew who she was, and that she was a murder victim, that helped me to pin down the right Duncan Baumann, and the right Daryl Hirsch.'

'Very good.' J appeared pleased by this. 'I knew I could rely on you to figure it out.'

Tom turned back to the window and sat in silence for a while, gazing out at the power lines that ran along the side of the road, black lines against the pale sky, dipping and rising in a steady rhythm between the poles.

'So who was she?' he asked.

Beside him, J raised an eyebrow.

'You didn't make any enquiries of your own?' he countered.

'Of course I did.'

'And?'

Tom sighed.

'I know she worked as a researcher at the university in Syracuse.' He frowned, trying to recall the details. 'She was in her late twenties, had a boyfriend who was briefly a suspect... and I think she was a runner...'

'Nothing else?' J pressed him. 'You didn't ask your friends at the police department?'

Tom looked over at him.

'I know her cause of death, if that's what you mean.'

J gave a snort of disapproval. 'You might know *how* she died, but I doubt you know the true *cause*.'

Tom sat up in his seat.

'Well, from what I heard, someone bashed her skull in with a piece of pipe.' He paused, then continued in a softer voice. 'That's a pretty nasty thing to happen to a nice person.'

J's expression became bleak. 'Oh, she wasn't nice, I can assure you of that.'

The change in tone was so sudden, so severe, that Tom faltered.

'Is that... is that why you killed her?'

Staring straight ahead, J nodded.

'So you knew her?'

'We hadn't met, if that's what you're thinking.'

Tom frowned.

'Then... how did you know what she was like?'

J's knuckles tightened on the steering wheel, but his voice remained low and measured.

'Meeting someone only gives you an impression of them, and that can be misleading,' he explained. 'I believe we should judge people on their actions – on what they do and say – not on how likeable they are.'

Tom considered this.

'So you killed her because of something she did?'

'Of course.' J rolled his eyes. 'I'm not a madman, Tom. I wouldn't strike a person down for no reason.'

Confused, Tom leaned back in his seat.

'So... what did she do? What could she possibly have done to justify you killing her?'

J smiled a cold little smile.

'You're starting to ask the right questions, Tom,' he replied. 'But before you can understand the answers, you're going to need a lot more context. And that's what this journey's all about.'

19

The view slowly changed as they drove south. Once past the sprawl of Wilmington, and the soaring heights of the William Roth suspension bridge, the landscape opened out, becoming steadily flatter. Tom gazed through the glass at broad, meandering rivers, and reed-covered wetlands, as the miles slowly slipped away.

'Are you going to tell me your name?' he asked.

The older man shrugged.

'J will do fine for now,' he said.

'Can you tell me anything about yourself... like where you're from?'

'Well, I was born in Louisiana, but my family moved around a bit when I was a kid. Spent some time in Mississippi, ended up settling in Arkansas... I guess that's where I think of when I think of home.'

Tom turned towards him.

'What did you do for a living?' he asked. 'Before all this, I mean.'

'I worked in the financial services sector for a long time,' J replied. 'But you're right, that was "before all this". I guess that was a few years ago now...' He smiled to himself. 'Is that a polite way of asking how long have I been killing people?'

Tom stiffened. 'Yeah, that's what I'm asking.'

J continued to gaze out at the road, but his expression became distant.

'Long enough,' he mused. 'Long enough to get good at it.'

It was mid-afternoon when they left the highway and turned onto a long leafy road that took them towards Seaford. Just before they reached it, J made a sharp right, and followed a smaller road that cut across open fields, skirting around the edge of the town. They passed an old freight yard, with long lines of rusting wagons, then made another turn to bump over the rail crossing and into a modern, tree-lined industrial park. There were a number of metal-clad business units, each with their own parking lot, separated by wide swathes of neatly-mown grass.

J pulled up on the side of the narrow private road and gazed over at one of the smaller buildings. A large wooden sign hammered into the lawn announced it as Dyn-Tec Electrics.

'Is this the place?' Tom asked.

'Yeah,' J replied, glancing up at the rear-view mirror, then reaching for the door. 'Stay here. I'll be right back.'

He got out and went around to the rear of the Honda. Tom heard the trunk opening and closing, then watched with interest as J walked over the grass towards the building.

What was he doing?

The older man made his way across the parking lot, then slowed. He paused by one of the parked cars – a tan Ford – and lifted an arm, as though checking his watch. Then he turned, stooped down briefly to tie his shoe, and wandered slowly back to the road.

A moment later, he opened the door and climbed back into the driver's seat.

'Well?' Tom looked at him expectantly.

'Well what?'

'What was that all about?'

J shrugged. 'There's someone I want to see, but I realized we're a little early.' He checked his watch again. 'We'll come back in a while.'

Starting the engine, he turned the car around in the parking lot entrance, then drove slowly back the way they'd come. Following the private road, he ignored the turn-off that led back to the railway crossing, and continued on for a few hundred yards, past the last of the buildings. The asphalt ended in a rough vacant lot at the other end of the park, and J pulled the car around into a quiet spot beside a tangle of trees and wild bushes.

Rolling down the windows, he switched off the engine and settled back into his seat, as though he were about to take a nap. Tom waited for a moment, then broke the silence.

'So what does Dyn-Tec do?' he asked.

J yawned.

'Electronics and software for vending machines.'

'Are you going to tell me why we're here?'

'I told you. Just someone I need to see. I won't be very long, then we can hit the road again.'

'Where are we going next?'

J stifled another yawn.

'We need to make a stop in Annapolis before we finish for the day.'

'Annapolis...' Tom mused, trying to recall his geography. 'Is that where we're staying tonight?'

J leaned back against the head rest.

'We'll be staying a little further on,' he said.

They sat there for a while, as a warm breeze drifted through the car. It was so quiet out here and, after years of living in New York, Tom found the stillness strange. The only sounds were a bird singing, and the gentle rustle of the wind in the trees.

'I'm curious about something,' he said, resting his arm on the door frame to feel the warmth of the sun.

'Yes?'

'Why did we spend the night up in Scranton?' Tom asked, frowning slightly. 'We drove all that way north to get there, then all the way south to come here today... why Scranton? Why not somewhere more convenient?'

J smiled to himself.

'You're a smart fella, you know that?' He paused, then angled his body towards Tom. 'Okay, look... most people like things they can understand. I guess it reassures them... makes them feel as though they have a grip on how the world works, or something. They like to see patterns, conformity, consistency – and they assume that others think the same way that they do.'

'So?'

'So, if someone goes missing in New York, and then they're spotted way up in Pennsylvania, you're going to assume that they're heading northwest. You're certainly *not* going to look for them down here in Delaware.'

Tom nodded. 'So it's just a way of evading the police?'

'It's one very small *part* of evading the police,' J corrected him.

'Okay,' Tom conceded. 'But what makes you think the police are even looking for us?'

J rolled his eyes and sighed.

'I'm sure your friend Leo Moretti will be wondering why he hasn't heard from you,' he said.

Startled, Tom could only stare at him. Had J gone through his emails? His text messages?

'What... what do you know about Leo?' he stammered.

But J just smiled, reclined his seat and closed his eyes.

. . .

The sun was getting lower in the sky. Just before five o'clock, J had sat up and turned to gaze out of the window. Now, he was staring towards the road that led back to the rail crossing, as cars began to leave for the day.

'Are we going to be here much longer?' Tom asked.

J ignored him, watching as a silver SUV turned off and disappeared into the distance, then leaned forward and started the engine. Bumping the Honda up onto the road, he drove slowly back down through the industrial park. When they reached Dyn-Tec, J once again turned the car around, then pulled over to the side and stopped.

'Wait here,' he said, opening his door, then pausing. 'Do you want me to leave the radio on for you?'

Tom shook his head, wearily.

'No.'

'All right, then.'

J got out and shut the door, then walked over towards the building. There was only one car in the parking lot now – the tan Ford – and a man in a pink shirt was kneeling beside it, changing a wheel.

J waved to the man as he passed, then slowed and changed direction, wandering over to him and saying something. The man smiled up at him and nodded; he appeared to be in his thirties. They were too far away for Tom to make out what they were saying. Was *this* the person that J had come to see? Or was he meeting someone inside the building, and simply passing the time of day with a stranger?

J moved around to stand with his back to him, stooping slightly as he pointed to the center of the wheel, directing the man to look... then suddenly swung his arm around and jabbed something into the side of the man's neck, lunging at him and knocking him off balance, pushing him down hard onto the ground.

Tom stared in horror as the man's legs jerked and kicked beneath J, shoes scuffing wildly on the asphalt. He couldn't see what was happening, but he knew exactly what would make a body move like that, and remembered the blazing agony of the stun gun. Choking back a cry, he shrank into his seat, unable to look away as the victim twitched helplessly, writhing, convulsing...

And then, abruptly, the limbs stopped thrashing and the awful struggle ceased.

Straddling the man, J took something from his own pocket, then leaned forward and did something that Tom couldn't quite see. The man didn't move.

Slowly, J straightened up and got to his feet. Glancing around briefly, he turned and walked back towards the Honda, his expression terribly calm. Tom continued to stare at the prone figure lying on the ground, willing it to move, but he knew it wasn't going to...

J pulled the door open, making him jump, and slid into the driver's seat.

'What did you do?' Tom's voice rose to a shriek. 'What the *fuck* did you do?'

J slowly turned, his deep dark eyes boring into Tom, pinning him with a steady gaze.

'I broke his neck,' he said, evenly. 'It's really not that difficult, once the person's been stunned.'

Tom breathed fast, fighting a rising sense of panic. 'Oh shit,' he croaked. *'Shit!'*

Beside him, J started the engine, and calmly placed a hand on the steering wheel.

'You knew you were gonna see this, Tom,' he said, in a quiet voice. 'This is the story you came for.'

20

They drove past the freight yard and away from the town. Tom stared out at the road, trying to process what he'd just seen, dimly aware that they were taking a different route than the way they'd come. The quiet road angled across empty fields, dotted here and there with patches of woodland. There was nothing out here, except a few small farming communities and the occasional white wooden church.

After a while, he turned to look at J. The older man seemed calm, but he was driving fast and glancing up at the rear-view mirror.

'Who was he?' Tom had to force the words out, his voice thick.

'His name was David Barron.' J continued to watch the road. 'He was a thirty-one-year-old systems designer from Millsboro, Delaware.'

There was no emotion on his face, but Tom thought he caught something in the older man's voice, like a grim satisfaction.

'Why did you do it?' he asked.

J raised his chin slightly, still gazing out at the road.

'Mr Barron brought this on himself.'

'But... *how?*' Tom shook his head in frustration. 'How did he bring *that* on himself?'

J took a deep breath and sighed.

'I told you before, Tom. It's all about context.'

Tom clenched his teeth. *Context*...Was there something special about these people? Something that connected them, marked them as J's victims? He thought back over those other names, the images he'd found, the news clippings he'd read... but they were just names. This – the awful, brutal reality of it – *this* was sickening. The thought that he'd built his career on reporting such things, gnawed at him.

'Are you *proud* of yourself?' he muttered, angrily.

J glanced over at him, his expression bleak.

'There's no *pride* in any of this. But I'm not ashamed of what I do.' His voice was grim.

After fifteen minutes, they emerged from a narrow country road and turned onto the highway. J seemed to relax a little, settling back in his seat and easing off the gas to match the pace of the other traffic heading west. They cruised past farms and roadside produce stalls, and Tom gazed out at the huge mechanical crop-sprayers that spanned the open fields.

'You wanted me to see, didn't you?' he said, quietly.

J didn't answer for a moment, then frowned.

'I wanted you to *understand*,' he replied. 'To *know* what you're writing about. You can't capture a moment like that in a police report, or a crime-scene photograph. You have to witness it to really grasp what's happening.'

Tom stared at him in horror.

'Oh shit,' he gasped. 'You didn't kill him just so I could watch, did you?'

J snorted and shook his head.

'Don't flatter yourself, Tom. I killed him to make the world a better place.' He flashed a bleak little smile. 'And trust me... it is.'

'But what was so bad about him?' Tom demanded. 'What had he done that could possibly justify this?'

'Oh, on the outside, nothing much,' J replied, as his expression became distant. 'And the curious thing is, I'm sure that Mr Barron would be asking me those exact same questions, if he could. But often-times that's the nature of evil. People just don't wanna see the malice that's down there inside of them. They look in the mirror and tell themselves that they're fine, upstanding people; that they're *good*; that it's the *rest* of the world that's crooked. And that's what makes them so evil.'

He sighed.

'The road to hell is paved with good intentions, Tom.'

They drove on. A small sign reading "Maryland Welcomes You" marked the state line. The highway continued through a flat landscape that alternated between woodland and farmland. Here and there, ugly cell towers loomed up by the roadside, and Tom gazed up at them as they passed.

If only he still had his shoes with the tracking device... but that wouldn't help him now. He was on a ride that he couldn't get off.

They passed through the outskirts of a town, with houses and fast-food restaurants visible through the trees, before the highway cut across a winding river.

J had a thoughtful expression on his face.

'Let me ask you something, Tom,' he said. 'Why are you more shocked – more appalled – by *this* death than all the others? Didn't you believe me when I told you that I'd killed before?'

Tom remained silent for a time. 'I believed you,' he replied eventually.

'Is it because seeing it makes it more... real?'

'I don't know,' Tom shrugged. 'I suppose so.'

'Have you ever seen someone die before?'

Tom bowed his head, thinking back to his grandfather's body as it lay in the coffin, so still and pale...

'No,' he said. 'I've seen a dead body but never... not someone actually dying.'

J nodded. 'It changes you, doesn't it? Witnessing that moment, that transition from something to nothing... it gives you perspective.'

Tom glared at him. 'You're a fucking monster,' he hissed.

J met his eye. 'Then I'm exactly who you thought I was, Tom.'

Eventually, they turned off the 404 and joined US-50. There was more traffic here, and they began to see signs for Annapolis. Auto dealerships and gas stations drifted by, before the highway rose up to cross a stretch of silver blue water, dotted with hundreds of little white boats. They descended into lush green woodland that soon gave way to a stretch of retail outlets and roadside restaurants.

Tom was still reliving the sight of the last spasms of that man in the parking lot, recalling the moment that his legs went slack and stopped moving. He'd written about death so many times, but the reality was nothing like his rational imaginings, and he'd been completely unprepared when he actually witnessed it. The emotional impact staggered him – that sudden connection with the victim, the overwhelming feeling of empathy with a complete stranger – and the crushing sense of loss as he saw the life of a fellow human snuffed out.

He wouldn't let that happen to Zak.

Outside, the last of the landscape suddenly seemed to drop

away as the highway split onto two narrow grassy banks that crept out onto a vast expanse of blue-green water. And then, even the banks were gone, and they were driving above the waves on an elevated roadway that stretched out before them. Far ahead, he could just make out the hazy towers of a bridge, faint against the sky. But there was no far shore, only a thin shadow on the horizon, like a distant island on the sea.

As they rumbled along the concrete roadway, Tom found himself pondering what J had said. How had he not grasped the horror of all those previous murders? Why hadn't they been real enough for him? And what had he expected, when he found himself trapped on a journey with a killer?

They'd been climbing steadily for several minutes now, rising higher and higher above the water as they passed through a cage of steel girders and approached the mighty towers of the bridge. Huge suspension cables swept up on either side of the car, disappearing from view and Tom leaned forward, to gaze up at the enormous structure.

'It's really something, isn't it?' J noted, as they crested the span between the towers. Before them, they could now see a peninsula of dark green land reaching out into the vast blue of the bay, and the road bent around to the right, angling down to meet it.

Tom sat back in his seat as they began to descend.

'Yeah,' he said, quietly. 'I suppose it is.'

It was just after 7pm when they drove into Annapolis. J had pulled over on a quiet side-road to change the Honda's license plates. Now he negotiated the streets confidently, following a route that took them through the suburbs of the city and skirted the parking lot of a large shopping mall. Just before a gas station, he slowed and turned onto an access road that led down the side of a retail warehouse towards a large steel gate.

Tom gazed up at the sign above the gate.

'A self-storage unit?'

'A precaution,' J replied. He reached under his seat and drew out two baseball caps, offering one to Tom. 'Put this on and keep your head down. These places have security cameras.'

Donning his own cap, he lowered the window and reached outside to tap a six-digit code into the keypad post. There was a beep, and the heavy gate rattled and slid aside. J wound the window back up and eased the Honda forward. Beyond the unmanned gatehouse, there were several long low buildings, each with a series of numbered shutter doors. J pulled up outside number 23 and killed the engine.

'Have you left anything in the car?' he asked. 'Anything at all?'

'No,' Tom replied, pulling on his cap. 'I just have that bag in the trunk.'

'Good.' J opened his door. 'Remember to keep your head down.'

They got out and walked over to the front of unit 23. J produced a key and undid the lock, then slowly rolled the shutter up. As it rose, Tom peered inside to see the front of a blue Chevrolet Equinox.

'Our new transportation,' J explained, in a low voice. 'Now, how about you go and unload the bags from the Honda?'

Once the Chevy was driven out into the narrow alley between the buildings, Tom stowed their bags in the back. He turned to watch as J reversed their old car into the storage unit, with a sinking feeling in his stomach. Even if the Delaware police *did* get a lead on a red Honda Accord, the change of plates meant that they'd have no reason to look for it here. And now, with a new vehicle, there was nothing to connect them with the murder in Seaford.

J emerged into the light holding a small black pouch.

'Are you done?' Tom asked.

'Not quite,' the older man replied. He opened the pouch, producing a box-like object about the size of a cigarette packet, which he turned over in his hands and studied. It had a military-style camouflage pattern on it.

'What's that?' Tom asked.

'Trail camera,' J replied. Stepping back inside the shadows of the storage unit, he reached up into the corner above the door and fixed the device in place. 'Okay, *now* we can go.'

'What's a trail camera?'

'It's like a wireless webcam,' J explained, as he rolled the shutter down and locked it. 'Folks use 'em for hunting, wildlife photography, whatever. The batteries last for weeks, and it's all motion-activated, so it'll just sit here doing nothing... unless someone opens this door. Then it'll upload whatever it sees, to an anonymous private server that I can access from anywhere.'

Tom considered this. It seemed like a lot of trouble to go to, unless...

'You're doing all this –' He paused, then frowned. '– just so you'll know if anyone is on your tail?'

J shot him a faint smile. 'That's right.'

Tom shook his head and followed J to the waiting Chevy. So much planning, so much thought. How did you stop a man like this?

'You're always so... so *careful*,' he said, as J climbed into the driver's seat and started the engine.

'I have to be,' the older man replied. 'Careless people end up losing – losing *everything* – and I can't afford for that to happen.'

'But all the planning, working through every eventuality...' Tom pressed. 'How did you learn all this?'

'I learned the hard way.' J said. 'There was a time, once, when I wasn't so careful... and I've been paying for it ever since.'

Tom looked at him intently.

'What do you mean?'

But J just shook his head. Gunning the engine, he drove back along the side of the retail warehouse, and out to re-join the road.

21

They left Annapolis behind them and took the 97 towards Baltimore. Exhausted, Tom rested his head against the window glass, feeling a nagging sense of déjà vu as he gazed out at another featureless interstate. Already, his old life in New York seemed so far away, like the fond memory of a favorite movie. As the evening sun dipped below the trees and the sky burned red, he turned towards J. The older man looked tired too.

'Where are we staying tonight?'

'Don't worry,' J replied. 'It's not much further.'

Before long, they took an exit, following signs for Fort Meade and Laurel, and found themselves on a long road of strip malls and gas stations.

'The motel is just along here,' J said, pointing through the windshield. 'But I reckon we should grab a few supplies, maybe something to eat, first. How's that sound?'

'Yeah, fine.'

'Pizza okay for you?' J asked, brightly.

'Sure.'

. . .

The motel was a two-story L-shaped building, set back from the road in a tree-lined parking lot, half-full of cars. They'd been given a room on the upper floor, and Tom waited on the narrow balcony, gazing out over a small blue pool surrounded by white plastic sun-loungers, while J set down his shopping bag and the pizza box, and unlocked the door. He wondered if anyone ever swam in there, or if it was just for kids... The thought suddenly brought Zak to his mind, and he looked away, frowning.

He should have made more time for Zak.

Following the older man inside, he dumped their bags on the polished wooden floor and sat down heavily on one of the beds, then reached up to rub his shoulder. It felt tense and stiff.

'There you go.' J opened two bottles of beer and handed one to him, then sat down on the opposite bed and lifted the lid of the pizza box. 'That's the trouble with spending time on the road; if you're not careful, your muscles can seize up.'

While Tom took a long swig of beer, J lifted a slice of pizza, then slid the box over.

'I used to do a lot of travelling,' he said. 'Driving, mostly... for my job. I'd sit there and tough out the miles, and my back would ache like hell afterwards. Then I learned that you just have to keep moving, keep changing your position, otherwise you end up hurting.'

'Oh yeah?' Tom took another pull on the bottle. 'What did you do?'

'I worked in insurance,' J replied. 'Nothing special, just a lot of time on the road.'

Tom looked at him thoughtfully.

'And since then?' he asked. 'What do you do now?'

'Well, I parted ways with my old employer.' J bowed his head slightly. 'Or rather, they parted ways with me. Anyway, for now, this...' He gestured around the motel room. 'This is a full-time job.'

Tom set the bottle down, thinking about the different cars, the motel rooms, wondering what J did for money.

'But I guess this doesn't pay so well,' he said, casually.

J paused, as though sensing the veiled question.

'Some things are more important than money, Tom.'

He stretched over for the remote and switched the TV on, channel-hopping until he found a local news station. Tom picked up a slice of pizza and ate in silence.

They watched until the end of the news program, but there was no mention of Seaford. Tom stared at the screen as a smiling woman gestured towards a weather map. Nothing about David Barron. Was it still too soon for the story to have been picked up? Or did a brutal murder in Delaware just cease to be news when you crossed the state line? He scowled at the thought.

J handed him another beer. 'Are you okay?'

Tom took it unhappily. 'No,' he said. 'I'm *not* okay.'

J sat down on the edge of his own bed and looked at him thoughtfully.

'It's about what happened earlier, isn't it?'

Tom shot him a withering look. 'Er... *yes.*'

'Would you rather not have seen it?'

'I'd rather you didn't kill people!' Tom snapped.

J nodded patiently.

'Of course you would, but that's not what I asked.' He leaned forward. 'Knowing that it was going to happen regardless, would you prefer that it happened without you seeing it?'

Tom looked away.

'I don't know,' he muttered, taking a swig of beer. 'What difference does it make?'

'That's just it,' J pressed him. '*Does* it make a difference to you?'

Tom stared at the bottle in his hand.

'I don't know, it's just...' He shook his head slowly. 'It's such a terrible thing to see.'

J gave a grave nod. 'It's a terrible thing, *period*.'

He leaned over and retrieved a bottle of bourbon from the shopping bag. 'But as a reporter, do you really want to shield yourself from the thing that you're writing about?'

Troubled by this, Tom glanced up at him. J got stiffly to his feet and walked through to the bathroom, returning a moment later with two empty glasses. Setting them down on the night-stand, he poured a slug of bourbon into each, then held one out.

'When you wrote about the Crawford case, you were writing about something that had already happened, something in the past. You had to read about it, research it, ask questions... all in the hope that you could get a sense of what really happened. Right?'

Tom took the glass. 'I suppose so.'

'Well, I read the articles,' J told him. 'You described the murder in a lot of detail, even though *you* weren't there.'

Tom regarded him doubtfully. 'So?'

'So you had to imagine that situation, construct it in your mind, and put yourself right in the middle of it.' J's dark eyes flashed. 'I mean, you *really* painted a picture, Tom.'

Tom sipped his drink and said nothing.

'And you did all that,' J continued, 'so that *other* people could imagine it, experience it... *see* it...'

Tom emptied his glass, then scowled at J.

'What's your point?' he snapped.

'My point is, you didn't shy away from the reality of what happened when you were writing about that case.' J looked at him, earnestly. 'So do you really want to shy away from the reality here?'

Tom frowned. He understood what J was driving at, but this was completely different to the true crime reports he'd worked on before. Anyone could see that. The Crawford case had already been several months old when he'd first picked up on it, and the research had been a slow, patient process. He'd uncovered the facts, and pieced together what happened, but it had all happened gradually. Today, everything had happened in a few awful seconds. The attack had been so brutal, so *sudden...*

He turned over the empty glass in his hands.

But did that really make it any worse?

'Would it have been better if I'd parked the car someplace else, and left you there while I dealt with Mr Barron?' J asked. 'If I'd come back, and told you what happened, rather than allowing you to see for yourself?'

Tom hesitated. 'I... I don't know...'

'Or would it just have been *easier?*'

Tom shook his head sharply. 'Nothing about this has been easy.'

'I know,' J said, his voice sympathetic now. He picked up the bourbon bottle and waited for Tom to hold out his glass before pouring them both another shot. 'But this is what you've been writing about all these years. This is the *reality* of it.'

22

Tom's Journal

I've brought my notebook and pen down to the pool and I'm stretched out on one of the uncomfortable plastic loungers, staring up at the night sky. It's getting dark but the last of that faint red glow is still visible above the silhouettes of the trees. What's the old saying... red sky at night?

I really thought that J would want me to stay in the room with him, but he seemed pretty relaxed when I asked about coming out. We've both had a few drinks, and I suppose that helps. I was certainly glad to numb my feelings after the events of this afternoon.

I witnessed a man dying today. Not just dying... being killed. I saw it happen right in front of me: the attack, and the struggle, and the awful moment when he stopped fighting.

I saw a life end.

Sitting here now, I'm still trying to get my head around it all, trying to understand what I saw, and why it's affected me so much. I'm certainly no stranger to murder, and I've reported on several high-profile killings... but this was so much more real – so absolutely different – that it makes me question whether I ever really understood what I was writing about before.

A whole human life – everything that he was – brought to an abrupt and irrevocable end. Who wouldn't need a drink after witnessing that?

Back upstairs, J asked me if I'd rather not have seen it, and I genuinely didn't know how to answer him. As a journalist, I suppose it's important to understand the reality of what you're writing about... but it was so much easier to write about these tragedies when they were just words, just abstract events that happened in some other time and some other place. Here and now, the reality is appalling.

From the balcony above, I can hear someone's TV – muffled music and canned laughter, drifting out into the night – while just across the way the light in one of the windows goes out. People are settling down and getting ready for bed. Life is going on, regardless... however strange that might seem to me, sitting here like a spectator, able to see the bigger picture that others can't. In the past, I've pitied those who knew less than me; right now, I envy their ignorance.

Of course, only J knows everything, and the longer I spend with him, the more I feel there is to uncover. Having watched him in Seaford, I know that he's a brutal murderer – yet I still find it difficult to reconcile that with the man himself; articulate, courteous... even considerate. What can all these people have done to make him feel justified in killing them? There was no delight in his eyes as he walked back to the car this afternoon; just a grim satisfaction, like the completion of an unpleasant task. When he spoke of it, he called the killing "a terrible thing... period" so it's not as if he's enjoying it.

But if he's not enjoying it, then why is he doing it?

Turning my head slightly, I can make out the sound of a siren in the distance, and I pause to listen. There's a curious sense of relief as I determine that it isn't getting nearer, and I rest back onto the lounger, gazing at the reflection of the lights rippling across the pool.

Would the police consider me an accomplice? Because I watched J kill and did nothing? Because I could have turned him in at that service plaza, or shot him when he handed me the gun? Should I have tried to get a message to Leo?

My eyes settle on a discarded child's armband, lying under one of the loungers on the far side of the water, and I think of Zak once more.

No. I've <u>got</u> to follow this story, no matter where it takes me. I've got to protect my son. If that makes me an accomplice, then so be it.

23

The sky was a cool, clear blue and the sun was just climbing above the trees when they set out next morning. Tom felt groggy as he lugged the bags down to the car. Wondering what the time was, he glanced down to check his watch, then remembered that it was gone.

'It's six-thirty,' J told him, smiling. He seemed bright and eager, unaffected by the previous evening's drinking.

'Why so early?' Tom asked, yawning.

'We've got some miles to cover today,' J replied. 'But don't worry, we'll make a stop for coffee soon enough.'

They drove west, and Tom dozed along the way, pacified by the steady rumble of the road. When he woke, and sat up blinking in his seat, he felt numb and shivery, though it was a warm fine morning. The sun was higher now, and they were cruising through a vibrant green country with lush, rolling hills.

'Where are we headed?' he asked, peering out at a line of hazy mountains in the distance.

'West Virginia,' J replied, patting the steering wheel.

Tom looked at him in surprise. 'Really?'

'I *told* you we had some driving to do,' J said, smiling. 'But it's a beautiful day for it.'

A truck passed them down on the other side of the highway. There seemed to be a lot less traffic out here, Tom thought, and he began to idly wonder where "here" was, until another thought seized him.

'Are we going to...' He broke off, then glanced over at J. 'Is this another murder?'

J nodded. 'Yes...' he began.

'Oh no!' Tom bent forward, feeling his stomach lurch. *'No!'*

'...but it's a murder that happened over a year ago,' J continued calmly, ignoring the outburst.

Tom hesitated. 'What?'

J sighed and shook his head.

'You'll see.'

The landscape steadily became more rugged, with the highway cutting through rocky outcrops and rounding the sides of broad, forested valleys. There were broad rivers, deep blue against the green of the pines, and tall hills that crowded in to force the road left and right.

It was lunchtime when they took the exit ramp and crossed the highway. They followed the signs for Oak Hill and soon Tom was gazing out at a succession of local gas stations and used car lots that marked the main road. As with so many small towns, it had the feel of a place that had once been bigger, more *alive*... but now, there were too many vacant lots, too many crumbling buildings. It was like glimpsing the ghost of youth in the face of an old man.

'Here we are.'

Slowing the car, J pulled over at the side of the road, and switched off the engine. He indicated a long fence of metal railings. Beyond it, the mown lawns rose gently into a large memorial park, dotted with lines of headstones.

'You brought me to a cemetery?'

'Candice Porter: gone too soon, living on in our hearts, forever twenty-six...' He paused, smiling to himself, then looked at Tom, '...and number eight on that list I sent you.'

Tom blinked at him, then stared out at the cemetery.

'A murder that happened a year ago...' he mused.

'Did you want to go see her?' J enquired.

'She's buried in there?'

'Just up there at the back.' J pointed. 'One of those awful headstones with a smiling photo of the departed set into it, probably at great expense. I don't care for them myself, but then... I didn't care for her either.'

Tom gaped at him. 'You killed her, then... visited her *grave?*'

'I didn't take *flowers*, if that's what you're wondering.' J flashed a cold grin. 'Come on. We still have some time... I'll show you where she lived.'

He started the car and they drove on.

The road became narrow as it wound through the center of the town. Brick buildings pressed in against the sidewalk, but several of them were empty with FOR LEASE signs in their windows. A modern fast-food drive-thru squatted conspicuously beside the grand old US Post Office, while a pale grey water tower loomed up against the sky like a forgotten sentinel.

J turned right down a side road, then made a left to run parallel with Main Street, one block over. It was a quiet residential area, with an apartment building on one side, and a terrace of red brick houses on the other, and he let the car roll to a standstill, halfway down the street.

'You see those houses up there?' He leaned on the steering

wheel, pointing up at the terrace. 'That was hers... second one along from the end.'

He sat in silence for a time, staring out at the past, remembering.

'I took her in the morning,' he said, then turned his head to glance at Tom. 'People feel safer in the morning, ever notice that? Makes them less vigilant.'

He smiled to himself and looked back onto the street.

'I had *the* most ordinary white panel van – stolen, but with different plates on – and I parked it just up there at the side of the building. I knew what time she went to work and I was waiting for her, with the side door open. Called her over like I wanted to ask her something, and when she was close enough I hit her with the stun gun and just pushed her into the van.'

Tom stared at him in dismay, but the older man just shrugged.

'It had to be quick, and I couldn't afford to leave her lying out in the street, now could I?' He turned and indicated the apartment block opposite them. 'You see all those overlooking windows? I knew I had to get her out of sight as fast as possible, but once she was in the van, I figured things would be okay. I gagged her and tied her before she recovered, then drove her right out of here.'

'You... you *kidnapped* her?'

'Just to get her out of town,' J replied. 'It all comes down to practicalities when you're targeting someone in a risky environment.' He turned to face Tom. 'You leave a dead girl in the street, in a place like this? That's gonna stir up every cop for fifty miles. But a missing person? That's a whole lot less serious... and even if you're unlucky, and someone sees you and calls the police, you can always drop your missing person off someplace – a failed kidnapping makes everyone focus on questioning the victim, rather than locking down the roads to find the perpetrator.'

Tom shook his head, trying to take this in.

'So... what did you do with her once you'd grabbed her?' he asked.

J sat back with a contented smile.

'There's a lake, just a few miles from here,' he replied. 'It's nice and secluded, with plenty of trees that go right down to the shore... a really beautiful spot. I drove her up there, stunned her again, then dumped her in the water.'

Tom recoiled at the idea. 'You drowned her?'

'Well... *yes.*' J shrugged. 'She was still tied, and I weighed her down. It was a few weeks before they found the body.'

Tom turned away, imagining the chill embrace of the water as it closed over the girl's skin, the hopeless panic, unable to struggle free or draw breath...

'That's barbaric!' he choked. It seemed such a cruel way to kill someone.

'It's *practical,*' J countered. 'A couple of weeks in open water is disastrous for forensic evidence... and it also gave me plenty of time to get rid of the van.'

Tom glared at him.

'How can you talk about being practical when you're killing innocent people?'

'*Not* innocent,' the older man corrected.

Tom threw up his hands. 'Oh, *right,*' he said, angrily. 'I suppose she brought this on herself too?'

J regarded him in silence for a moment, then nodded.

'But *how*?' Tom demanded. 'What the bloody hell did she do?'

J sighed. 'You'd need to know her better to understand.'

Tom gave a bitter little laugh. 'Well, thanks to you, there's not much chance of *that*.'

'Oh, but there is,' J replied.

Tom hesitated. 'What are you talking about?'

J gave him an exasperated look.

'Come on, Tom. You're an investigative journalist. When you want to learn about a murder victim, you speak to their family, their friends, work colleagues.'

'And how exactly am I meant to arrange anything like that?' Tom snapped. 'I've got no phone, no computer, no money...'

'It's already taken care of,' J told him. 'I've arranged for you to speak to Candice's best friend this afternoon.'

Tom gaped at him. 'You've *what?!*'

'I called her a couple of weeks ago,' J explained. 'I told her you were writing a story about unsolved murders and that you wanted to understand who Candice was, not just portray her as a victim. We're meeting her in half an hour, right here in town.'

Tom sat there, shaking his head in disbelief.

'You really want us to...? *No...*' He broke off, hardly able to speak. 'What kind of sick joke are you trying to pull here?'

'It's no joke, Tom.' J's expression was serious. 'You want to know who she was? This is how you find out.'

24

They left the car tucked away on a side road and walked back towards Main Street.

'Her name's Peyton Lynch, and she's twenty-seven years old,' J explained. 'I told her that Mr Tom Pritchard is working on a project about unsolved murders, and that he's interested in speaking to her about her friend Candice.'

'You gave her my real name?'

'Of course.'

'Who did you say that *you* were?'

'I told her that I was your agent.'

Tom glared at him. 'This is so messed up,' he muttered. 'I haven't prepared, or researched the case, or anything...'

'You know more about what happened than the police do,' J reminded him. 'Just relax, you'll be fine.'

They stopped outside a cheery little café, set in a line of small stores. J opened the door and Tom followed him inside. Despite the modest frontage, the interior was surprisingly large, stretching back a long way into the building. One side of the room was arranged like a diner, with booths and a counter, while the rest of the space was given over to large wooden tables and chairs.

'That's her,' J whispered. 'Sitting at the booth near the back.'

He indicated a young woman with long brown hair, wearing a pale blue jacket. She glanced up as they approached, and J's face warmed into a smile as he extended his hand.

'Miss Lynch?'

'That's right...' She rose from her seat to shake his hand, looking at them both a little uncertainly.

'I'm Jay Cunningham, and this is Tom Pritchard.'

'Pleased to meet you,' Peyton nodded, then turned to Tom, who awkwardly took her hand.

'Hello,' he said.

"We *really* appreciate you taking the time to meet with us today,' J continued, smoothly. 'Before we begin, can I get you anything?'

'Oh, no.' Peyton glanced down at the coffee cup on the table. 'I'm just fine – but thank you.'

J turned to Tom.

'Coffee?' he asked.

'Uh... yeah,' Tom nodded. 'Thanks.'

While J went to the counter, Tom eased himself into the seat facing Peyton, placing his notepad on the table between them. He was used to people being mistrustful, or even hostile, when meeting a journalist, but the woman opposite him seemed self-conscious, like a candidate at a job interview, anxious to make a good impression.

'It really is good of you to see us,' he said, summoning a smile.

'No, I'm happy to...' She broke off and made a face. 'Happy's the wrong word, but... well, you know what I mean.'

'Don't worry, I understand this must be difficult.' He decided to ask something easy to begin with, something to put her at ease. 'Maybe you could tell me how you first came to know Candice?'

Peyton's expression brightened a little.

'We actually met in High School,' she replied. 'Her family moved here from Glenville when she was fifteen and we were in the same class.'

'So you'd been friends for a long time?'

'Oh yes.' Peyton lowered her eyes. 'It's funny, 'cos we were always so different, but we always got along.'

'Different?' Tom prompted.

'Yeah, you know...' She gave him a bashful smile. 'I was always the quiet one and she was more confident, more outgoing?'

'Maybe you brought out the best in each other?'

Peyton nodded thoughtfully.

'Well, she certainly made a big difference to me.'

J returned from the counter and slid into the seat beside Tom.

'Can you tell me more about what she was like back then?' Tom asked, trying to ignore him.

'Well, she was always real smart.' There was a note of pride in Peyton's voice. 'And she had a kind of – ... maturity, I guess. Back in High School, most of us were just goofing off and worrying about stupid stuff, but she'd try and get people thinking about important things. You know, politics... issues... stuff like that.'

Tom jotted down a few notes. 'Did she have any interests? Hobbies, that sort of thing?'

'Well, in the summer she did a lot of hiking. There's some beautiful trails round here, and we'd go out together sometimes, down past Mount Hope, or over at the New River Gorge. She was really into nature, y'know?'

Peyton paused, a wistful smile on her face. 'And she was real good at baking... you know, designing fancy cakes for birthday parties? People would actually pay her to make them, she was so talented.'

'Uh-huh?' Tom scribbled in his notepad.

'Oh, and she *loved* books,' Peyton continued. 'Always reading – and writing stuff too. I don't know if I ever saw her so happy as when she got that job at the library.'

Tom glanced up.

'Had she worked at the library for long?'

'Two years, I think.' Peyton frowned and bit her lip. 'Or maybe three. It was only a part-time thing, and it wasn't a whole lot of money, but she enjoyed doing it – and I don't think they ever had enough hours for her at the Heritage Area office, so it worked out pretty good.'

'The Heritage Area office?'

'Yeah, it's like a kind of tourism and preservation thing? I think they fix up old historical buildings and stuff like that. She always liked it there, although...'

Peyton trailed off as the waitress brought two cups of coffee over and set them down on the table.

'Thank you so much,' J smiled, taking one of the cups and sliding the other to Tom.

Peyton watched as the waitress walked back to the counter, then continued, 'I think Candice sometimes felt like they weren't giving enough focus to women and minorities – when they chose which historical projects they got involved in, I mean. But I guess that's just the trouble with history: you can't change how things were back in the past.'

'Would you say that Candice was popular?' he asked, picking up his coffee cup.

'Oh, very popular.' Peyton beamed at him. 'She had a lot of friends here in town, and people from all over the world that she'd met online. Everybody liked her. I mean, sure, she may have rubbed a few folks the wrong way, but she always knew she was in the right, so it wasn't a problem.'

Tom gave her an encouraging smile.

'So she was opinionated then?'

'Oh yes,' Peyton replied, leaning forward slightly. 'She really *cared* about stuff and she was never afraid to stand up for what she believed in. She used to say that the only thing evil needs to triumph is for good people to do nothing.'

'That's very true,' J said, nodding gravely.

Tom shot him a bleak look, aware of the irony, then turned back to Peyton.

'What about relationships?' he asked. 'Did she have a boyfriend?'

As soon as he said it, he worried that he'd made a mistake. What if she wasn't straight? What if she and Peyton had been more than just friends?

Thankfully Peyton's expression didn't alter.

'Candy was seeing Daniel Winters on and off for a couple of years,' she said. 'I guess it was pretty serious... I mean, she was never one of those types who *needed* a man in their life, but she seemed to get along with Danny real well, and he's a nice guy. I'm not sure if they would have wound up getting married – she never said anything either way – but they always just seemed content to take things at their own pace.'

Tom sat and sipped his coffee as she began to speak more freely, reminiscing about parties they'd been to, and weekend trips to see bands up in Charleston.

J listened, appearing genuinely interested. Peyton continued, talking about the plans they had made, their hopes for the future, and then her face fell as the subject turned to her friend's untimely death.

'It was so awful, when they told us she had disappeared. I knew – I just *knew* – that something terrible had happened. I had this feeling, you know? Sheriff Harris was going around, asking people questions about where she might have gone, but

I knew there was no way she'd have upped and left without saying something to me first.'

Tom watched her hands, nervously turning her coffee cup as she approached the darkest moment of her story, and gently nodded for her to continue.

'Then they found her, up at the lake.' Peyton sniffed, then shook her head, composing herself. 'I was at work and I got a phone call from her brother Eugene... he could hardly get the words out, he was so upset... he said they'd found a body and they thought it might be Candy...'

Her voice wavered and she broke off, fanning herself for a moment. 'It was a while before they identified her, on account of her being in the water so long...'

Tom tentatively placed his hand on hers.

'I'm so sorry,' he said. 'I know this must be hard for you.'

Peyton looked up at him, her eyes shining with tears.

'No, I *want* to do this,' she insisted. 'I want people to remember her – and I want them to catch whoever killed her...'

Tom shot a sidelong glance at J, but the older man just sat listening, his face a mask of gentle sympathy.

'She hated injustice and... and violence.' Peyton dabbed at her eyes, then lifted her chin. 'She would never have kept quiet if she saw something she felt was wrong, so I shouldn't be quiet about her death. I feel like I owe her that, you know?'

'Of course,' Tom agreed, taking his pen and scribbling down her words.

'I just wish they'd investigate it all *properly*,' Peyton muttered. She lifted her cup and drank the last of her coffee.

Tom stopped writing. 'You don't feel that they did that?'

Peyton shook her head, then leaned in closer to him.

'The whole thing's messed up,' she said in a low voice. 'And it's all because of that stupid note.'

Tom stared at her.

'Note?'

'That note they found...' Peyton looked at him. 'You know, up near the lake?'

Tom hesitated, then nodded.

'I'm so sorry,' he said, smoothly. 'I don't have all my research here... can you just remind me?'

Peyton regarded him doubtfully, then shrugged.

'Robbie Kinkaid found this note, pinned to a tree in the woods up by the lake,' she explained. 'It said, "This is what happens to blackmailers", and I know that for a fact, because he told me himself.'

Tom sat back in his chair, considering this. 'Blackmailers?'

Peyton's face was indignant. 'I know, right?' she said. 'As if Candy would *ever* do anything like that. It makes no sense.'

From everything he'd heard, Tom thought, it did seem unlikely that Candice would be the type to blackmail anyone. He wondered whether J had left the note as a way of distracting the police, or discrediting Candice.

'The police are convinced that it's something to do with why she was killed,' Peyton continued. 'But I knew her better than anyone. She would *never* do anything like that, and I want people to know it.'

'I understand.'

Tom paused, wondering what Candice could possibly have done to bring herself to the attention of a killer, then picked up his pen again. 'How do you think she would want to be remembered?'

Peyton thought for a moment. 'I think she'd want to be remembered as someone who really made a difference, as someone who *mattered*, you know?' Her eyes glistened as she looked imploringly at J and Tom. 'She really mattered to me...'

They walked back to the car in silence. Deep in thought, Tom climbed in and pulled his door closed. Sitting beside him, J adopted a distant expression and placed his hand over his heart.

'"How do you think she would want to be remembered?"' he said, in a mocking parody of Tom's English accent, then stuck a finger in his mouth, as though he wanted to throw up.

Shocked out of his reverie, Tom stared in disbelief.

'Hey,' he protested. 'Candice sounded like she was a really *good* person. Intelligent... kind... opposed to violence and injustice...'

J reached forward to start the engine, then turned to look at Tom.

'Oh, I agree,' he said, his voice becoming serious. 'And yet... she wanted me dead.'

25

'What do you mean, she wanted you dead?'

They were driving along a narrow country road that curved through open fields and patches of woodland.

'I mean exactly what I say.'

'So, you knew each other?' Tom pressed.

'No.' J gave a slight shake of his head. 'We'd never met... not until the day I killed her.'

Tom tried to make sense of what he was hearing. 'Then how could she possibly want you dead?'

'Exactly!' J said, nodding emphatically. 'A *good* person, opposed to violence and injustice – and yet she was ready to condemn a complete stranger.'

Tom stared at him. 'I don't understand.'

J accelerated through a bend, his hand at the top of the steering wheel, knuckles whitening.

'People aren't always what they seem, Tom. They may *appear* to be good... they may even believe themselves to *be* good... but wickedness takes a lot of different forms.' He took a breath, almost as if he was calming himself, then sighed. 'You hate me because I'm a killer, and that's fair enough – but it isn't always obvious who's good and who's evil.'

Tom considered this. 'So you think Candice was – evil?'

'If she wanted you dead, *you'd* think she was evil too,' he said.

The road crested a slight rise, then dipped down towards a broad swathe of forest. Trees closed in on either side of the car.

'But if she'd never met you, then why the hell would she want you dead?' Tom objected. 'And how could you even know?'

J reached up to fumble in his jacket pocket, then drew out a folded sheet of paper. Scowling, he thrust it towards Tom, who opened it out to reveal a printout.

@JustCandiP123 ***Candice Porter***
No place in this world for abusive men. Forget about jail... a bullet is more effective and a whole lot cheaper. ***#JusticeFor-Kaitlyn***

@WFRecorder ***Wichita Falls News***
BLACKMAIL SEX: MAN HELD BY POLICE
A man who allegedly coerced insurance claimants to have sex has been arrested by...

Bemused, Tom read it through. 'What the hell is this?'

'It's a Twitter post that Candice made, a couple of years back,' J growled. 'Turns out she was quite the social media influencer... that was retweeted over 400 times. Thousands of people saw it. She told *thousands* of people that I should be shot.'

He snatched the paper back and stuffed it into his pocket, then looked up to check the rear-view mirror again.

'And all that from a person who was opposed to injustice and... oh *SHIT!*'

Flung forward against his seatbelt as J stamped on the brakes, Tom briefly glimpsed the other car, a grey Ford Taurus, pulling out from a side road. His body tensed as they swerved but the impact was shockingly sudden. With a deafening bang, something hot punched him hard in the face, jarring his teeth and leaving him dazed and winded, as the whole world lurched round in a long, sickening spin. There was a screeching of tires, a shuddering bumping noise, and then a sudden eerie silence.

It might have been minutes, or it might have been an hour. He became dimly aware of a voice speaking his name.

'Tom? Can you hear me, Tom?'

There was a scorched smell, like burning plastic, and a metallic taste in his mouth. He attempted to move, lifting his face from the sagging airbag, then gasped as he felt the pain shooting up through his neck and down through his side.

'Tom? Are you okay?'

He opened his eyes, blinking against the light, trying to focus. With effort, he turned his head until he could make out the concerned face of J leaning over him. The older man had a cut on his cheekbone, and blood was running down his jaw and dripping onto his shirt.

'My neck hurts,' Tom groaned.

'Don't move too quickly,' J warned. 'Just take it slow.'

Tom felt his seatbelt being freed, then J's hands were on his shoulders, gently supporting him and helping him to sit up. As he lifted his head above the crumpled airbag, he saw the web of shatter lines on the windshield, and the wrecked front of their car. Squinting, he tried to take in what had happened, but everything seemed distant and unreal, like a memory of something that happened to someone else. He tentatively raised a hand to feel his neck, but a sudden pain in his side made him flinch and gasp.

'Where does it hurt?' J asked. There was an unusual note of concern in his voice.

'My side,' Tom groaned, bringing his other hand across to hold the painful area.

'Just take it easy.' With some effort, J leaned across to see where Tom's hand was, then slumped back into his seat, breathing heavily. 'I reckon you've maybe bruised a rib or two, but hopefully nothing's broken.'

Tom slowly leaned back against the headrest and brought his free hand up to massage his neck. After a moment, he turned his head stiffly to look at J. The older man appeared to be unhurt, but he was staring out through the windshield and his expression was bleak.

'What happened?'

J shook his head.

'That car just pulled right out in front of us,' he said, wretchedly. 'There was no way to avoid it, nothing I could do...'

Tom carefully turned his head, peering through the cracked glass until he was able to make out the road and, a hundred yards away in some trees, the grey car. They sat in silence for a time, then J reached down between the seats and undid his own seatbelt. His door creaked in protest as he forced it open, and Tom saw him sway a little as he got out and stood up.

'Wait here,' he growled, then turned and began walking slowly back along the asphalt, following the stark black skid-marks towards the other car.

Tom watched him for a moment, then angled his body slightly and reached for his own door handle. He winced, as pain flashed through his side, but thankfully the door opened easily. With effort, he was able to swing his legs out and down onto the ground. Tiny fragments of glass fell from his clothing as he steadied himself then got slowly to his feet. The front corner of the Chevrolet was a mass of twisted metal – the hood was crumpled and scratched, and one of the wheels bent out at a strange angle.

They could have been killed.

He turned to check the damage on the Taurus. J was approaching it, gun drawn, bending forward to lean in the side window. Tom half-closed his eyes, waiting for the gunshot, but the older man just stood there, unmoving. Eventually, he returned the gun to its holster, then turned and trudged slowly back up the road.

As he drew nearer, crunching broken glass underfoot, he glanced up at Tom with a grim expression on his face.

'Dead,' he said, simply. 'Can you walk okay?'

Moving carefully, Tom shifted his weight from one foot to the other, still holding his side.

'I think so,' he said.

'Right.'

J bent forward to study the front of the Chevrolet, then straightened up and looked around.

'Come on,' he growled. 'We're in trouble.'

26

J strode purposefully round to the back of the Chevy and dragged out their bags, dumping them heavily on the asphalt. He stooped down to unzip one, taking out a shirt and hastily ripping off a strip of material. Straightening up, he turned around and undid the fuel cap, stuffing the fabric down into the opening. Only then did he look back at Tom.

'Can you manage one of those?' he asked, pointing at the bags.

Tom moved towards him, lurching slightly, then tentatively leaned down. His fingers closed over the handle, but as he tried to lift the bag, a searing pain in his side forced him to let go, and he stumbled backwards, struggling for breath.

'Sorry,' he gasped. 'I don't think I can –'

'Forget it,' J interrupted. 'Just get over there into those trees.' He pointed off to the side of the road. 'Down there. Get yourself out of sight.'

Clutching his side, Tom turned and walked slowly across the asphalt. Trees lined the grassy verge, and a long, forested slope fell away into the distance, shadowed and gloomy. A moment later, J was beside him, hefting both their bags over the grass and dropping them beside an old stump.

'Keep going,' the older man said, pointing. 'Down there. I'll catch you up in a minute.'

He turned and walked back towards the Chevy.

Tom picked his way slowly down the slope, wincing as he negotiated the uneven terrain. Reaching a point where the ground levelled out slightly, he paused to catch his breath, leaning against a large tree trunk and looking back up towards the road.

Silhouetted against the light from above, he saw J reappear, then watched him as he stooped for the bags and began hurrying down the incline. Behind him, there was a sudden flash, and a muffled report. A plume of ugly black smoke boiled up into the sky. Breathing hard, the older man made it down to where Tom was waiting, half- dragging their bags and gratefully dropping them at the base of the tree.

'You burned our vehicle?' Tom whispered, gazing up at the smoke.

'I had to,' J replied, panting. His face was beaded with sweat. 'Front axle was broken so it wasn't going anywhere. Too many prints, and DNA evidence, to risk leaving it intact.'

'Okay but...' Tom glanced around helplessly at the endless trees. 'It's been miles since the last town. How are we going to get out of here?'

J lifted a hand and wiped the blood from his face, then turned to gaze back up towards the road.

'I'm working on it.'

Tom followed his gaze.

'What about that other car?' he asked, suddenly. 'The one you hit?'

J whirled around and glared at him.

'He hit *me!*' he snapped. 'He just pulled out... there was *nothing* I could do!'

Tom flinched, startled by the ferocity of his reply.

'Sorry,' he stammered. 'But the car that hit us – is it drivable?'

J scowled for a moment, then shook his head unhappily.

'I don't know. Even if I could get it out of the trees, it's probably busted up pretty bad...' He trailed off, looking oddly pensive, then suddenly clenched his fists and snarled in frustration. 'Shit. *Shit!*'

Tom took a step back. It was the first time he'd seen such raw emotion from the normally calm killer, and the sight woke a sudden fear in him. J turned back towards the slope, glaring up through the trees, listening to the angry pops and hissing from the fire above them. Eventually, he seemed to reach a decision.

'I'm going up to see how bad that other car is, before somebody else comes past and calls the police.' He shook his head in annoyance. 'I should have moved the body to our car first, *dammit...*'

Tom managed an anxious nod. 'What should I do?'

'Just... stay here,' J muttered. 'And keep quiet.'

He drew his gun, then started to make his way back up the hill. Leaning against the tree, Tom watched until the older man disappeared from view, then slowly squatted down to sit on the ground, with his back pressed against the tree trunk.

He'd never seen J angry – or *worried* – before. Up until now, everything that had happened seemed to be in accordance with some intricate and horrible plan. But as terrifying as all that had been, this was worse.

From somewhere above him, he caught the sound of a car ignition being started. Straining, he listened as the engine stuttered and failed, then turned over again and failed once more.

Come on... start. Please start...

A cold dread began to settle on him. What if this was it? What if the police picked them up? With the other driver dead, there would be questions, and it wouldn't be long before the truth came out...

And if J was caught, then Zak's fate would be sealed.

Choking down a cry, he listened, willing the engine to start, then gasped with relief as he heard it revving into life.

They had to get out of this. They just *had* to.

Several long minutes passed. Tom felt sick, bent over from the pain, but he continued staring up the slope, where black smoke still billowed. He couldn't hear the engine any more over the crackling sounds of the fire.

It was all taking too long.

And then he stiffened as he made out a new sound... a different engine note approaching, followed by the sudden squeal of brakes. Not knowing what to do, he shrank back behind the tree, then cowered as he heard a woman's scream, and a man's voice, indistinct but urgent.

Someone had come. It was all over.

He screwed his eyes shut, grinding his teeth together as he silently cursed their luck. He'd gone along with all J's demands. He'd done everything he could to save his son...but it wasn't going to be enough.

He wondered how long it would be before the police arrived. Whoever was up there must surely have called in the accident by now. It was only a matter of time.

And then a noise, very close, made him twist his head sharply to the right. Pain shot up through his neck, and he gasped. J was standing there, eyes wide and alert, one finger raised urgently to his lips. With a wary glance up towards the road, he beckoned Tom towards him.

'Don't talk,' he hissed. 'Just follow.'

As Tom got to his feet, the older man stooped to grasp the bags, then began picking his way stealthily through the trees, all the time keeping parallel to the road above them. Despite the weight he was carrying, he moved quickly, and Tom was soon breathing hard as the pace made his injured side ache.

As they left the scene of the accident behind them, the ground rose steadily upwards. Eventually, pushing through a last tangle of undergrowth, they emerged onto the curve of a narrow road, lined on both sides by trees. The grey Ford was parked nearby, its engine ticking over quietly.

'I moved it back around onto the side road,' J explained, his breathing labored. 'Come on, we need to get out of here right now.'

Tom staggered over to the car. The rear passenger-side door was crushed inwards, where the Chevy had ploughed into it, and there was significant damage at the front where it had spun into the trees, but it wasn't as bad as he'd expected.

Pulling the passenger door open, Tom looked over at J, who was lifting their bags into the back.

'I heard two voices up there,' he panted. 'A man and a woman, I think. They must have reported it by now...'

'Just get in,' J replied, shoving the bags across the rear seats and slamming the door shut.

Tom lowered himself into his seat, doing his best to breathe through the pain as he lifted his legs in. Clutching his side, he turned to ask J where they were going... then choked back a cry as he noticed the dark smears of blood on the steering wheel, door pillar and dashboard.

'Oh shit,' he whispered.

'I know.' J shot him a grim look, then sighed. 'We're going to need another ride.'

Gripping the bloody wheel, the older man hesitated, lifting his hand and turning it to stare at the muddy red stain on his palm. Then his face set hard into a scowl, and he stared dead ahead. Gently revving the engine, he eased the car forward and set off slowly down the side road.

27

They drove in tense silence for a couple of miles, travelling at speed, before J slowed down suddenly, bumping the car onto a rough farm-track that curved away into the woods. Once the road was out of sight behind them, he pulled up and stopped, but left the engine running.

'I can't risk it not starting again,' he explained. 'Not until we're a *lot* further away.'

Tom nodded, wincing slightly as he did so.

J caught the change in his expression and looked at him intently.

'Are you all right?' he asked.

'I think maybe I just moved too quickly,' Tom replied, lifting a hand to touch his neck. 'The real pain's down in my side.'

J shuffled round in his seat, leaning across.

'Can you turn your head okay?' he asked. 'Look up and down?'

Tom angled his head, doing it carefully, aware of the tightness in his neck.

'Yeah,' he replied. 'It's just a little tender.'

J nodded to himself, then held up a finger, watching to see that Tom's eyes were able to follow it.

'I'm guessing you have a mild case of whiplash,' he mused, after a moment. 'It'll be uncomfortable, but it shouldn't be too serious. Lift your shirt up and let's take a look at your side.'

Tom hesitated, then leaned back in his seat and pulled his shirt up, gasping as the movement sent another sharp pain coursing through him.

J leaned over and prodded him gently, checking each rib.

'Bloody hell!' Tom hissed through gritted teeth, as one particular touch caused a stabbing pain that made him flinch.

'You felt that one, huh?' J sat back and frowned. 'I reckon you've maybe cracked a rib, but I can't say for sure.'

Tom exhaled slowly, breathing through the discomfort.

'Is that... bad?' he asked.

'Well, it isn't good. Not for someone on the run.'

J glanced up at the rear-view mirror again, then lapsed into silence. After a moment, he twisted around and reached into the back seat, tugging his bag towards him and unzipping one of the pockets. Tom tried to turn, wanting to see what was inside, but the movement was too painful. He sat still as J retrieved a small plastic medicine bottle. Half-full, it contained round, white pills, but the prescription label had been scratched off.

'These will help with the pain,' he said, handing it to Tom. 'Take two.'

Tom accepted the bottle, and unscrewed the lid, recoiling slightly as he saw the faint stain of blood on his palm.

From J, where he'd been holding the steering wheel.

Shuddering, he wiped his hand on his jeans, then tipped out a couple of pills and forced himself to swallow them, wishing he had some water to help them go down.

'What about you?' he asked.

'I'm not hurt too bad,' J replied. 'And I need to stay sharp.'

He had continued searching in the bag, and now dropped back into his seat holding a black electronic device that looked like a high-tech radio receiver, with a long rubber antenna, LCD screen and keypad.

'Police scanner,' he explained, plugging an earpiece lead into the top of the device then bowing his head and listening intently.

Tom replaced the top of the medicine bottle and set it on the dashboard between them, then relaxed back in his seat, waiting for the pills to take effect. Listening to the steady thrum of the engine, and staring out at the lush green woodland, he wondered where they were. They'd been less than an hour out from Oak Hill when they had the accident, but he hadn't noted in which direction they'd been travelling. With everything else that had happened, he hadn't thought to ask J where they were going next. Leaning his head back, he closed his eyes for a time, trying to breathe without aggravating his injury. The pain was tiring, and he had begun to drift off when J spoke again.

'Local police are on their way to the scene,' he noted, pausing to concentrate on something being said. 'No mention of us, yet... and no mention of this car, which is good.'

Tom felt a curious sense of relief.

J listened for a moment longer, then removed the earpiece.

'Out here, I doubt they have a lot of manpower available, but we've still got to be careful.' Turning to search in the bag again, he pulled out a cheap-looking cell phone with an orange sticker on the back. 'We need to find a way out of here.'

Tom watched as the older man pressed the power button.

'Where are we going to go?' he asked.

J pursed his lips. 'Good question. We *have* to get a new vehicle; this one's far too damaged, and it could easily be recognized or reported missing... *and* we're gonna need a place to stay tonight...'

Leaning forward suddenly, he peered down at the dashboard, and his brows creased into a frown. 'But we've less than half a tank of gas.'

He slumped back in his seat. There was a determined expression on his face, but Tom could sense the underlying tension as J began tapping urgently on the phone screen.

'Aren't you worried they'll track that?' he asked, after a moment.

'What?' J glanced up at him.

'Your phone,' Tom gestured toward it. 'And you're using the internet too... the police track that kind of thing.'

'This is a prepaid phone,' J explained, holding it up and indicating the sticker on the back. 'I have several, all bought with cash, all color coded. It's never been used before, never shown up on the network... and after I'm done with it, it won't appear on the network again. Nothing to link it to us, nothing to trace.'

He went back to scrolling the screen again, tapping now and then.

'There's a car rental place in Beckley,' he said slowly. 'I reckon we could make it down there, but they close at six, so there's nothing much we can do just now...'

He stared out through the windshield for a time, then appeared to reach a decision.

'We'll head down there, find a motel where we can rest up for the night...' He glanced over at Tom. 'And we'll see if we can't get something to strap up your ribs. Okay?'

Tom nodded gratefully.

J reversed back out onto the side road, pausing to consult the phone's map screen before turning left.

'You're navigating,' he said, passing the handset to Tom. 'I'll be okay once we hit the interstate, but these country roads are easy to get lost on.'

Tom squinted at the phone, panning the screen to look at their route.

'All right... it looks like we just follow this road for the next couple of miles,' he said. 'Keep going until we get to the T-junction, then we turn left.'

Staring down at the handset, Tom was suddenly aware of how long it had been since he'd held a phone; days now, without a single call or text message, without emails or social media. For the first time he could remember, he was truly off grid, disconnected from all the endless scrolling and clamoring alerts. Here, now, everything was sudden and vital... and terribly real.

He glanced across at J. The older man's color looked bad and he appeared fatigued, but there was an edginess to him that Tom hadn't noticed before. Clearly, the accident had shaken him. How close had they come to capture... and disaster?

Holding his side with one hand, Tom took a careful breath.

'When that car pulled out in front of us, there was a moment... I really felt like it was all over. Did you think that too?'

'We're not safe yet,' J growled. 'Not by a long way.'

'No, I guess not.' Tom agreed. 'None of this was in the plan.'

'Plans change.'

The older man seemed distracted, unwilling to talk.

'Do you want me to look for motels?' Tom asked. 'I could call a few places, see which ones have vacancies for tonight...'

J shook his head. 'Not a good idea.'

Tom sighed. Hadn't he done everything the killer had asked of him? Surely he'd earned some trust by now.

'Are you worried I'll turn you in or something?'

J glanced across at him, his face expressionless.

'I'm *worried* someone will remember that fine British accent of yours,' he countered. 'The aim is to blend in, not stand out.'

'Sorry,' Tom said, after a moment. 'I hadn't thought of that.'

'Forget about it,' J replied. 'What we're doing isn't easy...'

Steering round a tight bend, a knocking vibration came from one of the wheels, subsiding again as the road straightened out.

'...and it just got a whole lot harder.'

28

Tom dozed once they reached the interstate. When he awoke, his neck was painfully stiff, and there was a constant dull ache in his side. He sat up with difficulty, blinking at the sudden glare of headlights and peering out at the purple evening sky. They were driving down a curving suburban road, lined with bright neon signs for gas stations and fast-food restaurants.

'Where are we?' he croaked, his mouth dry.

'Just coming into Beckley,' J replied. 'How are you feeling?'

'Sore,' Tom groaned. He shifted in his seat, looking for the cell phone that had been in his hand, then spotted it in the cup-holder between the seats. 'Did you find a place for us to stay?'

'All taken care of. There's a motel close to the rental car place. It's nothing fancy, but if this piece of junk doesn't start up again in the morning...' He patted the steering wheel, grimly. '... well, at least we'll still have a way out.'

Tom could hear the uneven rattle coming from the engine; it didn't sound good. He reached down, carefully pressing a hand against his injured side, then frowned.

'Last I remember it was still light,' he said. 'How long was I asleep?'

'You've been out for a while,' J explained. 'I took it easy, coming down here, and the gas gauge wasn't too low, so I pulled over for a while just outside town. The car's badly busted up, so I figured it would attract less attention at the motel if I waited until it was getting dark.'

The motel was on a busy road, but J nursed the car into a distant corner of the parking lot, ensuring that the more damaged side was screened by trees. He spent a few minutes cleaning up, wiping the blood from his face and hands, then left Tom in the passenger seat and went to check in. When he returned, he lifted the bags from the back seat and led the way to their room.

'How do you afford this?' Tom asked, walking stiffly along the slab path that skirted the low building.

'What do you mean?' J asked.

'The motels, the cars, everything...' Tom shook his head. 'It must cost a lot to do all this.'

'It's not as much as you'd think,' J replied, lugging the bags awkwardly. 'But I worked hard all my life before...' He broke off abruptly, then continued in a more measured tone. 'I always worked hard, so I have some money set aside.'

'You said "before"?' Tom asked, picking up on the correction.

'Before things changed for me,' J replied, awkwardly. 'Before I became... who I am now.'

They reached the room and J unlocked the door. Tom followed him inside and walked over to the nearest bed, sitting down stiffly before laying back and stretching out, trying to find the least painful position.

'Rest up for a while,' J encouraged him. 'There's a pharmacy just down the road. I'll walk over there now and get a few things to make you more comfortable.' He started towards the door, then turned back again. 'What do you want to eat?'

Staring up at the ceiling, Tom slowly shook his head.

'I'm really not hungry...'

'You *have* to eat,' J told him. 'Especially with that painkiller I gave you.'

'I'm just thirsty,' Tom croaked. 'Very thirsty...'

'Okay...'

J walked through to the bathroom and returned a moment later with a glass of water.

'Here you go,' he said. 'Drink this.'

He helped Tom up into a sitting position and watched him sip the water.

'You want the TV on?' he asked.

Setting the glass down on the nightstand, Tom shrugged.

'I don't mind...'

J pressed the power button on the TV, then came over and handed him the remote.

'Just you sit tight,' he said. 'I'll be back before you know it.'

As soon as he left the room, Tom muted the TV and listened. There was no sound, no indication that J was returning. He glanced across to the other side of the room, where the two large bags were lying on top of J's bed, then frowned. Walking to the pharmacy and back would take him at least ten minutes... longer, if he stopped for food.

On the TV, a young man with lipstick and a middle-aged woman with short hair were gesturing and shouting at each other in silent fury, while a sharply-suited presenter looked on, nodding gravely.

Tom stared at the bags, knowing that he might not have the chance again. Breathing through the pain, he forced himself up onto his feet and walked slowly round to the other bed. J's black duffel bag was larger than his, with sturdy handles and several bulging side-pockets. He reached for one of the zippers, then hesitated.

He was dealing with an extremely clever man; he had to be careful, memorize the position of everything, so he could put it all back exactly as he found it.

Taking a deep breath, he unzipped the first side pocket, reached inside... then slowly drew out the stun gun. Weighing it in his hands, he studied it for a moment, then gripped it carefully and squeezed the trigger. There was a thin crackling noise as a bright arc of electricity sparked between the metal terminals. Tom winced, remembering how it felt to have that jammed into his neck. He peered down into the side pocket, noting the charging cable coiled in the bottom, then returned the stun gun to its place and closed the zip. The next pocket contained a number of different medicines, each in a different container. All of them appeared to have had their labels removed. Tom sifted through the boxes and bottles, then paused as he lifted out a familiar packet. Turning it over, he saw the printed label with his own name.

He stared at the packet, shocked by the sudden realization that he hadn't taken his anti-depressants for days. Was that why he'd felt so shivery this morning? Were the really bad withdrawal symptoms still to come? He remembered how strange he'd felt when he first began using them... the awful sense of *failure*, and the conviction that his life couldn't get any worse. At the time, he'd convinced himself that he was losing Zak and there was nothing he could do about it. But now, as he stood on the brink of *real* loss, he glimpsed the true unbearable horror of it. And he was determined not to let it happen.

Scowling, he returned the packet to the bag.

He couldn't risk taking any now, and drugs wouldn't fix the situation he was in.

The end pocket was crammed with a collection of cheap

cell phones – all identical, save for the colored stickers on the backs of their cases. He counted nine of them, plus a single charger. The orange-stickered phone was absent.

There was a noise outside. Tom looked towards the door and froze, waiting for the dreaded sound of the key in the lock – but then he heard indistinct voices, moving past and away. Breathing a sigh of relief, he hurriedly replaced the phones, closed the end pocket, then stood staring down at the bag.

How long had J been gone? It couldn't have been more than a couple of minutes...

He frowned, biting his lip. There was still time.

With a tremble in his hand, he reached for the main zipper, noting its position before he dragged it round far enough to open the top of the bag. The first thing he saw was the police scanner and the tangled earpiece cable, lying where J had hurriedly stowed them before the drive down here. They were nestled on a pile of neatly folded clothes – jeans, shirts, underwear... all ordinary, everyday items that could have come from any supermarket, obviously chosen to be forgettable. Grimacing from the pain in his side, Tom shifted the pile over slightly. There was a wash bag containing toiletries and, underneath it, a drawstring canvas backpack. Pulling this out, he opened it and peered inside, stiffening as he made out the contents. Thick rubber gloves, a roll of heavy-duty plastic sacks, cleaning wipes and bleach spray. Delving further, he found several sets of plasticuffs, two rolls of duct tape, and a small hacksaw.

Tom shuddered.

Closing up the backpack, he moved it aside. In the bottom corner of the duffel bag he could see a thick wad of hundred-dollar bills, secured with rubber bands, and two small cardboard boxes of bullets. There was no sign of the gun; J must have taken it with him.

Tom straightened up, looking towards the door and listening intently.

Everything was quiet.

Bending forward again, he moved the clothes to check the opposite corner of the bag. There was an old Philip K Dick novel with a tattered cover, and a spiral-bound journal. Easing this out, Tom leafed through the pages. There were names and addresses, printed headshot photos that had been cut out and stuck in, license plate numbers, hastily-drawn diagrams, and endless notes. Tom spotted David Barron's name at the top of one page, along with details for Dyn-Tec, and a home address in Millsboro, Delaware.

A record of J's victims, complete with all the notes and planning he'd undertaken...

It was so tempting to read on, to discover the full extent of the killings, but Tom knew that J could return at any moment.

Frowning, he closed the journal and slipped it back into the bag... but then his fingers brushed against something else, tucked away at the very bottom. He drew out a small brown card-backed envelope and opened the flap. Inside, there was a photograph of a woman in her forties, with long brown hair and a warm, sleepy smile. She was wearing a striped summer dress and standing in front of a lake. It was a standard-size print, and there were faint adhesive markings on the corners, like it had been removed from an album. Tom turned the photo over, but there was nothing written on the back. Wondering who she was, he slipped the picture back into its envelope, then meticulously replaced everything in the bag. Zipping it shut, he moved across the room as quickly as he could, flopping down heavily onto the bed, and clutching his side in agony from the exertion. As he lay there, staring up at the ceiling and breathing fitfully, his thoughts were continually drawn back to the spiral-bound journal. There were answers in those pages.

And he was going to find a way to read them.

29

Tom's Journal

I think J's asleep. His breathing has gradually slowed into a calm, steady rhythm, despite everything that's happened today. The accident certainly shook him, but he seems to have recovered quickly, adjusted his plans. His bag is lying on the floor at the end of his bed, still zipped up, with that spiral-bound journal inside. Maybe, if I get a chance to read it properly, I'll understand what he's doing, <u>why</u> he's doing it. All those names and faces, ordinary people who suddenly became victims... these aren't the thoughtless acts of a madman, and none of this is random.

But for now, I just can't think straight. Not about that, not about anything. My head's spinning and my mind is all over the place. Maybe it's withdrawal symptoms from not taking my anti-depressants, or maybe it's the pills J gave me. I've no idea what they were, and I've felt kind of weird since they kicked in... acid stomach, and a fuzziness in my head. They've helped a bit, with the ache in my ribs, but that's just the physical pain.

When I close my eyes, I keep seeing that car pulling out in front of us, the blood on the steering wheel... Peyton fighting back the tears while J nods sympathetically... Candice's bloated body being dragged from the lake.

And when I open my eyes, I think of Zak.

I thought I'd lost him, today. When I heard those voices up on the road, knowing they'd be calling the police... it really felt like it was all over. The thought of anything happening to him – because of me – is more than I could bear.

God, I wish I'd spent more time with him. But up until now, I thought I still had time.

Before he could talk, when we were still a family, I would hold him and gaze into those deep blue eyes and imagine all the stuff we would do together, all the things we would talk about. Getting to know him – connecting with him – was always something that I thought lay ahead of me, something that I was going to do when I was more ready. But I'm realizing that some of those moments are already lost, part of the past. And sitting here now, I'm really frightened that the little time I spent with him may be all the time we'll ever have.

Why is it only now, when it might be too late, that I can see what truly matters? Why did I put things off, why the fuck did I wait? I feel like I've spent all these years trying to prepare myself for living, rather than actually living.

Maybe Samaira was right all along, giving herself to each day, rather than worrying about tomorrow and getting things perfect. Maybe things were pretty perfect just as they were.

I'm glad Zak has her. I just wish I could have given him something too. But maybe, this is all I can do for him now – get to the end of this nightmare, do whatever it takes to buy his safety. I have to do that for him, no matter what.

30

Tom woke up gradually, screwing his eyes shut against the glare of daylight that streamed in through the window. Sensing movement, he squinted up to find a tall silhouette standing over him, holding a paper coffee cup.

'Good morning,' J said.

Tom attempted to twist around and angle his face away from the sun.

'Whoa, not so fast there...' the older man warned him, but the pain was already flaring through his side, and he sank back onto the mattress, moaning into his pillow as he remembered his injury from the previous day.

'You're gonna want to take it slow,' J advised.

'No shit...' Tom gasped, clutching at his aching side.

'Your coffee's just here,' J said, as he stooped to place the cup on the nightstand. 'And I've got another ice pack for your ribs...'

Tom groaned. *The ice pack again.* He'd been doubtful about its effects last night, but J had been very insistent and it did seem to have helped. Reluctantly, he levered himself up into a half-sitting position, propped up on the pillows, then accepted the pack and held it tentatively against his side.

'Aarrgghh...'

He clenched his teeth at the shock of the cold, but kept it pressed to his skin.

'Ten minutes,' the older man told him. 'When I get back, we'll strap you up a little, so you can move around without it hurting so much.'

Watching him as he bustled about the room, Tom blinked, weighed down by a crushing weariness.

'What time is it?' he asked.

'A little after seven thirty,' J replied.

Tom hung his head, feeling the cold from the ice pack beginning to numb his side.

'Couldn't we have slept a little longer?' he sighed. 'I had a rough night.'

J walked through from the bathroom, dumping his washbag into the duffel bag.

'I appreciate that, but we've got some things we absolutely *have* to do today.' He zipped it shut, then straightened. 'The rental car place opens in a little while, and I need to get over there.'

'All right.' Tom relaxed his head back, resenting the way the cold was waking him up.

J paused to check his pockets, then moved towards the door.

'Start getting ready,' he said. 'I won't be long.'

Tom had just finished in the bathroom when he heard the key in the lock. J entered the room and shut the door behind him.

'Did you get another car?' Tom asked.

'Sure did,' J nodded. 'A nice new Toyota SUV, sitting out in the parking lot.' He tossed the key up in the air and caught it again. 'Think you'll be okay to drive it?'

'Me?' Tom stared at him, confused. 'Why me?'

'I'll be driving the Ford,' J explained. 'Assuming I can get it started, of course.'

Tom made his way over to the bed.

'So... we're taking both cars?'

'We need to dispose of that Ford somewhere,' J told him. 'Can't leave it lying around here at the motel. Wouldn't be long before the police figured out that it belonged to one of the guests.'

Tom nodded, noting how much J thought like a cop. Had he perhaps spent some time in law-enforcement, before getting a job in insurance?

'Where are we going to dump it?'

'Not too far,' J replied. He stooped to pick up the pharmacy bag from the side of his bed. 'But I reckon we need to get you strapped up before we go anywhere. Take your shirt off.'

Tom did as he was asked, sitting on the edge of the bed with his arms raised. It felt curiously intimate, having J leaning in so close to him, wrapping the supports around his chest and carefully adjusting their fit.

'Now, you're gonna *want* to breathe shallow, but that's no good,' the older man cautioned him. 'Just remember: it's better to have it hurt a little, than to get a build-up of fluid in your lungs.'

'Understood. How do you know all this stuff? Have you had medical training?'

'A little, back when I was in the National Guard.' J straightened up. 'So how does it feel? Can you move okay?'

Tom lowered his arms and cautiously turned his upper body.

'Still sore, but...' He looked up and nodded, '...it's definitely better than it was.'

'Good.' J looked pleased. 'I'll find you another painkiller, and then we can get out of here.'

. . .

It was a bright morning when they stepped out of the room. J hovered in the doorway, taking a last look around. He'd spent the previous few minutes wiping down any hard surfaces, and he was using his sleeve to hold the door handle.

'Have you got everything?'

'I think so,' Tom replied.

J's expression became serious.

'Think hard, Tom,' he said. 'Have you *got* everything?'

Tom hesitated, then nodded.

'Yes.'

Satisfied, J pulled the door closed.

After dropping off the key at reception, he led the way out into the parking lot. A gleaming black Toyota RAV4 was now sitting beside their battered Ford Taurus, conveniently hiding it from view.

J opened the back and stowed the bags, then handed the key to Tom.

'Here you go,' he said, turning to look at the Ford. 'Now, if I can get this thing started, I'm gonna need you to follow me, and I'll need you to stay close. We *mustn't* get separated; I don't care if you have to run a red light, or cut someone up, you stay with me, okay?'

Tom nodded. 'Where are we headed?'

'There's a lake, about twenty minutes from here,' J told him. 'Just focus, and stay on my tail, okay?'

'Okay.'

J clapped him gently on the shoulder.

'Thanks, Tom,' he said. 'We'll grab some breakfast when we're done. Now, let's see whether it starts...'

He unlocked the Ford and got in, pulling the door shut with a creaking scrape.

Tom climbed into the Toyota. It smelled like a new car, and

he took a moment to look around, familiarizing himself with the controls. His side ached as he reached back to grab the seat-belt, but the strapping around his chest helped, and the painkiller was beginning to work.

As he started the engine, he was uncomfortably aware of the opportunity he had, sitting alone in a vehicle with a full tank of gas. He could just drive away, leaving J stranded, and the whole nightmare journey would end right now.

Except it wouldn't, because of the threat to Zak.

Even if he could get away, even if he could get to a phone, warn Samaira, and alert the police... no, he couldn't risk Zak's life.

So instead of doing the 'right' thing, he was going to do the 'wrong' thing – he was going to do what the killer wanted, actually *help* the killer get away. If that's what it took to keep his little boy safe, that's what he'd do.

Outside, he could hear the rattling of the Ford, as the ignition struggled to turn over. It sounded as though it wasn't going to start, but the engine suddenly seemed to catch, and stuttered into life. Through the glass, he could see J, who looked relieved and gave him the thumbs-up sign. A moment later, the Ford reversed out of its bay, then crept forwards across the parking lot. Tom put the Toyota in gear and followed it.

They retraced their route from the previous evening, cutting through the outskirts of the town, but when they reached the exit that led down to I-64, J kept going straight on, passing over the interstate and driving on into open countryside. The road became narrower, winding its way along the side of hills in slow, sweeping curves, plunging into wooded valleys then rising above the trees again. There were clusters of houses, huddled together here and there... agricultural workshops, the occasional diner or general store. After a while, the landscape flattened out a little, and a lonely railroad track snaked into view, running alongside the asphalt.

J drove at a steady pace, and Tom had no difficulty staying close behind him. As he stared out at the damaged rear of the Ford, he wondered what they would have done if the car hadn't started. J was being forced to improvise now; his grand design, whatever it was, had fallen apart when they had the accident.

Could he really be as good at thinking on his feet as he was at planning ahead? So far, he seemed to be. In a way, it was more impressive to see how he coped under pressure, dealing with things that would overcome most people.

What must it be like, to have such mental strength?

They rounded another bend, and Tom realized that the Ford was slowing down, though neither of its brake lights seemed to be working. A moment later, J turned right onto a smaller road that climbed between the slopes of a forested valley. Glimpsing a long expanse of silver-blue water through the trees, Tom followed, driving more slowly now. They passed several turn-offs that led down to picnic areas and an activity center, but J kept going. The road twisted left and right, following the line of the lake shore, and shaded by tall trees that squeezed out the sky above them. Finally, Tom saw J stick his hand out of the window, waving him to slow down. They stopped on a tight bend, and Tom pulled in close behind the Ford and shut off the engine.

J was already out, walking round to the edge of the road and peering down the steeply sloping bank towards the bright water below. Tom clambered out stiffly and went over to him.

'This far along, the road should be quiet,' the older man said, glancing around. 'But we're gonna have to be quick.' He pointed back along the shoreline. 'I need you to keep watch. You see anyone coming, I want you to call to me, then I want you to go and stop them, okay?'

'I can try...' Tom said, doubtfully.

'Wave them down, distract them, I don't care.' J's expression was grim. 'Just don't let them see what I'm doing.'

Tom nodded. 'All right,'

'Okay, then.' J took a deep breath. 'Here goes nothing...'

He got back into the Ford, leaving the door open as he reversed into the middle of the road, then crept the car forward to the very edge of the bank. Climbing out, he angled the steering wheel, then leaned in and put the gearshift into *Drive.*

Immediately, the car lurched forward. J stumbled along beside it, reaching in through the window to try and steer it straight, until it got away from him and went rolling down the slope. Crashing through some bushes and hitting a sudden bump, the trunk popped open and Tom gasped as he saw something flopping loosely inside.

It was an arm.

His stomach turned, as it dawned on him that this was the driver who'd hit them; they'd driven all the way from Oak Hill – and he had *slept* – with a dead body right behind him.

He stared in fascinated horror as the car ploughed into the water and slowed, its nose creating a wave as it dipped below the surface. Breathing hard, J clambered back up to the edge of the road and stood beside him, watching as the Ford slowly disappeared into the lake. Water flooded into the trunk, engulfing the corpse, and closing over the back of the car until all that remained were ripples on the surface.

Turning away, Tom shook his head in dismay. 'You had him in the back all this time...'

J brushed himself down, then shrugged. 'What else was I supposed to do with him?'

He lifted his head, listening for a moment, but there was no sound except the rustle of the wind in the trees, and the delicate lapping of the lake. Nodding to himself, he began walking back to the Toyota.

'We're done here,' he said, pausing to look back at Tom. 'Come on. I'll buy you breakfast.'

31

J lifted a forkful of egg and bacon to his mouth and chewed thoughtfully. They were at a table by the window, in a quiet corner of a restaurant near the interstate. The walls were adorned with framed photos of children in cowboy hats, and stenciled slogans about the importance of family. Tom gazed up at them in quiet anguish, thinking about Zak, wondering where he was and whether he was safe.

'Your accomplice,' he began. 'The guy you had pointing the camera at Samaira's place... has he been in touch? Has he said anything about my son?'

J paused to glance up from his breakfast, then slowly shook his head.

'I need to know that Zak's all right,' Tom hissed, leaning in towards the table and holding his side against the pain. 'I *have* to know.'

J swallowed his food, then nodded.

'I understand, Tom,' he said. 'But nothing's going to happen to Zak, not as long as we're on our journey. I promised you that, remember?'

'So you haven't been in touch? There's no news?'

'No.' J replied, toying with his fork and stifling a yawn. 'And no news is good news. Anyway, through no fault of our own, we've had a change of plan forced on us.'

Tom only had a cup of coffee in front of him, and sat, turning it.

'Yeah, I noticed.'

J caught the tone but ignored it.

'That accident...' He broke off, slowly shaking his head. 'Well, it means we won't be able to make our next stop.'

Tom shrugged.

'Okay.' He continued to turn his coffee cup, then stopped, his brows creasing into a frown as his curiosity kicked in. 'Actually, no... why?'

'It would impact on our schedule for the rest of the trip, and there are...' J hesitated, considering his words. 'There are places we have to be on particular days.'

Tom met his gaze and held it. Clearly there was a definite timetable for their journey... set times and places. But what for? Meetings with victims' friends? More murders? His thoughts returned to that handwritten journal, hidden in the bottom of the duffel bag. If only he'd had more time to read it.

'Can you tell me where we *were* going?' he pressed.

J gave a slight shake of his head and smiled. He loaded his fork with food and lifted it towards his mouth, then paused.

'Remember Duncan Baumann and Daryl Hirsch?'

Tom nodded. 'From the list you sent me.'

'I thought you might be curious about them... about who they were, where they lived... and how they died.' J smiled to himself, then lifted the fork again. 'We *were* gonna head up to Flint, Michigan, then on to Mitchell, South Dakota.'

Tom took this in, then frowned, mentally working out the distances involved.

'That's a hell of a drive,' he mused. 'How long would that even take?'

'I was allowing a day for us to reach Flint, then a full day there,' he answered. 'Then a couple of days to reach Mitchell, and a day there too. Five days, all told, but the accident put us behind schedule... and that's a lot of time for a man with bruised ribs to sit still in a car. You need movement – not too much, of course – and a chance to rest properly.'

He pushed his plate away and reached for his coffee cup. 'So, I figured I'd spare you that part of the journey... and spare myself a lot of hours staring out at the highway.'

'Oh,' Tom said, slightly taken aback. 'Thanks.'

J took a quick swallow of coffee.

'Forget about it,' he said. 'I told you I'd no intention of harming you, and I meant it. And I'm sure we'll find some time for me to tell you all about Mr Baumann and Mr Hirsch.'

'Why not now?' Tom pressed, but J just shook his head as he sipped his coffee.

Outside in the parking lot, a minivan pulled up and a young couple got out, herding their two small children towards the front of the restaurant.

'So what are we going to do now?' Tom asked.

'Now that we've got time to kill?' J met his eye, then shrugged apologetically. 'Sorry... poor choice of phrase.'

Tom ignored the joke.

'Do we just... find another motel?' he suggested. 'Lay low and wait it out?'

J shook his head.

'Oh, I think we can do a little better than that,' he said, leaning to one side and taking out his wallet. 'We're in a beautiful part of the country and I'm sure a little fresh air would work wonders on a city boy like you.'

Tom looked at him, puzzled.

'Finish your coffee,' J smiled. 'I'll get the check.'

. . .

They re-joined the interstate and drove for a couple of miles before J switched lanes and took the exit ramp, following the road around in a long loop. Soon, they were coasting down a hill, past churches and tanning salons.

'We're gonna need a few things,' J explained, as they left the main road and turned into the parking lot of a huge Walmart. He found a space close to the store entrance and switched off the engine.

'How are you feeling?' he said, turning to Tom. 'Ribs still hurting?'

'Still a little sore,' Tom replied. 'But it's not too bad right now.'

J gave him an encouraging nod.

'You okay to come in with me?' he asked. 'It'll be easier than you writing me a shopping list...'

'Sure.'

They got out and walked down the line of parked cars towards the front of the broad brown building.

'So are you going to tell me where we're headed?' Tom asked, as they made their way through the main doors and into the sprawling store.

'Ah, you'll see soon enough,' J replied. He veered off to collect a shopping cart, then brought it back over to Tom. 'Now... we're going to want meals for five days. You any good at cooking?'

Tom was thrown by this. 'Uh... not particularly. Why?'

'Doesn't matter,' J assured him. 'I reckon I can take care of that side of things... maybe give you a few pointers if you like. The place we're going has a good charcoal grill, so we can kick back and enjoy a few cook-outs.'

They spent some time walking the aisles, steadily filling the cart with different foods, J recommending different meats and consulting Tom on his preferences as they went. When they reached the liquor section, the older man picked up a case of beer and an expensive bottle of bourbon.

'How about you, Tom?' he asked. 'What's your poison?'

Tom turned to peer at the shelves and see what they had, then stopped.

What the hell was he *doing?* How could he be standing here in a supermarket, chatting about alcohol, with a murderer? What was *wrong* with him?

'I... I'm not sure...' he stammered.

Fresh in his mind, he saw the battered Ford Taurus, sinking into the lake, water swirling around the broken body in the trunk...

Another life ended.

Breathing fast, he rubbed his eyes for a moment, trying to force the images away. Pain radiated out from his side. When he looked up again, he found that J was watching him. The older man's expression was serious now, but there was a note of sympathy in his voice when he finally spoke.

'I understand,' he said gently, as though he guessed what Tom was thinking. 'This isn't easy.'

He held Tom's gaze, then turned to pick up another case of beer and put it in the cart.

'Come on,' he said. 'Let's go and find a couple of coolers for this stuff, then we can get out of here.'

32

They drove for a little over an hour, leaving the suburbs behind as they pushed out into rolling open country, with the highway snaking between tall green hills, and bridging deep, shady valleys. Unusually, J had tuned the radio to a music station, and Tom was grateful for the distraction. Resting his head against the window glass, he gazed out at the forested slopes as they slipped by.

The sudden crisis of responsibility that had gripped him in the supermarket was like jolting into wakefulness from the middle of a nightmare... but now it was slowly ebbing, giving way to a dreadful, reeling numbness. How could anyone be involved in something like this and not fall apart with the emotional turmoil?

'Does it ever overwhelm you?' he asked. 'What you've done, the lives you've taken, the impact of each death spreading out across all the friends and families?'

J remained quiet for a while, then nodded.

'It's been... very hard,' he admitted. 'There have been times when I struggled with it.'

'Then why did you continue? Why didn't you just stop?'

But the older man offered no reply, just a grim shake of the head to indicate that stopping wasn't an option.

Tom sank back into his seat and thought about the list of names, the vast collateral damage that each murder left in its wake.

'Wrecking so many lives,' he said, appalled by the scale of it. 'How do you *live* with something like that?'

'Lives get wrecked every day.' There was an edge to J's voice, then he sighed. 'But I've dealt with worse, and I survived. Well, *part* of me survived, I guess.'

Tom picked up on the change in tone. 'Like that old saying – when you kill someone, a part of you dies too. Is that what you mean?'

J gave a slight shrug.

'But you said you'd dealt with worse, and partly survived,' Tom continued. He noticed the muscles tighten along the older man's jawline, then looked away. 'Maybe that's how people cope... by being partly dead inside.'

After getting off the interstate, they joined a quiet country road, cruising past lonely houses and isolated farms, before J slowed and turned onto a narrow track that plunged down into the trees.

It was a difficult drive, with sudden patches of sunlight followed by long stretches of shade and, though there were occasional passing places, much of the track was only wide enough for one vehicle. Despite J's efforts, overgrown bushes continually brushed and scraped against both sides of their SUV. Eventually, after descending steadily for ten minutes or so, the track levelled out and grew wider again. Emerging from the trees, they found themselves near the bottom of a deep river valley. Ahead of them, wooden cabins could be seen, dotted along the sloping banks.

'Better than a motel,' J said, a distant look on his face as he gazed out through the windshield. For a fleeting moment, his expression appeared nostalgic, then he adopted a wry smile. 'And less likely to attract attention.'

'Attention?' Tom was curious.

'Two guys staying in the same cheap motel room for several nights? Maybe they think it's sexual, maybe they think it's sinister, but people notice it. They *remember* it.' He turned his face back towards the river. 'But a couple of guys out here? They're just hiking, or fishing, or whatever... they're just a couple of guys.'

After stopping at the office to pick up the key, J drove on down the track for a way, before bumping the SUV up onto a patch of lawn in front of their cabin.

'This is us,' he said, switching off the engine. Turning to Tom, he handed over a small key with a large wooden fob, bearing a carved number 4. 'I'll bring the bags and stuff in a minute. You go on inside, take a look around.'

Tom stepped out onto the sun-dappled grass and stood for a moment, just listening. Above him in the branches, he could hear the gentle rustle of leaves and, somewhere nearby, the constant rush of water. Nestled among tall trees, the cabin looked large and homely, with a steeply pitched roof and gable windows that promised an upper story. Steps led up to a front porch, that extended around the side of the building, forming a raised balcony as the ground dropped away behind it. He climbed up to the front door, unlocked it, and stepped inside.

The ground level was open plan, with polished wooden flooring, and a carved wooden staircase. The front half of the room was given over to a den area, with comfortable sofas and a large TV, while the rear was a kitchen-diner, with a rustic table and chairs, and sleek modern appliances built in along one wall. At the far end of the room, full-length glass doors opened out onto the balcony, filling the space with light and, as Tom walked over to them, revealing a view of the river through the trees.

He heard movement behind him and turned to see J bringing the two duffel bags in, wearily dumping them on the floor.

'Bathroom's up there,' the older man said, indicating the stairs. 'And there's two bedrooms – one at the front, one at the back – so just let me know which you want.'

Straightening up, he turned and went outside again.

Tom wandered over to the glass doors and undid the latch. Holding his side, he carefully slid them open, then stepped out onto the balcony. It was about six feet above the ground here, with several stacked lawn chairs and a covered barbecue grill. Walking over to lean on the wooden rail, he stared down the grassy slope between the trees to the shimmering silver water. Zak would have loved it here, away from the city, with space to run and laugh. He wished they'd taken the time to do things like that together, to really get close, really get to know each other... while they had the chance.

He could hear J moving around in the kitchen area for a while, the clinking of glass, cupboards opening and closing. Eventually, the older man stepped out onto the balcony. He came over to the rail, two beers in hand, and wordlessly held one out. After a moment, Tom took it, and the two men stood in silence, gazing out across the river.

It was later now, and getting cooler. The sun had finally dipped below the horizon, making silhouettes of the trees, and long wisps of dark, distant cloud were streaked across the glowing red sky. Tom sat on one of the balcony chairs, staring out into the evening.

You never saw skies like that... not in the city.

He lowered his eyes to where the river still shimmered in the gloom, then turned to look back along the balcony.

Standing over the smoking grill, J was holding a set of long metal tongs.

'This chicken's about done,' he said. 'Wanna pass me your plate?'

Tom stooped to retrieve his plate and held it out while the older man served up a couple of sizzling chicken legs. The smell was immediately appetizing.

'Thanks.'

'You're welcome.'

J removed the rest of the chicken, then dropped a couple of burgers onto the grill. Collecting his own plate, he walked round and sat down beside Tom.

'Nothing like cooking outdoors to fire up an appetite,' he said. 'Tell me what you think.'

Tom picked up a piece of chicken. The meat fell away from the bone as he bit into it, and the flavor was beautiful.

'Wow,' he nodded, taking another bite. 'This is actually really good.'

J seemed pleased.

'That's the honey-maple glaze I was telling you about,' he explained. 'Not as good as my dad used to make, but it still hits the spot.'

'Your dad taught you how to cook?' Tom asked. Gaining insight into the life of a killer, before he became a killer, was intriguing.

'Any time we had a barbecue, he'd get me involved,' J replied. 'He used to take us camping too, whenever he could. Taught me how to fish, how to build a fire, how to cook... said I'd appreciate things more if I did them myself. Yeah, we used to eat pretty good on those trips.'

He settled back into his chair contentedly.

Tom sat thoughtfully, trying to imagine such an idyllic childhood.

'What kind of work did your dad do?' he asked.

'He was a cop – a detective, actually.' J caught Tom's look of surprise. 'And yeah, I get the irony of that.'

'What would he think of all this, of what you're doing?'

'Oh, he'd hate it,' J replied, and his expression became one of regret. 'But I think maybe... well, he *might* understand. Least, I hope so. He was from a different time, and he wouldn't recognize the way the world is today, what passes for justice, what we choose to care about and choose to ignore.'

Tom paused.

'Sorry, you think he might *understand?*'

The question appeared to bring J back from some private thoughts, and he affected a hasty shrug.

'I'm just thankful he's not here to see any of it,' he said, turning away to glance at the barbecue.

'Or read about it,' Tom added, pointedly.

J bowed his head.

'Touché, Tom.' He turned back to reveal a wry smile. 'I certainly chose the right person to come along with me.'

'Because you think *I* might understand?'

J chewed thoughtfully for a moment, then swallowed. A faint smile touched the corners of his mouth.

'I really *do* admire your writing, Tom,' he said. 'And that's a big part of it.'

'But that's not the reason I'm here, is it?' Tom pressed him.

J put his plate down.

'Well, I liked that you were objective in your reporting,' he said. 'You always seemed to have a genuine desire to uncover the truth, rather than wallow in pointless hand-wringing, or foolish emotional nonsense.'

'Emotional nonsense?'

'Oh, you know the sort of thing,' J sighed. 'Always determined to portray the victims as perfect human beings, talking about their perfect family lives that were so *cruelly* shattered by the *heartless* killer... all those cheap tricks to try and make the crime seem more shocking.' He rolled his eyes, then added sadly, 'As if the truth wasn't shocking enough.'

Tom considered this. 'So you wanted someone to uncover the truth?'

'Of course.'

'But...' Tom hesitated. 'Why does that matter to you?'

J smiled to himself.

'Now *that's* a good question,' he said. Getting stiffly to his feet, he walked slowly round to the grill and started flipping the burgers over. 'I guess I do want people to understand.'

Watching him intently, Tom frowned.

'You want them to understand *you*?'

J put the tongs down and came back to his chair.

'I want them to understand what I've *done*,' he said, sitting down.

Tom scoffed. 'What you've done is *kill* a lot of people.'

'That's true,' J said, quietly. 'But I don't think you get it... not yet, anyway.'

'So *help* me to get it,' Tom retorted. 'Tell me *why*.'

'That's what I like about you, Tom,' he smiled. 'I believe you really *do* want to understand...'

'Of course. Why wouldn't I?'

J shook his head, sadly.

'More and more, people tend to confuse "understanding" with "agreement",' he said, leaning forward in his chair, and resting his elbows on his knees. 'If you say you understand something bad... like a racist or sexist comment, for example... then people accuse you of *being* racist or sexist. They deliberately confuse understanding with agreement. Now, I don't expect people to agree with what I've done – I know the difference between right and wrong, and I know that what I've done is terrible – but I do want people to understand it.'

Tom sat back in his chair, staring out towards the river.

'To understand something that they absolutely disagree with...'

'Exactly,' J said.

'And that's why you want me to have "context",' Tom mused. 'Because you want me to work it all out for myself.'

J nodded. 'It's like being a detective,' he explained. 'A good detective has to understand the person he's investigating, has to be able to put himself in their shoes... but that doesn't mean he agrees with them. That's just how he stops them.'

'Do *you* want to be stopped?' Tom asked.

J met his eyes for a moment, then walked slowly over to the grill. There was a loud sizzling and spitting of fat as he flipped the burgers again.

'How did the police react when you told them about me?' he said, changing the subject. 'Was it tough getting them to take you seriously?'

Tom hesitated, then sighed. There seemed little point in denying anything now.

'I spoke to a friend over there, someone I've worked with before...'

'Leo Moretti?'

'Yeah. He spoke to his boss and she... well, *she* took it seriously. Eventually.'

'Did they already suspect a connection between the three names I gave you?' J asked, eagerly.

Tom shook his head.

'I don't think so. As far as I know those deaths were viewed as unconnected...' He broke off, then shrugged. 'It was your mention of Lizzie Reeves that made the difference, about her laying on her back. That hadn't been made public.'

J nodded thoughtfully.

'Did they assign a protection detail for your little trip upstate?'

'Yeah. My friend called in some favors.'

J chuckled.

'Sorry, I shouldn't laugh,' he said. 'And I do feel bad about wasting everyone's time like that, but... well, at least they *tried* to look after you.'

'They did what they could.' Tom thought about the tracking device, how differently things might have gone...

'And I'm sure they're still looking for you right now,' J said. He turned and walked over to lean on the balcony rail, gazing out into the trees. 'Just not here.'

33

The morning had been hot and hazy, but now the blue sky was dotted with silvery clouds and a cool breeze whispered down the long green valley. Tom took his time as he wandered along the river bank, shoes crunching into the drifts of small stones, careful not to put too much stress on his ribs. There was a constant dull ache in his side, despite the strapping, but J had promised that today would be restricted to gentle walking, rather than hiking.

The river was broad here – maybe two hundred yards across – with blue-green water sliding steadily by, and dark forested slopes rising steeply from the far shore. A few yards ahead of him, J halted under an overhanging tree and looked back over his shoulder.

'Are you okay there?'

'I'm fine,' Tom replied. He stopped for a moment, turning carefully to gaze back along the valley. 'This reminds me of the Peak District, back in England. Only this is so much... bigger.'

'I've never been to England,' J said, looking up at the sky and wiping his brow. 'What's it like?'

Tom made a face.

'It isn't really one place,' he said, picking his way along the shore. 'It's like a lot of very different places, all squashed together. Does that make sense?'

'I guess...'

'But here, you have so much... *space.*' Tom walked over, gesturing around him. 'Everything's bigger, more spread out here. In England, everything's smaller, closer together.'

J smiled.

'I always wanted to visit there, to travel more...' He trailed off, then shook his head, wistfully. 'Guess it wasn't meant to be, though.'

He turned away and began to walk on along the shore.

Tom watched him for a moment, wondering why he couldn't travel. Was he wanted for some crime, that would prevent him leaving the country? Or was something else keeping him here?

'You've never been out of the US?' he asked, casually.

'Oh, I've been to Mexico and Canada a few times,' J replied. 'Took a trip to Europe when I was younger, visited Paris and West Berlin... but I never quite got around to seeing all the places I wanted to see.'

'You could still go now,' Tom suggested. 'Couldn't you?'

But the older man shook his head.

'It's not so easy for me,' he said. 'I have... commitments here.'

'Commitments...' Tom frowned. 'You mean you still have some names to cross off your list?'

'There are some things I *have* to do, Tom.'

They continued down-river, cutting through a stand of trees where the bank jutted out into the water.

'We're almost there,' J said, turning to him then holding up his hand. 'Do you hear it?'

Tom halted, listening. Above the steady low rush of the river, there was another sound: a louder, rougher, roaring noise.

'Come on,' J said, beckoning him forward.

As they made their way down a gentle slope and emerged from the trees onto a wide, grassy bank, Tom saw the waterfall. Stretching away towards the distant shore, it was a vast flight of staggered stone steps, with white water cascading down a few feet at a time before a final, deeper drop.

'Well now...' J stood gazing out across the river, with his hands on his hips. 'Would you just look at that.'

Tom stood beside him, his eyes following the shelf of dark rock that jutted forward, slick and shining, from the clouds of sunlit spray

'That's really impressive,' he agreed, raising his voice above the roaring. 'It almost looks as though you could walk across to the other side.'

'It's deeper than it looks,' J replied. 'Let's go on a little further.'

They made their way down the bank until they were just below the falls. The noise of the water lessened, but it still filled the air around them, and a fresh misty wetness touched their faces.

'This is a whole lot prettier than Flint, Michigan,' J said, with a soft chuckle. He walked over to sit on the trunk of a fallen tree, then uncapped his water bottle and took a long drink.

Tom perched on a large nearby rock, his hands feeling the moisture in the moss as he settled himself in place. The side of his ribcage was warm and sore, and he was glad of a chance to rest, but the mention of Flint reminded him of J's promise.

'You were going to tell me about them,' he said. 'About Hirsch and Baumann.'

J gazed at the falls for a time before responding.

'What would you like to know?'

'As much as you're willing to tell me.'

J continued staring across the river, but his face creased into a wry smile.

'Very well,' he said after a moment. 'Daryl Hirsch was a 37-year-old businessman who ran a small chain of "ethical" coffee shops... I mean, I'm not sure how ethical a coffee shop can really be, but he seemed to like his causes, and I'm sure it all helped him bring in more customers...'

There was obvious distaste in his voice.

'You really didn't like him,' Tom observed.

'I really didn't.'

'But that's not why you killed him.'

'Of course not!' J's voice was indignant, as though the idea was insulting. 'People absolutely *don't* need to like one another to peacefully co-exist.' He paused, then shook his head. 'If we all spent more time just accepting others as they are, rather than trying to change them into what we consider "likeable", the world would be a happier place...'

'But you did kill him.'

J met his eye briefly, then nodded.

'Oh yes.' He looked across towards the distant shore, remembering. 'And Hirsch turned out to be a difficult one. Quite risky... and messy.'

'So?' Tom pressed. 'What happened?'

'You *know* what happened,' J said, quietly.

Tom recognized a note of reluctance in his voice and turned towards the river. Sometimes, the vacuum of silence was more effective than the pressure of more questions. He sat patiently, until he heard J sigh.

'I'd planned to get him at his office,' the older man muttered. 'Didn't quite work out that way though.'

'Why not?'

'He had somebody with him,' J replied, shaking his head. 'Some guy he was seeing.'

Tom raised an eyebrow.

'Hirsch was gay?'

'Yeah... so?' J shrugged his shoulders. 'What's that got to do with anything?'

'Nothing,' Tom said. For a moment, he'd wondered if that might indicate a possible motive, but the older man clearly wasn't concerned by his victims' sexuality. And of course, Lizzie Reeves and Candice Porter both had boyfriends. 'So, what happened?'

'Well, at first, when I saw he wasn't alone, I thought about backing off.' J lifted his head slightly. 'But then I figured... I'd come all this way, I might as well follow him for a while, just to see where he went. So I did.'

'Go on...' Tom encouraged him. He had quietly taken out his notebook and was carefully writing down as much as he could.

'They drove half-way across town, with me behind them, trying to stay a couple of cars back but trying not to lose them...' He broke off, remembering the pursuit, then sighed again. 'Anyway, I followed them out to a retail park. Hirsch dropped his friend off – I guess the guy must have worked there or something – then he drove about a block away and pulled over at the side of a furniture store. I drove around the back of the place, trying to figure out what he was doing there because the store was closed and the parking lot was empty... and then I saw that he'd got out of his car and he was smoking a cigarette.'

Tom stared at him, blankly.

'I figured he didn't want his boyfriend to know that he smoked, and he'd been waiting to light up,' J explained. 'Anyhow, he was standing right there in an empty parking lot... I had the knife and the stun gun, and I finally had him on his own. It was like the opportunity was just presenting itself to me.'

'What did you do?'

'I decided I was gonna seize that opportunity,' J replied, then paused and shook his head. 'But it was a mistake.'

'Killing him?'

'*Stabbing* him,' J clarified. 'Have you any idea what it's like to go at someone with a knife?'

Tom blinked. 'Of course not.'

J lowered his eyes. 'Neither had I,' he murmured. 'It's a brutal way to kill. There's a kind of... intimate cruelty to it, and the feeling of the blade going in is so...' He trailed off into a brooding silence, then lifted his head to gaze across the river. 'And then there's the blood. *So* much blood, even if you've taken precautions.'

'Precautions?' Tom queried.

'I stunned him first, so he wasn't able to defend himself,' J explained. 'But it was a mess – *I* was a mess – and there was no place for me to clean up, which made the getaway harder. I had a long drive, hoping I wouldn't be stopped or seen. That's why I always carry cleaning supplies with me now.'

The roar of the waterfall seemed to grow louder as Tom sat there, trying to picture the scene.

'All that blood...' he mused, watching the older man's face.

'It was just awful,' J said with a slight nod. 'I'd decided I was gonna take his wallet and his watch – you know, to make it look like a robbery? – but he was *covered* in blood by then...' He took a deep breath, then sighed. 'I don't ever want to stab anyone ever again.'

Studying him reliving the memory, Tom frowned. J didn't enjoy the *act* of killing, though he *did* seem to take a certain grim satisfaction in his work. And his approach was practical, rather than passionate.

'Do you always try and make it look like a robbery, or provide some other false motive?' he asked.

'Of course,' J replied, seriously. 'It's important to give the police a nice obvious line of enquiry to follow. I certainly don't want them stumbling onto the truth.'

'And what *is* the truth? What had Hirsch done?'

J hesitated.

'Did Hirsch want you dead?' Tom persisted. 'Like Candice Porter did?'

J looked over at him, his dark eyes suddenly cold, empty.

'You remember you talked about the *impact* of my actions, spreading out across friends and loved ones?' he said. 'Well, it's a bit like tossing a match and starting a forest fire. Sometimes a tiny action can have an enormous impact. Sometimes, it's not just about what a person does, it's about the weight of the consequences.'

Tom held the deathly gaze.

'What *were* those consequences?'

J stared back at him for a long moment, then turned his head away to look along the riverbank.

'Probably best that you don't try to do too much today,' he said, getting stiffly to his feet.

'But I just want to–'

'You really *mustn't* overdo it,' J interrupted. 'It could be *very* bad for your health.'

34

Tom's Journal

It's our second evening in the cabin, and I'm alone at the table with my notepad and pen. Clouds have covered the moon, and it's dark outside, but the sliding doors are still wide open, and I can smell the trees beyond the balcony. J is over in the den area, sprawled out on one of the sofas. I've noticed that he doesn't like to bother me when I'm writing, but he's been unusually quiet tonight. He seemed bright enough while he was cooking earlier, but he's spent the last couple of hours just sitting in front of the TV, staring at a football game that he isn't really watching.

There's something on his mind. At first I thought it was just a reaction to the accident, and to having a sudden change of plans forced on him... for someone who likes to work out every detail in advance, that must *be unsettling. But now I'm starting to wonder if there's something more.*

He was shaken by that crash – not just the disruption, and the risk of being caught, but the death of the other driver really seemed to get to him, even though it probably wasn't his fault. It's a strangely human reaction for someone who's murdered so many people. He's done his best to take care of me since then, and that's been kind of confusing too. It's difficult to reconcile this considerate man, who's looking after me and diligently nursing my injuries, with the monster who snapped David Barron's neck back in Delaware, and threatened the life of my son.

Then there's his tendency to avoid certain questions. It happened again today, when I pushed him about what exactly Daryl Hirsch had done. He says he wants me to "figure out the truth", rather than him just telling me everything, and I do *kind of get what he means by that. But some questions just seem to shut him down, as though he's worried to go anywhere near those subjects.*

Why?

He wants me to understand what he's done, so why does he put the brakes on when I ask about it? Is he worried that, if he starts talking, he won't be able to stop? That he'll tell me too much, too soon? He wants me to write his damn story... so what the hell is he waiting for? I need to know more if I'm ever going to discover the truth of this man. I need to know who he is, and what he's done...

I need to read his journal.

Looking up from the table, I see J is still sitting across the room from me, staring at the TV, motionless. I glance up at the ceiling.

My bedroom's at the back of the cabin, leaving him with the one at the front. Both are about the same size and neither has a lock on the door. His bag is up there right now, probably lying open on his bed...

But I can't risk it. Sure, I could make an excuse to go upstairs, but he might come up after me, or hear the floor creak, and then he'd know. Anyway, it'd take time for me to read through the journal and find out just who he's killed... and when... and how...

And then a new thought grips me. What if it's not just a record of the people he's already killed. What if it includes the names of people he's going *to kill?*

What if I turn ahead through the pages and see my own name?

He says he isn't planning to hurt me, but he wasn't planning to hit that car, or dispose of a body in a lake, or come to this cabin.

Plans change.

I have to read that journal.

35

The next day dawned damp and cold, with an eerie grey mist hanging among the trees. By mid-morning the sky had darkened, as heavy clouds rolled across the valley, bringing with them the smell of rain.

Tom was back at the table again, nursing a warm mug of coffee as he stared down at his notepad. With so many pages of hastily scribbled notes from previous days to go through, the weather was an excuse to catch up on his writing, as well as an opportunity to clarify his thoughts.

Outside on the balcony, J had been pacing back and forth for some time. He'd seemed preoccupied at breakfast, and they'd hardly spoken all morning. Now, as he pulled the sliding door across and stepped inside, Tom noticed that he was gripping a phone in his hand.

'How are you feeling?' J asked. 'Is the pain any easier?'

'I'm okay.' Tom tentatively touched his side. 'It's not too bad just now.'

'That's good.' J slid the door closed, gazing out through the glass. 'I think it's gonna be too wet to do much walking today.'

The phone he was holding had a bright green sticker on it. As he turned, he noticed Tom staring at it.

'No cell service here,' he said, with a faint note of frustration in his voice. 'I suppose that's normally part of the whole wilderness charm but...'

He trailed off into an uneasy silence, then stalked over to the kitchen area to pour himself a coffee.

'You could always try the office,' Tom suggested. 'Where you picked up the keys? They must have a phone there.'

J flashed him a bleak little smile then shook his head.

'No,' he said, firmly. 'I don't use landlines.'

Tom shrugged his shoulders and turned his attention back to his notepad.

J leaned back to rest against the kitchen counter. 'Will you be okay on your own for a while?'

Tom glanced over at him.

'Er... yeah,' he replied. 'Why?'

J appeared to come to a decision. He straightened up and set his coffee on the counter.

'I'm going for a drive,' he said. 'I'm gonna head back out to the interstate... see if I can get a signal up there.'

'All right.' Tom put down his pen. 'Do you want me to come with you?'

'No,' J replied. 'No, you should stay here and write.'

'Okay.'

When J came downstairs, he was wearing a dark blue windbreaker. Approaching the front door, he paused and called over.

'I'm heading out... is there anything you want me to bring back?'

Tom looked up from his notepad and thought for a moment.

'Another bottle of bourbon?' he suggested.

The corner of J's mouth curled into a faint grin.

'I'll try and find a liquor store,' he promised. 'See you later.'

He pulled the door and it slammed shut behind him.

Sitting at the table, Tom closed his eyes and stilled his breathing, listening hard.

Shoes going down the steps...

After a moment, he made out the muffled thud of a car door, then the sound of the engine starting.

Good.

Opening his eyes, he got to his feet, and hurried over to the sliding door, pulling it back. Stepping out onto the balcony, he made his way along the rear wall, and cautiously peered around the corner of the cabin.

The Toyota bumped into view and drove away along the track. He watched until it disappeared into the distant trees, and listened until the engine noise faded, lost among the sounds of the river and the rustle of the wind in the leaves. Then he straightened up.

This was his chance.

He climbed the stairs and walked along the short landing to stand in the darkness outside J's bedroom. The door was closed, but he turned the handle and pushed, letting it slowly swing open, and spilling light out into the corridor. The room was almost a mirror image of his own, with exposed beams in the sloping ceiling and a single window in the far wall. There was a large double bed with a patchwork quilt, and homely oak furniture. A heavy brown rug lay on the wooden floor.

Taking a breath, Tom stepped into the room. He moved carefully to be sure he wouldn't accidentally disturb anything but, as he glanced around, he realized that he couldn't see any of J's things... except for the black duffel bag.

It was sitting on a low wooden bench in the corner beside the closet, the only sign that anyone was staying here. J hadn't unpacked; he was always ready to run.

Tom walked over to the bench, each footstep unnaturally loud against the watchful stillness of the cabin. He paused to listen again, then tentatively unzipped the bag and opened it. Laying on top there were two piles of clothes, neatly folded. Taking a moment to memorize the position of everything, Tom eased a hand under one of the piles and carefully lifted it out. Then, he reached under the other pile, feeling for the journal... but it didn't seem to be there. Puzzled, he lifted the second pile of clothes out, and set it down beside the other one on the bed. Turning back to the duffel bag, he peered inside. The wash bag was in there, along with the canvas backpack. He could see the ammunition boxes and the bundle of money, nestled in beside the old paperback novel; and there, at the very bottom, was the brown envelope... but the journal was missing.

Tom frowned. It had been right there, right on top of the envelope, but it wasn't now.

He turned around and stooped to examine the clothes on the bed. Working quickly, he checked each pile to ensure the journal wasn't tucked away between any of the items, but there was no sign of it.

He stood up, staring down at the duffel bag, then sighed and began carefully putting everything back in again. Once it was repacked, he zipped it shut and quickly checked the side pockets. The phones and the police scanner were there, and so was the stun gun...

Everything except the journal.

Frustrated, Tom searched the room. There was nothing in the closet, and he pulled out empty drawers to check their undersides. He lifted the rug, got down on his knees to peer under the bed, then pulled back the quilt and checked the mattress...

Eventually, he sank down to sit on the floor beside the bed, defeated. His ribs were hurting again, and he clutched at his side as he caught his breath.

J must have taken the journal with him. What was in it that he didn't want Tom to read?

By mid-afternoon, the rain had come – heavy rain that spattered down noisily through the leaves. Tom sat on the balcony, sheltered by the overhanging roof of the cabin, staring out through the trees. J had been gone for hours... too long for just a phone call.

Shivering, he leaned back in his chair, listening to the downpour drumming on the roof, the patter and trickle of water in the gutters. He felt restless, wanting to *do* something, *needing* to keep his mind occupied...

And there it was – that same familiar dread – the fear of being alone with his thoughts. Perhaps that was why he pushed himself so hard with his work, why it was so important to him. It was a way of distracting himself, of kicking any difficult issues further down the road. But what else had he distracted himself from? Was he guilty of kicking fatherhood down the road too?

Gazing out at the rain, Tom sighed. Maybe he'd been wrong. Maybe he shouldn't have questioned why Samaira had changed – maybe he should have questioned why he hadn't...

Suddenly, a noise behind him made him jerk upright. He hadn't heard the SUV returning, but as he looked round, he saw the front door opening and J stepped in, shaking water from his clothes. Tom stared at him. He had a bottle in his hand, but didn't seem to be carrying anything else.

The older man raised a hand in greeting and walked across the room to join him on the balcony.

'You were gone a long time,' Tom said.

'Yeah,' J nodded. 'It took longer than I thought.'

He was dripping wet, but he looked happier, more calm than he had this morning. He'd taken the gun with him...was he really just making a call?

Tom eyed him warily.

'You didn't...' He hesitated, not wanting to ask, but needing to know. '...you didn't *do* anything, did you? This wasn't another murder... was it?'

J stared at him in utter surprise, then burst out laughing.

'No.' He grinned at Tom, as though unsure whether he was joking. 'Is that what you thought?'

Embarrassed and annoyed, Tom turned away.

J laughed again, heartily this time, as though the idea was particularly amusing.

'I didn't go out to kill anyone, Tom. I went to make a phone call.' He stood there, smiling, then remembered the bottle in his hand and held it up like a trophy. 'Oh, and to get this.'

He walked over to the table.

'The look on your face!' he chuckled, setting the bottle down. 'Come on, let's crack this open. There's nothing else to do in this weather, and you look like you need something to settle your nerves.'

But Tom's mind was racing now.

Who would J need to contact, but couldn't risk speaking to in front of him?

'It was your accomplice, wasn't it?' he said, his voice tightening.

J gave him a wary look.

'My *what?*'

'Your accomplice who had the camera at Samaira's place,' Tom said. 'That's who you went to call. That's why you didn't want me with you, because it was about Zak–'

'Nothing's gonna happen to Zak,' the older man interrupted

him. 'Because nothing's gonna stop us getting to the end of our journey...'

J gazed down steadily at him for a moment, then placed a heavy hand on Tom's shoulder.

'...right?'

36

It was late. The rain had eased, but there was still a steady patter on the roof, and falling drops caught the light from the balcony to glitter in the darkness. Sitting forward in his chair, J carefully poured himself a shot of bourbon, then leaned over to offer the half-empty bottle.

'Another?'

Yawning, Tom held out his glass, doing his best to keep it steady while the older man refilled it.

'Thanks.' He glanced down, nodding to the bag of corn chips on his lap. 'You want any more of these?'

J settled back into his chair and shook his head.

'No, I'm good.'

Lifting the bag, Tom tilted his head back and tipped the last of the chips into his mouth, munching thoughtfully as he stared out into the gloom. Ahead of him, the black shapes of trees could be imagined against the dim sky.

'This is an amazing place,' he murmured. 'How did you even know about it?'

'We came here once when I was a kid.' J paused, as though gazing back into the past. 'Not this actual spot – another place, further north along the river – but this is just how I remember it. My parents always enjoyed the outdoors.'

Tom nodded, remembering his own childhood.

'My parents would take us to the seaside,' he said, softly. 'Whitstable... Margate... or sometimes Brighton. We lived in London and they had a thing about the importance of "getting fresh air". I used to think they were silly, but now...' He trailed off, lowering his eyes.

'You liked growing up in London?'

'I suppose so, although I've not really got anything to compare it with, so...' Tom gave a shrug. 'How about you? Where did you grow up?"

'I was born in Monroe, Louisiana,' J replied. 'Just a normal kinda place – not too big, not too small, but nice enough from what I remember. Later, we moved to Jackson, Mississippi, after my dad got transferred there.'

'How old were you when you moved?'

'I must have been ten or eleven – it was just as I finished fifth grade.'

Tom considered this. *Just starting middle school.* It couldn't have been easy, moving to a new town and being dropped into a new school without any of his friends.

'You stayed put in London until you came to the States?' J enquired.

'Yes. Well, I went to university in Warwick, but I moved back to London afterwards. I knew I wanted to write for a living, and it seemed the best place to be if that's what I was going to do.' Tom crumpled the empty corn chip bag. 'Did you want to be a cop? Like your dad?'

'For a while, when I was a kid,' J replied. 'But as I got older, I started to see the way cops were being treated. I mean, my dad was a good detective – a good *man* – but attitudes towards the police were getting really bad. He put in all those years, helping people who disliked him, who didn't even *know* him...' He shook his head. 'I couldn't follow him down that road.'

'You think he was disappointed?'

'Not a bit. I think he may even have been a little relieved. He could see the way things were going for law enforcement, and he knew they were only gonna get worse.' J paused, then smiled to himself. 'No, just as long as I was happy and I was getting paid, he was fine about it.'

Tom took a sip of his drink.

'After university, a friend got me a gig with this really crappy conspiracy magazine that sold about fifteen copies a month...' He gave a rueful chuckle. 'They didn't always pay me, and they *never* paid on time.'

'Deadbeats,' J muttered, grinning.

'Yeah...' Tom said to himself. 'That was the job that got me started though.'

He thought back, wondering what had become of the guys he used to work with. They'd scoffed at the idea of him making it as a serious journalist, but he'd proved them all wrong, clawing his way up through a succession of local papers until he came to the attention of the nationals. Back then, he'd been so sure about what he'd wanted.

'Well, I guess everyone's got to start somewhere,' J mused. 'And you never know where things are gonna lead.'

'Exactly!' Tom said, jabbing a finger at him. 'That's *exactly* it. By the time I was thirty, I was writing for several of the biggest newspapers in the UK. Corruption... cover-ups... miscarriages of justice... I was doing some big stories. *Important* stories.'

J raised his glass.

'Impressive,' he said.

Tom leaned over, steadying himself as he reached out to clink his glass against J's.

'It *was* impressive.' He slumped back into his seat and sighed wistfully. 'It really was.'

They finished their drinks, and J retrieved the bottle to pour them both another shot. Tom watched as his glass was being filled.

'So you decided you didn't want to be a police officer,' he said. 'What did you do instead?'

'Oh, just a bunch of dead-end jobs at first.' J replied. 'I wasn't as much of an achiever as you.'

'But you mentioned the National Guard?' Tom pressed.

'Well, I guess that's the thing about dead-end jobs... they leave you wanting more.' He shrugged. 'Anyway, I knew a couple of guys who joined up, and I figured it would be a challenge, y'know? Maybe I could do some good, make a difference, that kinda thing.'

'Like your dad.'

J hesitated.

'That never occurred to me,' he admitted, staring out into the shadows under the trees. 'Well, well... I guess sometimes it's easier to see things in others than it is to see them in ourselves.'

He picked up one of the glasses and passed it to Tom.

'Maybe that *was* part of it,' he mused. 'But it was a great experience, that's for sure. Really helped to broaden my horizons... and it made those boring day jobs easier to bear, knowing there was more to life than just the rat-race.'

'Amen to that,' Tom said, raising his glass again.

'So was that part of your reason for moving to the States? Wanting to broaden your horizons?'

Tom gazed up at the glistening drops of water that lined the edge of the roof.

'Perhaps,' he said, thoughtfully. 'Sometimes, when opportunities come along, you know you've got to grab hold of them... or they'll pass you by, and you'll spend your life wondering what could've been. It's like that saying: we only regret the things we *didn't* do.'

J nodded.

'And how did Samaira feel about the move?'

Tom fell silent at the mention of his ex-wife, then sighed. They'd been so into each other back then, so excited about their future together. He'd been more confident, and she'd encouraged him...

'She was fine about it,' he replied.

She'd certainly shared his ambition... or at least, that's how it had seemed at the time.

J leaned over and poured him another drink. Tom nodded his thanks and sat, staring down at the glass. For a time neither of them spoke, then J shifted in his seat.

'What happened with you two?' he asked, gently.

Tom bowed his head.

'I don't know,' he lied. 'We wanted different things, I suppose.'

They'd been so excited about their future together, but when that future arrived – when *Zak* arrived – everything changed. By the time he realized what was happening, that she wasn't the same person she'd been before, it was too late.

'After a while, it was like she forgot all the stuff we used to talk about, all the stuff we were going to *do* together...' He paused to take a drink, then looked out into the night. 'I'm not really sure what happened, but in the end we just kind of... drifted apart.'

'Sorry to hear that,' J said, softly.

Tom shrugged. 'What's done is done.' He took a deep breath and sat up in his chair, forcing a smile. 'Anyway, there's plenty of people worse off than me.'

They sat for a while, listening to the intermittent patter of rain drops and the rustle of the trees.

'So you're single at the moment?' J asked.

'That's right,' Tom replied. 'Totally unattached.'

'But you'd *like* to be attached...' J said, then paused. 'Attached to Kendra, maybe?'

'How...' Tom struggled to sit up. 'How the hell do you know about Kendra?'

J met his eye.

'I did my research.'

'But...' Tom gaped at him. 'How could you know *that?*'

'I *may* have been accessing your social media accounts,' he whispered conspiratorially. 'Sorry about that.'

Winking at Tom, he sat back in his chair.

Tom stared at him, bemused, then shook his head. 'You sneaky fuck.'

'Thanks,' J chuckled.

'It wasn't meant as a compliment.' Tom scowled.

'Oh yes it was.' J smiled to himself and took another sip of his drink. 'Anyway, what's the story with you and Kendra? Are you and her...?'

Tom sighed.

'No,' he said. 'We're "just good friends". Apparently.'

J grimaced. 'I gotta tell you, that doesn't sound like it's gonna work out.'

'Yeah,' Tom sighed. 'I really like her, and I think she likes me, but... not in the same way.' He gazed down into his glass, dimly aware that the alcohol was making him talkative, that he should probably be more careful. 'I dunno... I just can't figure her out.'

'In my experience, women are harder to read than men,' J shrugged, stooping for the bottle again. As he refilled their glasses, Tom noticed that he wasn't wearing a wedding ring.

'What about you?' he asked. 'Were *you* ever married?'

'Oh yes,' J replied as he put the bottle down, and picked up his glass. 'To the woman in the photograph.'

Tom frowned.

'The photograph you found,' J explained. 'When you went through my bag, back in Beckley.'

Tom stared at him, open mouthed.

'Oh, *relax*.' J lifted a hand, as though waving away Tom's concerns. 'What... you think I didn't know?'

'But...' Tom stammered. 'How did you...?'

'You put the photograph back in the envelope the wrong way around,' J told him.

'Shit...' Tom sank back into his chair. He thought he'd been so careful.

'Forget about it,' J lifted his glass, then paused, studying Tom with a thoughtful expression. 'Did you read my journal?'

Tom froze, as though caught in the headlights.

'I... flicked through it. Briefly, while you were out at the pharmacy.'

The dark eyes bored into him for a moment, then J's face creased into a grin.

'You sneaky fuck,' he murmured, arching an eyebrow.

Tom smiled despite himself.

'I didn't have time to read it properly though,' he admitted.

Leaning back in his chair, J yawned, stretching his legs out in front of him.

'Good,' he said.

'Are you *going* to let me read it?' Tom pressed.

'Are you gonna let me read *yours?*' J countered.

Tom faltered. He couldn't record his true thoughts and feelings if he had to worry about J reading them. Sighing, he knocked back the rest of his drink and shook his head.

'Yeah, I didn't think so,' J murmured.

'Tell me about the woman in the photograph then.' Tom was eager to move the conversation on. 'Tell me about your wife.'

J's expression became thoughtful.

'Her name's Robyn.' There was an unusual warmth to his voice. 'We were in our twenties when we met – just kids, really – but even back then there was something about her. Strong and intelligent... and principled...' His dark eyes softened. 'It sounds clichéd, but I knew right away.'

Tom looked at him, trying to picture J as a younger man, finding someone he cared about, getting married, settling down...

'Any kids?' he asked.

J hesitated, then bowed his head.

'Yeah, a daughter.'

'What's her name?'

J's expression turned serious. 'Her name's Juliette, but my little girl has no place in your story. Write what you like about me – I made my choices, and I'll take the consequences – but she has her own life ahead of her, and she's better off not being involved with any of this... or with me.'

He gazed down into his glass. 'But you're a father, so you know how it is; there's *nothing* we wouldn't do for our kids.'

'Right,' Tom agreed. Before the abduction, he'd never understood how much he would do – how far he would go – to save his son. Now, he was beginning to.

J sighed. 'But sometimes it doesn't matter what you do. Years go by, and things come between you, push you apart...It sure ain't easy.'

Tom studied him intently and felt a pang of guilt. *He* hadn't been much of a father to Zak, not since Samaira had left. He wondered if J was divorced too.

'So where is Robyn now?' he asked.

J picked up his glass and drained it, then stared out into the night for a long time before answering.

'She died,' he said simply. 'And that was the end of our happy family. There's no coming back from something like that.'

He got stiffly to his feet and went inside, leaving Tom alone on the balcony.

37

J seemed distant at breakfast the following morning. Tom leaned against the kitchen counter, quietly watching him as they drank their coffee, then turned towards the sliding door and looked out across the balcony.

'Skies are clear,' he noted. 'Should be a fine day.'

J stirred, then nodded absently.

'Did you want to go for a walk? I was thinking we could go further up the river, towards that big bridge.'

J blinked, as though disturbed from an important thought.

'Maybe later,' he said. 'I have to go out for a while this morning. There's some things I need to do.'

'Oh?' Tom glanced over at him, curious now. 'Such as?'

'Nothing you need to worry about.' J pushed his chair back from the table and stood up.

'Could I tag along?' Tom asked. 'It's hard to get much insight if I don't know where you're going or what you're doing.'

'Just...' The older man shook his head. 'Just stay here and do some writing.'

'But I need to know what's happening if I'm going to write about it. How will I do that if I'm stuck here?'

'You won't,' J told him, bluntly. 'Write *that* down if you want.'

The SUV bumped down onto the road and rumbled away through the trees. Standing back from the window, Tom watched it go, then checked the time on the clock on the wall. It was almost 10am and he guessed that he would have at least an hour before J returned. Briefly, he thought about going upstairs and searching for the journal again – there might be a hiding place that he'd missed – but, as he turned around, his gaze came to rest on the cabin key, with its heavy wooden fob, lying at the far end of the kitchen counter. Struck by a sudden idea, he snatched up the key and walked to the door.

Outside, the air was warm. Sunlight filtered through the trees, and the grass felt springy underfoot as he made his way down to the road. There were voices in the distance – children laughing – and the steady sound of the river behind it all. He took his time, following the road as it curved past the other cabins, but he emerged from the trees without meeting anyone. Ahead of him and off to one side there was a long, low building finished in rough timber, with a hand-painted sign above the covered porch reading "Pretty Shore Cabins". Taking a deep breath, Tom crossed the road and went towards it.

A little bell tinged above the door and he heard Hawaiian music playing as he stepped inside. The place felt cramped, with glass-fronted coolers, an antiquated ice machine, and racks of candy bars lining the wooden walls. A broad counter, with neat stacks of tourist pamphlets and a display stand of pocketknives, divided the room in two. Behind it, a woman with a plaid shirt and long grey hair got slowly to her feet. She appeared to be in her sixties, tanned, with a natural, well-worn smile.

'Good morning,' she said.

'Morning.' Tom walked over, his gaze flickering to the laptop on the desk below the counter.

'Now then...' The woman looked at him and narrowed her eyes slightly. 'You're number four, right?'

Tom froze for just a moment, thinking about J's list. Then it dawned on him what she meant.

'Yes.' He reached into his pocket and held up the wooden key fob. 'I'm in cabin four, that's right.'

'Well now...' She paused, then tilted her head to one side. 'Is that a British accent you got there?'

'Uh... yeah.'

'Well, how about that?' The woman beamed at him. 'You know I've always loved the way you people talk. Makes me think of that movie about the weddings and the funeral.'

Tom forced a smile, but suddenly remembered what J had been concerned about. This wasn't New York, and out here his accent was unusual enough to be memorable.

'I'm Sissy,' the woman said, holding out her hand.

'Er... Tom,' he replied, shaking it awkwardly.

'You don't sound too sure, honey,' she laughed.

'No, I'm definitely me,' he replied.

'So, what can I do for you, Tom?'

He hesitated. Without cash he couldn't buy anything, but he'd thought of another excuse for being there.

'I was just wondering if there was a local place where I could rent a kayak or something?' he said. 'Any kind of boat would do.'

'Oh, sure.' Sissy bent forward to peer down at the pamphlets stacked on the counter, then picked one out. 'Here you go. Jensen Waterways are about a mile and a half along the river. They do rafting, canoes, whatever you want. The number's right there on the back.'

'Thanks, that sounds great.' Tom took the pamphlet and

pretended to study it. 'I'll have a look at this and then give them a call... assuming I can get any service on my phone.'

Sissy chuckled.

'Yeah, no cell coverage down here in the gorge – just part of our wilderness charm, I guess.' She inclined her head towards the telephone on the desk. 'But you can always use the office phone if you need to.'

'Really?' Tom glanced up at her. 'You don't mind?'

'Of course not.' She lifted the phone and set it on the counter for him.

Tom hesitated, then moved closer.

'Well, if you're sure it's all right...'

'You go right ahead, honey.'

Tom picked up the handset. This was what he'd hoped for, but now that the moment had come, he felt suddenly fearful. He watched as Sissy busied herself at the back of the office, then he stared down, struggling to recall the once-familiar number. Biting his lip, he tapped the buttons, then turned away, with the handset pressed to his ear. It rang several times before anyone answered.

'Hello?'

The sound of Samaira's voice jerked him back to a different version of himself, to a time long before J, to the life he used to have when things still made sense.

'It's me,' he said, clearing his throat and trying to steady his voice. 'It's Tom.'

'Oh, hello Tom.' Her tone changed very slightly, but he knew her well enough to recognise it. In his mind, he saw that bright smile dimming and the hint of disappointment in her deep brown eyes. 'It's been a while. How've you been?'

'Oh... busy with work, you know how it is,' he muttered, staring down at his shoes. 'Listen, this is just a quick call. I... I just wanted to see how Zak and you are doing.'

'Really?' He could imagine her frowning, puzzled by this.

'Yeah,' he pressed on. 'I just wondered if there was anything you guys needed... if everything was okay...'

'Uh... sure,' Samaira replied. 'Zak's not actually here right now...'

Shit! Tom felt his stomach lurch. *Had something happened to him?*

'...he's out at a birthday party for one of his little friends, otherwise you could have spoken to him. I'm sure he'd like to hear from you, if you wanted to call back in a few hours?'

Tom leaned heavily against the counter and exhaled with relief.

'I'll try to, but... well, I'm kind of in the middle of things at the moment.' He hung his head. 'But if you could just tell him I called and... and tell him I miss him.'

'I'll tell him,' she said slowly, and he heard the concern in her voice. 'Is everything okay, Tom?'

'Everything's fine,' he replied, lifting his head. 'Why?'

'You sound kind of...' Samaira paused. 'I don't know... you sound tired, I guess.'

'It's nothing,' he said, quickly. 'It's just... just something I'm working on. It's been taking up a lot of my time.'

'Oh.' Her voice went flat, the way it did so often in their last months together. 'Well then, don't work too hard.'

He could hear the veiled rebuke in her words, and gritted his teeth to avoid rising to it. 'Just... just please take care of Zak, okay?'

There was a moment of frosty silence, and he realized that he'd said the wrong thing.

'What do you think I've been doing since you left, Tom?' Her eyes would be colder now, her brows tightening into a scowl. 'You've no *idea* how much I care for our son, how much I *do* for him...'

Tom screwed his eyes shut.

'No,' he told her. 'I... I didn't mean it like that...'

'No?'

'No.'

Tom took a breath, trying to figure out what he could say to her, but it was no use. He knew how the conversations always went from here.

'Listen, I have to go,' he said. 'I'll call again when I can. And tell Zak that I love him, okay?'

'Of course I'll tell him, but don't you think it would be better if you–'

'Just *tell* him,' Tom interrupted her, then cursed himself for doing so. 'I'm sorry, okay? And I really *do* have to go, so I'll... I'll see you around.'

He quickly replaced the handset and sucked down a breath. It wasn't as though he could tell her what was happening, but he *had* to know that Zak was all right. And, thankfully, he was... at least for now.

The wooden floorboards creaked and he became aware of Sissy standing behind him.

'Everything okay?' she asked, brightly.

Tom turned around, mustering a cheerful expression.

'Perfect,' he lied. 'Couldn't be better.'

'Glad to hear it,' Sissy grinned. 'Anything you need, you just let me know.'

Tom flashed her a grateful smile.

'I appreciate that.' He took a step back, as though he was about to leave, then paused to glance at the laptop again. 'Um... this is going to sound stupid, and I *really* don't want to be any more bother... but is there any way I could possibly use your computer? Just for a couple of minutes?'

Sissy gave him a curious look.

Tom feigned embarrassment.

'I'm feeling a bit lost without my phone,' he explained. 'It's pathetic, I know, but I just wanted to check in on a couple of things...'

Sissy's expression softened.

'Aw... you gettin' social media withdrawal symptoms?' Her eyes twinkled with amusement, then she reached down and lifted the laptop up onto the counter for him. 'There you go, darlin'. Just don't visit no sites that'll make me blush, okay?'

Tom stared at her.

'No, it's nothing like that, I promise!'

Sissy laughed.

'Relax, I'm just messin' with you.' She turned and walked over to the back of the office where she picked up a vape and clicked it on. 'And you wouldn't be the first person who came in here askin' if they could get online.'

Tom leaned over the laptop and opened a new private browser window.

'Really?' he asked.

'Oh yeah,' Sissy said. She inhaled from her vape and blew out a pale, sweet-smelling cloud. 'I get business-folk checkin' their big important emails. And kids loggin' on to tell their friends how their mean ol' parents brought them to a place where the phones don't work.'

'Kids don't like to be without their phones,' Tom murmured. He stared down at the keyboard, frowning, trying to remember the printout that J had showed him in the car. What the hell was that hashtag again?

He hesitated, then tapped in **#JusticeForKaitlyn** and added **Candice Porter** to narrow the search. The screen cleared then brought up a page of entries. The tweet he wanted was at the top of the list and he clicked on it.

@JustCandiP123 ***Candice Porter***

No place in this world for abusive men. Forget about jail... a bullet is more effective and a whole lot cheaper. ***#JusticeFor-Kaitlyn***

@WFRecorder ***Wichita Falls News***
BLACKMAIL SEX: MAN HELD BY POLICE
A man who allegedly coerced insurance claimants to have sex has been arrested by...

There it was, just as he remembered it. The printout J had showed him was genuine.

'So, you're from England, right?' Sissy asked.

'That's right,' Tom replied, glancing up from the screen.

'But you don't live there now?'

'No, I live in New York.'

Sissy raised an eyebrow.

'New York?' She brought the vape to her mouth again. 'Wow. You guys are really off the beaten track comin' here.'

'Yeah,' Tom agreed. He selected Candice's retweet, expanding it.

@WFRecorder ***Wichita Falls News***
BLACKMAIL SEX: MAN HELD BY POLICE
A man who allegedly coerced insurance claimants to have sex has been arrested by police after one of his accusers posted an account of her experience to an online forum. Read more at ***https://bit.ly/2PxbxVc***

Tom clicked through to the article and began skimming it.

BLACKMAIL SEX: INSURANCE ASSESSOR HELD BY POLICE
"Unless I agreed to have sex with him, my claim would be rejected and I'd lose everything."
Wichita Falls Police confirmed that they have taken a man into custody following ***serious allegations*** *made on a popular online mothers' forum, which quickly went viral. Posting anonymously, a woman from Iowa Park explained how she*

lost her house in a fire, and how the man sent to assess her insurance claim used his position of authority to blackmail her for sex.

The woman's harrowing account has sparked widespread outrage. Alex Wright from the online campaign group Back-Lash condemned the man's behavior. Writing on her blog, she called for his arrest, and suggested a national boycott of Blue-Stone Mutual Group companies.

"This is sexual exploitation at its worst; misusing a position of trust and authority to abuse a woman at her most vulnerable. It's immoral, it's illegal, and it's intolerable. The police must show the perpetrators of these acts that they cannot escape justice. And we must show big companies like Blue-Stone Mutual that they have a responsibility for the behavior of their employees."

[more]

Tom scrolled back up and clicked on the serious allegations link, but it took him to an empty forum page that read "This post has been removed."

'So you and the other fella...' Sissy began.

Tom looked up to find her studying him thoughtfully.

'Yeah?' he said.

'Are you guys like... a couple, or...?' she asked.

'Oh, no...'

'Cos it makes no difference to me,' Sissy told him. 'I just didn't want to say the wrong thing. Some folk take offence awful easy if you say the wrong thing.'

'No, we just...' Tom shook his head then looked down at the screen again. 'We just know each other from work.'

Clicking back to his original search, he began scanning down the page, but few of the entries seemed relevant. Frowning, he decided to try something different, and tapped in **#JusticeForKaitlyn David Barron.** The top result was a tweet.

> *@Dave_Barron_XD* ***David Barron***
> *Scum like Sherman don't deserve to draw breath. Hopefully rape won't seem so good when he's on the receiving end of it... IN PRISON!*
> ***#JusticeForKaitlyn***
>
> ---
>
> *@BacklashOrg* ***Backlash***
> *The* ***#BlueStoneMutual*** *insurance investigator who demanded sex from vulnerable women, and threatened to cancel their claims if they refused...*

At last, he might have a connection between the victims! Had each of them made a posting like this?

'So what brings you all the way out here?' Sissy asked.

Tom lifted his head.

'Oh, you know...' He paused, wondering what to say. 'I've been having a difficult time lately and... well, I think the idea was that this place might be good for me.'

Shrugging, he turned his attention back to the laptop and began scrolling down the page of search results. He was about to skip past the Images section when one of the thumbnails caught his eye. Clicking to enlarge the picture, Tom stared down at the screen.

It was a photograph of J, taken at a distance with a long lens, but it was definitely him. Next to the picture, a caption read "Former insurance investigator Joseph Sherman was released without charge after the..."

Tom took a deep breath, then straightened up, pulling a hand across his jaw.

Joseph Sherman. So *that* was what the J stood for.

'You all right, honey?' Sissy put her vape down and walked back over towards the counter.

'Yes,' Tom said, quickly closing the browser window and folding the lid down on the laptop. 'Yeah, I'm fine.'

'You sure?' she asked. 'You're looking kinda tense there.'

'No, I'm good.' Tom raised a hand, waving away her concern. 'But I should really stop bothering you and let you get back to your day.'

'Oh, you ain't no bother,' she assured him. 'I could probably listen to that accent of yours all day.'

Tom forced another smile.

'You're very kind,' he said.

'All part of the service,' the woman grinned. 'Say, would you like a cup of coffee? I was just gonna put another pot on.'

Tom glanced down at his wrist, then hesitated as he remembered that his watch was gone. How long had he been here?

'Thanks, but I should really be getting back.'

'Well, okay then.'

Tom turned and moved towards the door, then paused and looked back to the counter.

'Um, listen,' he said. 'It's silly, but would you mind *not* mentioning that I was using your phone and your computer? This week is meant to be about relaxation and staying off the net and stuff...'

Sissy regarded him for a moment, then winked.

'The way I remember it, you were never even in here.'

J didn't return until the evening. He seemed quieter than usual – distracted by something – and Tom's speculation about his captor's past was overtaken by a gnawing curiosity about where he'd been.

'You were gone a long time,' he said, trying to prompt a conversation.

J didn't look up.

'Yeah,' he said. 'Just some things I needed to take care of.'

'What sort of things?' Tom waited for him to elaborate, but the older man didn't seem to be in a talkative mood.

'Well, according to the TV, the weather should stay good,' Tom persevered. 'Maybe we can go for a walk tomorrow, and you can tell me all about it then.'

At first, J didn't answer. Then he frowned. 'Sorry... what?'

'I said, the weather should be okay to do some walking tomorrow.'

J shook his head. 'We're leaving tomorrow.'

'Oh?' Tom looked at him, confused. 'I thought we were here for the whole week?'

J walked slowly across the room, pausing at the foot of the stairs.

'Nothing lasts, Tom,' he sighed. 'Trust me. I know it better than anyone.'

38

Tom's Journal

I know who he is. Joseph Sherman, a former insurance investigator for the Blue Stone Mutual group. He was arrested some time ago after attempting to blackmail a woman, threatening to cause trouble and deny her claim unless she had sex with him. This is the man I've been travelling with. Somehow, I find myself hating him even more for this than for the killings. I was starting to think that someone had done something to him, that the whole journey might be some sort of vengeance trip, to punish those who had somehow wronged him. Not that there would be any excuse for that, of course, but the truth seems to be worse. He's a creep, and a predator. And he's not angry because he was wronged, he's just angry because he was found out.

How did the bastard avoid prison? Did he skip bail and disappear? And how long has he been on the run? Maybe this is why he can't travel abroad any more...

He says that we'll be back on the road again tomorrow, though he hasn't told me where we're going. All my questions have been avoided or ignored this evening, and the only thing he's volunteered is that we have a long drive ahead of us, so we'll need a fairly early start. I thought seriously about confronting him, about telling him what I know and seeing his reaction, but something warned me against it. Not tonight, not yet. For the first time, I know more than he thinks I do, and that may just be advantageous.

At the beginning, I wondered if he was just another psychopath, going after random strangers, lashing out at the world for no reason. But now, it's clear that his victims aren't random after all. Candice Porter and David Barron both made very similar posts on social media... and though I didn't have time to confirm it, I expect the other people on his hitlist did the same.

Joseph Sherman seems to be on some kind of sick crusade, hunting down particular people just because they dared to express their outrage at his awful crime. From the way he speaks about the victims – always with that undertone of bitterness and resentment – it's almost as if he feels some justification for what he's doing. It's ironic that he can't see how wrong he is.

Maybe he just doesn't want to see.

39

It was already dark when they drove across the water at Louisville, caged in by the rusting steel framework of the long bridge. As the tree-lined shores of Kentucky slipped away behind them and they descended towards the lights of Indiana, Tom adjusted his seat belt so he could stretch.

'How do you feel about them?' he asked. 'The people that you've killed.'

J's knuckles flexed as he gripped the steering wheel.

'How do you *think* I feel about them?' His voice was tight with contempt.

Tom lapsed into silence for a time, quietly considering what he'd discovered about J's loathsome past, trying to imagine the mindset of someone as they transitioned into a murderer, trying to grasp how anyone took that first, irrevocable step. J had been a predator... but did that kind of selfish disregard for others make it any easier to kill?

'Was it difficult?' He glanced over at the older man. 'The first time, I mean. Did you have doubts? Did you hesitate?'

J said nothing for a moment.

'I had doubts,' he admitted. 'And I hesitated for a long time.

But that was before I even decided to go after these people. Once I made my mind up... well, there was no stopping.'

'What finally made your mind up?'

'I guess it was the realization that nothing was ever gonna change unless someone did something.' J took a deep breath, then exhaled. 'It's difficult to explain.'

Tom reflected on this. 'Has it got easier?'

J gave a slight shrug.

'Everything gets easier, the more you do it,' he said, glancing up at the rear-view mirror. 'But not in the way you're thinking, not on an emotional level. It's just... practice, I guess. Being better prepared. Being ready.'

'What about the emotional level? Does that get easier too?'

'In some ways, yes.' J nodded to himself. 'Every name crossed off the list brings a little bit of closure, I guess.'

And one less voice to call out what you've done, thought Tom. He leaned back in his seat, gazing out at the dim shapes of buildings beyond the passing street lamps. They'd been on the road all day, but the landscape seemed endless, stretching out before them into the night. The last suburbs gradually gave way to the deeper darkness of open country. Out here, the only real light came from other cars, or the illuminated signs advertising rest areas, but J showed no signs of weariness and didn't offer to stop. He'd been evasive in his answers all afternoon – preoccupied by something – and the further they drove, the more often his eyes flicked down to the dashboard to check the time.

Tom felt a creeping sense of dread spread through him.

'We're not heading for a motel,' he said, slowly. 'Are we?'

J's expression was grim and purposeful.

'We'll find a motel later. Afterwards.'

'No, *no*...' Tom recoiled in horror, picturing that last awful moment in Delaware, as David Barron's legs kicked and twitched then finally lay still. 'Not again, please! I don't know everything that's going on here, but there has to be another way–'

'That's right, Tom,' J interrupted. 'You *don't* know everything.'

'Because you won't tell me!' Tom shouted. 'Who is it this time, and how will killing them solve anything?'

'You *really* need to keep it together, Tom,' J growled, the muscles around his jaw tightening visibly. 'I'm serious.'

He flashed a baleful look at Tom, who slumped into a brooding silence.

There was hardly any other traffic now, and their surroundings had become more rural. The headlights picked out a few mail-boxes at the side of the road, and the occasional dim glow of a window winked out from a house set back in the trees, but the night seemed to be pressing in all around them, shrinking their world to a blurred stretch of asphalt.

Tom rubbed his eyes, trying to shake off the mental exhaustion and the gnawing frustration. He had to *do* something – but what? He couldn't interfere directly, not without endangering Zak. But maybe there was another a way to stop his captor, or at least delay him.

'Look, I'm... I'm sorry I yelled before,' he said, as calmly as he could manage. 'I just want to know so I can try and understand. I mean, that's what you want, isn't it? That's why I'm here. So please, tell me: who is it?'

If he could get J to talk about the target, maybe there was a way to humanize them. Maybe he could make it more difficult to go ahead with the kill.

'He's called *Travis*.' A look of disgust touched J's face as he spoke the name.

'Tell me about Travis,' Tom urged. 'What does he do?'

J said nothing.

'Is he married? Does he have kids?'

But J shook his head.

'None of that matters.'

'It *does* matter,' Tom argued. 'I want to understand who he is, and what you think you'll accomplish by killing him. I want to know if there's an alternative.'

'You should be thinking about Zak, about Kendra... about protecting the people you care about.' J scowled and his voice became cold. 'Not some hate-filled lowlife. Now shut up and let me think.'

They drove on in silence for some time, with Tom wondering what he could say to change J's mind. There was too much resentment towards the names on the list – all of them guilty, all of them condemned. How could he persuade the killer to spare someone?

Beside him, J suddenly shifted in his seat and leaned forward, peering through the windshield as the fluorescent glare of a gas station bloomed out against the darkness. It sat at an intersection and, as they drew closer, J began to slow down, moving the SUV over to the middle lane and coming to a halt. They waited, gazing up at the red glow of the stoplights hanging against the vast night sky until they went green, then J swung across onto a smaller side road. A hundred yards ahead of them, on the right-hand side, there was a dimly illuminated sign. Beyond it, partly screened by a line of silhouetted trees, was a small wooden building.

J took his foot off the gas and let the SUV coast forward. There was a soft click from the dashboard as he switched off the headlights, plunging their surroundings into sudden gloom.

'What are you doing?' Tom gasped, sitting up and straining to make out the line of the asphalt.

J let the SUV bump down onto a strip of dirt at the left side of the road and brought it to a gentle standstill. Switching off the engine, he allowed himself a deep breath, then turned to look at Tom.

'We're here,' he said, quietly.

Tom stared at him, then turned to peer out at the building. It was a low wooden hut, converted into a small office. Inside, a bearded overweight man in his thirties was sitting at a cluttered desk, the glow of a computer screen reflected in his glasses. Light spilled out from the windows onto a small porch. The painted sign in front of the building displayed a phone number and a simple illustration of some handcuffs beneath the words *Bateman Bail Bonds 24/7*.

There was a click as J undid his seatbelt. Tom looked over at him.

'You don't have to do this,' he said, urgently. 'Please, just... let's just talk about it.'

In the shadowy interior, J's dark eyes glittered.

'This *is* going to happen, Tom,' he said. 'You understand that, right? No matter what you say, no matter what you do, it's going to happen. I know it's difficult, but you're only here to witness events; you don't get to change them.'

Feeling helpless, Tom turned his head, squinting to see the man in the office.

'That's him?' he asked. 'That's Travis?'

J checked his watch, then leaned back into his seat with an air of impatience.

'That's him.'

They sat in silence for a time.

'Now, I'm gonna need you to stay in the car,' J warned. 'No matter what, you stay in the car. Is that clear?'

'I just wish you'd–'

'Is that *clear*, Tom?' J snapped. 'Or do I need to cuff you to the damn seat?'

Tom stared at him for a moment, then looked away and managed a grudging nod.

'Say it,' J hissed. 'And remember that Zak is depending on you.'

Tom bowed his head in defeat.

'I'll stay in the fucking car.'

'All right.' J checked his watch again. 'I won't be long.'

He got out, taking care to close the door quietly behind him, then walked around to the back of the vehicle. Tom heard the trunk open, and the sound of things being moved, then a gentle thud as it closed again. A moment later, he watched the shadowy figure of J ghosting across the road and carefully skirting around the pool of light from the office windows. In one hand he was carrying some sort of large container – it looked heavy by the way it dragged him down – while the other was gripping a baseball bat. He made his way past a parked car and disappeared around the back of the building.

Several minutes passed. Tom shifted himself across into the driver's seat, straining to see.

What the hell was J doing?

He stared out, the static scene burning into his unblinking eyes. Nothing was happening...

And then, in the window, the overweight man looked up suddenly from his screen. Twisting in his chair, he turned and reached for the phone on his desk.

At the same moment, a movement at the rear corner of the building caught Tom's eye. J had reappeared and was making his way along the side wall. He had the container, and the bat was now tucked under one arm, but his other hand was raised to his ear, as though he was holding a cell phone. When he reached the front, he stooped down and allowed the bat to fall, then gripped the container and tilted it forwards.

Now Tom could see the glisten of liquid, sluicing out onto the plank walls and running along the wooden porch.

Oh no...

Unable to look away, Tom leaned closer to the window, a hand over his mouth to prevent his breath from fogging the glass. From somewhere at the back of the building, a flicker of yellow light began reflecting off the trees.

Oh, dear God, no!

J tipped the container on its side and slid it over towards the door. Crouching down, he reached out a hand. There was a brief, bright spark and suddenly a river of rippling flame spread along the porch, leaping up against the front of the building. When it reached the container, a gush of fire spewed out, quickly engulfing the base of the door.

Tom gave a strangled cry and pressed his hand against the glass. At the back of the building, the first flames were licking up high enough to be visible over the flat roof. All around, a greedy yellow glow was spreading out, eating into the darkness.

The overweight man was staring towards the window. At first he seemed to be rooted to the spot, then he lurched suddenly to his feet, knocking his chair over in his panic. Backing away, he turned and disappeared from view. There might be another exit at the rear of the building, but it would surely be blocked by the fire now.

Moments later the man reappeared at the window, his head jerking frantically from left to right, trying to make sense of what was happening, searching for a way out. Tom lost sight of him when he moved hurriedly towards the front door. For a moment, nothing happened. Then, with obvious difficulty, the door was wrenched inwards to reveal the man's silhouetted figure, recoiling from the flames that swept into the open doorway.

Desperate screams for help echoed out into the night, and Tom's fingers dug into the car seat, gripping it tightly.

With the fire raging in front of him, the man wavered. Then, appearing to reach a decision, he lifted his hands to shield his face and began to stumble forwards through the blaze. As he did so, J walked swiftly into the circle of light, breaking into a run and raising the baseball bat. Swinging it around and down, he caught the advancing figure on the side of the head, knocking him backwards. The man crashed down onto the burning porch, the weight of his fall sending out a billow of flame that quickly closed back over him.

J stood motionless, a dark shape against the dancing glare of the fire, watching the body burn. It was only then that Tom noticed the other figure, standing a little way further along the road.

She was staring towards the blaze, hands raised to her mouth, as though frozen in horror.

How long had she been there? How much had she seen?

Silhouetted against the flickering light, J began to turn away from the burning building, and Tom saw him hesitate as he noticed her. As if released from a spell that had paralyzed her, the young woman became animated, taking a halting step backwards and glancing around nervously. It looked as though she might bolt into the darkness but, when she spotted Tom sitting in the SUV, she turned towards him and broke into a run, clutching a large bag to her chest with one hand and waving wildly at him with the other.

'Help,' she called out. 'Please help!'

She was younger than he'd first thought – late teens or early twenties – and thin, with large, anxious eyes. The ends of her long brown hair were dyed blue, and she was wrapped in a shapeless fleece-lined coat.

'Please, mister!' Stumbling up to the door of the SUV, she began banging her palm on the window. 'Let me in!'

Helpless, Tom stared out at her through the glass, then his gaze flicked to the shadowy figure of J approaching, a gun now visible in his hand. The girl glanced over her shoulder, then immediately started pounding harder on the glass.

'Please!' she cried. 'Don't let him hurt me!'

J stopped a few yards away, raising the gun and pointing it at her back, his expression bleak.

'I'm sorry, miss,' he called out to her. 'But I'm afraid he's with me.'

She faltered, arm raised midway through banging the window, and all the desperation seemed to drain out of her.

'No...'

Slumping against the door, her face slackened in defeat and she stared mournfully up into Tom's eyes.

No...

Her expression tore at something deep inside him.

'No!' He banged his hand against the glass, but she was already turning her head away from him, looking round to the figure behind her.

'Step away from there,' J demanded, gesturing with the gun. 'Move.'

'Oh God, *please*...' Shaking her head, the girl began to sob.

'Hey!' Fumbling with the handle, Tom forced the door open and clambered out. The air was heavy with the smell of the fire. 'Stop! Just wait a minute!'

'I'm sorry,' J said, sadly. 'Really, I am.'

'But she hasn't done anything!' Tom protested. 'She's *innocent!*'

'I *know* that!' There was a shrill edge to J's voice, as though the word stung him, and he lowered the gun slightly. 'But she's also a witness.'

The girl gaped at him, then turned and clung to Tom's arm.

'I won't say anything about this, I swear!' she begged. '*Please*, don't let him hurt me!'

J took a deep breath then aimed the gun at her again.

'I'm sorry...'

'NO!' Tom stepped forward, positioning himself between J and the girl. 'You can't!'

He found himself staring down the barrel of the gun, and was suddenly afraid that J would pull the trigger. They stood there for a moment, locked in a dreadful, silent standoff, neither willing to back down... and then J lifted his head slightly, peering off into the gloom, alert.

Tom turned to see what he was looking at. Some way off in the darkness, the glow of headlights was creeping along the distant highway.

J glanced round at the flickering blaze behind him, then back to the approaching headlights.

'Fuck!' he hissed.

'Please don't do this,' Tom urged. 'I'm begging you.'

J glared at him, then at the girl, and gestured angrily with the gun.

'Get in the car,' he hissed. 'Both of you.'

40

Behind them, the glow of the fire had been swallowed up by the night. Tom gripped the steering wheel tightly, every muscle tense as he drove along the empty road, peering out into the darkness. Beside him, J sat twisted around in the passenger seat, keeping the gun trained on the girl as she cowered in the back.

'Look,' Tom began. 'You don't have to–'

'Shut up and drive,' J snapped. There was an unfamiliar edge to his voice and when Tom glanced over he saw the older man's face was creased with worry.

They crested a small rise, and the road fell away before them, an endless grey strip disappearing into the gloom beyond the headlights.

J studied the girl. 'What's your name?' he demanded.

In the rear-view mirror, Tom could see her shrinking into her seat, wide eyes fixed on the gun.

'Just... just please let me go.' She had a slight southern accent, and her voice wavered with fear. 'I won't say anything–'

'I *asked* you what your name is.'

The girl hesitated.

'Hannah,' she said, softly.

'Well, Hannah, I'm gonna need you to pass that bag over,' J told her. 'Slowly.'

'My bag?'

J held out his free hand and she reluctantly passed her bag forward.

'Thank you.' He reached up and switched the interior light on, then wedged the bag between his knees so he could open it while keeping hold of the gun. Tom stole a couple of brief glances as his captor sifted through the contents.

'Ah.' J sat up, drawing out a driving license and holding it at arm's length so he could squint at it. 'Hannah Karen Leigh, from Montgomery, Alabama...' He turned to look at her. 'You're a long way from home.'

Hannah didn't respond, her eyes still on the gun.

J shrugged and went back to rummaging through the bag, taking out her purse and counting the few dollars inside. After a moment, he frowned.

'Where's your phone?' he asked.

'I... I don't have one.'

J sighed and shook his head.

'Everyone has a phone,' he told her.

'I did have one,' she admitted, quietly. 'But I sold it.'

Watching her in the mirror, Tom saw her lower her eyes.

Poor kid, he thought. *She's just a runaway... a drifter.*

J closed the bag and put it carefully by his feet. Then he sat back, a troubled expression on his face, staring out at the road. Open country spread out in shadow all around them and there were no lights to be seen. After a few minutes, he turned to Tom.

'Find somewhere to pull over and get off the road,' he said. 'Somewhere quiet.'

Tom's eyes flickered up to the mirror and found Hannah staring back at him. She gave him a terrified, pleading look.

Ahead of them, the road bent to the left, angling around a small patch of woodland.

'Up there,' J said. 'By those trees.'

Tom tightened his grip on the wheel but he did as he was told, lifting his foot from the pedal and slowing down. Behind him, he felt Hannah leaning forward.

'Please, just let me go,' she begged. 'I won't say anything–'

'Hush now,' J murmured, raising the gun so she could see it.

Tom gently applied the brakes, pulling off the asphalt and bringing them to a halt on a broad strip of grass in the shadow of the trees.

'Kill the engine,' J told him. 'But leave the lights on.'

Tom stared at him for a moment then shut it off. A vast, dreadful silence settled over them.

J turned around again to peer into the back.

'Where do you live?'

'Nowhere.' Hannah seemed to wither under his gaze. 'I... I was staying with my boyfriend in Jasper but...' She looked away. 'It didn't work out.'

J studied her thoughtfully.

'So where were you headed when we found you?'

'I got a friend,' Hannah replied. 'Down in Evansville.'

J nodded to himself, then held up her purse.

'This is all the money you've got?'

'Yeah.' There was embarrassment in her voice now, but also a note of defiance. 'Take it if you want.'

J bowed his head slightly and sighed. He remained silent for a time, then appeared to reach a decision.

'Hannah, I'm gonna need you to open the door and step outside for me.' The words were eerily calm, but he held the gun up again, making sure she could see it. 'Nice and slow.'

Hannah stiffened.

'Why?' she stammered. 'What are you gonna do?'

'Just step out.'

Her wide eyes met Tom's in the mirror.

'Please!' she whimpered. 'I don't wanna get shot.'

Tom gave J an imploring look, but the older man's face was blank.

'She's just a drifter.'

'I know.'

'She's innocent!'

'I know!'

Tom shook his head.

'If you'll just–'

'Oh for fuck's sake!' J snatched angrily at the handle and kicked the door open. Launching himself out of the vehicle, he turned and levelled the gun at Hannah. 'Out. NOW!'

The shock of his outburst left them in a stunned silence. Trembling, Hannah slid across the seat, and fumbled with her door handle.

Tom watched her scramble out, then opened his door and followed. The air felt cool, after the warmth of the interior, but there was an oppressive stillness as the night pressed in around them.

J's face had a dead expression now, and he gestured impatiently with the gun.

'We're going to walk into those trees,' he said.

Hannah appeared frozen for a moment, then her shoulders drooped and she began to cry.

'Oh *please*, mister!' She stretched out a slender hand towards Tom. 'I'll do anything you say, just... just don't let him kill me!'

Her look filled him with anguish and the fear in her eyes was unbearable.

'Wait!' Tom yelled, turning towards J and striding over to him. 'Just... just wait a minute!'

J regarded him with a deadly seriousness.

'You should step aside, Tom. Right now.'

'She's not on the list,' Tom protested. 'She's innocent!'

Again, the word seemed to sting J.

'You think I don't *get* that? You think I don't fucking HATE that?' he shouted. 'But she's still a damn witness!'

Hannah gave a strangled little cry and moved closer, hiding behind Tom and clinging to his arm.

'There's got to be another way,' Tom insisted.

J bowed his head and let his gun arm drop slightly. He took a breath, then spoke in a more measured voice.

'Tom, are you really prepared to bet everything – to bet the life of your *son* – on a complete stranger? Because I gotta tell you, *I* sure wouldn't be.'

Tom hesitated as the implications loomed up in his mind. He turned to glance at Hannah. She'd seen the murder, and seen their faces. If they let her go, even out here in the middle of nowhere, the police would be on their tail in a matter of hours...

'No!' Seeing him wavering, she became even more scared. 'I won't tell anyone anything, I promise!'

Tom faltered.

J looked at him pointedly, then shook his head and raised the gun again.

'I'm really sorry.'

Tom stood there, paralyzed. *Helpless*. He saw himself in the car, doing nothing, watching the death throes of David Barron in Delaware. He saw himself pressed against the glass, doing nothing, as the flames closed over the man at the bail bonds office. And he saw J studying this poor girl's driving license, the way he must have studied Lizzie Reeves' license back in Syracuse.

No. Not again. He *had* to do something.

'Stop!' he yelled, holding up his hands. 'You stop and *listen* to me!'

J rolled his eyes and groaned.

'What now?'

Trembling, Tom reached out slowly, open palm towards the gun.

'Everyone on the list – everyone you've executed – has done something to you, right? They've brought it on themselves, they've... they've *deserved* it, somehow.' He took a quick breath. 'And you said it yourself, that you wouldn't strike someone down for no reason, that you're not a monster... well, this is where you show me, this is where you *prove* it.'

J glared at him, eyes narrowing.

'That guy in the silver Ford wasn't your fault,' Tom continued, noting how J winced at the memory. 'The car just pulled out in front of us and there was nothing you could do, I *know* that...' Nervously, he edged a step forward. 'But this would be different. You'd be *choosing* to murder someone who's absolutely innocent. *Punishing an innocent!* And you wouldn't be doing it because you *had* to, but because you *wanted* to...'

'That's bullshit!' J argued. 'I don't *want* to...'

'Then *don't!*' Tom urged. 'Don't do something stupid, that turns everything you've said into a lie. This isn't how you want your story to go.'

J stared down the gun at him.

'You don't know all of my story, Tom,' he said, a cold edge in his voice.

'No, I don't,' Tom countered. 'But I'm the one who's supposed to be telling it for you.'

J scowled at him for a moment.

'What's your point?' he hissed.

'My point is, you *can't* do this.' Tom met his eyes. 'It goes against everything you've been saying, everything you've told me... you can't.'

J shook his head in frustration.

'I'll tell you what I can't do,' he said. 'I can't let her go. And we can't take her with us.'

Tom felt Hannah's fingers tighten on his arm, and his resolve hardened.

'Why not?' he said.

'Why *not?*' J gave him an incredulous look. 'Think about what you're saying!'

'I... I just–'

'She'd turn us in, first chance she got!' J snapped.

'No!' Hannah clung to Tom, pulling him around so she could stare up at him. 'I wouldn't... I won't...'

'Think *real* carefully,' J warned him. 'Your son's life depends on it...'

Tom swallowed, and Hannah saw the doubt in his face.

'What does he mean?' she whispered.

Tom placed his hands on her shoulders, feeling her tremble under his touch.

'You'd... you'd have to do *exactly* what he tells you,' he explained. 'No police, no contact with anyone...'

A desperate hope flickered in Hannah's eyes.

'I won't say anything,' she assured him. 'I swear, if you just let me go, I'll disappear...'

Tom bit his lip then shook his head.

'I think...' He glanced over at J, then looked back at her. 'I think you'd need to come with us.'

Hannah stared up at him, her expression shifting from confusion to dread.

'Come *with* you?'

41

At some point they'd crossed the state line into Illinois, but Tom hadn't noticed when. They'd been driving for almost an hour, keeping to small roads, when the illuminated sign finally rose into view, an inverted red V with white letters spelling out the word MOTEL. Slowing down, J let the SUV roll into the half-empty parking lot and come to a gentle stop. He sat for some time, staring out at the long row of rooms, all in darkness, and the welcoming light shining out from the reception at the far end of the building.

'This is a mistake, a huge fucking mistake,' he muttered. Killing the lights, he switched off the engine then turned to scowl at Tom. 'We're jeopardizing everything by bringing her along. You know that, don't you?'

Tom met his gaze.

'She's *innocent,*' he insisted.

J appeared to relent, but shook his head bitterly.

'She's a risk, *that's* what she is.'

He took a deep breath, then opened the door and climbed out. Tom watched in the mirrors as the older man walked stiffly to the rear of the vehicle and opened the back, rummaging through the bags for something. A moment later, he closed the hatch quietly, then made his way round to Hannah's door and pulled it open.

'All right, miss,' he said in a low voice. 'I'm gonna need you to turn around and put your hands behind your back.'

Hannah withdrew from him, eyes wide with fear.

'Why?' she stammered. 'What are you going to do?'

J sighed and held up a set of zip-tie plastic handcuffs for her to see.

'It's just to make sure you don't go running off,' he said. 'Now, if you don't mind?'

Hannah shot a desperate look at Tom, who quickly lowered his eyes, then she reluctantly shifted in her seat, turning away from the door and placing her hands behind her back.

'Please...' she moaned. 'You... you don't need to do this.'

J leaned in, looping the plastic around as he bound her wrists together.

'And I don't need another passenger,' he muttered. 'But here we all are.'

He pulled the cuffs, checking that they were secure.

'There,' he said, stepping back and straightening up. 'Now, you just sit tight.'

Shutting her in, he moved forward to his own door and leaned over to peer in at Tom.

'She better be here when I get back,' he growled. 'Think about your son.'

Tom gave him a sullen look, then slumped back in his seat.

'Nobody's going anywhere,' he murmured.

J held his gaze for a moment longer, then abruptly shut the door.

Tom watched him as he strode away across the parking lot, a dark figure against the light from reception. The mention of Zak was a painful reminder, and he closed his eyes, trying not to think about how much was at stake. The people he cared for, the people who mattered...

A quiet sob jolted him back to the present and he turned to see Hannah hunched over awkwardly, unable to lean back with her hands tied behind her.

'Are you okay?' he asked.

She lifted her head, staring up at him with pleading eyes.

'What's going to happen to me?'

Tom swallowed hard.

'I... I don't know,' he muttered.

'Oh God!' Hannah's voice became shrill. 'Is he going to kill me?'

'No!' Tom replied quickly. 'No, I won't let him...'

'But he killed that guy back there,' Hannah cried. 'I *saw* him!'

'I know...' Tom bit his lip, trying to keep things calm, trying to think. 'But it's... it's going to be okay.'

'Okay?' Hannah gaped at him. 'How is this *okay*?'

Tom tilted his head back to stare up at the ceiling. The situation was getting away from him. All the fight, all the defiance as he'd stood up to J... it had all drained out of him across those long miles through the dark from the bail-bonds office. In that moment, he'd been so determined to save this poor girl, but now he was exhausted, and worried. And he had no answers for her.

'Please!' Hannah was leaning close to him. 'Just untie me, let me go!'

'I... I can't...'

'Yes, you can,' she urged him. 'I won't say anything, I swear.'

'It's just that–' Tom looked at her helplessly. 'I... I really can't.'

Hannah blinked up at him, then bowed her head and began weeping again.

Tom turned away to stare out at the motel. There was no sign of J.

Behind him, the sound of Hannah's crying filled the vehicle and he could feel her body shaking through the seat.

'I'm sorry,' he whispered. The words seemed so inadequate, so small in the face of such a nightmare.

'I don't wanna die,' she moaned, choking through her tears.

'You're not going to die,' he promised.

'Then let me go!'

'I told you, I *can't!*'

'But he's a killer, and you're...' Her voice became strangled. 'You're fucking *helping* him!'

'You think I don't know that?' he snapped. 'You think I *wanted* any of this?'

Hannah threw herself against the back of his seat.

'Then why are you doing it?' she wailed.

Tom swung his clenched fist hard against the door panel.

'Because I've got no fucking *choice!* Because...' He took a breath, collected himself. 'Because my son will die if I don't.'

Hannah fell silent.

Wearily, Tom rested his head against the window, feeling the chill of glass on his skin as he stared out into the night. There were three other cars in the parking lot, dark shapes in the gloom. He wondered where they'd come from, and where they were headed... ordinary people making ordinary journeys, unaware of how lucky they were.

'I'm a writer,' he said, softly. 'A journalist. I guess that's why he got in touch with me.'

He thought back to New York, a lifetime ago, when he'd been so eager, so sure of himself.

'I did everything right, everything I possibly could. I was going to stop him. I was going to deliver him to the police and I was going to...'

Get the story?

That had been the plan, that had been the reason for doing it all.

'It wasn't supposed to happen like this,' he murmured, staring out through the windshield, then shook his head. 'Anyway, now I'm caught, just like you. And I *am* sorry.'

Hannah said nothing.

From outside, the dim glow of headlights shone in the mirrors as a lone car came along the road. It swept past without slowing, and Tom watched as the red taillights dwindled into the distance.

A moment later, J emerged from the office. He walked across the parking lot, glancing about cautiously to make sure there was nobody around before opening the driver's door and peering in at them.

'We're in number 12,' he said, holding up a key. 'Let's go.'

The room was large but basic, with dated décor and threadbare carpets, all worn down by years of use. Both the double beds had crisp new linen that seemed out of place and couldn't disguise the dip in the mattresses. A cheap black microwave sat awkwardly on top of an elderly refrigerator with peeling wood veneer, and there were groups of screw-holes in the faded wallpaper where the small TV had been moved and re-attached.

J followed them inside and quickly set the bags down. Turning around, he went back to peer out at the parking lot, one hand hovering over the gun jammed down the back of his jeans. After a moment, he seemed to relax slightly, pushing the door closed and locking it.

'Well,' he said, glancing around the room without enthusiasm. 'Not exactly the Ritz-Carlton but I suppose it's just for the one night.' He nodded towards Hannah, who stood nervously with her hands still bound, and indicated the bed furthest from the door. 'Go on and take a seat.'

She flinched as he spoke, staring at him for a moment, before moving over and perching on the edge of the bed.

J turned his attention to Tom.

'So. Here we all are.' He spoke lightly, but there was a cold edge to his voice and his dark eyes were hard. 'You got what you wanted. I'm just curious about how you see things going from here...'

Tom shot him an uneasy look. 'What do you mean?'

'Well, I mean that the whole dynamic of our little journey has changed a bit, hasn't it? We've gone from two persons to three, adding in an unknown factor and significantly upping our chances of getting caught. But you?' J paused, shaking his head in mock admiration. 'You were adamant about it. This is what you wanted, and now that you've *got* it... well, I'm just wondering how you think it's all gonna work out. What's the plan?'

Tom lowered his eyes.

'How the hell should I know?' he muttered. 'You haven't told me where we're going, or how long it's going to take.'

'But you know we can't afford to get caught,' J snapped. 'And *she* knows what happened back at that bail bonds office, so we can't exactly turn her loose, now can we? What were you *thinking,* Tom? That we'd just... just pick her up and bring her along for the ride?'

He grunted with frustration, then turned and sat heavily on the bed by the door, resting his face in his hands.

Tom glanced over at Hannah. The poor kid seemed to have retreated into herself; sitting there, gently rocking forward and backward, glazed eyes staring into the distance. He'd been so determined to save her – he still was – but he hadn't thought about what saving her might mean.

J gave a deep sigh and slowly lifted his head.

'So what are we gonna do, Tom?' he asked. 'How do you

propose we continue, knowing that your new friend could betray us at any moment?'

Tom looked away, unhappily. If Hannah turned them in now it was all over for Zak. But he'd promised her that he wouldn't let her die.

'I won't make any trouble.'

Hannah's voice, which had been so desperate in the car, was now subdued, distant. Tom turned and found her staring up at him with glassy eyes. 'I'll do whatever you say, go wherever you want, anything. Just... just don't hurt me.'

He felt sick with guilt, uncertain what to do, unable to look away.

'*Please*, mister.'

He stood there, trying to find words, but it was J who finally spoke.

'His name's Tom. And I'm J, but *he's* the one you really need to persuade right now.'

The bedsprings creaked as the older man leaned over and wearily set his gun down on the nightstand. 'How much has he told you? Has he explained how important this is, what's at *stake* for him?'

Hannah's eyes flickered nervously between them.

'I... I don't understand any of this,' she stammered. 'You said something about his son. And he told me I had to come along with you, but I don't know what's happening, or why...'

'Let me catch you up a little,' J said, stretching out on the bed. 'Tom here, he's a reporter – does true crime pieces for the newspapers, written a couple of books about some famous cases, that kind of thing.'

Tom leaned back against the wall and hung his head.

'I've been following his work for months, and he's good at what he does,' J continued. 'So, I figured I'd get in touch with him... y'know, give him an opportunity for an exclusive, an opportunity to see some true crime *up close*.'

'You fucking kidnapped me,' Tom muttered.

J made a face and shrugged.

'It took him a little time to come around to my way of thinking,' he admitted. 'But we've been on the road for a week or so now, and we've kind of settled into a routine. He gets to see what I do, how I work.'

'How you... work?' Hannah asked.

'He kills people,' Tom said, miserably.

'People who deserve it,' J clarified. He smiled, then nodded towards Tom. 'And *he* gets the inside line, behind-the-scenes access. He gets the *story*.'

Hannah stared in disbelief, then turned to look at Tom. 'And you... you went *along* with all this?'

Tom shut his eyes, not trusting himself to respond.

'Well, to be fair, he didn't have a whole lot of choice in the matter,' J explained. 'You see, if anything happens to me – if I don't make it to our destination in one piece – then poor Tom's gonna lose some of the people he loves most... including his little boy.'

Tom clenched his fists as Hannah stifled a cry of dismay.

'Now, you have to understand, I don't *want* that,' J assured her quickly. 'I don't want to hurt *anyone* who doesn't really deserve it, least of all a kid.'

Tom glared at him but said nothing.

'My plan was just to make it through to the end of the journey, then Tom and I would go our separate ways.' J yawned and laid back, gazing up at the ceiling. 'He gets his story; I bring a little justice to the world... everybody's happy.'

Hannah sat on the edge of the bed, mouth slightly open, an expression of disbelief on her face.

'I had it all worked out. Every hit, every route, every detail...' J said, wistfully. He turned his head to stare at Hannah. 'But I *hadn't* figured on bringing a passenger along.'

. . .

'So what happens now?' Tom asked. 'Where is she going to sleep?'

J had emerged from the bathroom after brushing his teeth, and now stood yawning in the doorway.

'This is all on you,' he said, with a weary shrug. 'If *you* want to give up your bed for her... well, that's your call to make. But it's late, and I'm tired, and there's a lot of driving to do tomorrow, so I'm gonna get some shut-eye.'

Tom turned to look at Hannah. She sat, head bowed, with her hair hanging limp over her face, hands still bound tightly behind her back.

'Shouldn't we at least untie her?' he asked.

J walked slowly over to the bed by the door and stooped down to rummage in his bag. He stood up again with a small pocket knife and a spare set of plastic cuffs.

'Whatever you want,' he said, tossing the items on the bed for Tom. 'I assume you're going to stay up and watch her? Or you can cuff her to the bed... I don't really care, just so long as she's still here in the morning.'

He pulled back the covers and sat down sleepily.

Tom picked up the knife and the restraints, then looked uncertainly at Hannah. Her body language was resigned, and he ached with sympathy for her – what must be going through her mind right now? – but he was horribly aware of the risk she represented. He *couldn't* allow her to jeopardize Zak's safety.

'Well, goodnight, Tom.' J lay down and flicked the bedside switches until the main light went off and the room was lit by a lamp over the other bed. 'And goodnight, Hannah.'

She stiffened slightly at the mention of her name, but didn't reply.

As J yawned and settled himself, Tom stood anxiously, wondering what to do. Walking over to the bathroom, he reached in and switched on the light over the basin. There were no windows in there – no way of escape to worry about – just a single vent, high in the back wall.

Satisfied, he turned back to the room, trying to think. Apart from the two beds, the only furniture was a desk, a chair, and a slightly threadbare couch. The couch didn't look big enough to sleep comfortably on, but maybe he could take the cushions off and put them on the floor...

He was so very tired.

Eventually, he reached a decision. Stepping forward hesitantly, he leaned towards the frightened girl.

'Uh... excuse me?' He waited a moment, then added, 'Hannah?'

She lifted her head and blinked up at him, eyes red from crying.

'Listen,' Tom said in a low voice. 'I'm so sorry about all this but... well, you know the situation now.'

He'd hoped to see something in her face – maybe a little sympathy, or the beginnings of forgiveness – but her expression was hollow with misery.

'I really don't want to keep you tied up,' he murmured. 'You understand why I can't just let you go, right?'

She stared at him for a moment longer, then lowered her eyes and nodded very slightly.

Tom sighed with relief.

'If I free your hands, you won't... you won't *try* anything will you?' He met her gaze as she looked up hopefully. 'Promise me.'

She swallowed with some difficulty then answered with a croaking whisper.

'I promise.'

Tom nodded awkwardly, then reached for the pocket knife. Hannah watched the blade with obvious distrust, but she twisted around on the edge of the bed, bending forward slightly so that he could get to her wrists. The skin was red where the restraints had chafed her, and Tom took care not to hurt her further. She had several cheap friendship bracelets, made of woven leather and fabric, and one delicate gold chain, decorated with tiny golden hearts that sparkled as he worked to free her. As the plastic finally snapped, her shoulders slumped forwards and she gave a little whimper of relief.

'There.' Tom stood up, watching her as she rubbed at her wrists. 'Just remember, I'm *trusting* you, okay?'

Hannah turned towards him and nodded.

'I'm really thirsty,' she said. 'Is it okay if I get some water or something?'

'Of course.' Tom gestured towards the bathroom. 'There's a glass by the basin. Go ahead.'

Hannah got shakily to her feet and stood for a moment, before making her way through to the bathroom. She left the door open and soon the gurgle of running water could be heard.

Tom went over to the couch and began lifting out the cushions. He thought about spreading them out on the floor between the two beds, then hesitated. He really didn't want to restrain Hannah again... but would he hear her, if she *did* try to escape in the night? Frowning, he walked over to the front of the room and began laying the cushions on the carpet directly across the locked door.

He was just arranging the pillow and spare blankets when Hannah came out of the bathroom sipping a glass of water. She glanced at the position of the makeshift bed, then looked at him.

Tom turned away.

'It's better than sleeping in restraints,' he muttered. 'Just... try to get some sleep.'

It was difficult to find a comfortable position on the uneven cushions. Tom lay there, wide awake in the darkness, trying to keep the blankets in place. A faint but continuous draught crept under the door, and there was an earthy smell from the carpet, mingled with the artificial scent of chemical cleaners. He could hear J breathing slowly, in the gentle rhythm of sleep, but his own mind was still trying to process everything that had happened.

Had he made a mistake?

Hannah also remained awake far into the night. In the heavy quiet, he could make out her restless stirring and, after an hour or so, she slipped out from under the covers and padded through to the bathroom, bolting the door. Moments later, he heard the toilet flush, and she returned to bed.

Tom lay still and silent. He couldn't let J kill her... but he couldn't let her put Zak in danger either. Staring into the darkness, he wondered what the hell he was going to do.

42

In the morning, Tom was groggy; it was as though he hadn't slept at all. His neck felt stiff after a night on the draughty floor, and the burning ache in his injured ribs was starting to flare up again. Hannah also seemed to have had a troubled night. Her eyes were puffy and she looked tired and disheveled. Only J appeared rested. He moved around the room, bright and alert, hurrying them into readiness.

'Time to move out,' he said, in a brisk tone. 'Get your things together, both of you.'

Tom groaned and began gathering up the cushions, tossing them back onto the couch.

Hannah stood at the side of her bed, looking at them anxiously.

'So, uh... what happens now?'

'We're gonna hit the road,' J told her, picking up his gun from the nightstand and tucking it down under the back of his jacket. 'Got a lot of miles to cover today, and the sooner we start the sooner we'll be done.'

'Where are we going?' Tom asked, stifling a yawn.

'West,' J replied. He paused, then glanced over at Hannah.

'Do you need to use the bathroom before we go? No offense, but we've only just met, so I'm not entirely comfortable about you disappearing into busy restrooms on your own.'

Hannah regarded him with a sullen expression, then her shoulders dropped and she went through to the bathroom, bolting the door behind her.

'Hey, *someone* has to think about these things, Tom,' J said, even though he hadn't asked. 'If this is going to work, we really shouldn't let her out of our sight in public places.'

'Yeah, I suppose.'

'And one of us needs to check that bathroom after she's done, *just* to make sure she didn't leave a message scrawled on the wall, or a note or anything. We can't afford any mistakes.'

Tom gave a grudging nod. It was beginning to dawn on him just how difficult this whole thing with Hannah was going to be.

They made their way across the parking lot, J and Hannah linked firmly arm-in-arm. The older man glanced around, smiling calmly as they walked, but his eyes were watchful and he kept the stun-gun pressed in against the young woman's side.

In the morning light, the motel looked more cheerful, an old-fashioned building on a tree-lined country road. A little way beyond the office there was a small diner and Tom found himself yearning for coffee, to help shake off the fog of weariness.

J unlocked the SUV and held the back door open for Hannah. She looked at him for a moment, then wordlessly climbed in. J closed the door on her then turned to Tom.

'Stay with her while I go get the bags and return the key,' he said. 'If she's any trouble...'

He held out the stun-gun and placed it into Tom's hand.

'Oh.' Tom looked at it with dismay. 'I don't think I could...'

J shrugged his shoulders.

'Better to have it and not need it,' he said. 'I won't be long.'

He turned to walk away.

'Uh... what about breakfast?' Tom asked, pointing towards the diner. 'There's a place right there.'

J paused, then turned and looked thoughtfully at Hannah sitting in the back of the SUV.

'I think we'd be better off sticking with drive-thru and take-outs,' he said. 'At least until we get to know your new friend a little better.'

The highway cut south, two straight grey lines draped across a flat landscape of empty fields, disappearing into the distant morning haze. Before long, they began to see houses – just one or two at first, then more frequently – as a small town closed in around them. Coming to an intersection, they found a McDonalds and, with a brief warning glance at Hannah in the rear-view mirror, J pulled the car around to the drive-thru window. After collecting their food, he found a quiet corner of the parking lot, and reversed back into the bay so he could watch the main road.

'Okay...' He stopped the engine and released his seat belt. Lifting the warm paper bag, he peered inside. 'Let's see what we have here... Tom, do you want the sausage muffin or the bacon muffin?'

'I don't mind,' Tom said, with a shrug. 'Sausage, I suppose.'

'There you go.' J handed over one of the muffins and kept the other for himself, then twisted around in his seat to pass the bag back to Hannah. 'Which leaves your bacon and egg McGriddle.'

She hesitated, then took the bag.

Yawning, Tom handed out the coffees.

'Here.' He gave one cup to J, then turned to Hannah. 'Cream and sugar?'

She gave a slight nod, then murmured, 'Thank you.'

'No problem.'

He watched her as she ate, noting the way she wolfed her food down. The poor kid was obviously hungry... was she so short of money that she'd not been eating properly?

J sipped his coffee as he stared out across the parking lot.

'We need to stop somewhere, pick up some supplies...' His eyes flickered to the rear-view mirror, '...and some new clothes for our guest.'

Hannah glanced up from her food.

'What's wrong with my clothes?'

J shrugged his shoulders.

'If you're gonna be travelling with us for a while, then you'll need more than you've got in that bag of yours.' He leaned over to slot his drink into the cup holder, then started the engine. 'And I reckon you could do with a new look... just in case anyone misses you, and gives a description of what you were last seen wearing.'

There was a Walmart on the edge of town. J cruised slowly around the parking lot and pulled into a bay that commanded a good view of the store entrance. Switching off the engine, he took out his wallet and frowned as he counted out a handful of bills.

'What size are you, Hannah?' he asked.

'Uh... I'm usually a size six,' she replied.

'And shoe size?'

'A nine.'

'Okay.' J turned to Tom and gave him the money. 'She's gonna want clothes and underwear for maybe ten days – no, make it two weeks – with a couple of pairs of sneakers, and a coat or jacket. Nothing memorable... just get things that are suitable for warm weather and avoid anything that's similar to what she's wearing now.'

'You want *me* to go in?' Tom was surprised.

'She's your problem,' J replied. 'C'mon, we don't have all day. Maybe get some drinks and snacks for the road. Oh, and try to keep your mouth shut in there... we don't need anyone picking up on that Downton Abbey accent of yours.'

Tom stared at him, then looked at Hannah sitting quietly in the back. She seemed calmer now, resigned to the situation, but he felt a deep unease at the thought of leaving her alone with the killer. Reaching for the door handle, he hesitated.

J glanced across at him and rolled his eyes.

'Jeez, Tom. Just get going, already.' He shook his head. 'I promise she'll still be here when you get back... so long as you're quick.'

43

They joined the interstate at Marion and headed southwest. Once the town was behind them, the landscape that slid by began to take on a deep blue-green color – patchwork fields, shallow hills, all broken up with meandering lines of trees. Tom gazed at it wistfully. Apart from being on the wrong side of the road, it was almost like looking out on England.

By early afternoon, they'd crossed into Missouri, and J finally pulled off the highway at a small gas station convenience store.

'Comfort stop,' he announced, then glanced at Hannah in the rear-view mirror. 'Might be a good time for you to try on some of your new things.'

Her expression was sullen, but her eyes flickered briefly towards the front of the small store.

'Now remember, just behave while you're in there, and I won't have any cause to shoot the place up.' J drew out his gun so she could see it. 'Nobody has to die, and we can all go on our way, understood?'

Hannah's shoulders dropped slightly, but she nodded.

'Understood.'

Tom opened the door to get out, moving stiffly after hours on the road, and placed a hand over his aching ribs. J emerged from the other side of the car and shot him a brief warning look across the roof.

'Keep a *real* close eye on her in there,' he said quietly. 'I need to fill up.'

He turned his attention to the pumps.

Tom opened the back door then moved aside to give Hannah space as she stepped out, clutching the Walmart bag. She glanced towards the store entrance then looked questioningly at Tom.

'Just be cool,' he told her. 'Come on.'

She gave a slight nod, then fell in beside him as he walked across the dusty forecourt.

Inside, the store was like a labyrinth, tightly packed with rows of tall shelving. Tom positioned himself between Hannah and the bored-looking man who stared at them from behind the counter. Taking in the layout of the place, he gestured towards the far corner.

'Restroom's over there,' he whispered. 'Go ahead.'

He turned away slightly, pretending to study the different bags of potato chips, but watching out the corner of his eye as Hannah disappeared into the tiny restroom and closed the door. The man at the counter lost interest and went back to peering at his phone.

Tom breathed a sigh of relief and rubbed absently at the crick in his neck. Outwardly, Hannah appeared subdued – she'd hardly spoken on their journey down here, seemingly indifferent to any attempts to engage her in conversation – but her eyes had remained watchful and alert.

He couldn't take any chances with her.

Taking care to move casually, he walked over to stand outside the restroom door, as though waiting his turn to use it. He glanced back towards the forecourt, where J was still filling up the tank, and wondered once again where they were headed. *West*, that was all the older man had told him, but how *far* west? They were nearly half-way across the country already, and he still had no real sense of where they were going. J had said to buy her warm-weather clothing for at least ten days... were they making for the West Coast? California? Would their plans change? Would J still be willing to talk, with Hannah in the car?

Frowning, he turned back towards the restroom, just as the door opened. Startled at coming face-to-face, they both flinched, but Hannah's expression was immediately wary and she regarded him with disgust.

'What the fuck!' she gasped. 'You scared me!'

Caught off guard, Tom took a step backwards, almost knocking over a rack of cheap sunglasses.

'What were you doing?' Hannah demanded. 'Ew... were you listening at the door?'

'Eh?' Tom stared at her, then shook his head. 'No. *No!* I would never do anything like that!'

Hannah eyed him doubtfully. She looked different now, dressed in the non-descript sweatpants and hoodie that he'd bought her.

'But you'd take a road trip with a killer,' she muttered. 'As long as there was a cool *story* in it, right?'

Tom winced. He glanced nervously over his shoulder towards the man at the counter, then turned to Hannah again.

'Keep your voice down,' he hissed, then pointed at the bag in her hand. 'That's all of your old clothes?'

'Yeah. Why?'

Ignoring her question, Tom stepped past her, leaning around the door to give the restroom a cursory look. There was no incriminating message scrawled on the bare off-white walls, and nothing appeared out of place.

'Checking up after me?' Hannah sneered. 'Like your *friend* told you to?'

Tom took a deep breath and swallowed his frustration.

'Let's… let's take this outside.'

He touched her arm and she stiffened a little but allowed him to steer her towards the door.

J was replacing the fuel filler cap as they approached the vehicle, though Tom noticed that the older man had been watching the store intently as they emerged, ready to react if anything seemed wrong.

'Much better,' he said, glancing at Hannah's new clothing, and giving an approving nod. 'You don't look like a runaway anymore.'

She shot him a contemptuous look but remained silent.

'Stay with her,' J instructed Tom. 'I'll be right back.'

Tom opened the back door for Hannah, then got in the front and slumped down into his seat while they waited.

'He's not my friend,' he muttered.

Behind him, Hannah lifted her head.

'What?'

'You called him my friend in there,' Tom said. 'But he's not. I mean, he's really, *really* not.'

She stared at him blankly for a moment, then turned away to look out of the window.

'And this… all of this…' Tom gestured around him and scowled. 'This isn't about a damn *story*. Okay?'

Whatever it had been in the beginning, things were different now.

Hannah's unblinking eyes met his in the rear-view mirror, but she said nothing.

J emerged from the store a moment later, sipping on a large slushie as he walked calmly across the forecourt. Dropping into the driver's seat, he set his drink down in the cup holder, then glanced at Tom and Hannah, noting the expression on their faces.

'Well, I'm glad to see you kids are getting along,' he said, brightly. 'That always makes the miles pass quicker...' He leaned forward to start the engine. 'And we've got a *long* way still to go.'

44

The sun was getting low in the sky when they reached the outskirts of Tulsa. J finally broke away from the steady crawl of traffic on the turnpike, escaping down an exit ramp and heading south. Before long, he pulled in at a small motel, stopping in a secluded spot at the far corner of the parking lot, well away from the road. He sat for a moment, yawning and stretching, then glanced over at Tom.

'Sit tight,' he said.

Tom watched him walking stiffly across the parking lot towards the office, and thought how *easy* it would be to catch the older man off guard, to beat him into the ground and deliver him to Leo... except that he'd be sentencing his little boy to death.

Clenching his fists in frustration, he sat in brooding silence.

The motel stood on a desert of dusty cracked concrete. Beyond it, a row of battered pickup trucks lined the white brick wall of an auto parts warehouse, while dumpsters huddled close to the back of a small diner. Dead streetlights and drooping wires framed the evening sky. There wasn't a human being in sight.

'I've never been to Tulsa before.' Hannah's voice was distant, as though she was speaking to herself.

'Me neither,' Tom replied, gazing out at the taller buildings that made up the jagged horizon. He'd always wanted to drive across America, see more of the country... but not like this.

They sat in silence for a time, then Hannah stirred.

'Where are you taking me?'

Tom twisted round in his seat.

'I'm not taking you anywhere,' he told her. '*He's* taking you... taking *us*.'

Hannah rolled her eyes.

'Okay, but where?'

'How the hell should I know?' Tom replied. 'It's not like he consults me on stuff.'

Hannah bit her lip and frowned.

'But you're writing his story, aren't you?' she persisted. 'How can you not know where we're going?'

Tom sighed.

'Because he doesn't trust me, I suppose. I'm a prisoner, just like you.'

Hannah appeared to consider this.

'He still left you to watch me,' she countered. 'Seems like he trusts you more than you think.'

Tom met her piercing gaze, then looked away.

'It's part of this...' He shook his head. '...this *idea* he has. He doesn't want to just *tell* me his story – you know, like just lay out the details and have me write it up for him – no, he wants me to figure him out somehow. He wants me to *understand*.'

Hannah slowly sat back, her expression thoughtful.

'And *do* you?' she asked. 'Do you understand what he's doing?'

Tom hesitated. His view of J kept shifting. At first, it had seemed simple – an evil monster who slaughtered people, perhaps at random, for his own sick gratification. Later, with the discovery that several victims had posted on social media, the connection had suggested the possibility of a deeper motive behind the killings. But now, it looked as though the whole nightmare was just the rage of a frustrated abuser, lashing out at a world that had exposed him, desperately trying to rewrite his own narrative by silencing those who'd told the truth...

His thoughts were interrupted by the sight of J emerging from the office.

'He's coming back.'

Hannah fell silent and turned her head away.

J walked across the parking lot and opened the door.

'Well, I got us checked in,' he said. 'Hannah, maybe you could help Tom with the bags?' He glanced at Tom. 'But leave mine in the car for now.'

The room wasn't homely, but it was clean and unfussy – with muted colors and dark, angular furnishings, tailored to the unloved business traveler whose expense account wouldn't stretch to a real hotel in the center of town.

Tom watched as J absently removed the glass jug from the coffeemaker and wandered through to the bathroom to fill it up. If he *was* a former insurance investigator who'd spent a lot of time on the road, this transient existence was probably second nature to him.

Hannah set the bags down against the wall, then stepped aside as J emerged from the bathroom.

'Coffee?' J asked, holding up the jug.

She shook her head.

'It's late for me,' Tom said, with a yawn.

J shrugged and switched on the machine.

'There's a pull-out cot in the corner there,' he said, glancing over his shoulder at Tom. 'I figured that would be more comfortable for you than sleeping on the floor again.'

'Gee, thanks,' Tom muttered, without enthusiasm.

J grinned. He stood patiently by the machine while it brewed, and the sickly smell of air freshener gave way to the pleasing aroma of coffee. When it was done, he poured himself a cup, then turned around and regarded them thoughtfully.

'I think I'll let you two unpack and get settled in.'

Tom looked up.

'What are *you* going to do?'

'I figured we may as well eat here in the room this evening,' J replied. 'If you tell me what you want, then I'll go pick up some food... I need to collect a few supplies anyway.'

Tom leaned forward on the sofa, flicking through the TV channels, searching for one that wasn't on commercials. Eventually, he found a rerun of an old *Big Bang Theory* episode, and sat back to watch, but his thoughts were elsewhere and he couldn't concentrate on it.

He glanced over at Hannah, sitting on the bed. She hadn't spoken since J went out for food.

'How are you doing?' he asked. 'Are you okay?'

She stirred, as if waking from some private deliberation. For a while she said nothing, then frowned.

'You didn't answer my question,' she murmured.

Tom stared at her, momentarily confused.

'What question?'

'From earlier. I asked if you understood what he's doing. I mean, you've been with him for a while, right?'

Tom lowered his eyes, staring down at the carpet. Right now, he felt as though he'd been on the road with J for so long that his old life was a distant memory. But in all that time, what had he really learned? What could he be sure of?

'I don't know,' he mumbled. 'At first I was so scared, so fucking *terrified*, I just...' He broke off, reliving the horror of waking in the van, struggling to move, struggling to breathe. 'He kidnapped me. Tasered me right outside my apartment. I woke up, gagged and blindfolded in the back of a van.'

'Shit!'

Tom met her gaze.

'I was so sure he was going to kill me.' He hesitated, recalling the awful moment when J had untied him and handed him a loaded gun... the moment that could have changed everything. 'But he didn't.'

They sat in silence for a time.

'Did you know who he was?' Hannah asked.

'He got in contact with me, back in New York, weeks before. In the beginning I didn't realize...'

'And then?'

'We spoke on the phone, and I started to piece things together, to figure out what he'd done, what sort of person I was dealing with. He asked me if I wanted to know who he was, if I was prepared to meet...' Tom paused and gave a bitter laugh. 'He said I'd walk away with a hell of a story.'

Hannah blinked at him in disbelief.

'So... you *agreed* to all this?'

'No!' Tom snapped. 'Well... kind of... but only to play him along. I've got friends in the police department... we were going to set him up. We were going to *catch* him.'

'But you didn't.'

'No. He set *me* up. He caught *me*.'

An annoying jingle began playing. Tom reached for the remote and muted the TV.

'He's smart. Very patient, and very careful.'

Hannah bit her lip. 'But do you know *why* he's doing this?'

Tom shook his head.

'That's what I can't figure out. I've written about psychopaths – monsters who really got off on the killing – but he doesn't seem to enjoy it at all. It's like it's just a job to him... something that needs to be done.'

He swung his feet up onto the sofa and lay back, gazing up at the ceiling. 'The people he kills aren't chosen at random. I mean, he says he doesn't know them, but he certainly seems to know *about* them... where they live, where they work, their routines...'

And what they posted on social media.

'Whatever his reasons, he definitely doesn't like them. He believes they deserve what they get, that the world's a better place without them. I think he's trying to bury something... something from his past. I haven't quite put it all together yet though.'

Hannah was quiet for a moment.

'His past?' she asked.

'There were allegations made against him, a while back, but I don't know all the details.'

'What kind of allegations?'

Tom hesitated. She was just a kid. It was traumatic enough to have witnessed a killing and then be taken prisoner by the man who did it. What would it do to her if she thought he was a sex criminal as well?

'It's... something that happened a few years ago, back when he was an insurance investigator,' he replied. 'But like I said, I don't know the details yet.'

Hannah looked up sharply.

'He's told you all this?'

'Some. Not all of it.'

'Then how do you know so much?'

Tom turned his body so he could gaze over at her. It was time to change the subject.

'I'm a journalist,' he explained with a shrug. 'Anyway, I'm sick of talking about him. Tell me about you.'

Perched on the edge of the bed, Hannah had been leaning

forward, almost eagerly, but now she seemed to falter and Tom sensed the tension in her. Perhaps she still thought he was secretly working with J.

'Why?' she asked, wary now. 'What do you want to know?'

Tom held up his hands.

'Hey, I'm just making conversation,' he assured her. 'You don't have to tell me anything if you don't want to.'

Hannah looked at him doubtfully, then lowered her gaze.

'I'm from Alabama originally,' she said softly. 'But I've been living up in Jasper for a while...'

'Nice place?'

'Kinda quiet, I guess, but it wasn't so bad.'

She didn't mention her boyfriend and Tom decided not to either.

'I'm from London,' he said. 'Originally.'

'London, England?'

'That's right. Moved over here a few years back. New York.'

'I always wanted to see New York,' she murmured, then lapsed into silence.

Tom tried to steer her back into the conversation.

'Any brothers or sisters back in Alabama?'

Hannah shook her head. 'I'm an only child.'

'Mom and dad?'

Her eyes hardened. 'I don't want to talk about them.'

There was bitterness in her voice, but also a note of deep hurt, and he felt a sudden pity for her. What had happened? What was she running away from?

'That's cool,' he said, lightly. 'It's been a long day, you're tired, I get it. Here...' He tossed the TV remote over so it landed on the bed beside her. 'Find us something to watch. Anything you want.'

She glanced down at the remote, then leaned over and picked it up. Flicking through the channels, she settled on an animated show he didn't recognize.

'Is this okay?'

'Whatever you want,' Tom replied.

She slumped back on the bed. 'Right now, I just want something to eat,' she muttered.

'Yeah,' Tom said. 'I could do with something too.'

He went to check his watch, remembered he didn't have one, then looked over at the time on the TV.

J had been gone for a long time. *Too* long.

Suddenly restless, Tom got to his feet. Walking over to the window, he pulled back the drapes and peered out at the parking lot, now blanketed in darkness. There was no sign of the SUV. When he turned around, Hannah was watching him.

'What's wrong?' she asked.

'Nothing,' he replied quickly. 'Just hungry. And thirsty.'

Frowning, he wandered past her and into the bathroom. Taking one of the glasses from the shelf above the wash basin, he rinsed it under the tap, then filled it up and took a sip. In the mirror, his reflection stared back at him, unshaven, with dark circles under tired eyes.

J had said something about picking up supplies, hadn't he? Maybe that was why he hadn't returned yet. Setting the glass down, Tom walked back through to the room and stopped short. For a moment, he couldn't quite comprehend what he was seeing. Then he choked out a broken cry.

Hannah was gone.

45

Tom burst out of the motel room and stood for a second, blinking. His eyes swept across the parked cars, piercing the gloom, searching for any sign of her, any movement...

Ahead of him, across the open space of vacant lots, he could see the lights of cars slipping between dark buildings. Beyond that, a cluster of illuminated signs marked the route of the freeway and twinkling lights glittered on the distant downtown skyline. A whole world, oblivious to the fact that everything was falling apart...

She was gone.

All the urgency bled out of him as he stood there, swaying slightly, lost and alone. What was he going to do now? If he couldn't find her, if she went to the police, if J was captured...

And then, just as despair crashed in, threatening to engulf him completely, he saw something.

There!

It was only a fleeting glimpse – a barely-imagined movement on the edge of his vision – as a shadow disappeared around the corner of a building, but he suddenly had a spark of hope. Launching himself forwards, he sprang after her, powering across the concrete.

He couldn't lose her!

Racing between two parked cars, he leapt across the low barrier that marked the edge of the motel property and sprinted across the broad open space behind the auto warehouse. She was probably a hundred yards ahead of him, and she'd looked as though she was moving quickly, but he had purpose now, and pushed himself to go faster.

He *mustn't* lose her.

He rushed through the darkness, angling his run away from the place where he'd seen her disappear, anticipating where she might emerge on the far side of a long low building, needing to close the distance between them. His shoe scuffed the raised edge of a broken slab, startling him, and he forced himself to look down, picking out a path across the uneven ground. He couldn't afford to stumble, not now.

Rounding the corner of the building, he slowed, straining to see into the darkness. For a moment, he worried that he'd got it wrong, but then his eyes picked her out.

There!

She was heading for an alleyway at the side of a large warehouse. He thought about shouting but decided against it. There was no point in scaring her, in spurring her on. Breathing hard, he lurched forward again, feeling pain in his ribs and heat in his leg muscles. He'd never been much of an athlete, but adrenalin lent him strength and carried him forward. He ran across another parking lot and passed under a tall streetlight, his shadow stretching out ahead of him and distorting into a nightmare silhouette that reached out to catch her with its elongated limbs.

She slowed a little as she disappeared into the alley and he felt a surge of excitement. He was closing on her now, and there was no sign that she even realized he was behind her. He would catch her and then... what? What the hell would he even say to her?

Doubt flickered in his mind, but he forced himself on. Reaching the corner, he turned into the alley and suddenly faltered, skidding to a weary standstill.

No!

His gaze swept along the length of the alley, past the line of dumpsters, to the high mesh fence that blocked off the far end from the street.

She was gone.

He stood there, panting, staring at the fence. It was ten feet high... she *couldn't* have climbed that, not without him seeing her. So where was she?

Swallowing his nerves, he began to advance down the alley, alert to every sound and shadow. His movements were slow now, placing each foot with care and treading softly. The high walls pressed the darkness in around him as he tensed up and leaned around the side of a dumpster.

Hannah screamed.

Cursing, Tom stumbled backwards, thrusting out a hand to save himself and grazing it against the far wall. As he did so, she was already rising from her hiding place behind the dumpster, eyes wide and teeth bared, a rusty length of steel pipe gripped tightly in her hands.

'Hannah,' he gasped, trying to catch his breath. 'Wait!'

'Get back!' she snarled, shifting her weight from one foot to another like a cornered animal, eager to escape but reluctant to draw closer to him. 'Get the *fuck* away from me!'

Tom held up his hands, palms outwards.

'Please. Just let me talk to you.'

'Get away! Just leave me the fuck alone!' She raised the pipe, holding it like a baseball player winding up for the swing. 'I mean it. Get back!'

Tom retreated, leaning against the wall, still out of breath.

'Please! I just want to talk to you. Just *talk*.'

Hannah's gaze flickered towards the glow of the street, just yards away beyond the wire mesh fence.

'I'll scream this whole place down,' she warned him. 'I'll cry rape and someone will hear... they'll come!'

'No!' Tom pleaded. 'You don't understand.'

Hannah gave a sarcastic nod.

'Oh, I think I understand just fine.'

Tom shook his head in desperation.

'No, it's just... my son...' His voice wavered. 'My little boy... he'll *die!*'

He stared at her wretchedly.

Hannah's eyes flashed with anger, but when she spoke there was a note of uncertainty in her voice.

'Whatever you've gotten yourself into, it's not my problem,' she growled.

'I know it's not, but–'

'This is *your* fault,' she snapped at him. 'You agreed to it, you put everyone in danger... this whole thing's on you!'

'I just...' Tom faltered, then slumped against the wall.

The whole thing *was* down to him, to his desire for recognition, his need for approval. He'd wanted the story, wanted to be the hero... but he hadn't considered what it might cost.

Hannah regarded him unhappily.

'I saw someone killed,' she hissed. 'I had a gun pointed at me – at my *face* – and I've been fucking *kidnapped...*'

'I'm sorry,' Tom murmured.

'Oh, you're sorry?' Hannah's eyes widened and she took a step towards him. 'You're *sorry?* Is that supposed to make everything all right?'

'No, it's just...' Tom faltered. 'I don't know what else I can say to you.'

Hannah glared for a moment, then shook her head in disgust. Keeping the pipe aimed towards Tom, she edged her way around the dumpster and began to move back along the alley.

'*Please*,' he implored her. 'Zak will *die*.'

She slowed, and there was doubt on her face.

'What do you expect *me* to do about it?' she demanded.

'Help me,' he said, simply.

Hannah gave him a cold look.

'He won't hurt you,' Tom assured her. 'I wouldn't let him do anything to you, I promise...'

Her expression became one of disbelief, as though she was waiting for him to admit that he was joking.

'You think I'm going *back* to him?' she said with a shrill laugh. 'What the hell is *wrong* with you?'

Tom felt his panic rising. The situation was getting away from him.

'Please...'

'This is my chance to disappear,' Hannah told him. There was a glimmer of sympathy as she met his gaze. 'Yours too, if you're smart. Get away, call your wife, call the police... whatever you need to do...'

Tom shook his head.

'I'm out of options here. I *have* to do what he says. I don't want to but...'

He trailed off in despair. It was all unravelling.

Hannah scowled. 'Just... oh, I don't know... have your wife disappear for a few days, just until they catch him... then your troubles are over.'

Tom lifted his gaze to meet hers.

'You don't get it,' he said. 'J isn't the one who's going to kill my son. The hit's already been arranged – J's the only one who can *stop* it.'

She stared at him blankly.

Tom pushed himself away from the wall and faced her.

'If anything happens to J, if he's caught, or killed, or *anything*... it's over for my little boy.'

Hannah frowned with uncertainty.

'He's five years old, for God's sake,' Tom told her. '*Please.* Help me.'

For a moment, he thought he was getting through to her, but then her expression hardened. She snorted and turned away.

A desperate anger flared up in Tom, and he stepped forward.

'I saved your bloody life back at the bail bonds office,' he shouted. 'You remember that? *Do* you?'

Hannah flinched at the sudden violence of his outburst. Taking a step back, she raised the pipe once more, swinging it nervously.

Tom forced himself to take a deep breath, containing his anger. When he spoke again, his voice was measured and cold.

'You'd be face-down in some forest right now, with a bullet in the back of your head if it wasn't for me.' He straightened up, and something in his quiet manner was enough to make her shrink away from him even more. 'So let me make this really clear for you: you *are* going to help me save my son.'

46

They made their way back along the side of the darkened auto warehouse, Tom leading Hannah by the hand. She followed like a reluctant child, half-heartedly pulling against him, and he gripped her small limp fingers as gently as he could. The adrenalin of the chase was gone now, and burning pain had flared up in his side once more. His movements were weary, and his clothes felt clammy against his skin. He wondered how long they'd been out here, how long it would be before J returned...

Hannah's shoes scuffed across the concrete, her head lifting suddenly as they reached the corner and the lights of the motel came into view.

'No,' she whimpered, jerking back and trying to retreat into the shadows. 'I don't wanna die.'

Tom sighed and looked round at her.

'You're not going to die,' he assured her. 'It's going to be okay, I promise.'

'Your friend's gonna kill me.'

'He's not my friend,' Tom reminded her.

She rolled her eyes in frustration.

'Well, then maybe he's gonna kill us *both.*'

'He isn't...' Tom broke off. He'd been about to say that J wasn't going to kill *anyone...* but caught himself just in time. Turning around, he looked her in the eye. 'He isn't going to kill *either* of us, okay? I won't let anything happen to you.'

Hannah's brow creased into a frown.

'How do you know he won't kill you?' she demanded.

Tom paused.

How *did* he know? His mind went back to the older man, patiently explaining the rules to him... rules he should have taken more seriously.

'He promised me he wouldn't.'

'He promised?'

'Yeah.'

'What, and you just *believed* him?'

Tom glared at her. 'Yeah, I believed him. I believed him enough to put myself in the way of that gun he had pointed at you, *remember?*'

Hannah appeared chastened, but she shot him a bitter little smile before turning her head away. Tom sighed and looked towards the motel.

'Come on,' he said. 'We really need to get back.'

They walked across the parking lot, their footsteps loud against the far-off rumble of the freeway. Tom reached to his pocket with his free hand, then slowed to a stop.

'Shit.'

'What's wrong?'

'No key for the room,' Tom explained. 'J must have it.'

He'd raced after Hannah without thinking. Had the door closed behind him? His eyes swept along the building with its long row of identical rooms and he realized that he wasn't even sure which one they'd been in. It had been in the middle somewhere... hadn't it?

'Come on,' he whispered.

They crept along, passing one closed room after another. A few of them had illuminated windows, with warm light spilling out from below the drapes. Before long, Tom found one of these with its door slightly ajar and breathed a sigh of relief. It was just as he'd left it.

'Here we are,' he said. 'It's all right, the door's still open.'

With a quick backward glance around the parking lot, he led Hannah inside, rubbing his eyes as he walked wearily over to the second bed.

'Well, hello,' said a voice behind him.

Tom whirled around and froze; Hannah stifled a cry of surprise and jerked her hand free of his grip.

J was standing in the corner of the room, just behind the door, his dark eyes on them. He was holding a gun at his side.

'The door was open,' he noted, stepping forward.

'I... er... sorry,' Tom stammered.

J took another step closer, then halted, his piercing gaze searching their faces.

'So... did anything happen while I was gone?' he asked. 'Anything that I need to know about? Be concerned about?'

'No,' Tom replied quickly. His voice sounded shrill and anxious. 'No, I think everything's okay. Fine.'

J nodded thoughtfully.

'Well. I'm glad to hear that.' He turned to Hannah. 'Anything *you* want to tell me?'

She stared down at the floor and slowly shook her head.

'No.'

J studied them both for a long moment, then calmly tucked the gun into the back of his jeans, and gave a cold smile.

'Okay then,' he said, as though everything was suddenly

settled. 'Shall we eat? I was away a little longer than I wanted and I'm sure we must all be hungry.'

Tom stole a quick glance at Hannah and found her looking at him, eyes wide. J seemed oblivious to their tension as he walked over to the desk and lifted a couple of brown bags.

'Here we go,' he said, holding them out. 'I didn't check, but hopefully they got your order right. Oh, and there's beer in the fridge.'

It was as though nothing had happened.

Feeling numb, Tom took one of the bags and sat down heavily on the sofa. J was already making himself comfortable on the bed beside the door. Clutching her food, Hannah retreated to the other bed and positioned herself at the opposite corner of it, trying to take herself as far away from them as possible.

'It's a funny thing,' J observed, reaching into his bag and drawing out a taco wrapped in paper. 'For the longest time, I thought that eating late was a bad thing... you know, *breakfast like a king, lunch like a prince, dine like a pauper...* you ever hear that?'

Tom looked at him blankly.

'Yeah?'

'I guess the idea is that, if you eat more, earlier in the day, then you have more time to burn it off, or whatever. But then I saw an article that said it wasn't *when* you ate, just *what* you ate that made the difference.' J shrugged. 'Just goes to show, you can't believe everything you read. And anyway, tacos and beer taste better at the end of a long day.'

Tom looked down. The brown bag was warm on his lap and the aroma of food that rose from it reminded him that he was hungry. He closed his eyes for a moment – trying to shut everything out, trying to quiet his mind – then lifted out his taco and began to unwrap it.

For some time, they ate in silence. Hannah was huddled on

her bed, knees drawn up in front of her like a wall, but she was eating too, wolfing her food down hungrily. J sighed contentedly, then stood up and went over to the fridge.

'There was a car wreck, up on the 44 near that big casino,' he said, stooping down to take another beer. 'We were lucky we got down here before it happened. We could have been stuck in traffic for hours.'

Tom frowned to himself. Where *had* the older man been for all that time?

'You went to a casino?' he asked.

'No, I just heard about it on the radio.' J walked back to the bed and sat down. He glanced at Tom, then added, 'I don't like to gamble.'

Tom nodded thoughtfully. J certainly wasn't the type to leave things to chance.

'I just wondered,' he said, with a shrug. 'You know, because you were gone for quite a while.'

Leaning forward, he took a bite of his taco, trying not to let any of it drop onto his lap.

'Yeah, sorry about that.' J yawned and stretched. 'The person I went to find wasn't where they were supposed to be.'

Tom looked up, swallowing hard.

'The person you went to find?'

J took a long sip on his beer then nodded calmly.

'Yeah. I was pretty sure he'd be home but the stupid sonofabitch kept me waiting.' A grim smile touched his lips. 'He's where he should be now, though. Where he *belongs*.'

Tom felt his fists clenching. He didn't want to ask, but he had to know.

'Not again,' he pleaded. 'Not another one...'

'Oh relax, will you?' J yawned and rolled his eyes. 'It's done. I'll give you all the details tomorrow. Anyway, you kept complaining when I let you witness these things, so I figured it might be easier all round if you just... sat this one out.'

'Easier?' Tom's voice rose in pitch. 'You think this is fucking *easy* for me?'

He looked across to Hannah, who sat huddled on her bed, looking scared. Then he turned back to J.

'You've *killed* someone. Another human being is *dead*. And you just sit there... eating and drinking, like it's nothing!'

J regarded him coolly.

'That's right,' he replied. 'I accept who I am – *what* I am – and I get on with what needs to be done. While *you* stamp your feet like a spoilt child, and wring your hands for some low-life hater you never even met.'

Tom choked with fury. Rising to his feet, he jabbed an accusing finger at the older man.

'You're psychotic, you know that? You think you can go around playing God, deciding who lives and who dies...'

J's eyes went dead.

'Tom...'

'No, *fuck* this.' Tom moved closer, shouting now. 'And fuck *you*! I don't want to hear any more of your bullshit about how you think people *deserve their fate*. Nobody deserves this. *Nobody*.'

J lifted a hand to massage his temple. 'Tom...'

'No!' Tom stood over him, fists clenched with anger. 'This has to stop right now! I'm not going to–'

The older man lunged forward, sweeping one hand around and up, as though to punch him in the stomach. But the impact was a sudden explosion of agony, as every muscle tightened in spasm, and electricity seared down into Tom's pelvis, out across his chest, up through his neck and into his teeth. He dropped to the floor like deadweight, barely able to breathe, barely able to think. His arms and legs wouldn't work and he blinked stupidly up at the ceiling as J loomed over him and knelt down with the stun gun to shock him again.

Tom contorted helplessly under the assault, limbs kicking

and twitching, spine arching as though it would snap, overwhelmed by the blinding pain and confusion. He tried to cry out, and a sound finally came, but it wasn't his voice. Hannah was screaming, and the pain abruptly ceased as J turned to glare at her.

'Be quiet!' he barked, silencing her with barely contained fury. Panting like an animal, he looked down again, jamming the metal prongs of the stun gun in below Tom's ear, but not activating it.

'I *don't* get to decide who lives and who dies,' he hissed, taut with anger. For a moment, there was something wild in his dark eyes, then he seemed to get control of himself once more. His expression slackened, and he leaned back slightly. 'I *warned* you that you needed to keep it together, remember? *Remember?*'

Gasping for breath, Tom could only blink helplessly. Was J going to kill him?

But the older man shook his head in disgust.

'I'm disappointed in you, Tom, I truly am. I thought we were past all this, I thought you understood. All that bleeding-heart sympathy for people you know nothing about... for shitty, hate-filled people, evil people who try wrapping up their poison in a veneer of social fucking justice, just so they can validate their wickedness... I may be a killer, but at least I'm *honest* about what I am.' He got slowly to his feet, gazing down for a moment longer, then glanced towards Hannah who sat cowering on the bed. 'I warned him...'

He broke off as she began to sob and turned his attention back to Tom.

'We had an agreement,' he growled. 'And you're going to honor it.'

Tom lay powerless, his body simultaneously numb and aching.

'If it makes you feel any better, there's only one more,' J told him. 'One name left on the list. After that, you can go and do whatever you want, express your righteous anger, feel sympathy for whoever you like, put it all in your damned book... but until then, you do as I fucking say, okay?'

Tom stared at him.

J gave a reluctant sigh, then bent over, offering his hand. Breathing hard, Tom managed to turn his head away, shunning him.

J shrugged and straightened up.

'Help him up as soon as he's ready,' he told Hannah. 'And don't let him piss on the damn carpet.'

47

'Are you all right?'

Hannah was bending over him, her voice an anxious whisper.

Tom blinked up at her then tried to raise his head, but shooting pains and a surge of nausea forced him to slump back down onto the carpet.

'Jeez,' he gasped, laying still until the waves of discomfort eased. 'Still think he's my friend?'

Hannah looked stung.

'I'm sorry,' she murmured.

'Forget about it,' Tom groaned. He felt a deep, aching exhaustion throughout his body, and his limbs were heavy like lead.

'Do you think you can get up?' Hannah asked.

Tom took a slow, cautious breath.

'I suppose so...' He tried to sit up carefully, groaning with the effort, gritting his teeth as each muscle tensed and hurt.

Hannah reached out instinctively, putting her hand on his shoulder to steady him.

'Take it slowly,' she urged. 'Let me help you.'

She stooped down, half-supporting, half-lifting, as Tom got to his knees, then struggled to stand.

'Here, sit on the bed.'

She guided him over and Tom sank down heavily on the edge of the mattress, gasping as another flash of pain burned through him. He sat there for a moment, breathing through the worst of it, trying to shut out the sensory overload of discomfort, then reached up and gingerly touched the back of his scalp.

'What is it?' Hannah watched him with concern. 'Did you hurt your head?'

Tom felt around with his fingers then winced as the motion of his arm triggered a burst of agony in his chest.

'Just bruising, I think,' he grunted. 'I'll be okay... it's my ribs that really hurt.'

His eyes flickered around the room and back to Hannah.

'Where's J?' he whispered.

'In the bathroom,' she replied. 'What are we going to do?'

She turned her head and gave a meaningful nod towards the door that led out to the parking lot.

'What do you mean?' Tom hissed.

Hannah stared at him.

'He *electrocuted* you!'

Tom grimaced.

'I know, but–'

'He could have killed you,' she continued. 'You're lucky you didn't die!'

Tom frowned.

Something *had* happened. There had been a moment, when all the light in J's eyes had gone out, and he'd thought that maybe this was it... but he was still here. And Zak was still okay.

'It doesn't change anything.'

'What?' Hannah shook her head. 'How can you *say* that?'

'We're alive,' Tom replied in a low voice. 'That's all that matters.'

'But what if...'

Hannah broke off as they heard the snap of the bathroom door unlocking.

J emerged, pausing in the doorway to look at them.

'Don't stop your conversation on my account,' he said, stepping into the room. He appeared calm and controlled again, but Tom still flinched a little as he approached.

J sighed and slowed, holding up his hands to show that both were empty.

'Take it easy,' he said, glancing towards the other bed. 'I'm just going over there.'

Too weary for anything more, Tom acknowledged him with a nod. He shifted his weight slightly, trying to relax, but the pain in his side flared up and made him catch his breath.

J turned and gave Tom a speculative look.

'Ribs bothering you again?' he asked.

Tom grimaced, trying to find a more comfortable position.

'It's like it was before, after the accident...'

J nodded to himself, then sighed.

'Yeah, sorry about that.' Sitting on the bed, he bent over and lifted his bag up onto the mattress. Opening it, he rummaged around and took out one of the plastic medicine bottles. 'Want me to go and get you some ice for it?'

Tom shook his head, remembering the aching cold that involved.

'No,' he murmured. 'Not ice.'

'Okay.' J turned his gaze to Hannah and tossed the bottle of pills to her. 'Give him two of those. And a glass of water to help him swallow them.'

Hannah turned the bottle in her hands, noting the missing label. She looked questioningly at Tom, who nodded.

'It's all right,' he told her. 'They're just painkillers.'

Seemingly satisfied, Hannah padded through to the bathroom. She returned a moment later with water.

'Here you go...'

She stood over him as he swallowed the pills and washed them down.

J rubbed his jaw thoughtfully.

'Maybe you should take that bed tonight, Tom,' he mused, then glanced at Hannah. 'You don't mind sleeping on the couch, just this one time?'

'No.' She shook her head quickly. 'I don't mind.'

'Good.' J looked at Tom again. 'See if you can find a position where you can relax those muscles. And remember what I said about not breathing shallow.'

Tom lifted his head.

Remember what I said...

'You said there's only one name left on the list.'

J held his gaze for a moment, then turned away, arranging the pillows and reaching over to find the bedside light switch.

'We'll talk in the morning,' he said abruptly.

48

Tom's Journal

He's killed again. Another senseless murder. Another death that could have been prevented... that should have been prevented.

My hands are shaking as I write this. The guilt I'm feeling right now, the sickening, overwhelming guilt... it's unbearable. Three people have died since I held that gun and pointed it at him. Four, if you include the driver of the car that hit us. Real people, with real lives stretching out into the future, abruptly cut down in a few moments of violence.

And I could have saved them, if I'd just pulled that trigger when I had the chance.

But I couldn't do it. I couldn't risk anything happening to my little boy. Zak's safe for now, and Kendra. Hannah too, I suppose.

Three lives saved, at the cost of three brutal murders. Perhaps J isn't the one playing God, deciding who lives and who dies... perhaps it's me.

Hannah's asleep now. I can hear her breathing, slow and calm, after all the desperation of earlier. The way she cried out when J hit me with that stun gun... I think she's finally beginning to understand that I'm a prisoner, just like her, that I never wanted any of this, that I really had no choice. I'm glad I stopped J from shooting her.

But that doesn't make me feel any better about the people who're dead. My hands are still shaking, with the aching in my muscles from the stun gun, and the aching guilt I feel inside. I can't write any more tonight.

49

Tom had a restless night, his sleep disturbed by strange dreams. He woke with a jolt, unable to remember what had unsettled him, feeling confused and groggy. There was a dull ache in his side. A burning ray of sun glared down on the empty bed across from him, and he lay still for a time, listening, hearing nothing.

He frowned and lifted his head slightly. There was discarded bedding on the couch, but no sign of Hannah.

He was alone.

A flutter of panic shook the sleep from him and he tried to sit up, but moving quickly sent his ribs into spasm and the sharp pain made him gasp. He held himself still, bracing his weight against the mattress, until the discomfort lessened.

Where were they? Had something happened?

Cautiously, he eased himself up into a sitting position, eyes sweeping the room. All the bags were still here... J's jacket was draped over the back of a chair, and Hannah's hoodie was on the couch...

Tom stopped, turning his head towards the window. There were voices outside, an indistinct conversation in the parking lot. He strained to hear. Was that J's voice?

Holding his side with one hand, Tom rose carefully to his feet and shuffled across the carpet. Pulling back one corner of the drapes, he peered outside, squinting against the dazzling light.

J was standing beside their car, speaking quietly to Hannah. Tom couldn't quite make out what they were saying, but the older man appeared to be in a good mood, gesturing with his hands, a faint smile on his face. Sunlight glinted off the metal of the gun, tucked into the back of his jeans. Hannah had her back to the motel, but her body language seemed reasonably relaxed... considering the circumstances.

Tom wondered what they were talking about, whether J knew that she had tried to run the night before, and whether it would change anything if he did...

As though alerted by some sixth sense, J turned slightly and spotted him at the window. The older man held up a cardboard cup-holder with three tall coffees, and beckoned him outside.

Tom opened the door and walked over to them. The sun touched him with a soothing warmth as J took one of the cups and offered it to him.

'Good morning.'

'Thanks.' Tom accepted the coffee. 'What are you doing out here?'

'You seemed kinda wasted,' J replied with a smile. 'Didn't seem any point in waking you too early.'

Tom yawned and raised his free hand to shield his eyes against the light. The movement sent a twinge through his side, but at least he could breathe without any stabbing pains.

'What time is it?'

'Almost eight thirty,' J told him. 'And we have things we need to get done today.'

Tom took a sip of his coffee, trying to focus, remembering the events of last night.

'You said we'd talk today.'

J looked at him for a moment, then nodded.

'I did.' He turned away, staring out across the parking lot to the hazy city skyline. 'Let's get out of Tulsa first. Once we're on the road, then we'll talk.'

He glanced back at Tom. 'But we have a stop to make first.'

J drove cautiously, losing them on the anonymity of the freeway, disappearing into the steady stream of cars that rumbled along below the wide, open sky. His eyes flickered often to the rear-view mirror during that short journey, particularly when they took the exit ramp.

He was still worried about being followed, Tom realized.

After a long pause at an intersection, J swung around onto a small bumpy road that sloped down to run parallel to the freeway, separated from the flowing traffic by a rough grassy embankment and a wire-mesh fence. A moment later they slowed, and Tom saw an entrance on the right, with a little sign on a tall pole that read *OK Storage*. Beyond the security gate, he could make out a line of garage-size units with red roller-shutter doors. His mind went back to the storage unit in Annapolis.

'We're changing cars again?' he asked.

'We sure are.'

'You've got another one waiting here?'

'I have.'

Tom stared out through the windshield, thinking about the preparation that had gone into this journey.

'You've got quite a few vehicles stashed away,' he noted.

'A few,' J shrugged.

'How long did it take to plan all this, to set everything up?'

'Months,' J admitted. 'There's been so much to think about, so much to get ready...'

Tom shook his head as he considered the kind of determination – the kind of *anger* – required to go through with something like this. And what about money? J must have ploughed thousands and thousands into the transport alone... the van, three different cars plus their current SUV, although the SUV was a rental.

'The cars, the accommodation,' he mused. 'How much has it cost you?'

J pulled up at the security gate, then turned to give him a disappointed look.

'Trust me, Tom, some things cost you a lot more than money.'

Tom scowled and turned away. It was a valid question. They'd been driving this same car for a while now – since Beckley, when they got rid of the wrecked Ford – and in that time it had been involved in a murder and a kidnapping...

He stiffened.

...or was it now *two* murders and a kidnapping? He'd know soon enough, once J told him the truth about what happened last night. They might have dealt with the witness to the killing at the bail bonds office, but now there was a new crime to get away with. No wonder J was keen to switch vehicles.

Once past the main gate, J drove round to a unit at the back of the lot and stopped the engine. At his request, they all put on baseball caps before they got out, and kept their heads down. Hannah didn't question the instructions, and began unloading their bags while J walked over to unlock the unit, hauling up the shutter to reveal a blue Kia sedan waiting within.

Tom stood off to one side, feeling slightly useless as he watched the others. His ribs weren't hurting so badly just now, but J seemed concerned enough to spare him from any tasks that might strain his injury.

Hannah came over and stood beside him, as J reversed the Kia out into the daylight.

'Swapping cars to avoid the cops,' she said, quietly. 'He's pretty careful about this stuff, huh?'

'You have no idea,' Tom replied.

Hannah nodded thoughtfully.

'They aren't gonna catch him, are they.'

It was a statement, rather than a question. Before Tom could respond, J was climbing out of the Kia and beckoning Hannah over. He had another of the camouflage-patterned trail cameras in his hand.

'Dump the bags in the trunk,' he told her. 'I'll just be a minute, then we can get out of here.'

Once he'd nosed the Toyota into the empty unit and paused to fix the camera inside the doorway, he rolled down the red shutter and locked it. Walking over to the Kia, he looked earnestly at Tom.

'Sorry,' he said. 'But I've never been motivated by money.'

Something in his tone caught Tom's attention. Was this a sensitive subject for J?

'So, what *are* you motivated by?' he asked.

J paused as he was about to get into the car.

'That's a good question.'

'Revenge?'

'Perhaps,' J mused. 'It's tough to say where consequence ends and vengeance begins, but I guess I crossed that line at some point.'

Tom stared at him.

'And you crossed it again last night.'

J sighed and got into the car.

The Kia smelled faintly of cleaning products and air freshener. J seemed more relaxed as he pulled onto the interstate, calmly moving over to the left-hand lane and accelerating through the traffic. It wasn't long before they had left the city behind, heading west.

Tom gazed out at the endless blur of orange cones, where work was being done on the central reservation.

'So... last night. You said we'd talk once we were on the road?'

J didn't respond at first. 'That's right,' he said eventually. 'I did.'

'Last night, when you were gone all that time...' Tom hesitated, choosing his words. 'I assume that was another –' He wanted to say *murder*, but sensed that J wouldn't see it that way. 'Another execution?'

'Right again.'

A faint smile touched J's lips, and he glanced up to catch Hannah's expression in the rear-view mirror.

'See? Tom's a true journalist, naturally curious,' he told her. 'Now, you don't mind if we talk about work for a little bit, do you? I *did* kinda promise him.'

Hannah shrank back into her seat, eyes wide. She shook her head slightly and said nothing.

J's attention returned to the road.

'His name was Ryan Court,' he said, softly. 'He was 27, and he was a research geologist.'

'A what?'

'One of those people that work for the oil companies.' J shrugged. 'There's a lot of that down here, with the Oklahoma oil fields and all.'

'What did you do to him?'

'Oh, I think you know *what* I did to him,' J mused. 'I assume you're asking *how* I did it?'

Tom rolled his eyes.

'Fine,' he said. '*How* did you do it? What happened?'

J eased back in his seat, making himself comfortable.

'Well, after I left you, I figured I'd drive over to his place. It's not that far – maybe fifteen minutes – though I was lucky I didn't go up by the casino or I might have been caught in that traffic grid-lock.' He shook his head. 'Anyway, I got there in plenty of time. He had one of those townhouse apartments – nice place, actually, and good parking. I found a spot with a clear view of his door and I settled in to wait for him. Now this guy's *usually* home around eight... but of course, last night he was late for some reason.'

'How did you know what time he gets home?' Tom asked. 'Have you met him before? Or followed him?'

'I never met him before last night.'

'Then I don't get it.' Tom frowned. 'How come you know so much about his habits?'

J chuckled softly to himself.

'You'd be surprised how careless some people are about their privacy,' he said. 'In this case it was real easy; Mr Court liked to include his location when he posted on social media.'

There it was: social media again. Tom's thoughts quickened at the thought of a connection. Had Ryan Court posted something that J didn't like?

'I knew he was usually home by eight because he usually posted from there around that time,' J continued. 'But last night? I don't know... maybe he was working late, maybe he stopped for something to eat. Anyway, the stupid sonofabitch kept me waiting for almost half an hour.'

'So... what, you just sat in the car that whole time?'

'Yeah.'

'Wasn't that kind of risky? I mean, what if someone saw you?'

'I was thinking the exact same thing, sitting there,' J muttered. 'Hell, I was just about to cut bait and leave when he finally showed up.'

Tom glanced across at the older man, who was still staring calmly out at the road.

'So how did you kill him?' he asked.

J pursed his lips slightly. 'I deprived him of oxygen,' he said, as though it was no big deal. 'I waited in the car until he'd gone into his apartment, then I went and rang his bell straightaway, before he had a chance to get settled. It's always best if you can catch people off balance, and interrupting someone just as they're getting home is an effective way to do that... as *you* know from experience.' He smiled to himself, then continued. 'Anyway, I rang the bell, and he answered the door. Then I hit him with the stun gun and pushed him inside.'

Tom swallowed hard. 'Just like that?'

'Well, no. When he opened the door, I gave him some B.S. about how I had a delivery for him,' J explained. 'I handed over a big padded envelope for him to hold, and as he took it, *that's* when I stunned him.'

Tom shuddered, recalling the helpless agony of electricity jolting through his body.

'He went down, and I zapped him again, just here...' J lifted a hand from the wheel and tapped two fingers just below his ear, '...until he was too dazed to cry out or defend himself. Then I put a very *specific* plastic bag over his head, taped it nice and tight around his throat, and sat with him until he was finished struggling.'

In the back seat, Hannah had clapped her hands over her mouth, clearly appalled.

Tom turned away, shutting his eyes briefly as he tried not to imagine the horror of being suffocated, of the warm wet breath condensing on the smothering plastic that clung to your face...

He shook his head, forcing the image away.

'Now you see why I didn't bring you along,' J said, quietly. 'The reality of these moments can be... well, it can be challenging.'

Tom took a deep breath, resting his head against the cool glass of the window as he tried to gather his thoughts. He gazed out across the gently rolling landscape towards the bright horizon, then frowned. 'What did you mean, when you said it was a *specific* plastic bag?'

J paused.

'Oh, that.' He took a breath and sighed. 'It was a plastic bag from an adult store, a *gay* adult store. Pink, with a big black logo.'

'So this Ryan Court was gay?' Tom asked.

J shook his head.

'I don't think so, no. But that's not the point. *Now* the death will have to be treated as a hate crime...' He trailed off, and something in his expression changed. 'People stop thinking rationally when they deal with emotive issues... they just grab at any idea that supports their view of the world, then persecute anyone who dares to question it.' He gave a bleak little laugh. 'Anyway, this ought to ensure that there's pressure on the police to waste their time looking in all the wrong places.'

Tom stared at the older man with disgust. This was more than just a brutal, pointless killing. It was cynical. It was evil. His revulsion came bubbling up as sudden, uncontrollable anger. How could he hold back – *why* should he hold back – when this monster had put him through so much?

'You sick bastard,' he snarled. 'All this... *all this*, just because someone posted something mean about you online.'

J looked at him.

'No.'

'Oh, I'm *sorry*,' Tom said in a mocking tone. 'Because some accusations went viral on social media. Boo hoo.'

All the life drained out of J's eyes.

'No,' he growled.

'Then why?' Tom pressed.

'Because of what they cost me,' J snapped. 'Because of what I lost.'

Tom shook his head.

'So you lost your job... so it cost you some money...' he said. 'So what?'

J's knuckles whitened on the steering wheel.

'After all the time we've spent together,' he hissed. 'After what I told you earlier... do you really think I give a damn about *money*? Or some stupid *job*?'

'Then for fuck's sake, why?' Tom demanded. 'What did you lose that was so fucking important?'

'*My wife*!' J screamed, and there was a dreadful anguish in his voice. Breathing hard, he glared at Tom for a moment, then turned his eyes back to the road ahead, speaking softly now. 'I lost my *wife*.'

50

There was a sudden silence following J's outburst, like the startled hush after something shatters on a restaurant floor. Tom sat absolutely still, shocked to have found such raw suffering in someone who had always seemed so careful, so confident.

Or was this, finally, the *real* J? Was this Joseph Sherman?

Slowly he became aware of the road noise again, the steady bumping rhythm of the wheels on the concrete sections as they crossed a long, sweeping bridge. J was staring straight ahead once more, pretending to focus on the freeway, but Tom could see the restless energy in him, the need to talk.

'Tell me,' he said.

J glanced over at him. There was something different in those dark eyes, something hesitant and vulnerable. Instinctively, Tom knew that this was the moment to press, and with that knowledge came a name, summoned from their unfinished conversation at the cabin.

'Robyn,' he said quietly. 'Tell me about Robyn.'

J stiffened slightly, then looked back to the road. For a time, he said nothing. Then, his shoulders sagged and he seemed to become smaller, older.

'It wasn't my fault,' he murmured. 'None of this was my fault.'

Tom nodded, wanting to encourage him, but determined not to say the wrong thing. He forced himself to remain quiet, leaving a gap and waiting for J to fill it. Eventually, the older man spoke again.

'Some folk... they set themselves up for trouble, y'know? They do things they shouldn't, or take stupid risks... they *invite* that trouble, so it's no big surprise when it finally comes for them. But then there's other people, people who keep their heads down, who avoid trouble, who try to play it fair...' He gave a bitter little laugh. 'But life isn't fair. And when trouble hits people like that, it can hit them *hard*, because they're not ready for it, they're not expecting it. I mean, why *should* they expect it?'

He flexed his fingers, gripping the top of the steering wheel, then cleared his throat.

'You know I was in the insurance business for nearly 14 years? I put in the hours and worked my way up... made it to claims investigator. That's not an easy job, but I was diligent, and I guess it kind of suited me. I always tried to be fair – I didn't help the company to screw over any honest folk, but I didn't let grifters take advantage and defraud the company either. Maybe it wasn't the greatest job in the world, but it was steady, and the money was okay. Those things are important when you have a family – you understand that, right?'

He glanced over at Tom, who nodded slowly.

'I had a wife and a kid,' J explained. 'And the best thing about the job was it allowed me to support them. That's why I stuck at it for all those years. I had to travel a lot, going from one place to the next, interviewing people where there was some question or discrepancy on their claim. I didn't like being away from Robyn so much, but I got to set my own schedule so I could always make it back home, at least for weekends. We had a house in Fort Smith, and she was working for a tax firm there in the middle of town, while Juliette was studying at UAFS. We had a lot of good times there, lots of happy memories...'

J stared out through the windshield, a distant look in his eyes.

'So that was me. Avoiding trouble. Keeping my head down and playing it fair. And that was when it happened.' He frowned slightly. 'I had a case on my worksheet, a woman whose house was burned out in a fire. Now, usually those kinds of cases don't get passed to me unless there's some sort of red flag on the claim, some irregularity or something that looks... wrong. So I went over the paperwork, and there were a couple of problems.'

There was a different note in J's voice, as though he was talking to a work colleague.

'First of all, this was quite a new policy – less than three months old when the place burned down – and that's usually worth checking into. But the real issue was the report from the fire department; they weren't happy about the way the fire started. Now, they didn't come right out and *say* it was deliberate, but when I read through the notes... well, they were *very* clear that they wouldn't rule that out.' He allowed himself a grim smile. 'So the insurance company had these two issues, and it was my job to figure out whether the claim was legitimate, or whether someone had just torched the place for a quick pay-out. I made some calls and spoke to a bunch of different people, but eventually I had to go down to Texas and see the woman who filed the claim.'

J broke off, his jaw tightening as he glared out at the traffic around them.

'Her name was Kaitlyn Brance,' he muttered. 'She was a real estate agent – 36 years old, divorced, no children.'

Tom stiffened in his seat.

Was. Past tense. Another victim.

'So I head down there,' J continued. 'And right from the start, she's acting real edgy, real nervous. Most folk, when I go to see them, they're impatient. They want their claim dealt with right now and they're pissed at me because they've lost their house or whatever, and it's a big deal. They want to know what I'm doing to get them fixed up and why it's all taking so damn long. But when someone *doesn't* want to talk to you, when they *don't* ask many questions because they just want to get rid of you? Well, that always makes you wonder if they've got something to hide. And this Kaitlyn, she was like that. I went and saw her at the motel she was staying in, and she didn't seem pleased, or relieved that the insurance company were finally doing something. We spoke for a while, and the more questions I asked her, the more her story began to fall apart. I think she realized that she was in trouble, because she suddenly switched from being evasive to being downright hostile. When I pointed out the discrepancies in what she'd told me, she started denying she'd said any of it, even though the words had just come out of her mouth. She accused *me* of lying, of falsifying things for the insurance company so they wouldn't have to pay her the money she was "entitled to".'

J shook his head slowly.

'When she started getting angry, I figured there wasn't much point in me staying. It was pretty clear that she was hiding something about how the fire started, and she knew that I was onto her. I thanked her for her time and got up to leave, and that's when she changed on me again. She went from being angry to smiling and apologetic, like *that*.'

He snapped his fingers, making Hannah jump in the back seat.

'It was the damnedest thing. One minute she's calling me every name under the sun, the next she's all sugar and spice.

She followed me to the door, put her hand on my arm, told me that there had obviously been "some sort of misunderstanding". She was being *real* friendly now, making it very clear that she wanted my report to be a favorable one. I pulled away from her and told her no thanks – I mean, Robyn and me, we had a good thing going, and I wasn't gonna do anything to jeopardize that.'

His shoulders dropped slightly, and he sighed.

'That was a mistake. Kaitlyn changed again, started shouting and screaming at me. Told me to get the hell out of there, told me I was gonna be sorry. But I didn't believe her. And that was a mistake too, but not as big a one as meeting her alone in her motel room.'

J fell silent for a time. He seemed to be just gazing out at the road, driving on autopilot, but his dark eyes were alert and watchful. After a while, he spoke again.

'Six weeks later, I got summoned to the regional office. I was working on another case file, and I'd forgotten all about Kaitlyn Brance... but she hadn't forgotten about me. My manager was there, along with a whole team of people from human resources, people I'd never seen before, all looking at me like I was carrying an infectious disease. It was like getting called into the principal's office and finding your parents there – you know you're in trouble, but you don't know why. They asked me a bunch of questions that I didn't understand, then told me that they were suspending me pending an internal investigation. Nobody mentioned Kaitlyn Brance, nobody told me what it was about, and I was escorted out of the building by security. I went home to Robyn without knowing what I was supposed to have done.'

He shook his head again. 'But by the time I got home, social media was doing its thing and the whole story had taken on a life of its own. In the beginning, a few friends saw stuff and contacted me, assuming it was a mistake, wondering what the hell was going on, but pretty soon all of our friends went quiet. And I finally understood that it didn't matter that I was innocent... what *mattered* was that people who didn't know me were telling other people that I was a monster, that I was someone who blackmailed a vulnerable woman for sex.'

There was frustration in his voice now, a deep, smoldering anger that had burned for a long time.

'When the police showed up the first time, I wasn't worried. I figured they were just doing their job, following up on a complaint to see if there was any truth to it. I told them all about my meeting with Kaitlyn, about what she'd said and the discrepancies in her claim. I thought they'd go back and check things out with the company, realize why Kaitlyn was lying, and I'd be in the clear. I didn't know that the company had already decided to fast-track her claim and pay her off. The online campaigns against them had pushed them into full-on damage-limitation mode, and I'd become a *liability*.' He snorted as he said the word. 'A few days later, I got fired. Two lawyers from Bluestone Group showed up at my home and told me that I had violated the conditions of my employment by bringing the company's name into disrepute. They gave me a choice – take a small payoff and disappear quietly, or they'd go legal on me and take me for everything I had. I couldn't afford to lose our house, so I signed the papers they gave me and took the cheque.'

Tom sat quietly, listening to the unfolding story, committing the details to memory. So far, it seemed to tie in with the things he'd read during his brief time online at the camp site. But now J was speaking again.

'I think Robyn still believed in me, up until then, but something changed after that. Maybe it was all the accusations and hatred on social media, maybe the way our friends and neighbors turned their backs on us, maybe because things got so difficult for her at work... she started looking at me differently.

But it was when the police came back and took me in for questioning... *that* was when it happened.'

J paused, eyelids briefly closing as he took a deep breath, like someone steeling themselves for a blow.

'Robyn left me,' he said, quietly. 'I don't know if she just needed some space to think, or if she was going for good... and I don't blame her, either way. It was harder on her than on anyone, and she'd done *nothing* wrong. Anyway, she packed up her things and left, while I was away being questioned by the police.'

He winced, as though struggling with the memory, then took another breath to compose himself.

'I remember when the detective who had been interviewing me came back into the room. She was Hispanic, in her thirties – very intelligent, very professional – and I was glad to have someone like her on the case because I figured she'd be thorough enough to get to the truth. But when she came back and looked at me, her whole expression was different, and I knew that something was wrong. She sat down and told me that there had been an accident, a traffic accident, and that she was really sorry. An officer drove me to the hospital but by the time I got there...'

He broke off, shaking with grief.

Tom gasped as it finally dawned on him what had happened. This wasn't some petty vendetta over a minor grievance.

'Robyn died while you were still in custody,' he said softly.

'She died before the truth came out, before the police cleared me. She died thinking I must be some kind of... pervert.' J slowly lifted his head and sat up straight, snarling as his eyes flashed with tears. 'She'd still be alive if it wasn't for all those social media *scum*, those self-righteous vigilantes who turned everyone against us, and drove my daughter away, and pressured the police to bring me in... she'd know it was all a lie. She'd be here today, and she'd *know*.'

Tom leaned back against the passenger door, recoiling from the suppressed fury that crackled in the older man's voice, from the raging pain, and from his own sudden, awful understanding.

This was the context that J had spoken about. This was *why*.

51

Nobody had spoken for miles. A funereal hush had descended on the car after J's revelation, causing each of them to retreat into themselves, with nothing but the constant rumble of the tires on the road for accompaniment.

They were heading south now, cruising steadily through the shifting flow of vehicles that followed the highway across the vast open farmlands of Oklahoma. Set against a never-ending backdrop of flat green fields, the occasional passing buildings could almost be mistaken for barns. A warehouse, an auto dealership, even a small casino; out here, everything had an agricultural feel to it.

One hand resting on the wheel, J glanced over at Tom, then turned his gaze back to the road.

'I'm sorry, okay?' he murmured.

Tom looked up, surprised.

'That was a lot to lay on you in one go. But you wanted the truth and... well, maybe now you have a better sense of what happened, what they took from me.'

Tom considered this, then nodded. It was hard to imagine

such terrible loss. But did the older man honestly believe that justified such an appalling spree of violence?

'I'm sorry too. Really. It's just...' He paused, unsure of the reaction his question might provoke. 'Do you think that makes this – right?'

'Of course not,' J said, firmly. 'There's *no* excuse for what I'm doing.' He broke off for a moment, then sighed. 'But how can I just accept it and move on? If it was Zak, would *you* do nothing? *Could* you do nothing?'

Tom hesitated, recalling that moment in the back of the van when he'd held the gun in his hand, remembering how ready he'd been to pull the trigger, how *eager*. He lowered his eyes, unsure how to reply.

'Everyone's a good citizen,' J said. 'Until it happens to them.'

Tom frowned, not wanting to embrace this logic.

'But *killing* people...' He shook his head unhappily. 'It won't bring her back. It won't *solve* anything.'

'Exactly!' J nodded. 'And that's the terrible thing that I've come to realize: it's just not *enough*. For the guilty, they get a brief moment of panic and then it's all over – while our suffering continues?' His face became grim. 'No, that's not justice.'

'Then what *is*?'

Very slowly, a cold smile spread across the older man's face. For some reason, it was the most terrifying expression Tom had ever seen.

Small towns came and went, until the sun climbed high and morning was gone. The landscape they were passing through became steadily less remote and more built-up. After a while, J stifled a yawn and moved the car across to the right, pulling off the highway and following signs to a gas station and restaurants. They parked outside an IHOP, where J killed the engine then twisted round in his seat to address them both.

'Now, I'd rather we all sat down and ate like civilized folks, but I'll get an order to go if I have to...' He paused, staring at each of them in turn. 'Can I trust you to behave yourselves?'

'Oh come on,' Tom muttered wearily. 'I'm not going to try anything, you *know* that.'

Hannah's large eyes flickered up to meet J's, then she looked away and nodded.

'Good,' J said, unfastening his seat belt and letting them see his gun. 'We've made it this far together. It'd be a real shame to have a tragedy, especially when we're so close to the end of the journey.'

He opened the door and climbed out.

The restaurant was quiet inside, with the murmured conversations of a handful of families and single diners. A tempting savory-sweet aroma hung in the air. J assessed the layout of the place with a practiced glance, then directed them over to a booth by the window, several tables away from anyone else.

A waitress brought them coffee and took their order. Once she had gone, J settled back in his seat and regarded Hannah thoughtfully.

'Are you doing okay?' he asked. 'You look kind of... anxious.'

Hannah's expression became sullen.

'Of *course* I'm anxious,' she muttered. 'What d'you expect?'

'I'm sorry you got mixed up in all of this,' J sighed. 'No, really. I wish things had gone differently.'

Hannah met his gaze. 'So do I.'

J gave her a wry smile. 'That's fair,' he said, leaning to one side while he drew one of the burner phones from his pocket and set it face down on the table. 'Now, I'm curious; you're from Alabama but you say you were headed for... Evansville, was it?'

Hannah nodded.

'So what's the story there?' J asked. 'Did you have a job waiting for you in Evansville?'

Hannah lifted a sugar sachet from the table and began to fold its edges over.

'Not exactly.'

'Not exactly?'

'Okay, no!' she snapped. 'I didn't have a job.'

Undeterred, J continued to study her. 'What were you gonna do when you got there?'

Hannah turned her head and looked out of the window. 'I don't know,' she said, slowly. 'Start over, I guess.'

J watched her fingers absently creasing and smoothing the sugar sachet.

'It wouldn't have been easier just to go back home to Alabama?' he asked.

Hannah stiffened, then quickly shook her head. Tom caught a hunted look in her eyes. J obviously saw it too, for his own expression softened and he held up his hands.

'Just making conversation,' he said, and there was a note of sympathy in his voice. 'So. Anywhere but Alabama, huh? Maybe you should talk to Tom here. He's running away from *England*.'

Before long, the food arrived, and they lapsed into their own private thoughts as they ate. Tom gazed out across the parking lot, reflecting on the events of the morning. He found that he was less fearful now, almost *calm,* in spite of everything that had happened. J was certainly a brutal killer, but not a mindless one, and his brutality didn't appear to be aimed at Tom. Or Hannah.

Outside, a silver Ford Taurus crept into view, slowing before turning left into the nearby gas station. Tom stared at it, suddenly recalling the crash in West Virginia, the dreadful jarring impact and the burning smell from the airbags. His hand went to his side, lightly touching his ribs, as he remembered how J had reacted, how much it all seemed to have affected him. At the time, he'd assumed it was just the older man's frustration at not being in control, or some primal fear of being caught… but what if it was something else?

What if it was distress at the loss of an innocent life?

After they had eaten, J leaned back in his seat and stretched.

'That was good,' he said, swinging his knees out from under the table, then glancing at his empty coffee cup. 'I'll be back in a minute. If the waitress comes by, ask her to fill me up, would you?'

He got slowly to his feet and walked away in the direction of the restrooms. Hannah's eyes followed him until he disappeared from view.

'What do you think he means, about reaching the end of the journey?' she asked in a low voice.

Her question caught Tom off guard.

'Where's he taking us?' she continued. 'And what's going to happen when we get there?'

'I don't know where he's taking us,' Tom replied. 'But I think getting to the end of the journey really means getting to the end of his list.'

It was Hannah's turn to look puzzled. 'His list?'

'The list of…' Tom hesitated, then sighed. There was no gentle way of saying it. 'The list of people he's going to kill.'

Hannah stared at him in disbelief. 'You've *seen* this list?'

'Not exactly,' Tom said. 'He has a journal. I only got a quick look at it, but it has names and details for the people who he's been targeting.'

Hannah thought for a moment, then her eyes widened in fear.

'What if *our* names are on that list?' she whispered.

Tom shook his head.

'I don't think he wants to hurt us.' He paused, and once again his mind returned to the car crash, how upset J had been that the other driver died. 'I'm not sure he wants to hurt anyone really... except the people who hurt *him*, the people he blames for what happened to him.'

Hannah reached out a small hand, absently turning one of the syrup jugs.

'Did you buy all that stuff he was saying before?' she murmured. 'About the way he lost his wife? The accusations?'

Tom's mind went back to those moments at the campsite, skimming online articles and tweets. What J had told them *did* seem to fit...

'I think so,' he said. 'Yes, it might actually make a weird sort of sense...'

He caught Hannah's eye and broke off.

'I'm not condoning what he's done,' he added quickly. 'Far from it. But if something like that happens to someone... well, who knows what it might do to them, how they might react?'

Hannah held his gaze, then her eyes flickered to something behind him.

'He's coming back,' she whispered.

J returned from the restrooms, walking swiftly. He was holding the burner phone in his hand and his expression was grim.

'We're leaving,' he hissed. 'Right now.'

Rummaging in his pocket, he drew out a few bills and placed them on the table.

'What's the matter?' Tom asked.

'I said *now!*' J growled. He ushered Hannah quickly out of her chair and hurried them both towards the exit.

'Has something happened?' Tom whispered.

J didn't meet his eye, just reached for the door and held it open.

'Yes,' he snarled.

They followed him as he strode across the parking lot, Hannah half-running to keep up.

'What's wrong?' Tom demanded, but J just glared and pointed at the car.

'Get in,' he snapped. 'Quickly!'

A moment later, they were on the move, leaving the restaurant behind and pulling up at the junction. J gripped the wheel, as though he was about to turn left and return to the interstate, but then he hesitated, and went right instead.

He looked agitated, even worried, and it was clear that his mind was racing as he made a haphazard series of turns onto smaller roads, as though he was trying to avoid the town, avoid traffic, avoid *people.*

'You need to tell me what's going on,' Tom insisted.

J shot him a brief, troubled glance.

'Cops,' he growled.

Tom glanced over his shoulder.

'Back at the IHOP?'

J shook his head irritably.

'No. *Serious* cops. Cops who're looking for *us*.'

Seeing Tom's confusion, he scowled and reached into his jacket pocket. Drawing out the burner phone, he squinted down at it, then passed it over.

'The trail cam in Tulsa,' he explained. 'I just got an alert from it.'

Tom stared at the phone screen, where J had signed into an anonymous web portal. There were a series of grainy images: the interior of the storage unit, light spilling in as the shutters were rolled up, illuminating their SUV. The same view, fully illuminated, with a uniformed figure in the corner of the frame. Then several uniformed men, fanned out around the vehicle. They were all armed, alert, weapons drawn.

Serious cops.

'They're onto us,' J muttered to himself. 'I don't understand it. How the hell are they onto us?'

Tom tried to think. Had J been seen during his last murder?

'You told me you were parked outside...' He felt bad that he couldn't remember the Tulsa victim's name. '...the geologist guy's place for a long time. Maybe someone saw you, or got a look at the SUV?'

J considered this, then shook his head.

'No, I was careful...' He lifted his head suddenly, looking even more worried. 'And I had different license plates on the SUV while I was out last night. This doesn't make any sense at all.' His eyes flickered up to the rear-view mirror, then he swore under his breath.

Watching him, Tom felt a strange thrill of excitement. However it had happened, this turn of events had profoundly shaken his captor.... something he hadn't foreseen, hadn't planned for.

'What about the car in Annapolis?' Tom asked. 'Have they found that one too?'

'No.' J had a faraway look in his eyes for a moment, then his frown tightened. 'How the *hell* did they manage to pick up our trail between then and now? How much do they know?'

He shot another nervous glance at the rear-view mirror, as though he expected to see flashing lights behind them.

'Well then...' Tom sensed the older man's heightened tension and searched for something reassuring to say. 'If they haven't found the Annapolis storage unit, they can't know *that* much.'

J's face became bleak, his voice flat.

'You're missing the point,' he replied. 'If they've found the place in Tulsa, it won't be long before they have the license plate for *this* car.'

Tom swallowed hard. The police were much, *much* closer than he'd thought.

His excitement turned abruptly to dread as he remembered Zak, and what this might mean.

'What are you going to do?'

J gripped the steering wheel and stared straight ahead.

'We're done talking for now,' he growled. 'I need to think.'

52

J dropped the burner phone and stamped it into the cracked concrete with his heel. Grinding his weight down on it until it disintegrated, he kicked the pieces away, sending them skittering into the long grass. Tom watched him as he took a cigarette lighter from his pocket, and carefully held the phone's sim card over the flame.

They'd found a deserted country road on the outskirts of town and J had pulled over beside a line of bushes that partly sheltered their car but offered them good visibility in all directions.

J dropped the blackened sim card before it burned his fingers, scuffing it into the grass with his shoe, then drew out a bundle of credit cards from his pocket and began sorting through them.

'So?' Tom pressed him. 'What happens now?'

'Good question,' J said. He put down the cards, leaning wearily against the side of the car and staring off into the distance with unblinking eyes.

Tom watched him, sensing the uncertainty of the moment.

'Can't you just stop?' he asked, softly.

For a while, it appeared that J hadn't heard him. Then the older man's head turned, a questioning look on his face.

'Stop?'

'Just let us go and... I don't know... disappear,' Tom urged, then added, 'While you still can.'

J held his gaze, then gave the faintest of smiles.

'I've come all this way...' He paused, corrected himself. 'Sorry, *we've* come all this way. Together.' His eyes returned to the horizon. 'We can't stop now, so close to the end.'

Tom waited for him to say more, then bowed his head. It was no use. J was going to see this through, no matter what.

'All right,' he said with a sigh. 'So what are you going to do?'

J frowned.

'I'm not sure.'

Tom moved over to stand beside him.

'Maybe rent another car?' he suggested.

'Not a good idea,' J replied. 'The SUV was a rental, so they might expect me to do that again. For all we know, they could have sent our descriptions to every rental office in the state, or be checking transactions against dormant credit cards to try and find us... it's too risky.'

'Okay...' Tom thought for a moment. 'Can you change the plates on this car?'

'It's an option,' J conceded. 'But they may have figured out that I've been doing that too.' His expression darkened. 'Damn, this is impossible without knowing how much they know. How the hell did they pick up our trail?'

He lapsed into a brooding silence.

A noise behind them made Tom turn around. Hannah had emerged from the bushes, where she'd gone to relieve herself, and she was now picking her way through the grass back to the road. Her eyes were on J and she bit her lip, looking troubled. Tom wondered if she'd overheard their conversation, heard him refuse to walk away and let them go. Had he got her hopes up, only to knock them down again?

Presently, J turned on his heel and walked around to the back of the car. Opening the trunk, he dug out another phone from his bag and was soon bent over, peering intently at the screen.

Hannah paced restlessly, then wandered over to stand beside Tom.

'What's gonna happen to us now?' she whispered.

Tom shrugged. 'He'll think of something, I guess.'

Hannah shifted her weight from one foot to another, turning so that her back was towards J.

'How *did* the police pick up on that car?' she asked in a low voice.

'I don't know,' Tom replied, wondering if there could possibly be something that J hadn't considered. 'He's always so thorough, so careful about everything... it doesn't make sense.'

Hannah studied him for a moment. 'Well, somebody made a mistake somewhere,' she murmured.

They heard the sound of a bag being zipped shut. J closed the trunk and strode purposefully round from the back of the car, holding the police scanner.

'Okay,' he said, opening the driver's door. 'Saddle up, everyone.'

They got in.

J started the car but didn't drive away. Leaving the engine to idle, he glanced over at Tom, then twisted round in his seat and stared at Hannah.

'Would you mind laying down as flat as you can?' He motioned with his hand. 'That's right, just lay across the back seat for me...'

Hannah gave him a doubtful look, but did as he asked, rolling over and drawing her knees up to lie across the rear seats.

'Thank you,' J said. He faced forward again, taking the police scanner from between the seats and switching it on. 'If local law enforcement *are* searching for three people in a Kia, then let's not *look* like three people in a Kia.'

Tom frowned.

'Okay, but what are we going to do?' he asked.

J met his eye.

'Well, the way I see it, we've got ourselves a transportation problem... and I'm gonna solve it.' He found the earpiece and fitted it into his ear. 'Now, hush. I need to listen.'

They drove for ten minutes or so, taking a zigzag route that followed a series of small streets around the edge of the town. They passed a new housing development, looking lost and lonely in the empty landscape, then turned down a dusty road that led along the side of a fenced-off concrete processing yard. J listened closely to the police scanner, his gaze flickering to the rear-view mirror every now and again, but he seemed to be regaining his confidence again.

Before long, they were passing through the outskirts once more, cruising down a straight road dotted with small business units, most of them vacant. J took his foot off the gas as they approached a tiny used car lot, peering out at it thoughtfully as they coasted by. An assortment of different vehicles was lined up there, all of them older models, and a faded American flag drooped on a pole outside the office.

Apparently satisfied, he continued a half-mile further on, then swung the car around sharply to drive back the way they'd come. This time, he turned onto a side road just before the car lot, then pulled over after a short distance and killed the engine.

'I reckon this might be just what we need,' he said, reaching up and adjusting the rear-view mirror so that he could study the place.

Hannah stirred in the back seat.

'Can I get up now?' she asked.

'Sure,' J replied.

She rolled slowly into an upright position, pushing her hair back from her face and glancing out of the windows to see where they were.

Still watching the mirror, J's attention shifted slightly, and he smiled. Twisting around in his seat he gave Hannah a long, speculative look.

'What?' she demanded, her voice suddenly wary.

'I've got an idea,' J mused. 'You think you could keep it together if we took a walk over there? Just you and me?'

Hannah frowned. 'Keep it together?'

'Yeah, just be cool and act calm,' J replied. 'You know, like you were my daughter or something.'

'Sorry, I don't understand...' Hannah trailed off. 'What are you talking about?'

J flashed her a grin.

'Today's your lucky day,' he explained. 'Daddy's gonna buy you a car.'

Alone in the driver's seat, Tom peered at the dashboard clock, then leaned back and sighed. They'd only been gone for fifteen minutes – it would take time to choose a new vehicle and do the paperwork, and it wasn't the sort of thing you could rush, particularly if you wanted to avoid suspicion.

His thoughts drifted to the police raid on the storage unit in Tulsa. All those armed officers... and they'd found the place so quickly, just a few hours after J had ditched the SUV...

Leaning back against the headrest, he stared at the ceiling.

How *did* the police get onto them? J had been so careful, but there must have been a mistake somewhere along the line. They hadn't found the previous car, so whatever alerted them must have happened somewhere between Annapolis and Tulsa...

Tom bit nervously at his lip.

He hoped it wasn't Hannah. Of all the things that had happened on their trip, she was the single biggest unforeseen factor. J could never have imagined that there would be a third person joining their little road trip. Had her presence unsettled the older man, causing him to make a mistake? Or had she somehow found a way of selling them out, leaving a message for the police somewhere, maybe even scrawling down the license plate of their SUV? A license plate could have led the police to the storage unit in Tulsa.

Tom shut his eyes. He'd promised Hannah that she'd be okay, that he'd protect her – but how would J react if he discovered that she'd jeopardized his plans for revenge?

He thought back, trying to recall every time she'd been alone, all the ways that she might have betrayed them and tried to get help. A note hidden in a gas-station restroom, perhaps? Or had she done something when she bolted from their motel room?

Frowning, he tried to think of alternatives. Aside from Hannah, the only other wildcard on their trip was the car crash in West Virginia. He cast his mind back to all those desperate moments where J had been forced to improvise, to get them out of danger, to find another vehicle, to dispose of evidence...

What if the police had found the body they'd dumped in the lake? It didn't matter that the death had been an accident because that wasn't how it would look, not when the driver was found in the trunk of his own car. A discovery like that would certainly trigger a murder investigation, and a serious police response... but was there anything connecting it to J and himself? There had been no witnesses to the crash, and their disposal of the body had been considered and careful. Even if the police somehow traced the victim's Ford Taurus back to the motel in Beckley there wasn't anything to link it with the SUV they had rented. After all, J seemed to have an abundance of fake identities. He wouldn't have used the same one in both places.

No. It had to be Hannah.

Tom sighed. Somehow, she'd found a way to get a message the police. It was the only possibility that seemed to fit...

And then it dawned on him. The phone call to Samaira from the camp site.

He hesitated, then shook his head, dismissing the idea. The call was probably a mistake, but he hadn't given anything away.

No, surely it couldn't have been him. He'd been careful on that call, said nothing that would alert Samaira, given her no clue that anything was wrong.

It couldn't have been him. Even if the police *did* speak to her, she'd just tell them the truth – that he'd called and everything seemed normal. Why shouldn't he phone her and ask about his son? Even if they somehow managed to trace the call, that would only lead them to the camp site office. And even if the woman there remembered him, she wouldn't have the license plate of their SUV. A camp site like that wouldn't keep CCTV footage... would it?

Tom shifted in his seat, telling himself that it didn't stack up, even as the first chill of guilt uncoiled in his stomach.

Could it have been him?

He decided not to say anything, not to Hannah, and *definitely* not to J. Nobody else knew about the call, so what was the point in mentioning it? After all, there was no way to be sure that this was his fault.

He swallowed hard, and waited anxiously for the others to return, trying not to think about what would happen if his call led to J being caught.

53

It was an old, dark red Buick. The paintwork had faded from years in the sun, and there were several dents and scratches, but aside from that it looked to be in reasonable condition for its age. Tom watched as it pulled up behind him, and saw the other two getting out. Hannah seemed a little subdued as she emerged from the driver's side, but J looked pleased, striding forward, and gesturing for Tom to roll his window down.

'Nicely inconspicuous,' he said turning around to look at their new transport. 'And it wasn't even that expensive.'

Tom nodded in agreement. The older man had a knack for finding vehicles that didn't attract attention.

'So did you want to transfer the bags across now?'

J rubbed his chin, then glanced up and down the road.

'Not here, I don't think,' he said. 'No, it's too quiet. Any locals who come by are probably gonna remember seeing these two cars together, and we don't want that...'

He trailed off, gazing into the distance, then appeared to reach a decision. 'Start the car and follow us. It's not far, and it's somewhere we needed to go anyway.'

He turned and walked back to the Buick, directing Hannah

to switch over to the passenger side. Tom rolled up his window and started the engine.

They drove in convoy through quiet neighborhoods, taking it smooth and steady. At first, there were few houses, but soon the grass and trees were replaced by buildings and businesses, and they continued until they reached a busy intersection. The lights were green, and they crossed over into the sprawling parking lot of a large Walmart. J turned away from the store, cruising slowly around the outer edge of the lot, his head turning from left to right as he scanned the lines of parked cars. Eventually, he flashed his turn signal and pulled the Buick into an empty bay. Tom stopped alongside him and got out.

'We're gonna do this quickly and carefully,' J explained, as he walked to the back of the Kia and opened the trunk. 'Hannah will unload the bags and we can transfer everything to the Buick, but there's something I have to do first.'

He unzipped one of the black bags and rummaged for a moment, before withdrawing a screwdriver.

'I need you to keep watch,' he explained, stooping down at the back of the car. 'Warn me if anyone comes, or if anyone's going to drive past.'

He positioned the screwdriver and began unfastening the license plate.

Tom stared down at him, then lifted his head, turning to scan the parking lot. There were a few people pushing shopping carts, but none of them seemed to be heading this way.

'Got it,' J grunted, removing the plate and getting stiffly to his feet. 'Come with me and keep watching. Hannah, start unloading the bags.'

He made his way past the Buick to a blue Ford parked just beyond it. Squatting down, he began swapping the plates.

Tom cast nervous glances around the parking lot, spotting a

pickup truck as it came in from the road... and breathing a sigh of relief as it drove straight on towards the store entrance. Behind him, Hannah was lifting their bags down onto the asphalt.

J had the Ford's original plate off and was hurriedly fixing their own one in its place. After a moment, he got to his feet, brushing down the knees of his jeans.

'That's the difficult part done,' he said, smiling grimly. 'Front plates are easier, being screened by the cars in the next row, but I still want you on lookout duty.'

It took nearly five minutes to swap the license plates over. Several vehicles came in from the road, and Tom held his breath every time someone emerged from the store, but J had chosen the right part of the parking lot. Nobody came in their direction.

'What are we doing with the Kia?' Tom asked, as J slammed the trunk down. 'Leaving it here?'

J glanced around, then shook his head.

'I think we can find someplace better,' he said.

Leaving Walmart behind, Tom trailed the Buick down a broad boulevard, lined with retail parks and fast-food restaurants. Tall office buildings rose up around them as they passed through the center of town, but before long the storefronts became less frequent again and they entered an older, more run-down neighborhood. Just before the railroad crossing, the Buick slowed and turned aside into a quiet lot with a traditional, white-walled station building. Tom followed, noting the sign at the entrance: *Amtrak Patron Parking*.

Ahead of him, J had rolled his window down and was gesturing towards an empty bay. Tom nodded that he understood. A car could sit for days in a station car park without arousing suspicion.

Carefully maneuvering into the space, he switched off the engine. Then, glancing around the interior to make sure he hadn't left anything behind, he climbed out and locked the Kia. J had turned the Buick around and pulled over beside him.

'Is that it?' Tom asked as he got in. 'We're just leaving it there?'

'We're leaving it there.' He put the Buick into gear and rejoined the road. 'Why do you ask?'

'No reason,' Tom said, with a shrug. 'I just thought that you might... torch it or dump it in a river or something.'

'I did consider that,' J admitted. 'I checked on the map – there's a big old lake not far from here. Nice and remote, a lot like the place up near Beckley I guess.'

'So?' Tom asked. 'Why didn't you?'

J pulled up at a red light.

'Couple of reasons,' he mused. 'First of all, because we've done it before. I don't know how much the police know, but I'm not gonna hand them any obvious similarities that would help them piece together where we've been. Secondly, it's about the time factor. If they're close behind us – like just a few *hours* behind us – then we really need to open that gap up again. A car on fire, or sticking up out of the water? That gets attention, and it brings them running. I'd just as soon have our trail cool off a little before the cops pick it up again.'

Tom nodded to himself. It was one thing to burn a van in a rough part of New Jersey, but in a small town like this? That would get attention.

'Thirdly, this was a station parking lot,' J continued. 'If someone abandons a vehicle in a station parking lot, then there's an expectation, however small, that they left town on a train. And *that* means a lot more checking up for the cops to do, slowing them down even further.'

The lights changed and he put the car in gear again.

'But aren't you worried that the CSI people will find something in the car?' Tom asked. 'Fingerprints, DNA, stuff like that?'

'Oh, they'll find something, I'm sure,' J replied. 'But by the time they do, it won't matter anymore.'

He smiled to himself – a grim, joyless smile.

'By the time they do, it'll be too late.'

54

Tom's Journal

The last few days have been a weird blur after the relative quiet of the river camp – driving hundreds of grueling miles across six different states. The road is relentless and uncaring, stretching out ahead of us even though two more people are dead, two more names summarily crossed off J's list. Somehow, being on the move again makes it all even harder to take in.

And of course, everything's changed since we picked up Hannah.

I do feel bad for her, about pushing her so hard, about bringing her back when she tried to make a run for it up in Tulsa. She didn't ask for any of this and she's just a kid – but so is my son. And my first responsibility has to be protecting him.

Anyway, I don't think that J will hurt Hannah, not now. If he was going to kill her, he would have done it that first night, by the side of the road back in Indiana. After all, vicious though he is, our captor does seem to have his own moral code, a twisted sense of right and wrong that guides his actions. He knows that she's an innocent, and he only goes after people who he feels have wronged him. If she plays by his rules, she should be okay. That's my hope, anyway.

. . .

We stopped earlier this evening. J took us off the interstate soon after we crossed over into Texas, and we drove towards the fiery orange sunset for a while, coasting down a long, straight highway, through an empty landscape. Eventually, we hit a small town – a lonely little place, strung out along the side of the road – and found this motel.

J appears more settled than he did before. He's sitting propped up on his bed as I write this, watching the TV with a beer in his hand. I think we must be back "on-plan" again, after those anxious hours when the trail-cam first alerted him to the police. He always seems deeply uncomfortable when he's thinking on his feet, despite the fact that he's so good at it. In any case, he looks calm now. Maybe he's just glad that we're nearing the end of the journey.

That's been growing on my mind today. What will happen when we get there – if we get there – to the end of this? Will J just... turn us loose somewhere? Drive off into the distance and disappear? Hannah and I know so much about him and what he's done. Too much for him to stay disappeared for long. And yet, he's promised that he won't hurt me. How does he think he's going to get away with all this? How can he hope to evade the police that are already closing in and hunting him down? Maybe he has no intention of getting away with it at all... maybe he's planning to go down in a hail of bullets, and that's why it's so important to him that his story is told. I honestly don't know.

For him, it will be the completion of his great task – devastating payback for all the thoughtless social media anger that cost him so much. I'm not sure whether he truly believes that this run of executions will make the world a better place, or whether he simply hopes that it will help him to deal with his own unending loss. I'm not sure whether it even matters. I guess it's just about doing something, rather than nothing.

That thought pains me. Doing nothing can be hell – believe me, I know. Witnessing such horrors, unable to intervene, imprisoned by circumstances... but somehow I've made it this far. And if we really are nearing the end of the nightmare, then I can't do anything that would risk Zak, not for one last name on a madman's list.

55

In the morning they set out once more, swinging left onto the highway and letting it carry them west. The little town fell away until all that remained was the dark strip of asphalt, rolling out before them. On their right, far to the north, towering forests of wind turbines loomed up above the horizon, their blade arms swinging slowly, bone-white against the deep blue sky.

Yawning, Tom rested his head on the window and gazed out across the Texas plains. There was more water than he'd expected to see – with winding creeks, small lakes dotted here and there – and many more trees. Minor settlements slipped by, and they saw the occasional cattle ranch, but it was lonely country nonetheless. They found one larger town, where J pulled in at a general store to buy some drinks and snacks, yet soon the gas stations and restaurants, the gun stores and banks, were all gone.

Trees were replaced by electricity pylons that came marching up out of the south to run alongside the road for a time, but it wasn't long before they were gone too. Even the traffic, the one constant on their journey so far – the one reassuring hope of human contact – became infrequent and scarce. There really was almost nothing out here.

After an hour or so, they left the highway. The roads grew smaller and smaller, angling south then west across the endless open farmland. Eventually, J slowed at an unmarked turning, pulled the wheel round hard, and eased the car down off the asphalt onto a dirt road that led out across the vast, empty landscape.

'Not much further,' he murmured, as the tires crunched over loose stones. They drove on for some time, bumping along the narrow track. Tom frowned, wondering what could possibly be out here. Why was their captor taking them somewhere so remote?

A momentary thrill of panic flared in his chest as he pondered whether J was driving them into the middle of nowhere to kill them. It would be an ideal place to do it – nobody around to witness anything, and nobody around to find the bodies afterwards.

But J didn't want to kill them... *did he?*

'What's out here?' he asked.

'Someone I know has a place down here,' J replied. 'You'll see soon enough.'

They pulled up at a bend in the road. A few hundred yards away, behind a small line of trees, the roof of a large wooden house was just visible and, beyond that, the silvery reflection of a broad lake.

J killed the engine and sat for a moment, eyes alert as he peered out through the windshield. Tom went to unfasten his safety belt, but the older man glanced at him and shook his head.

'You wait here.'

He leaned forward, reaching under his jacket, and carefully drew out the gun. Tom stiffened, but J gave him a wry smile.

'Calm down, Tom. That's not what this is.'

Removing the keys from the ignition, he opened the door and got out. Tom watched as he walked briskly towards the house, cutting across the rough grass at the side of the road to disappear into the trees.

'What d'you reckon he's gonna do?' Hannah asked. 'Why's he brought us so far out into the boonies?'

'I don't know,' Tom whispered. He realized that he was holding his breath, listening for a gunshot. Forcing his gaze away from the trees, he twisted round in his seat. 'It'll be okay, though.'

Hannah didn't look reassured. Shaking her head, she stared past him at the lake and the empty country all around them.

'We're *really* on our own now,' she murmured. 'There ain't *nobody* comin' to help us out here.'

J was only gone for a few minutes. When he returned, walking back along the road, he appeared relaxed and the gun was no longer in his hand.

'We're all set,' he said, sliding into the driver's seat and starting the engine. 'I just wanted to take a quick look around before we went in.'

Putting the car in gear, he drove them past the trees and round to the house. It was a two-story, timber-frame building, with overhanging gable roofs, and a covered porch. There was a large gravel parking area at the side of the road, but no sign of any vehicles other than their own.

'What is this place?' Tom asked.

'It belongs to... well, he's not exactly a *friend*, more like someone I used to know,' J explained, steering onto the gravel and stopping. 'He doesn't come down here very often, but I just wanted to make sure the house was empty. It pays to be cautious, especially when you're dropping in unannounced.'

. . .

The front door was slightly open, and Tom pushed it wider as he stepped over the threshold. The house stood in complete stillness – no humming appliances, no air conditioning, just silence. There was a faint musty smell, and a chill to the air, as though nobody had been here in a while. He walked slowly into the middle of the hallway, his footsteps uncomfortably loud on the wooden floor, and paused at the bottom of the staircase.

There were family photos on the walls – a smart-looking couple in their forties, with a teenage son and daughter, smiling for the camera. Tom stared at them, wondering if they were all still alive, or if J had murdered one of them...

He jumped as J elbowed the door open behind him, heaving their black duffel bags into the hallway and dumping them heavily onto the floor. Hannah followed, carrying the drinks and snacks from the general store.

'Kitchen's right down there,' J told her, pointing towards the back of the house. Hannah nodded and took the supplies through.

J straightened up and pushed the door shut.

'Make yourself at home, Tom,' he smiled. 'We're gonna be here for a day or so.'

The house was spacious, with three bedrooms and an open loft area that looked over the comfortably furnished living room below. Tom walked across to the large windows, gazing out at the nearby lake, then glanced down to the splintered door frame leading out onto the porch. The back door had clearly been forced. J must have broken in to open the place up for them.

Hannah was sitting at the long dining table, absently

peeling the label off a bottle of Coke. She lifted her head at the sound of footsteps on the stairs, and turned to see J come in, checking his watch.

'All right, then,' he said brightly. 'I'm gonna head out for a while. Are you two gonna be okay here?'

Hannah shrugged and returned her attention to the bottle.

Tom thought about the smart-looking couple from the photos in the hallway.

'What do we do if someone shows up here?' he asked.

'Nobody's gonna show up,' J assured him.

'But what if they do?'

'Well then, just...' J made a face. 'Just tell them you're friends of Charles, and that *he* said you could use the place. Okay?'

'Who's Charles?'

'Unimportant.'

'What if they don't believe us?'

J rolled his eyes. 'Nobody's coming out here,' he said firmly. 'So, both of you just sit tight, and I'll be back later.'

Tom sensed a note of impatience in the older man's voice, and he felt his stomach sink a little. 'Where are you going?'

'I have several things that I need to do, Tom. What's bothering you?'

'I want to know why you're leaving us here,' Tom demanded. But he already knew the answer. J was going after another victim. Another life was about to be snuffed out.

J held his gaze for a moment.

'I'm leaving you here because of *her*.' He nodded towards Hannah, who looked up, startled. 'You were the one who wanted to bring her along, so now *you* get to babysit her.'

Tom glared at him. 'While *you* go out and murder someone.'

J paused, then gave a faint smile. 'Is that what you think?'

'Yeah.' Tom stared him down, defiantly. 'That's what I think.'

'Worried you'll miss the next kill?' J asked, with mock concern, his dark eyes boring into Tom. 'That big finale for your story?'

Then he shook his head, as though suddenly tired of the exchange. 'Oh relax, will you? I'm going out to get supplies and make a few arrangements, *okay*? Nobody's dying today.'

Tom stood a little way back from the window, watching as the car drove off down the road and disappeared behind trees.

'Has he gone?' Hannah's voice came from the foot of the stairs.

'Yeah, he's gone.'

'Then come and see this.' She sounded tense.

Tom followed her up the stairs and into the master bedroom. J's black duffel bag was sitting on the bed, unzipped and half-empty – wherever he had gone, it appeared that their captor had taken a lot of the contents with him.

But Hannah wasn't interested in the bag. Walking to the end of the bed, she pointed excitedly at the nightstand.

'Look, there's a phone!'

She watched him expectantly as he made his way around the bed, hesitated, then lifted the receiver to his ear... but there was no sound. The line was dead.

Tom leaned over and peered down the back of the nightstand, then slowly lifted the base of the phone up. As he did so, the ragged end of the trailing cable came into view, bare wire visible where it had been cut.

'Great,' he said with a sigh.

Hannah stared at the severed cable, and her shoulders dropped. 'He really does think of *everything*, doesn't he?'

Tom shrugged, then nodded.

'So far, yeah.'

He walked over and peered cautiously into the duffel bag, wondering what was missing. The gun and the stun gun were both gone, along with the burner phones and the police scanner. But had J taken them because he planned to use them, or because he didn't want to leave them unattended?

Frowning, Tom reached down the side of the bag, searching between the layers of folded clothing. The spiral-bound journal wasn't there either.

Disappointed, he put everything back and arranged the bag to be just as he'd found it. Then he walked over to the window and leaned on the sill. The lake was bigger than it had looked from the road – from up here he could see that it stretched away beyond the trees, like a giant oval mirror, pushed down deep into the sweeping grass.

'Has he said anything about what'll happen?' Hannah asked.

Tom glanced round at her.

'What do you mean?'

'When he's done... when we get to the end of this trip.' Her fingers picked nervously at the sleeve of her top. 'You still think he's gonna just let us go?'

Tom went back to looking at the sky reflected in the lake, a bright swathe of blue in the muted colors of the landscape.

'Yes,' he said, after a moment. 'I think so.'

'You *think* so?' Hannah spoke sharply. 'You don't sound too sure.'

'He's come this far without breaking his word.' Tom turned to face her. 'I believe he'll let us go.'

Hannah shifted her weight from one foot to another.

'Well, I don't like it,' she muttered.

'Neither of us likes it.'

She stood for a moment, restless, then looked at him hopefully.

'Couldn't we just walk out of here?' she asked. 'I don't know... maybe go and *find* a phone or something?'

Tom shook his head slowly.

'It's a long walk back to the highway, and we didn't pass any houses on the way out here,' he said. 'Anyway, what use is a phone going to be? Who would we call? You know we can't get the police involved.'

'Yeah, yeah, you keep on saying that,' Hannah retorted. 'But you could call your family, tell them to go someplace safe or something? It would be a start...'

Tom sighed. 'It's not that simple. Remember, I'm a missing person, so the police may already have tracked my family down and spoken to them...'

He fought back a momentary pang of guilt about his foolish call from the river camp. 'They could probably trace the call, figure out where I was, and then the whole area would be crawling with cops.'

'But...' Hannah trailed off in frustration.

'If the cops get J before he calls off the hit, my little boy is dead,' Tom reminded her. 'I *can't* let that happen.'

He saw tears start in Hannah's eyes; saw her turn away in despair.

'I'm so sorry, really I am,' he said quietly. 'But we *are* almost at the end. I can't allow anything to go wrong, not now.'

Hannah hung her head for a while. When she finally looked up, her eyes were red and angry.

'So... I guess I'm your *prisoner* then.'

She spat the word at him.

Tom shut his eyes for a moment, slowly clenching his fists. He wanted to scream at her, to make her understand just how much he was going through, but somehow he kept a lid on it.

'We're *both* prisoners,' he said, in a level voice.

Hannah scowled at him as he stalked out of the room.

Going to the loft balcony, he stood, staring down at the living room area below.

Why couldn't she just see things from his point of view? Didn't she realize what was at stake?

He turned around, trudging back along the hallway and into one of the other bedrooms, where J had left his duffel bag for him. Walking over to the bed, he began to unzip the bag, then stopped.

There was something inside, nestling on top of his clothes.

It was J's spiral-bound journal.

56

Tom turned another page. He wasn't sure how long he'd been sitting there, poring over the notebook, but his neck felt stiff as he lifted his head and rubbed his eyes.

The scale of it was appalling.

Seeing the slaughter laid out in J's measured handwriting, seeing those names and details and dates, all carefully documented in that methodical matter-of-fact way... somehow it made the horror even worse. These weren't isolated moments of blind rage, this was a patient campaign of terrible vengeance. And yet there was no sense of confession in those pages, just an air of inevitable causality.

Peter Van Meuren, Sophie Bouchard, Trevon Williams, Lizzie Reeves, Amanda Bailey...

A detailed study of each victim, covering their home-life, their job, their daily routines and interests, all written out like a cruel memorial-in-advance, alongside lists of family and friends.

Duncan Bauman, Alex Fisher, Candice Porter, Daryl Hirsch, Shanice Coleman...

For each name – each *murder* – there was a plan and a schedule, with methods and logistics, neatly set out and prioritized.

Mia Aguilar, Courtney-Anne Wright, David Barron, Travis Nelson, Ryan Court.

And finally, for every punishment, there was a 'crime'. Here was a record of what each person had done – what they had posted where, how many people had shared or retweeted it, and the approximate social reach of their comments. Tom did a quick calculation; together, their false accusations about Joseph Sherman had been seen by over a million people, stretching out across the country, influencing, inciting – a lynch-mob for the digital age.

Tom sighed. Staring down at the notebook, his brows tightened into a frown. The final entry was for Ryan Court, the geologist from Tulsa... yet J had said there was still one more name on his list. Tom leafed quickly through the remaining pages but they were all blank.

Why wasn't the final victim written down?

He sat for an anxious moment, trying to stop his imagination from running wild.

J wasn't going to kill him; he was almost certain of that.

Almost certain.

He forced himself to calm down, to breathe, to think. What about Hannah? Her name wouldn't be written down like the others because J hadn't known about her when he made his plans – could she be the one?

But Hannah was innocent. J spoke of his actions making the world a better place. Would he really hurt someone who'd done nothing wrong? It didn't seem to fit...

Tom closed his eyes, shutting out the questions, the confusing thoughts, the rising panic.

He'd made it this far on the journey. He *had* to see how this ended.

. . .

Hannah scowled again when he came downstairs, her eyes following him as he walked over to the kitchen counter and picked up a soda.

'I *said* I was sorry,' he reminded her.

'Oh.' She threw her hands up and gave him a sarcastic nod. 'Well, I guess that changes everything then.'

Tom sighed. 'What do you want me to say?'

Hannah remained silent. When he looked up again, she was still watching him.

'Seriously,' he muttered. 'What do you expect me to do? What *can* I do?'

Sitting at the far end of the counter, Hannah clenched her fists in frustration.

'This whole thing, it's...' She stared at him. 'It's fucked up!'

Tom nodded.

'I don't understand how you can be so – so *calm* about it all,' she complained. 'Why aren't you freaking out?'

Tom paused. His mind went back to those breathless hours, sliding about on the floor of the van, screaming into his gag until there were no screams left...

He hugged himself and took a deep breath to stop himself from shivering.

'Just because you don't see it, doesn't mean I'm not freaked out inside.'

Hannah turned away, shaking her head.

'Well, I don't think I can take much more of this.'

There was a palpable tension about her, and fear gripped Tom as he realized how close she must be to breaking. *This poor kid.* But he couldn't let things fall apart, not now.

'Don't give up, Hannah.' The words were hollow, but he did his best to sound positive, encouraging her. 'You're going to get through this. I know you are.'

She lifted her head.

'How do you expect me to do that?'

'You just...' Tom faltered. 'You just need to hold on. It won't be much longer.'

'Just hold on?' There was contempt in her eyes.

'We're almost at the end,' Tom reminded her. 'He *said* so.'

Hannah was silent for a moment, then rose to her feet.

'Sure, why not?' she said, icily. 'I mean, it's only *one more death*, right?'

She turned and walked out of the room.

It was getting dark when Tom first made out the distant sound of a vehicle approaching. He'd spent the afternoon shrouded in his own thoughts, writing under the heavy stillness of the house, but the noise disturbed him, and he set his pen down, standing up to peer out of the window. He saw headlights flickering through the line of trees, then stiffened as a large black SUV swept into view, turning in and crunching to a halt on the gravel.

'Hannah?' He took a step back from the window. 'Someone's outside... a car I haven't seen before. I think they're coming in.'

He heard Hannah's footsteps quicken as she ran through from the other room.

'Who is it?' she hissed. 'What are we meant to do?'

'I don't know!'

Going back to the window he stared out at the shadowy vehicle, blinking as the headlights went dark, and the engine fell silent. The driver's door opened and a figure emerged, briefly revealed by the glow of the interior light. Tom allowed himself to breathe.

'It's okay.' He realized he was addressing Hannah in a

hushed tone and forced himself to speak normally. 'It's J. When I saw that big SUV driving up…' He trailed off. 'I guess he must have switched vehicles again.'

Hannah leaned up against the wall, her face unreadable.

'It's all right,' Tom assured her. He took a step towards his chair, then paused, struck by how wrong it was to be relieved at the sight of a killer. 'Well – you know what I mean.'

J came in, stretching wearily and yawning. He set his gun down on the counter and began taking off his jacket. Glancing round, he caught Hannah watching him.

'Pleased to see me?'

Hannah glared at him, then abruptly turned and left the room. They heard her footsteps thudding up the stairs. J's eyes followed the sound as it passed above him, then he glanced at Tom. 'Something I said?'

'You gave us quite a scare there,' Tom said.

J draped his jacket over the back of a chair. 'What are you talking about?'

'When I saw that SUV pulling in' – Tom gestured towards the window – 'I thought maybe the owners of this place had come back. I didn't know what to do.'

Understanding dawned on J's face.

'Of course,' he said. 'Sorry about that. I should have mentioned I was going to pick up another ride.'

'I don't get it though,' Tom said. 'You only just changed vehicles.'

'That last switch was a response to the police getting so unexpectedly close.' J shook his head slowly. 'But this? This one's been planned from the beginning.'

'I see.'

'How was *your* afternoon?' J asked, changing the subject. 'Productive?'

Tom met his gaze.

'I found your journal.'

J paused and nodded to himself.

'Good,' he said. 'I trust you found it useful.'

'It was... informative.' Tom shuddered as he recalled the details of the crimes. 'Do you want it back?'

'No, you go ahead and keep it. Saves you copying everything out into your notebooks.'

'I appreciate that.'

'No problem.' J picked up the gun from the counter and checked it, before tucking it down the back of his jeans. 'I'm done with it now.'

'Yeah, I noticed there are no more names after Ryan Court...' Tom trailed off, watching for some clue, some indication in the older man's response.

'That's right.' J yawned disinterestedly.

'But you said there's one more name on the list.'

'Right again.'

There was a pause.

'Well?' Tom pressed. 'Are you going to tell me who it is?'

For a moment, J said nothing, then smiled faintly.

'*All good things*, Tom' he said, turning towards the stairs.

Tom frowned. Evasive answers again... but there had to be a reason why the final name wasn't written down. All the other victims had been carefully considered. There had been pages of research, detailed notes, yet nothing for this last one. Didn't he *need* to research the final target?

A sudden thought came to him. How many times had he read about killers coming to the end of a spree and then ending their own lives?

'Is the final victim Joseph Sherman?' He blurted out the question before he could stop himself.

J halted, then very slowly turned around to face him again.

'I don't recall mentioning *that* name to you, Tom.' There was a dangerous note in his voice and his piercing stare became intense.

Tom's stomach twisted, as he grasped what he'd just done.

'However did you get hold of that?' J pondered. 'Has someone been indiscreet?'

Tom swallowed, to prevent his voice breaking. 'I read it online.'

J stood motionless, studying him the way a cat studies a trapped mouse.

'I wasn't aware that you had internet access, Tom.'

'I... I don't.' Tom realized he'd been holding his breath, and exhaled. 'When we were at the river camp, when you were out... I took a walk down to the office, and the woman there... she let me use her computer.'

J's eyes bored into him, unblinking.

'Go on...'

'That's it,' Tom said. 'I just used her computer to look at a couple of web pages.'

'*Which* web pages?'

'I searched for the hashtag in the tweets you showed me. *#JusticeForKaitlyn*.'

J's expression grew colder but he said nothing.

'I read about the Backlash campaign,' Tom continued. 'About you being implicated, about the boycott of Bluestone Mutual.'

'What else?'

'Nothing else,' Tom replied. 'That was it. I was only online for a couple of minutes and I barely had time to skim those pages.'

J continued to stare him down.

'Did you sign into any accounts?' he demanded. 'Email? Social media? Anything with your name on it?'

'No, of course not,' Tom said. 'Why would I do that?'

'I don't know why,' J growled. 'But I *do* know that could be enough for your friends in the police department to find the camp site. And *that* would be enough for them to get a make on our vehicle.'

Tom felt himself caught by the cold, penetrating stare that seemed to reach deep into his soul. Unable to look away, he tried desperately to think of something else, *anything* else... but the only thought, the thought that filled his mind, was of the phone call to Samaira. He felt his face flush red.

'What did you do, Tom?'

It was no use trying to fool him... but a spark of anger glimmered in Tom and he lifted his head in defiance.

'What would *you* have done?' he retorted.

J appeared unmoved. 'Tell me,' he said, then added, 'please.'

'I called Samaira, *okay?*' Tom replied, the words spilling out of him. 'I didn't warn her or tell her anything. I just... I just needed to know that Zak was all right.'

J closed his eyes. 'I see.'

'I *had* to know,' Tom continued. 'I had to know if my boy was all right.'

J bowed his head, thinking for a moment, then sighed deeply.

'So?' Tom demanded. 'What are you going to do?'

'Don't misunderstand me, Tom. I applaud your ingenuity, your determination to find the facts. It's exactly the reason I chose you.' His shoulders dropped slightly. 'And I understand the need to check up on your son, I really do. I'm just disappointed that you weren't smarter about it, that you didn't think things through.'

'Hey, I was careful!' Tom protested.

'You were careless!' J snapped. 'You risked *everything*. The police almost got us in Tulsa, remember?'

'But that wasn't necessarily–'

'Oh, come *on*, Tom! How *else* could they have picked up our trail?'

Tom took a step back, chastened by the intensity of the older man's outburst.

'I'm sorry, okay? *Okay?*'

J looked at him with empty eyes.

'We got away with it this time... *just*. We got *lucky*.'

Tom nodded.

'Journey's almost over,' J growled. '*Don't* screw up again.'

57

A sound woke Tom, stirring his sluggish mind into slow awareness. His nose caught the scent of a strange bed, and there was an unfamiliar feel to the pillow... but there had been so many strange beds recently.

Another sound came to him. It was an engine starting, somewhere outside, loud against the silence. Briefly, he cracked his eyes open, but it was still dark, and that seemed odd somehow.

He shifted position slightly and groaned into the pillow. Some part of him was curious now. With an effort, he rolled onto his side and swung his legs out from under the comforter, wincing at the touch of chill air on his skin.

The note of the engine changed.

Forcing himself to his feet, Tom padded across the cold floor to the window and peered out. It was maybe an hour before dawn, with only a glow of warm color beyond the black horizon to hint at the coming morning. Below him, the searching beams of headlights swept across the gravel, as the SUV reversed out onto the road, halted for a second, then accelerated away. The engine noise gradually receded, and he watched the red taillights glimmer among the trees until they were gone.

He remained at the window for a moment longer, gazing out into the darkness, then turned away and retreated to the warmth of the bed, wondering where J was going...

When he woke again, the room was different, filled with the sharp light of morning. He lay back for a time, shielding his eyes and yawning, then wearily pushed himself out of bed to get dressed.

Hannah was sitting at the kitchen counter when he came downstairs. There was a glass of water in front of her.

'He's not here,' she said, in a flat voice. 'The car's gone.'

'Yeah, I heard him leave,' Tom said, with a yawn. 'Not sure what time, but it was pretty early.' He looked over at her. 'Still angry at me?'

Hannah met his gaze, then shrugged. 'I'm not *pleased* with you.'

Tom sighed.

'Hey, I'm just trying to keep us alive.'

Hannah lifted her glass but didn't drink from it.

'I get that,' she said. 'It's just all so...'

She trailed off, shaking her head.

'I know,' Tom said, softly. He approached the counter, then pulled up a stool and sat down.

'Are you okay?' he asked her. 'You know, *apart* from all this?'

Hannah's expression was distant. 'It's been a while since I felt okay.'

Tom looked at her expectantly, but she forced a brief smile and shook her head.

'It doesn't matter.'

'Are you sure?'

'It's just that...' She stared down at the counter. 'I've just had some bad luck, is all. Well, a run of bad luck, really.'

Tom thought for a moment.

'Luck changes,' he said.

'I sure hope so. With all this...' She gestured around herself, and her features tightened into a bitter little smile. 'Well, I figure it can't get much worse.'

Tom wondered what she was running away from. 'Wanna talk about it?'

Hannah toyed with her glass, slowly turning it to catch the light.

'Talking won't change anything for me.' She flashed another brief smile. 'Anyway, I don't wanna be in your dumb book.'

Tom frowned. 'My book?'

'The book you're writing,' she reminded him. 'Your big story or whatever... that's why you're here, isn't it?'

Instinctively, Tom drew himself up, ready to remind her how he'd been kidnapped, how he'd been trying to catch a killer – then he hesitated. Would he be telling her? Or telling himself?

Her sad eyes bored into him until he looked away.

'Yeah,' he admitted quietly. 'That's why I'm here.'

Tom was lying on his bed, writing, when he heard J return. Setting his notepad aside, he got to his feet and wandered downstairs. The older man seemed to be in a good mood, sipping an energy drink as he paced around the kitchen, and smiling brightly.

'Good morning, Tom.'

'Morning. You were out early.'

'Yeah, sorry if I woke you but I had an errand to run over in Archer City.'

Tom looked at him, curious.

'What's in Archer City?'

J took another mouthful of his drink, then set the can down on the counter.

'It's where they filmed that movie, *The Last Picture Show*.'

'Never seen it.'

J raised an eyebrow.

'Different generations,' he said, shrugging. 'Anyway, it doesn't matter. We've got ourselves a schedule to keep and a lot of miles to cover.'

He clasped his hands together, eagerly. 'Go pack your stuff, so we can hit the road.'

Crunching across the gravel, Tom paused and looked back. The house stood tall and lonely in the empty landscape. Beyond it, several birds wheeled above the lake, tiny silhouettes against the broad blue sky, their mournful cries breaking the stillness. Part of him wished he could stay here, remote and removed from the violence and vengeance, shutting himself off and letting it carry on without him. But he knew that wasn't an option, not for him, and not for his captor. The only way out of this nightmare was to follow it through to the end.

J emerged from the house, holding the door for Hannah, who was lugging one of the large bags. Stepping down from the porch, he made his way over to Tom.

'Remember yesterday?' he enquired. 'When you asked me about the final victim?'

'I remember,' Tom said.

They walked slowly across the gravel towards the black SUV.

'I wasn't very forthcoming, was I?'

Tom glanced over at him. 'Not really, no.'

'Sorry about that.' Stopping at the rear of the vehicle, J set his bags down and took out a small electronic key fob. 'Let me make it up to you today.'

Tom rolled his eyes.

'And how are you going to –'

But the older man was lifting open the tailgate of the SUV, and Tom jerked backwards in startled horror as he made out the disheveled figure, bound and gagged and squirming desperately on the floor of the trunk.

'Here she is,' J said, brightly. 'The very last name on the list.'

The woman was in her thirties, barefoot, and wearing pajamas. Wedged in among a bundle of blankets, she lay on her side, hands secured behind her back, brown hair tangled and plastered across her face.

But her eyes...

Tom shuddered. Her eyes were red with tears, blinking up at the light and staring around wildly. He had never seen true terror in a face before, but he was seeing it now. The tape across her mouth bulged as she struggled to cry out, but the woeful animal moan that emerged was more distressing than any scream.

Tom swallowed hard, unable to look away, as he recalled how it felt to be bound and gagged in the back of a vehicle. Beside him, Hannah was staring, eyes wide, one hand over her mouth.

'Allow me to introduce you both to Miss Kaitlyn Brance,' J said. 'A valued customer of my former employer, the Bluestone Mutual Group.'

Tom's head jerked round.

'Kaitlyn?'

J nodded with a grim satisfaction.

'None other.'

'But I thought...' Tom broke off, trying to put it all together. 'You spoke about her as though she was dead. I thought you'd...'

'Killed her?' J snorted with contempt. 'Not yet. But every story needs an ending, and this one seems so very appropriate. She *started* this whole nightmare, after all.'

58

J reversed back over the gravel, slowing as the rear wheels bumped down onto the road. Behind them, a muffled thud came from inside the trunk.

Tom sat rigid in his seat, his mind still reeling from the shock.

'What the fuck,' he groaned. 'What the *fuck!*'

J tutted with disapproval.

'Language, Tom.'

He put the SUV in gear and set off along the road, driving back the way they'd come the day before. Tom stared out at the empty landscape.

'You kidnapped her,' he murmured, struggling to take in what was happening.

J nodded calmly.

'I did.'

'That's why you went out so early this morning.'

'Of course,' the older man replied. 'It's one of the best times to catch people at home. I drove over to Archer City and let myself into her house. Luckily, she lives alone, so I didn't have to worry about anyone else. It was just a matter of walking quietly into her bedroom, stunning her until she was subdued, then carrying her out to the car. Nothing to it.'

Tom tried to process this. 'You carried a body out of a house in broad daylight?'

J shook his head.

'It was still pretty dark, so not exactly daylight,' he explained. 'And I'd wrapped her in blankets so it wouldn't be *too* obvious, but... yeah. It's easy to overthink these things and make them complicated, but oftentimes the simple solutions are the best. I was in and out in a few minutes, no fuss.'

'But... weren't you worried that you'd be seen?'

'On a quiet side street in Archer City? At that time of the morning?' J chuckled to himself. 'No, I wasn't too worried. And like I said, this is the last stop on the tour, so it's not such a big deal, even if someone does remember the SUV. By the time the police figure out what's happening...' He broke off, a thoughtful look on his face. 'Well, it should all be over by then.'

They reached the main road and J made a hard left. There was another audible thud from the trunk. Tom twisted around in his seat and caught Hannah's expression. It was clear that she was painfully aware of the noises just behind her.

Tom was aware of them too, and his mind filled with images of how it must be for Kaitlyn, bumping around in that claustrophobic darkness, struggling, sweating, shaking. He felt his panic rising in sympathy, and even the mild pressure of the seat belt across his chest became unbearable.

He turned to J.

'Is she all right back there?'

The older man frowned. 'Hannah?'

'No, *Kaitlyn!*'

J said nothing for a moment, then shrugged. 'That woman destroyed my life, Tom. I'm not unduly concerned about her comfort.'

Tom slumped, leaning back against the headrest, his hand pulling at the seat belt.

'Are you sure she can breathe okay?' he demanded.

'Oh, I expect she'll make it to our destination,' replied J slowly.

Behind them, Hannah shifted her position and leaned forward.

'Where are you taking us?' she asked.

J glanced up at her in the rear-view mirror, smiling slightly. 'South.'

Tom gazed out at the road, noticing for the first time that they were following a different route from the day before.

'South?' he enquired.

'We're going to the middle of nowhere,' J told them.

There was another bump from the trunk.

'What are you going to do with Kaitlyn when we get there?'

The smile on J's face turned cold.

'Let's just say, I wouldn't get too attached to her, if I was you.'

They avoided Archer City and followed narrow country roads to the highway. Small towns slipped by and the landscape flattened out, while the road stretched off into the distance, chasing a horizon that seemed impossibly far away. Everyone had lapsed into an uncomfortable silence – even the noises from the trunk became less frequent, and eventually ceased.

After a couple of hours of steady driving, J shifted position slightly, glanced up at the rear view mirror, then moved the SUV over to the right-hand lane. He left the highway at the next exit and followed a smaller road for a while, before turning onto a quiet dirt track that led away across an expanse of dusty fields.

Tom gazed out at the emptiness all around them. No houses, no cars, no people...

'Is this it?' he asked.

J shot him a puzzled look.

'You said we were going to the middle of nowhere,' Tom reminded him.

Understanding dawned on J's face.

'Oh, right. No, this is just...' He gave a slight shrug. 'A comfort stop.'

They followed the dirt track for nearly a mile before J slowed down. Bumping up onto the rough ground at the side of the road, he turned the SUV around and brought it to a halt, then switched off the engine.

'All right,' he said, stretching in his seat, then looking round at them both. 'Let's go check on our cargo.'

They got out. Tom stepped down, shielding his eyes against the light as he peered off into the distance. Aside from the dirt-track, there was nothing – just ground and sky, for as far as he could see.

'Hey.' J was beckoning him from the back of the SUV. 'Come and help me get her out of the trunk.'

Tom took a step towards him, then hesitated.

'Why?' he asked. 'What are you going to do?'

'You want me to keep her in there, or you want to let her straighten up and get some air?' he demanded.

Tom went warily to the back of the SUV. 'How do we do this?'

'Support her upper body,' J said, reaching to open the trunk. 'I'll get her feet.'

The smell of human confinement wafted out over them, warm and sickly, as he lifted the hatch. Kaitlyn seemed dazed, drenched in sweat, hair plastered over her face. Tom put an arm around her shoulders and helped her into an upright position, horribly aware of the clamminess he could feel through her pajamas.

'Careful of your ribs,' J warned him, as he swung her legs round and turned her.

They got Kaitlyn into a sitting position, bare feet dangling out the back of the SUV. Tom kept a hand on her shoulder, supporting her as she swayed slightly, blinking at the light.

J squatted down in front of her so he could gaze up into her face.

'Hey...' He clicked his fingers a couple of times, encouraging her to look at him, but keeping his voice gentle and quiet. 'Hey, how are you doing there? Are you okay?'

Kaitlyn moaned behind her taped gag.

J nodded sadly, as though he completely understood.

'Oh, I know, I know, *shhhhh...*' He regarded her with what looked like deep sympathy. 'It's been a difficult day and you must have so many questions, but... *shhhhh...* I just have *one* question for you first...'

He leaned in closer, staring up until she finally focused on his face.

'Do you remember me, Kaitlyn?'

For a moment, Kaitlyn seemed too disoriented, her head lolling slightly. Then, suddenly, her eyes widened and she jerked backwards, the tape across her mouth bulging out with a muffled shriek.

J remained still, a bleak smile spreading across his face.

'I see that you do, and that's gratifying, Kaitlyn, it really is.'

He leaned in closer, and there was an edge to his voice. 'Because I've *never* forgotten you.'

Struggling desperately against her restraints, Kaitlyn slipped off the back of the trunk and fell to the ground. Landing on her side, she flapped like a beached fish, unable to get up.

J rose to his feet, shaking his head. He turned to Hannah.

'I don't like to impose on you, but our guest here... well, she might need a bathroom break, and I can't risk removing her restraints...'

Hannah stared at him in disbelief.

J shrugged.

'Well, *someone's* gonna have to help her...'

Tom and J stood with their backs to the SUV, staring out at the empty landscape.

'Are you going to kill her?' Tom asked in a low voice. It was a terrible thing to think about, but he had to speak.

J glanced over at him then answered with a bleak grin.

Tom swallowed hard.

'Then why all this?' he demanded. 'Why kidnap her, and drive her all this way in the back of a car? Why make her suffer?'

J regarded Tom thoughtfully, then reached back and drew out his gun.

'You saying I should put her out of her misery right now?'

'No!' Tom exclaimed. 'No, I'm just... just trying to understand.'

J paused, then smiled and put the gun away.

'And I *want* you to understand,' he murmured. 'I want *everyone* to understand.'

They heard footsteps and turned to see Hannah standing at the corner of the SUV.

J acknowledged her with a nod.

'Thank you for doing that,' he said.

Hannah shrugged, but her expression was troubled.

'Kaitlyn seems pretty dehydrated,' she muttered. 'You should probably give her some water or something.'

J considered this. 'Of course,' he said. 'Come and help me with her, and Tom'll bring some water.'

There was a bottle between the front seats. Tom retrieved it and brought it around to the back of the SUV, where J and Hannah were helping Kaitlyn up into a sitting position. She wasn't struggling any more, perhaps due to fatigue, but her eyes were quick and alert.

She flinched as J reached towards her face, but he held up a hand, palm open.

'If you want a drink, I have to remove your gag, okay?'

She looked fearfully around at all of them, flinching once again as J reached for the tape and peeled it away from her mouth.

'Ughhhh....' She gasped for breath, coughing as she drew in too much air.

Tom held out the water bottle but stopped as she began to speak.

'Let me go,' she croaked, weakly. 'I... I don't know why you're doing this...' She broke off, coughing again. 'Please, just – let me go.'

J's face betrayed no emotion. He took the bottle from Tom and unscrewed the lid.

'Just a little at a time,' he warned her. 'Drink it slowly.'

He tilted the bottle and held it close to her mouth.

Kaitlyn leaned forward and sipped eagerly, water dribbling over her chin as she gulped it down.

'Slowly,' J reminded her. 'Don't rush it.'

She drank a little more, then coughed again. J lowered the bottle, watching her patiently. Eventually she raised her head, staring up at Tom, then Hannah, then back at J.

'Untie me,' she begged him. 'I won't tell anyone. I won't say anything.'

J regarded her sadly. 'But Kaitlyn, you already *did*. Don't you remember?'

Kaitlyn stared up at him uncertainly.

'When you crucified me?' J reminded her. 'With all those lies you told? Come on, you *must* remember that.'

Kaitlyn hesitated, anxious eyes flickering to the others for a second, then back to him.

'Wh-what do you mean?' she stammered.

'It doesn't matter,' J said, softly. 'Because there's nobody left for you to tell your lies to, Kaitlyn. And nothing more that you can do to me.'

Kaitlyn shrank away from him.

'What's he talking about?' she cried. 'What *is* this?'

J stared at her, unblinking.

Wriggling in the dirt, Kaitlyn angled herself towards Hannah.

'Let me go!' she pleaded. 'Please, just untie me and let me go!'

Hannah stared down at her helplessly.

'She's not really in a position to do that, Kaitlyn,' J explained. 'This is Hannah, and she's an unwilling guest on this trip...'

'Guest?' Hannah spat the word out. 'You fucking *kidnapped* me!'

J held up his hands, as though feigning embarrassment.

'I'm ashamed to say I did. In fact, I kidnapped Tom here, too.'

He turned back to Kaitlyn. 'So, you see, they *can't* help you because they're both prisoners, just like you.' He paused, then stood up straight. 'Well, not *quite* like you.'

He turned away from her to stand, hands on his hips, twisting his body left and right as if to loosen his muscles.

'You see, they didn't lie about me, or start some bullshit crusade against me. They didn't destroy my life.' His fists momentarily clenched, but he forced them to relax before turning to face his victim. 'Which is why *they* have a chance of walking away from this with their lives, while *you*...'

He shook his head, gravely.

'But I never lied!' There was panic in Kaitlyn's voice as she turned to look at Hannah. 'He's the one lying, not me!'

Hannah glanced across at Tom.

'I lost my house and everything in that fire,' Kaitlyn insisted. '*And*, I was a... a vulnerable individual being pressured by a person of authority.'

Tom frowned. Something about the way she'd phrased that last sentence sounded odd, as though the words were someone else's.

'Oh, Kaitlyn.' J sighed. 'You know you're done, right? And *nothing's* gonna change that... but hey, if you wanna waste your last words on some chicken-shit lie rather than telling it straight...' He trailed off, sneering with contempt. 'Well, I guess trash like you don't change.'

Kaitlyn's eyes became hard.

'Oh yeah?' she rasped. 'You think you're *so* much better than me. But I figured out what you were up to when you came around with your stupid forms to fill out, asking all those dumb questions, trying to trick me, trying to stop me getting my money I was *owed*...'

'Trying to get the truth,' J murmured.

'What the hell would you know about truth?' Kaitlyn snapped. 'You don't know how it is to see everyone getting on except you, to see your friends doing better than you, to see your chances slipping away. That money didn't mean nothing to the insurance company, and it didn't mean nothing to you... but it was everything to me. And I fucking *earned* it!'

J shook his head.

'You don't *earn* an insurance pay-out.'

Kaitlyn glared up at him, defiant.

'I made all the payments,' she insisted.

'And then burned down your own place,' he reminded her.

Kaitlyn's eyes narrowed.

'And nobody can prove it,' she sneered. 'Cos if they could, then the insurance people wouldn't have sent you to snoop around and try to trick me.'

She made a face at him.

J gazed down at her with a faraway look in his eyes.

'You think you won, don't you? You *actually* think you won.' He shook his head, bitterly. 'But nobody won, Kaitlyn. Thanks to you, everybody lost.'

Sighing deeply, he looked over at Tom.

'I'm gonna take a leak. Five minutes, then we need to hit the road again.'

He turned and walked away, disappearing round the far side of the SUV.

Tom glanced at Hannah, who still appeared to be in shock, then looked down at Kaitlyn.

'Uh... do you want some more water?'

Her eyes were on him, wild and desperate.

'Listen, you *have* to let me go,' she whispered.

'I can't... you don't understand...'

'No, *you* don't understand!' she hissed. 'That piece of shit has it in for me, and there's no tellin' what he'll do. You *gotta* let me go!'

Tom shook his head.

'It's not as simple as–'

'Why?' Hannah stepped forward, interrupting him. 'Why's he got it in for you?'

Kaitlyn glanced up at her, then looked away.

'He was trying to mess with my insurance pay-out,' she muttered. 'So I figured I'd mess with him.'

Hannah regarded her doubtfully.

'Oh, for fuck's sake,' Kaitlyn said, losing patience. 'I made some complaints, got him into trouble for a while. It doesn't matter.'

'You lied?' Hannah asked.

'I said what I had to say to get my money, okay?' Kaitlyn's voice was raised now. 'Who gives a shit! I just need you to let me go!'

Her outburst startled Tom and he leaned forward nervously.

'Look around you!' he hissed, willing her to be quiet. 'There's no place to go out here!'

Kaitlyn's bloodshot eyes stared past him for a moment, then slowly grew wider. He saw the anger drain from her expression, and fear take hold again, as the reality of her situation came crashing in. She threw back her head and let out a rasping cry.

'Help!' she yelled. 'Somebody help me! HELP!'

Startled, Tom took a step back from her, shooting a panicked glance at Hannah.

'Help me! Somebody help!'

J appeared, walking calmly round the corner of the SUV. Tom looked on nervously but the older man seemed completely unconcerned by the noise.

'Feeling better, Kaitlyn?'

She stared up, gulping down a breath, then screamed again.

'Help me! HELP!'

J smiled and slowly shook his head.

'That's okay, you just let it all out.' He went to one of the bags and retrieved a large roll of tape, then advanced on her. 'But nobody's listening, not this time.'

59

They drove on for several hours, and it grew steadily hotter as the miles slipped away. Tom lay back in his seat, gazing out the window at the desert landscape – tufts of grass burnt yellow by the sun, clumps of prickly pear cactus, a jagged horizon of hazy black peaks – it was like something from an old cowboy movie.

His mind kept returning to Hannah's words – *it's only one more death, right?* – and he shut his eyes, hating the guilt, hating himself.

Only one more death.

But he'd made it all this way, he'd *survived*. And Hannah was still alive, and Zak, and Kendra...

That was what mattered now: the people he cared about. He couldn't take any stupid risks, not after everything he'd been through, not when he was so close. And Kaitlyn had admitted that she'd lied...

A noise from the back reminded him that she was bound and gagged just behind him, in the suffocating darkness of the trunk. He imagined the plastic ties cutting into her wrists and ankles, the tape across her mouth, the dwindling air, hot and heavy and stale with her own sweat...

No! He shifted in his seat. *It's not my fault.*

The whole world was messed up, with people lashing out at each other all the time. This was just one more example of that. There was nothing he could do about it, except report on it.

'This is what it's all been building up to, isn't it?' He looked across, trying to read the older man's face. 'How do you feel right now?'

'Still asking the questions,' J replied, with an approving nod. 'That's good. But as to how I feel? Well, I'm glad it's almost over, but I'm not happy, if that's what you're wondering. There's no cause for celebration in any of this, just... closure, I guess.'

'Closure,' Tom mused. 'You'll be able to move on, is that it?'

'Maybe.' The older man returned his attention to the road. 'I hope so.'

'Any idea what you'll do afterwards? You must have thought about it.'

'What I'll do depends on whether I'm caught.'

Tom frowned. Up until this point, everything his captor had done had been carefully prepared and thought through. Whatever came next might not be written down in the journal, but that didn't mean it wasn't all planned out.

'Are you going to try and disappear?' he asked. 'Are you hoping to contact Juliette? Do you think you'll be able to, after this?'

'My daughter will know the truth,' J said softly. 'She'll know that Kaitlyn lied... maybe that'll be enough.'

Tom gazed at him thoughtfully, appreciating the importance of Kaitlyn's confession. If his wife had died thinking the worst of him, it would matter that his daughter knew the truth.

'And that's why you brought me along. To make sure the story was told.'

J nodded again.

'Won't be long now,' he murmured.

Tom leaned back in his seat.

This was it. They really *were* coming to the end of the journey.

After all this time on the road, he dared to believe it might soon be over. He'd be released unharmed. The people he cared about would be safe. And he'd have the story of a lifetime – even if there *had* been a terrible price to pay for it.

The sun was getting low in the sky. They were following a smaller road now, dipping and curving to follow the contours of the desert landscape. They hadn't seen another car for half an hour.

'Where are we?' Tom asked.

'You ever hear of Big Bend National Park?'

Tom shook his head.

'It's part of the Chihuahuan Desert,' J explained, lifting a finger to point over the steering wheel. 'Right down on the southwest edge of Texas, a thousand square miles of big, beautiful nothing.'

Tom considered this for a moment. 'The middle of nowhere.'

J nodded solemnly.

'The middle of nowhere.'

They slowed down at a long sweeping curve, where the wind had blown thin drifts of pale sand across the asphalt. J checked the rear-view mirror, then swung the SUV down off the road onto a dusty trail that led out into the endless rolling desert. The trail ran straight for a while, then descended in a series of lazy zigzags between two low ridges.

Tom peered out at the gentle slopes, where withered bushes clung to the dry, rocky ground.

'What's out here?' he asked.

'Nothing,' J said, softly. 'Just desert.'

They drove on. A deep rut caused the SUV to lurch and

bounce, and there was a sudden thud from the trunk. Tom twisted around in his seat to find Hannah's eyes boring into him. She had heard it too. The poor kid was obviously struggling to keep it together, and he wished there was something he could do for her. Slumping back into his seat, he waited, wondering what the hell he was going to do when they reached their destination.

The track was little more than a strip of dust now, winding between scrawny bushes and outcrops of rock. J slowed and turned off to the left, bumping and swaying over rough ground, forging his own path. *This* was why he'd chosen a big 4x4 SUV – an ordinary vehicle would struggle out here.

They continued for some time. Tom began to worry that they were lost – everything looked the same and he was no longer certain in which direction the dirt track lay, never mind the road.

Finally, J took his foot off the gas and they rolled to a gradual stop. Switching off the engine, he gazed out at the vast desert landscape. The sun was just above the horizon, casting long shadows over the rough ground, and the sky was a deep, darkening blue.

'End of the line,' he said, taking the key from the dash. 'Everyone out.'

They opened the trunk and helped the exhausted Kaitlyn up into a sitting position once more. J peeled back the tape from her mouth and produced a half-full bottle of water, holding it for her until she'd drunk it all.

'Where are you taking me?' she gasped, once she'd finished the water.

J straightened up then pointed down at the ground beneath his feet.

'Right here,' he said, quietly.

Kaitlyn glanced around groggily, craning her neck to see behind her.

'Where are we?'

'In the desert,' J replied. 'Oh, and feel free to holler if you want to... there's not another soul for miles and miles.'

'The desert?' Kaitlyn frowned. 'But – why?'

J folded his arms.

'I figured it'd be a good place for you to reflect on the choices you've made, on what you've *done*. And it's somewhere that we aren't gonna be disturbed.'

Kaitlyn lifted her head with an effort and glared at him.

'What I've done?' she rasped. 'Is *that* what this is about? You're trying to get me to admit to the fire?'

J looked down on her and sighed.

'Because I won't admit a damn thing,' Kaitlyn said, worn-out but defiant. 'I earned that money and *nobody's* taking it away from me.'

J shook his head sadly.

'I don't care about the money,' he said. 'I don't care about the fire, or any of that stuff.'

'Then what the *fuck* do you want with me?' she demanded.

'I want you to understand. I want you to understand that your bullshit complaint got me in trouble...'

'You were trying to cheat me,' Kaitlyn muttered.

'Your bullshit complaint got me fired from my job,' he continued.

Kaitlyn hesitated slightly.

'Yeah, well...'

'And after that, most of my friends cut me off because they figured maybe there was something to the accusations.'

Kaitlyn was still scowling, but there was uncertainty in her expression now.

'With the online campaign, it was only a matter of time before the police brought me in,' J said, sadly. 'And I think that was the final straw, that was when my wife decided she couldn't take it anymore, and she left. All because of your bullshit, and the hatred *you* stirred up.'

Kaitlyn stared up at him nervously.

'But it *wasn't* bullshit,' she argued. 'The insurance people paid me. Why would they do that if they didn't believe my story?'

'And I told you, I don't *care* about the money.' J leaned closer, his dark eyes flashing with suppressed rage. 'I care about the fact that my wife *died* while I was in police custody. I care about the fact that she died believing the lies *you* told about me, and now I can never tell her the fucking truth.'

Kaitlyn recoiled from his words.

'I... I thought it was the fire...'

J shook his head, holding her gaze until she became uncomfortable and looked away.

'Well, you can't blame me for all this,' she objected. 'Maybe I made a complaint to get you off my back, but that don't make it my fault if the thing gets talked about on the internet. If other people read stuff and want to have their say, that's down to them.'

'I quite agree,' J told her. 'And that's why I dealt with them.'

Something in his tone made Kaitlyn hesitate. 'Dealt with them?'

'Eliminated them,' J said, his voice bleak. 'The world's a better place without people like that.'

A look of fear passed across Kaitlyn's face, but she quickly replaced it with a sneer.

'You're just trying to scare me.'

She watched him for a moment, but his expression remained grave. She turned and looked appealingly to Hannah and Tom, as though trying to read some reassurance in their faces. Tom met her eye and gave a warning shake of his head.

Kaitlyn turned back to J. 'You... you *killed* people?'

J nodded slowly.

'People filled with hate, inspired by *your lies.*' He turned away in disgust. 'Like I said, the world's better off without them.'

Kaitlyn gaped up at him, panic on her face.

'I... I'm sorry,' she croaked.

J remained still, saying nothing. The gun was visible, tucked down the back of his jeans.

'You want me to take it back?' Kaitlyn offered. 'About the sex stuff?'

'I don't care,' J murmured. 'It's too late now.'

'But I can tell the truth,' Kaitlyn insisted. 'I can tell people that you just asked your stupid questions, nothing else.'

'I *know* that's all I did,' J snarled. 'I was *there*, remember?'

Kaitlyn began struggling against her restraints, her voice increasingly desperate.

'I'm sorry, *okay?* I'm fucking sorry!'

'No,' J said. 'It's *not* okay, Kaitlyn.'

She looked really frightened now.

'Please,' she begged him. 'I'm sorry! I'm really sorry!'

'I lost my wife, my family, my friends.' J leaned over her, his voice rising. 'I lost EVERYTHING!'

Kaitlyn flinched, almost tipping over into the back of the SUV.

'People wanted me dead,' J continued. 'They wrote about how they hoped I'd be raped and murdered in prison.'

'I'm sorry – I'm sorry...'

'And that's why I took their lives.'

Kaitlyn started sobbing.

'But you – ' J broke off for a moment, composing himself. '*You* began this, Kaitlyn. Just you, and your greed, and your lies. All the misery, all the hate, all the deaths... it's all on you.'

Kaitlyn jerked her head round to look at Tom and Hannah.

'Please!' she whimpered. 'I didn't know...'

J took a step closer to Kaitlyn, who shrank from him.

'*That's* what I brought you out here to think about.'

Lifting her from the back of the SUV, he placed her on the dusty ground and stood over her. She cowered, struggling with her restraints.

'What are you going to do?' she whispered.

J regarded her with contempt, then turned away to look at the orange glow of the sun beyond the horizon.

'I'm done with you, Kaitlyn,' he said, wearily. 'I'm going to move on. I'm going to leave you here, and move on.'

'Leave me?' Kaitlyn raised her head, and there was a flicker of hope in her voice.

J sighed and nodded.

Tom stared at him in surprise. *What the hell was happening?*

'I won't say anything,' Kaitlyn promised eagerly, sniffing away her tears. 'Just... just untie me and go.'

For a long time, J said nothing. Then he slowly shook his head.

'No.'

Kaitlyn looked up in confusion as he turned around to face her.

'No, I won't untie you,' he explained. 'I'm leaving you here. *Right here.*'

Tom went cold as he understood what J was planning.

'But... but you *have* to untie me!' Kaitlyn twisted on the ground, straining against her restraints. 'You can't leave me like this!'

She began to struggle desperately, toppling over to lay in the dirt, hands behind her back, kicking her tied feet helplessly.

'You'll have plenty of time to think about all the lives you've destroyed,' J told her, calmly. He glanced around, as though calculating something. 'Out here, I reckon you'll probably live for a day or two, unless the coyotes or the vultures find you first.'

Thrashing around weakly on the ground, Kaitlyn began to scream. Her voice was hoarse and broken, but it echoed out around them, filling the empty desert sky.

J looked round and caught Tom's anguished expression.

'Don't worry,' he said. 'That water I gave her was spiked. She'll quiet down soon enough.'

He stepped over her and walked around to the side of the SUV, leaving Kaitlyn to howl and writhe in the dust.

Tom remained rooted to the spot, watching her struggle until it became unbearable, then he turned away and stumbled after the older man. He couldn't take any more of this. It was too much, and he needed it to be over.

J had opened the rear passenger door and was taking a soda can from one of the bags on the back seat. He glanced up as Tom approached and offered the drink to him.

'Thirsty?'

Tom shook his head, fighting to keep his voice steady.

'I need to know that you're going to keep your promise.'

'What are you talking about?'

Tom took a breath. 'Zak. Kendra. The people who are important to me. I need to know that they're safe!'

J raised an eyebrow. 'Well, once we're done here–'

'No!' Tom insisted. 'I need to know that they're safe *now!*'

J regarded him thoughtfully. 'I told you before–'

'And now *I'm* telling *you*,' Tom interrupted. 'Call off the hit. I've done everything that you've asked, and we're at the end of this awful journey, aren't we?'

J popped open the soda can and took a sip, his eyes never leaving Tom.

'So, call it off,' Tom demanded. 'Call it the fuck off!'

A cold grin spread across J's face.

'All right,' he said, with a shrug.

'Do it, then!' Tom urged him. 'Get one of your phones and stop it. Right now!'

J stared at him for a moment, then slowly raised his left hand. He snapped his fingers.

'Done.'

Tom glared at him in confusion.

'Stop fooling around and do it!' he demanded. 'Come on!'

J met his gaze calmly.

'It's *done.*'

Tom faltered, as a terrible doubt began to form in his mind.

'I don't... I don't understand.'

'Yes, you do,' J told him.

'No...'

Had it all been a lie? The threat to Zak... just an awful, cruel bluff, that J had used to control him?

'Oh fuck, no!' Tom gasped, leaning up against the side of the SUV for support. 'Oh, you sick, sick bastard. You're – you're...'

'Oh, grow up, Tom.' There was a note of irritation in J's voice. 'I'm not a *monster*. I just told you what you needed to hear, gave you an excuse to come along and get what you really wanted.'

The words sent Tom reeling, and he suddenly felt as though he was going to be sick.

J took a step closer, his dark eyes glittering.

'Of all people – of *all* fucking people – you think *I* could hurt a child? You think *I* could destroy an innocent family member, after knowing what it is to lose one? Have I *ever* done anything like that?' He shook his head, bitterly. 'I punish the *guilty*, Tom!'

60

'I told you what you wanted to hear,' J said, pointedly. 'And you believed it because it suited you.'

He took another sip from the soda then set the can down on the roof of the SUV.

Tom stood there, trembling, staring at him. Had his eagerness for the story blinded him to what was going on? Had he missed something?

J's expression appeared to relax a little.

'Aw hell, don't beat yourself up over it,' he said. 'It didn't really change anything much. It's not as though you'd have been able to *save* any of them.'

Tom gritted his teeth.

It's only one more death...

Behind him, he could hear Kaitlyn sobbing and struggling. Her voice sounded weaker now, as though the fight was beginning to drain out of her.

'And now you've had a chance to meet the lying bitch who started the whole thing,' J added, nodding towards the rear of the SUV. 'And you know how it's gonna end for her.'

Only one more death...

Tom shook with utter frustration. He'd been *played*. He'd gone along with the whole sick adventure, taking notes while J took people's lives. He should have stopped it. He *could* have stopped it!

'That reminds me,' J added. 'I should get that roll of tape and shut Kaitlyn up again. We're outside the areas where the border patrol works, but I don't want some passing hiker to hear her before she's done.'

One more death...

Tom felt his hands clenching into fists. He *had* to do something!

Adrenalin coursed through him as he followed J around to the back of the SUV. Kaitlyn had stopped struggling. Still bound, she lay limp on her side, eyes staring vacantly, her mouth partly open. J walked over, gave her a nudge with her foot, then knelt down beside her.

'Should her eyes be open like that?' Hannah whispered.

'I put something in her water,' J explained. 'To sedate her.'

Hannah glanced down and shivered. 'It's creepy.'

J began tearing off pieces of tape. As he leaned forward, placing them over Kaitlyn's face, Tom's eyes settled on the gun, sticking out of the back of his jeans.

Do something!

The older man began straightening up. He was only a few feet away...

Do something NOW!

Tom launched himself forward with a sudden snarl, everything focused on the gun, snatching at it with his outstretched hand and clamping his fingers around the grip. Jerking upwards, he managed to wrench it free, even as his momentum carried him into J, knocking the older man off balance and sending him sprawling onto the ground.

Tom stumbled, but managed to keep his footing, twisting around and levelling the gun as his finger found the trigger.

'You sick bastard!' he spat. 'How could you *do* this to me? How could you let me think that my *son* was in danger?'

'What are you doing?' Hannah gasped, stepping back from them.

'He lied to me,' Tom hissed. 'Zak was never in danger. It was all just a scam, to control me, to keep me in line.'

Twisting around in the dirt, J nervously raised his hands.

'It was the only way,' he said, speaking softly, carefully. 'It had to be the thing that mattered most to you. Anything less and you could have stopped me.'

Tom brought his free hand up to steady the gun and prevent it from shaking.

'Move away from her,' he commanded, nodding towards Kaitlyn.

Reluctantly, J began shuffling himself across the ground.

'I *would* have stopped him,' Tom murmured, feeling tears pricking in his eyes. 'I would have–'

'*He's got a gun!*' Hannah screamed, pointing.

Tom saw J reach down to his ankle, saw the sheen of metal as the older man began to pull a small pistol from his sock...

There was a brief, bright flash in the dusk light, and a deafening cracking sound as Tom felt the startling kick of the weapon in his hand...

J jerked backwards, as though struck by an invisible blow. Eyes staring wildly, his body sagged and became limp, and he slowly toppled over to lie on his side. A dark stain began to spread across the front of his shirt.

Hannah took a nervous step backwards, her hands over her mouth.

'Oh shit!' she whispered.

Tom wasn't sure how long he stood there. The silence of the desert settled over him until he became aware of his own heartbeat, slower now, marking out the seconds. He moved stiffly, as though waking from a troubled dream, turning away from the dead body at his feet to look at the prone figure of Kaitlyn, laying in the dust.

'Come on,' he said, his voice hoarse. 'We need to get her out of here.'

They managed to lift Kaitlyn into the SUV, laying her across the back seat and wrapping one of the seat belts around her to keep her in place. Tom closed the door carefully, then turned to look at J's bloody corpse, lying on the ground nearby.

'No.' Hannah was standing beside him, shaking her head.

'No what?' Tom asked her.

'I'm not touching him,' she said, an expression of revulsion on her face. 'I... I just can't.'

Tom scowled at her, then walked over and squatted down. Easing his hands in under the older man's arms, he gripped as well as he could and tried to lift, but the body was heavy, and a sharp pain flared in his ribs. Cursing, he took a breath and tried again, but it was no use.

'I can't do this on my own,' he panted. 'If you could just...'

But Hannah shook her head and turned away.

Defeated, Tom sat back heavily on the dusty ground.

'Well, I guess he's not going anywhere,' he muttered.

Getting slowly to his feet, he stared down at the body for a time. After all that had happened, he felt a strange reluctance to leave the older man out here, but Joseph Sherman looked peaceful, lit now by the last rays of the setting sun.

Their journey was finally over.

It was dark by the time they finally found their way back to the road. The headlights lit up the dusty asphalt as it wound its way through the shadowed desert landscape, while Hannah's face was illuminated by the screen-glow of a cell phone they'd found in one of the bags.

'Anything?' Tom asked.

'Let me try again,' she said.

Tom frowned. With no cellular coverage, they were lost out here, and Kaitlyn still hadn't regained consciousness. He peered out over the steering wheel, scanning the horizon for any lights, or signs of a settlement.

'Got it!' Hannah suddenly hunched forward, studying the phone. 'There's a medical center about an hour from here.'

'An hour?'

'It's the nearest one.'

Tom nodded grimly. 'Which way?'

The sky was a vast canopy of burnt orange, and the roads grew straighter as the landscape flattened out. They began to see other cars, passing them in the darkness. The town appeared in the distance, little pinpoints of light, strung out along the horizon.

'How's she doing?' Tom asked, as they approached the outskirts.

Hannah undid her seatbelt and twisted around, leaning over into the back.

'Still out cold,' she said, after a moment. 'But her breathing's okay and she seems... y'know... stable.'

'Thanks,' he said. 'I guess they'll be able to figure out what he gave her.'

They drove past the bright lights of a gas station, and several fast-food restaurants, as the town slowly closed in around them, shutting the desert out. As they approached a red stop light, Hannah turned in her seat to look at Tom.

'There's gonna be police when we get to the medical center, isn't there?'

There was a hollow note to her voice.

'I guess so.' Tom pulled up and stopped, then glanced across at her. 'Why? What's wrong?'

Hannah lowered her eyes. 'Will you do something for me?'

'Sure,' Tom replied. 'What is it?'

'Will you let me go?'

'Let you *go?*'

'Please,' she urged. 'You can drop me off right here. I'll be okay, really.'

The light went green, but Tom sat staring at her.

'I… I'm not holding you prisoner,' he assured her. 'I'm just taking Kaitlyn to get medical attention.'

'But she was kidnapped, and *we* were kidnapped, and now *he's* dead…' She stared at him, desperation in her eyes. 'The police are gonna be involved and there's gonna be questions…'

'It was self-defense,' Tom reminded her, but even as he said it, he realized that something else was worrying her. 'Why don't you want to speak to the police?'

Hannah said nothing for a moment, then she looked away.

'I… I don't want to be found.'

Tom gripped the steering wheel and peered out at the street. The light had gone red again. He waited until it was green, then drove across the intersection and pulled in at the curb.

'We're a long way from Alabama,' he said, softly.

'The further the better,' she murmured.

Tom frowned, looking out along the deserted sidewalk.

'What will you do here?' he asked her. 'How will you even manage?'

Hannah raised her head in defiance.

'I'll manage,' she told him. 'I *always* manage.'

Tom thought for a moment, then shrugged. Hannah had been through a lot, and he wasn't about to put her through any more.

'Look in the back,' he said. 'The black duffel bag behind my seat... look in the bottom of it.'

Hannah regarded him doubtfully, but she did as he asked, reaching back and unzipping the bag.

'Holy shit,' she gasped, glancing round at him. 'There's a lot of cash in here.'

Tom nodded.

'Listen, I'm sorry,' he said. 'Sorry about everything. I don't know what you're running from, and it's none of my business anyway, but...' He met her gaze. 'Maybe you can find something to run *towards*. Take the bag... maybe it'll help.'

Hannah stared at him. 'For real?'

'For real,' he said.

Hannah zipped the bag shut and lifted it over onto her lap, wrapping her arms around it.

'I don't know what to say.'

'Forget it,' he said. 'Go on, get out of here, so I can find a doctor for Kaitlyn.'

Hannah nodded. She opened the door and stepped down, slinging the bag over her shoulder.

'I was right about one thing,' Tom told her.

'What's that?'

Tom shrugged. 'I told you he wouldn't kill you.'

Hannah smiled.

'Thanks,' she said.

Tom watched until she disappeared round the corner of the street, then he put the SUV in gear and drove on.

The medical center was on the far edge of town. Tom sat on a chair in a brightly lit corridor, rubbing his eyes as the nurse completed her questionnaire.

'So, is she going to be okay?' he asked.

'The doctor is in with her now,' the nurse replied. 'But I'm gonna need you to wait here for a while. The sheriff is on his way over to talk to you about... well, everything.'

Tom shrugged and leaned his head back against the wall. 'I'll wait,'

The nurse shot him a wary look from behind her clipboard, then turned and walked back along the corridor.

Tom yawned, then reached into his pocket and took out the burner phone. He turned it over in his hands, noting the colored sticker on the back, then switched it on. After studying the screen for a moment, he found the number he needed, and dialed it.

A voice with a New York accent answered.

'Hi there,' Tom said, wearily. 'I'm trying to reach detective Leo Moretti. I don't have his cell number with me right now, but is there any way you can get me through to speak to him? I know it's late, but believe me, he's gonna want to take this call...'

61

Tom's Journal

Normally, when I go to book launches, I drift around with a drink in my hand, searching out familiar faces, looking for people to talk to. Tonight, almost all the faces are familiar, and everyone is drifting around, waiting to talk to me. We're at a beautiful indie bookshop in Lower Manhattan and the place is buzzing, with the clink of glasses and the murmur of a hundred conversations.

It's all happened so fast – a very quick turnaround in publishing terms – but already the events of my journey feel strangely distant to me. Getting the words down and reading them back, over and over again... I've relived the whole nightmare every day for months, yet now I feel detached from it, like it happened to somebody else.

I certainly don't feel like a hero, whatever my publicist might say.

Kendra's here with her boyfriend, Dave. She brought me a miniature bottle of bourbon, like the ones you find in hotel minibars, and slipped it into my hand when she arrived "just in case you get bored of all these phony publishing people". She said it loud enough for my agent and my editor to hear, but it's probably been the high point of the night for me, albeit a bittersweet one with Dave hovering at her elbow. He seems like a genuinely nice guy, and he clearly makes her happy. I fucking hate him.

Leo arrived late, but he's having a great time, walking around and telling everyone who'll listen that he's "the cop from the book". He's kept me updated on the investigation, though there hasn't really been anything new, and it sounds as though the FBI have plenty of higher-priority cases to occupy their time.

My actions were ruled as self-defense – not unexpected, but still a relief. Hannah, if that was even her real name, could be anywhere by now. In any case, there's no suggestion of any wrongdoing on her part, so while the Feds might like to get her version of the story for completeness, there's no serious effort going into finding her. I'm pleased about that.

I would have liked it if Samaira could have been here tonight, but I understand it's a long way to come just for a book launch. Still, I'll catch up with her this weekend in Boston when I go up to see Zak. That's probably the best thing that's happened since I came back from the desert – I've spent so much more time with Zak. It was a little strained at first, but I'm beginning to figure out what he enjoys, and we're having fun together, which is great. Things are better with Samaira too, probably because she can finally see me acting like a father – I've certainly got some catching up to do.

But for now, for tonight, it's all about the book. My publicist is steering me around the room, thrusting me into groups of people that I'd be too awkward to approach by myself, then summoning me away when she spots someone else that she wants me to meet.

Everyone has the same questions. What was it like? What was he like? They all want to know how I felt when I pulled the trigger.

Nobody ever asks me about Kaitlyn. The internet turned on her after reports of what she'd done broke in the press, and there were even rumors that Bluestone Mutual briefly considered a fraud action, though they wisely decided that the best thing was to put the whole mess behind them and move on. But the internet isn't nearly so forgiving and, last I heard, Kaitlyn had been forced to change her name and move to another state. Her life's pretty much ruined... but at least she's still alive.

I manage to keep smiling until the very end of the evening. All my friends have gone, but I take a moment to thank the staff from the store and sign a couple of books for them before I leave. It feels strange, seeing so many copies piled up on the tables, my name in block letters on each one.

It's a pleasant enough evening, and my apartment isn't far, so I walk home. Crossing through Roosevelt Park, I remember Kendra's tiny bottle in my jacket pocket and pause to crack it open. The bourbon feels warm going down.

It's been an incredible evening, and my career is absolutely back on track – a big story to put me in the public eye, a top-tier publishing deal, and a bidding war for the TV rights... everything I always wanted.

I should be happy. I should be completely euphoric, and yet... I'm not. Not completely. A few people have noticed. They mostly assume that I must be somehow traumatized by what I went through, but it isn't that. I can't tell them the real reason, even though I know exactly what's troubling me.

It's not my fault. It's just that... well... I haven't been entirely honest.

62

'I told you what you wanted to hear,' J said, pointedly. 'And you believed it because it suited you.'

He took another sip from the soda then set the can down on the roof of the SUV.

Tom stood there, trembling, staring at him. Had his eagerness for the story blinded him to what was going on?

J's expression appeared to relax a little.

'Aw hell, don't beat yourself up over it,' he said. 'It didn't really change anything much. It's not as though you'd have been able to *save* any of them.'

Tom's fists clenched tightly.

It's only one more death...

Behind him, he could hear Kaitlyn sobbing and struggling. Her voice sounded weaker now, as though the fight was beginning to drain out of her.

'And now you've had a chance to meet the lying bitch who started the whole thing,' J added, nodding towards the rear of the SUV. 'And you know how it's gonna end for her.'

Only one more death...

Tom shook with utter frustration. He'd been *played*. He'd gone along with the whole sick adventure, taking notes while J took people's lives. He should have stopped it. He *could* have stopped it!

His muscles tightened as though readying for action. He knew he had to do something.

'That reminds me,' J added. 'I should get that roll of tape and shut Kaitlyn up again. We're outside the areas where the Border Patrol work, but I don't want some passing hiker to hear her before she's done.'

One more death...

As J turned away, Tom launched himself forward with a snarl. His outstretched hand snatched the gun from the back of J's jeans, wrenching it free, while his other hand slammed into the older man, catching him between the shoulder blades. Both men pitched forward, J stumbling and landing heavily on the ground, Tom managing to keep his footing and hurriedly aiming the gun.

'You sick, *sick* bastard!' he spat. 'How could you *do* this to me? How could you let me think that my *son* was in danger?'

Laying sprawled on the dirt, J nervously raised his hands.

'It was the only way,' he said, speaking softly, carefully. 'It had to be the thing that mattered most to you, otherwise you could have stopped me.'

Tom brought his free hand up to steady the gun and prevent it from shaking.

'I *would* have stopped you,' he insisted, feeling tears pricking in his eyes. 'I would have–'

He broke off as he felt something cold and metallic being pressed firmly against the back of his neck. Right behind him, a voice hissed, '*Don't* you hurt my daddy.'

On the ground, J's expression became troubled, and he shook his head anxiously.

'No, baby,' he implored. 'Don't do it... *please!*'

As slowly as he could, Tom raised his hands and turned his head.

Hannah was standing behind him with a small gun in her hand, pointing directly at his face. Her eyes were cold and hard.

'Drop it!' she demanded. 'Then step away from him.'

Tom gaped at her in disbelief.

'Drop it!' she snapped, making him jump. He bent forward, placing J's gun on the ground, then took a step backwards.

'Over there,' she ordered him, gesturing with the barrel of her gun. 'Move!'

He did as she asked, moving several paces away, to stand with his hands raised.

Hannah kept her eyes on him as she darted forward to collect the gun, then went over to J.

'Are you okay?' she asked, bending down and putting out a hand to steady him.

'I'm fine,' J assured her. 'He just got the drop on me, it's my own fault.'

He took his gun back, then allowed Hannah to help him to his feet.

'There,' he said, after a moment brushing himself down. 'No harm done.'

Hannah glared at Tom, her gun still pointing at him. 'If you touch him again...'

Tom retreated, lifting his hands higher.

'Daddy?' he whispered.

J sighed and gazed up at the darkening sky.

'Well, now,' he murmured. 'This *is* awkward. And unfortunate.'

Tom looked at Hannah, still aiming the gun at him.

'You're his *daughter?*' he said incredulously. 'But I thought...'

'You thought what you were supposed to think,' Hannah told him. 'What we wanted you to think.'

'I'm not the only one who lost their family when Robyn

died,' J said, putting an arm around Hannah. He smiled at her sadly, then glanced towards the back of the SUV. 'Come on, baby. Let's finish up here. Then we'll figure out what we're going to do.'

Kaitlyn had stopped struggling. Still bound, she lay limp on her side, eyes staring vacantly, her mouth partly open. Hannah went over, gave her a cautious nudge with her foot, then looked back.

'Should her eyes be open like that?' she whispered.

'It's the effects of the drug,' J explained.

Hannah glanced down, doubtfully. 'It's creepy.'

J stepped forward with the roll of tape in his hand. 'Don't worry, I'll cover her eyes *and* her mouth.'

He knelt down beside the body and began tearing off a piece of tape.

Tom watched him for a moment, then looked warily at Hannah.

'What's the matter?' she asked.

'I don't know, I just...' Tom shook his head. 'I can't believe it.'

Hannah gave him a calculating look.

'But you *did* believe it, didn't you?' she said. 'And folk don't like to change their minds. That's why you're so turned around right now... because you thought you knew stuff, and you were wrong.'

Her words caught him off guard, and he nodded slowly, before his eyes were drawn back to the gun that she still pointed at him.

'You were the accomplice,' he said. 'It was you on that video call outside Samaira's house in Boston. And when he left me alone to go and phone someone, he was speaking to you, sorting out the change of plans.'

Hannah didn't answer. Instead, she smiled and looked across to her father.

'You almost done there?' she asked.

J got stiffly to his feet. He gazed down at Kaitlyn for a moment, as though committing the sight to memory, then turned to the others.

'I'm done.'

There was something very final about his tone.

'So, this is it,' Tom said. 'You're going to leave her out here to die?'

J tilted his head to one side and looked at him thoughtfully.

'Let me ask you something, Tom.' He indicated the unconscious Kaitlyn. 'How much is her hateful, manipulative life worth? How much is it worth to *you?*'

Tom frowned. 'What do you mean?'

The older man walked slowly towards him.

'I mean, what would you do to save her?'

'I don't understand...' Tom shook his head. 'I thought she was the whole point of this. She was the one who caused all of this, who ruined everything for you...'

'That's right.'

Tom glanced at Hannah, then back at J.

'You're offering to *spare* her?'

J looked at the prone figure on the ground.

'I'm asking, what would you do to *save* her?'

Tom hesitated. Was this some kind of test, to see if he'd be willing to sacrifice himself for a woman he didn't even know?

'What do you want?' he replied, cautiously.

J pursed his lips, as though considering what would be best.

'How about this?' he said. 'You write your story – the *whole* story – from the very beginning up until now, without missing anything out...'

'Okay...'

'But change the ending,' J added.

'Change it how?' Tom asked.

Once again, J appeared to be thinking.

'Maybe you got the drop on me back there,' he suggested. 'I mean, you kind of *did*, after all. And it's not like some poor *runaway* like Hannah here would have any reason to stop you.'

Hannah met Tom's eye and gave him a faint smile.

She wasn't surprised. With a sudden certainty, Tom knew that they had planned for everything, even this moment.

'Maybe you figured out that I don't hurt innocent people,' J continued. 'Maybe you realized that I could never hurt your little boy, so you took a heroic risk...' He made a mocking gesture towards Kaitlyn. '...to save this poor, unfortunate woman.'

He smiled at Tom, then turned away to gaze out across the vast desert wilderness.

'You know, if you killed me out here, then my body would probably never be found. And I imagine you'd be in a hurry to get medical attention for poor Kaitlyn, so you wouldn't waste time loading my body into the car. You'd just leave it here... wherever the hell *here* is.' He shrugged. 'You're the writer, Tom. You'll figure something out.'

Tom stared, trying to take it all in, then looked across at Hannah.

'Of course, this poor, *innocent* girl would probably disappear as soon as you got to the nearest town.' There was a note of warning in J's voice now. 'I guess that's just what runaways do, isn't it? But it would be another life you'd saved, Tom. And it's a great ending for your story. You'd be a real hero.'

Tom rubbed his eyes and took a breath. It was an audacious plan, certainly, but he found himself questioning it as his eyes went to the unconscious figure laying in the dust.

'What about Kaitlyn?' he asked.

'What about her?'

Tom frowned. 'You'd really let her live?'

'You think I should kill her?' J countered.

'No! Of course not.' Tom said, quickly. 'But I thought... after all she did to you, I thought she was what this was all leading up to.'

'That's right.'

'And yet... you *don't* want to kill her?'

J shook his head slowly.

'You speak about it as though I'm offering her mercy,' he said. 'But I assure you, I'm not.'

Tom stared at him, blankly.

'We spoke about this once before, Tom. Death is a fleeting moment, the briefest transition between one place and another. And that's not *enough*. Not for what she did to my wife, to my daughter, to me.'

'You want people to know what she did,' Tom mused.

'I want *everyone* to know what she did,' J explained. 'I want them to see what she is. I want people to hate her, and eventually I want her to hate herself. And I want that hatred to last forever.'

Tom turned away, struggling with the enormity of this. Here, at last, J was being completely honest with him, he felt sure of that. But how could he, Tom, allow himself to be a part of something so twisted, so... fucked up?

'What's the alternative?' he asked.

J hesitated, then sighed.

'That would be... unfortunate.'

Tom glanced over at Kaitlyn.

'Not just for her,' J warned.

Tom looked at him and saw that his expression had become pained.

'It's my fault, really.' J shook his head unhappily. 'You weren't supposed to know who "Hannah" was. That was *never* part of the plan. I've always understood that there would be a price to pay for my actions, that I'd be hunted, maybe captured, maybe worse. At *best* I'd spend the rest of my days on the run. And I accepted that fate... for *myself*. But not for my daughter.' He paused, looking hard at Tom. 'I did all of this so that she wouldn't have to.'

Tom glanced over at Hannah. Her smile had gone now, and she was gazing at her father, her eyes bright with their shared pain.

'She's young, Tom,' J explained. 'I want her to have closure, and a life beyond all of this. After everything she's lost, everything that she's been through, I believe she deserves that. And I won't allow anything, or *anyone*, to jeopardize that.'

'So...' Tom looked between them. 'What are you saying?'

'I need to know that you're committed,' J said. 'As far as the rest of the world is concerned, my daughter is out of the country just now, and *this* poor soul...' He indicated Hannah. '... is just some drifter we met by chance on the road. But if you can't write it that way, if you allow *any* suspicion to fall on her... I *will* come for you. For *you*, Tom. Is that absolutely clear?'

Hannah walked over and took her father's arm.

Tom stared at them, silhouetted in the fading orange light of dusk.

'You have to decide what's more important,' J told him. 'Saving a life, or having your say.'

It was getting dark by the time they made it back to the road, their headlights illuminating the dusty asphalt as it wound its way through the shadowed desert landscape.

J reached up and adjusted the rear-view mirror so he could see Kaitlyn, propped-up and unconscious in the back seat, tape still covering her eyes and mouth.

'There's a medical center, over in Alpine,' he said. 'We can go there and you can get her fixed up.'

Tom considered this.

'As soon as I take her in there, you know someone's gonna notify the local PD.' He hesitated. 'There's gonna be a lot of questions, and I'll have to tell them stuff.'

'So?'

'Aren't you worried?' Tom asked. 'The police won't just take my word on all of this...'

'Don't forget about Kaitlyn's word. She knows who kidnapped her.'

'Well, exactly.' Tom frowned. 'There's going to be a lot of interest in you, even if I tell them you're dead.'

J nodded thoughtfully.

'I expect there will be,' he said. 'And your detective friend from New York will be in touch, once he learns where you are. Things will get busy.'

'So what will you do?' Tom asked. 'Where will you go?'

J gazed out at the road, the twin yellow lines stretching away beyond the beam of the headlights.

'South,' he said.

Tom remembered his comment from earlier, about how close they were to the border.

'Mexico?'

'Don't you worry about us, Tom.' J's voice was calm and assured. 'Just worry about getting your story right.'

They drove for an hour, beneath a vast burnt orange sky. The road became straighter as the landscape flattened out, and they started to see other cars, passing them in the darkness.

The medical center was on the outskirts of town – a long, sandy-colored building surrounded by a large, open parking lot. J pulled up a short distance from the main entrance.

'Here we are.'

Tom looked over to the covered entrance where light spilled out from the glass doors, then bowed his head.

'What's wrong?' J asked.

Tom took a breath.

'It's just...' He broke off, then shook his head. 'It doesn't matter.'

J twisted around to peer at Kaitlyn in the back.

'Go on in and tell them that you have an unconscious passenger,' he said. 'Have someone come out and help you with her.'

Tom hesitated.

'Go on.'

Tom looked at him.

'Is this it?' he asked. 'I mean... will I see you again?'

A faint smile spread over J's face.

'Go,' he said.

Tom met Hannah's piercing stare, then J's dark eyes. 'All right then.'

When he came back, moments later, they were gone.

63

Tom's Journal

I push the door of my apartment closed and snap the lock. My fingers rest on the metal for a moment, and I remember the surprise I felt when I got home to find that my broken door had been replaced and paid for. That, and the brand-new laptop that showed up a few days later.

'A man should honor his agreements...'

I put my keys down and walk across to my desk. There are emails to be answered, and tweets that need replies, but they can wait 'til the morning. My eyes come to rest on the postcard, propped up against my printer. It bears a colorful sugar-skull design to celebrate Día de Muertos, with the words "Greetings From Mexico". There is no message on the back of the card, just my name and address, in neat capital letters. The skull grins out at me until I turn away and switch off the lights.

Not all stories have happy endings. I just hope that my part in this one is over.

THE END

ALSO BY FERGUS MCNEILL

EYE CONTACT

KNIFE EDGE

CUT OUT

BROKEN FALL

ASHES OF AMERICA

ACKNOWLEDGMENTS

I'm deeply grateful to Steph Broadribb, Alexandra Benedict, and Louise Voss from Crime Fiction Coach for their superb editing services. Special thanks to Colin Scott, for making me smile on a regular basis.

And finally, thanks to my wife Anna, for her strength, support, and wisdom.

A video documentary of our travels across America, visiting the key locations from this book and discussing the story in more detail, is available on my YouTube channel.

FM

ABOUT THE AUTHOR

As well as writing novels, Fergus McNeill has been creating video games since the early eighties, writing his first interactive fiction titles while still at school. Over the years he has designed, directed and illustrated all sorts of games, spoken at the Cannes Film Festival, and failed to excel at any sport whatsoever. He wishes he could cook.

Fergus lives in the south of England with his wife and their cats. He is the author of the Detective Harland series (EYE CONTACT, KNIFE EDGE and CUT OUT, plus the short novella BROKEN FALL) and the historical thriller ASHES OF AMERICA.

Fergus is represented by Eve White Literary Agency.

facebook.com/fergusmcneillauthor
twitter.com/fergusmcneill
instagram.com/fergus.mcneill
bookbub.com/authors/fergus-mcneill
youtube.com/fergusmcneill

UP CLOSE AND FATAL

First published in Great Britain in 2022.
US-1

A CIP catalogue record for this title is available from The British Library.

Printed in Great Britain
by Amazon

84329279R00243